WITCHES

of

BROOKLYN

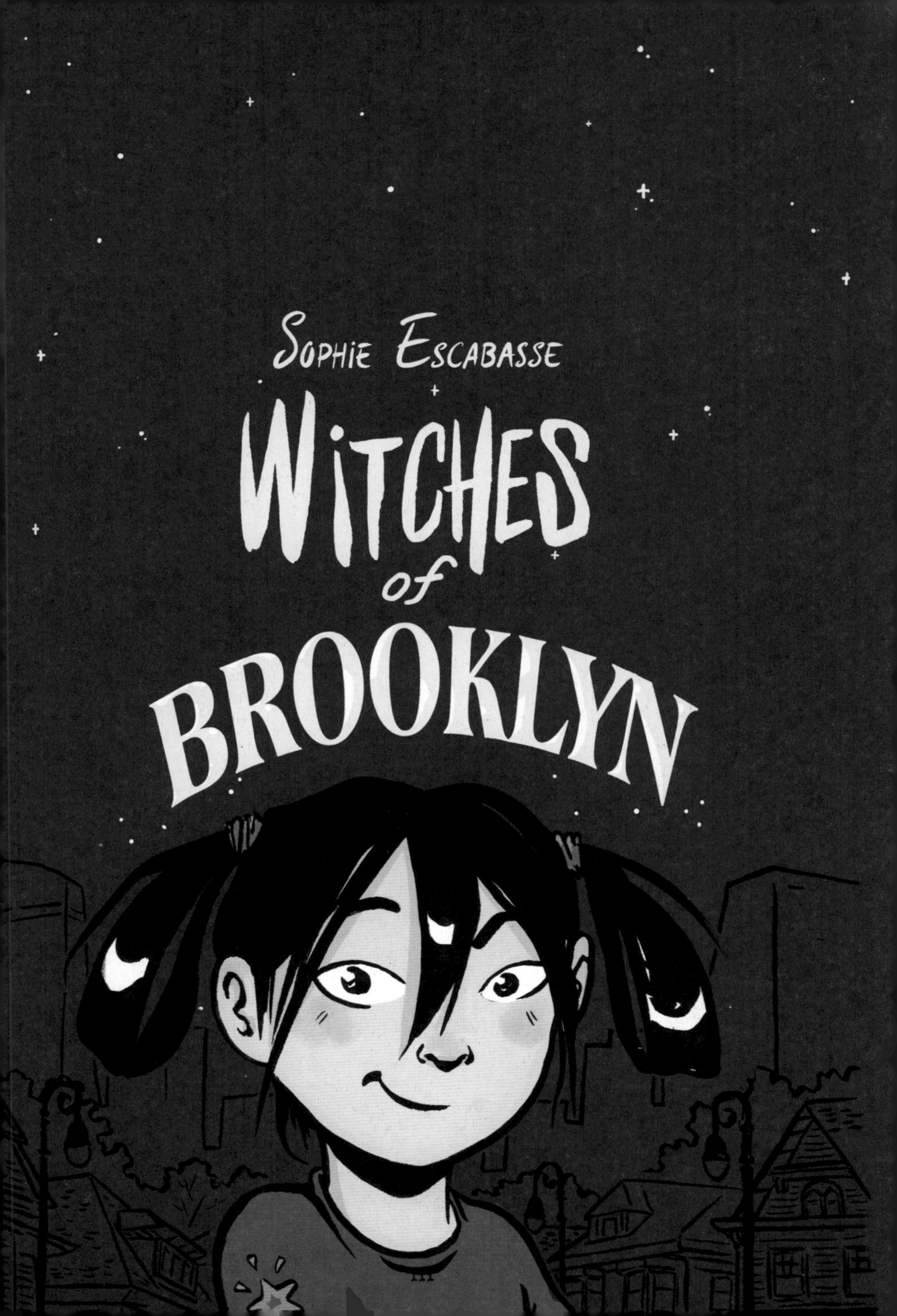
Sophie Escabasse
Witches of Brooklyn

Witches of Brooklyn was drawn with blue or purple pencils of all sorts, any brand will do, until they were two and a half inches long. Then all the sketches were scanned. Inking and coloring were done with Procreate and Photoshop.

Cover art, text, and interior illustrations copyright © 2020 by Sophie Escabasse
Case art used under license from Shutterstock.com

All rights reserved. Published in the United States by RH Graphic, an imprint of Random House Children's Books, a division of Penguin Random House LLC, New York.

RH Graphic with the book design is a registered trademark of Penguin Random House LLC.

Visit us on the Web! RHKidsGraphic.com • @RHKidsGraphic

Educators and librarians, for a variety of teaching tools, visit us at RHTeachersLibrarians.com

Library of Congress Cataloging-in-Publication Data is available upon request.
ISBN 978-0-593-11927-3 (pbk.) — ISBN 978-0-593-12528-1 (trade) — ISBN 978-0-593-11928-0 (lib. bdg.) — ISBN 978-0-593-11929-7 (ebook)

Designed by Patrick Crotty

MANUFACTURED IN CHINA
10 9 8 7 6 5 4 3 2 1
First Edition

A comic on every bookshelf.

For Patrick, my fabulous husband,
and our three amazing raccoons,
Ella, Josephine, and Arthur

Chapter 1

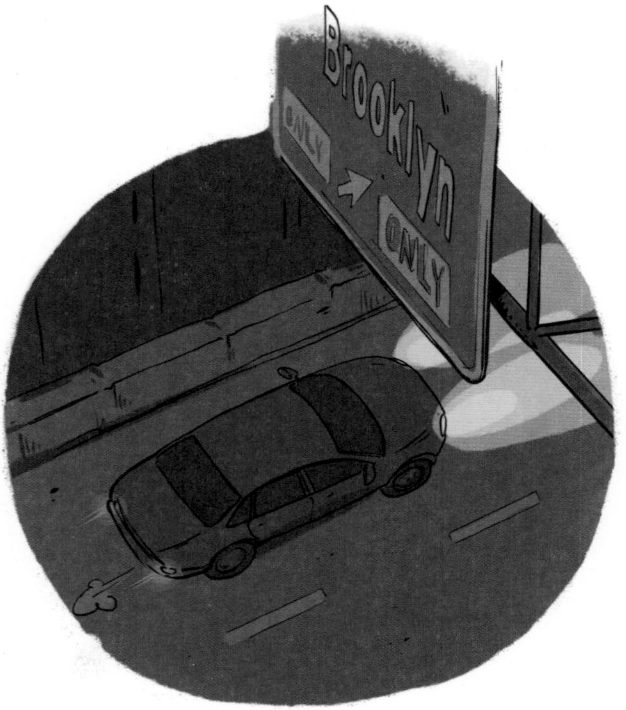

Brooklyn
ONLY
ONLY

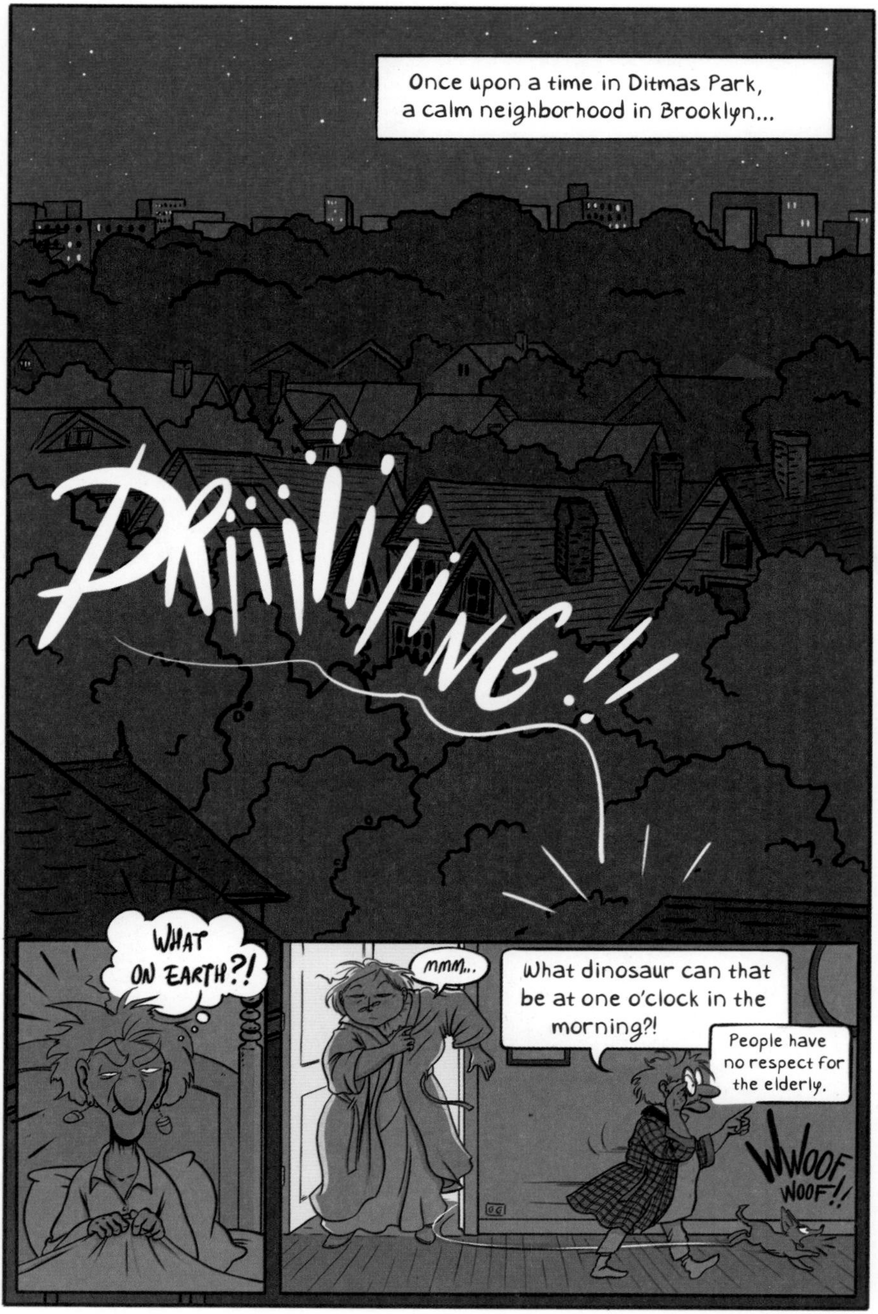

Once upon a time in Ditmas Park, a calm neighborhood in Brooklyn...
DRiiiiiiiiNG.!!
WHAT ON EARTH?!
mmm...
What dinosaur can that be at one o'clock in the morning?!
People have no respect for the elderly.
WWOOF WOOF!!

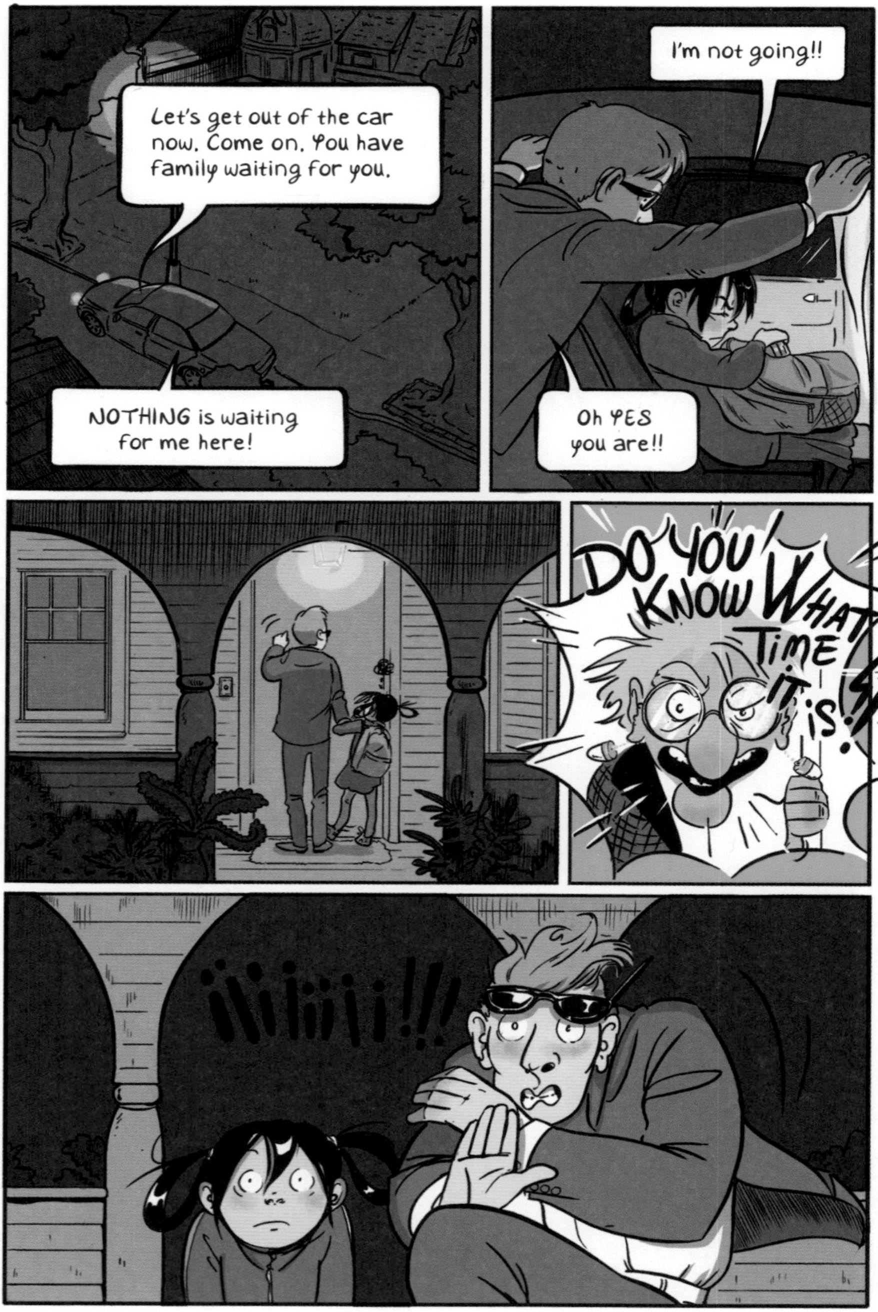
Let's get out of the car now. Come on. You have family waiting for you.
NOTHING is waiting for me here!
I'm not going!!
Oh YES you are!!
DO YOU KNOW WHAT TIME IT IS!!
¡¡¡¡¡¡¡!!!

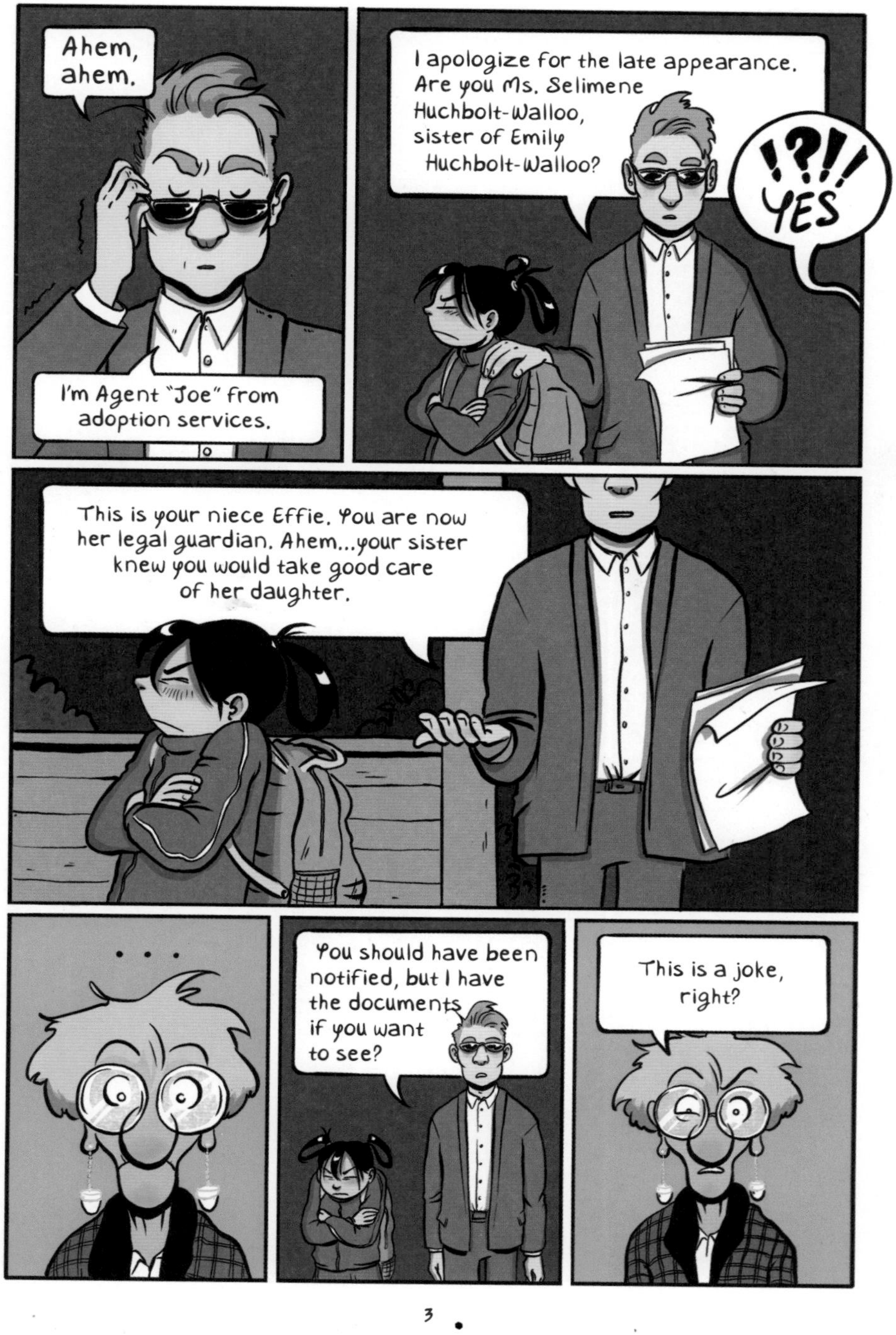
Ahem, ahem.
I'm Agent "Joe" from adoption services.
I apologize for the late appearance. Are you Ms. Selimene Huchbolt-Walloo, sister of Emily Huchbolt-Walloo?
!?!! YES
This is your niece Effie. You are now her legal guardian. Ahem...your sister knew you would take good care of her daughter.
. . .
You should have been notified, but I have the documents if you want to see?
This is a joke, right?

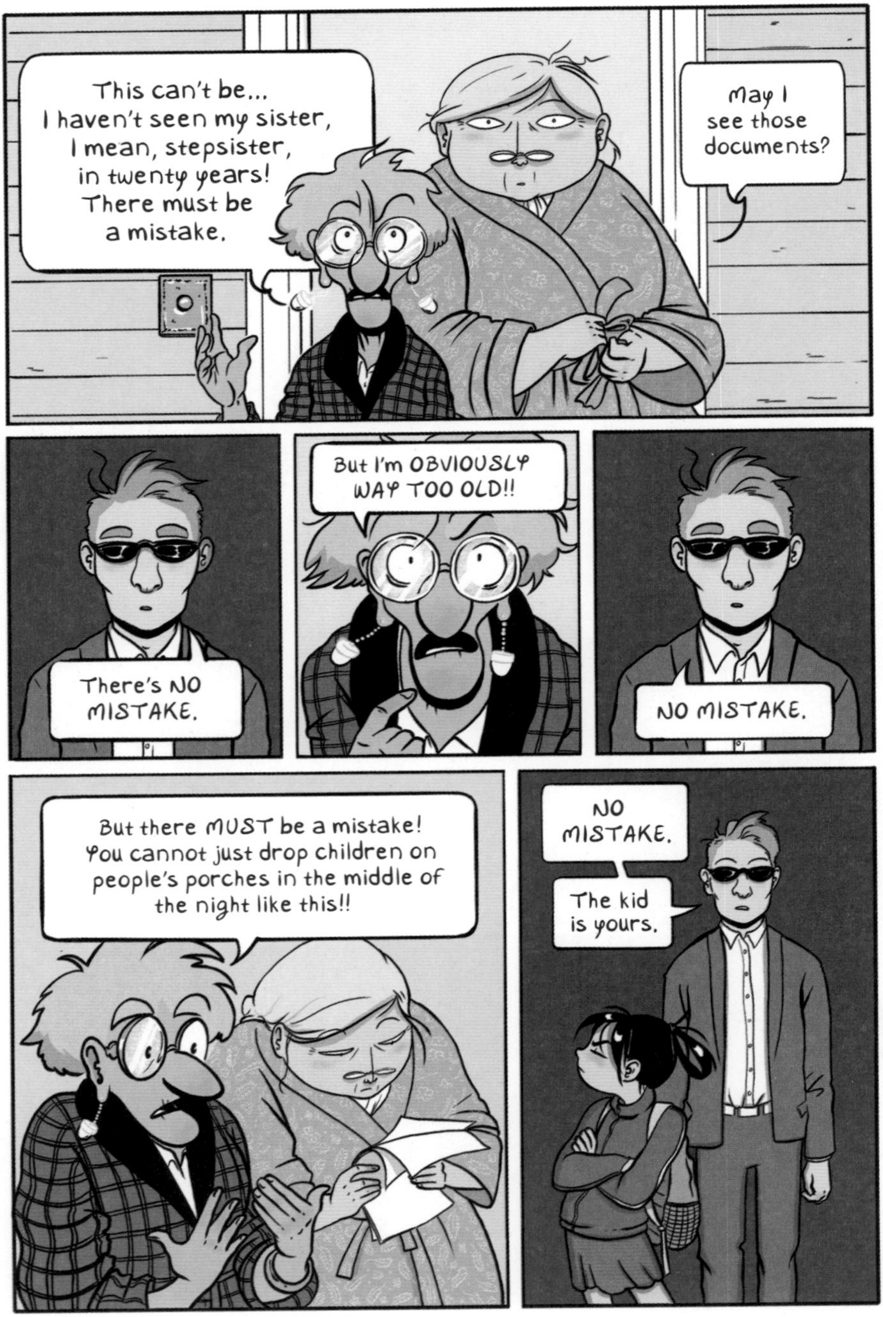

This can't be... I haven't seen my sister, I mean, stepsister, in twenty years! There must be a mistake.
May I see those documents?
There's NO MISTAKE.
But I'm OBVIOUSLY WAY TOO OLD!!
NO MISTAKE.
But there MUST be a mistake! You cannot just drop children on people's porches in the middle of the night like this!!
NO MISTAKE.
The kid is yours.

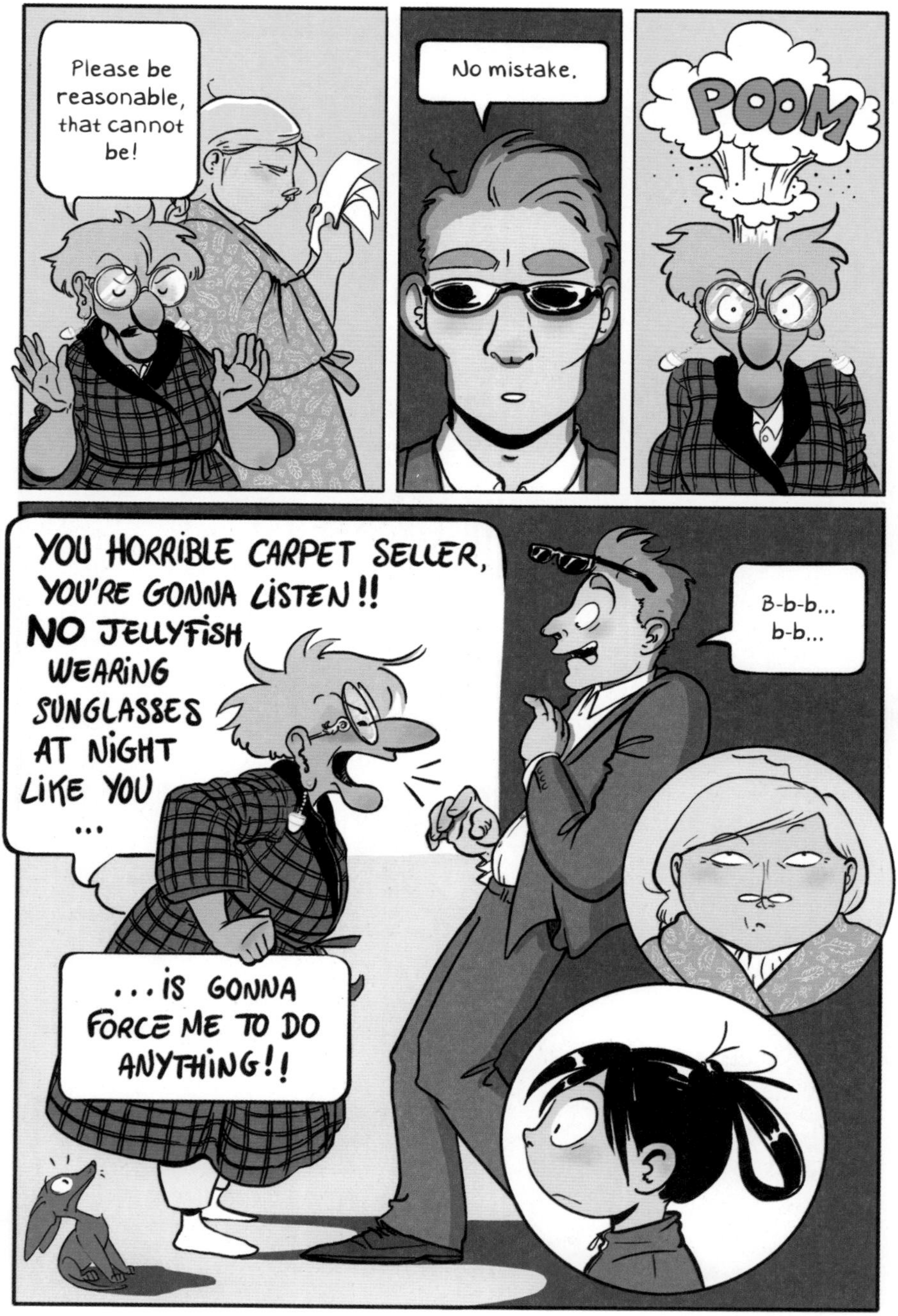

Please be reasonable, that cannot be!
No mistake.
POOM
YOU HORRIBLE CARPET SELLER, YOU'RE GONNA LISTEN!! NO JELLYFISH WEARING SUNGLASSES AT NIGHT LIKE YOU ...
B-b-b... b-b...
...IS GONNA FORCE ME TO DO ANYTHING!!

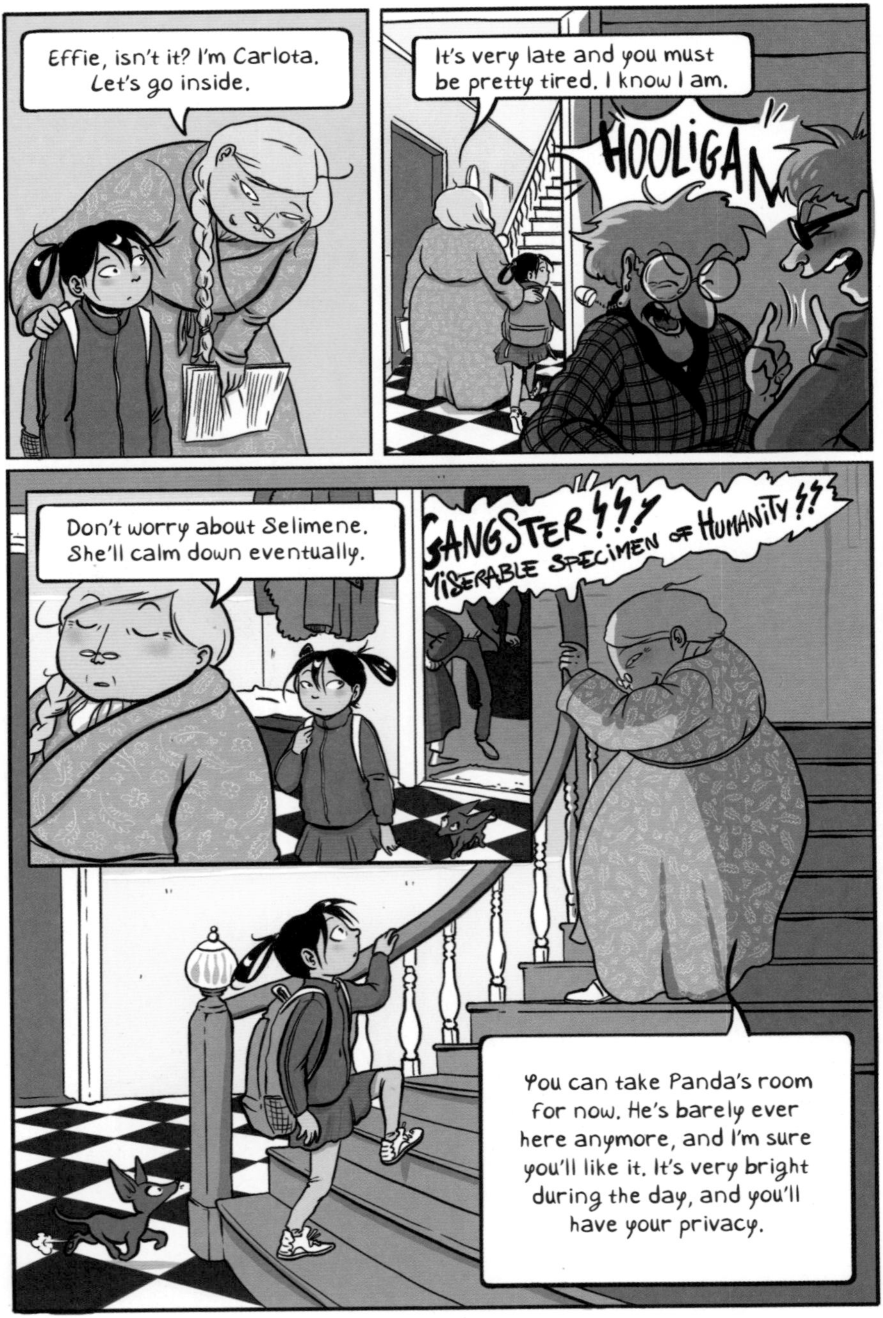
Effie, isn't it? I'm Carlota. Let's go inside.
It's very late and you must be pretty tired. I know I am.
HOOLIGAN
Don't worry about Selimene. She'll calm down eventually.
GANGSTER!?!
MISERABLE SPECIMEN OF HUMANITY?!
You can take Panda's room for now. He's barely ever here anymore, and I'm sure you'll like it. It's very bright during the day, and you'll have your privacy.

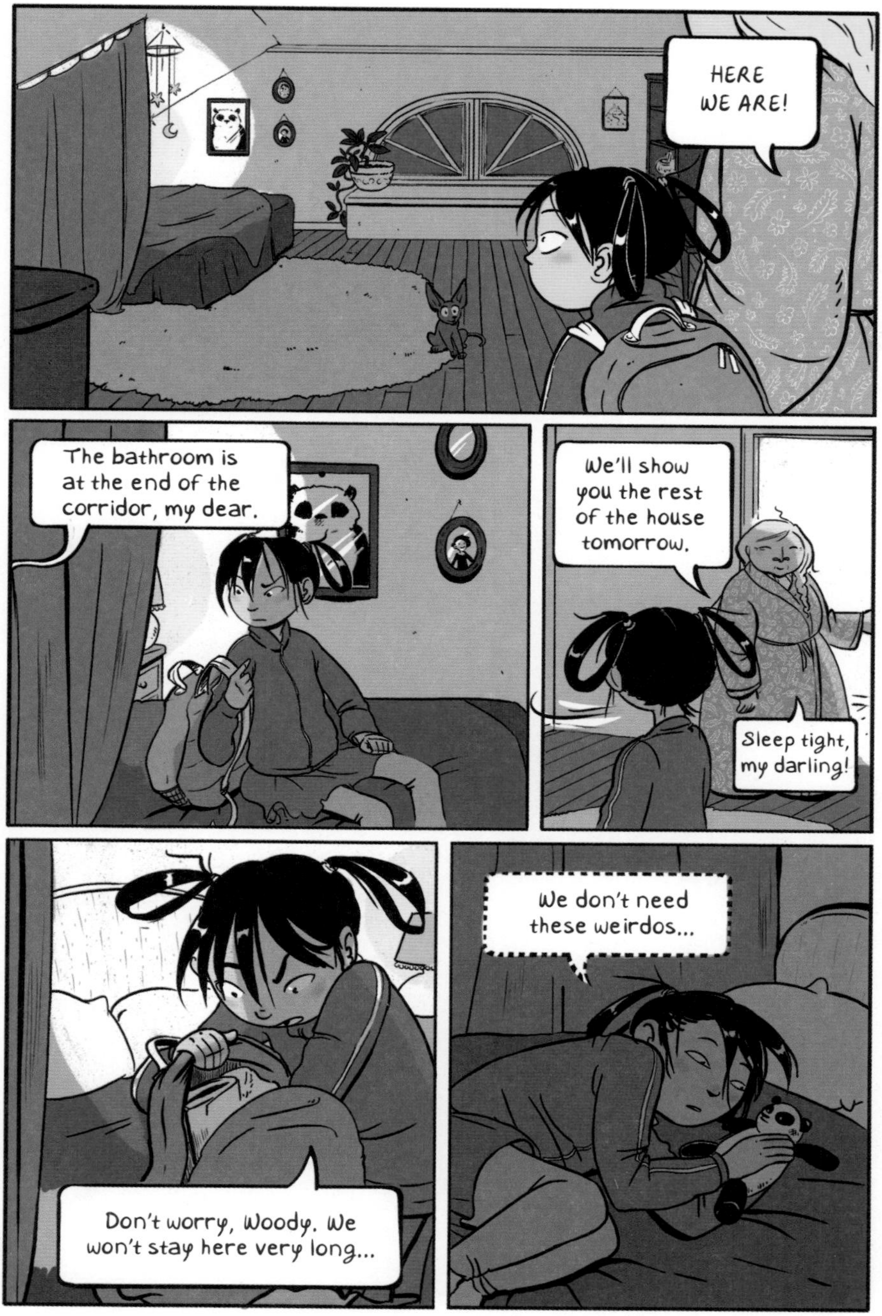
HERE WE ARE!
The bathroom is at the end of the corridor, my dear.
We'll show you the rest of the house tomorrow.
Sleep tight, my darling!
Don't worry, Woody. We won't stay here very long...
We don't need these weirdos...

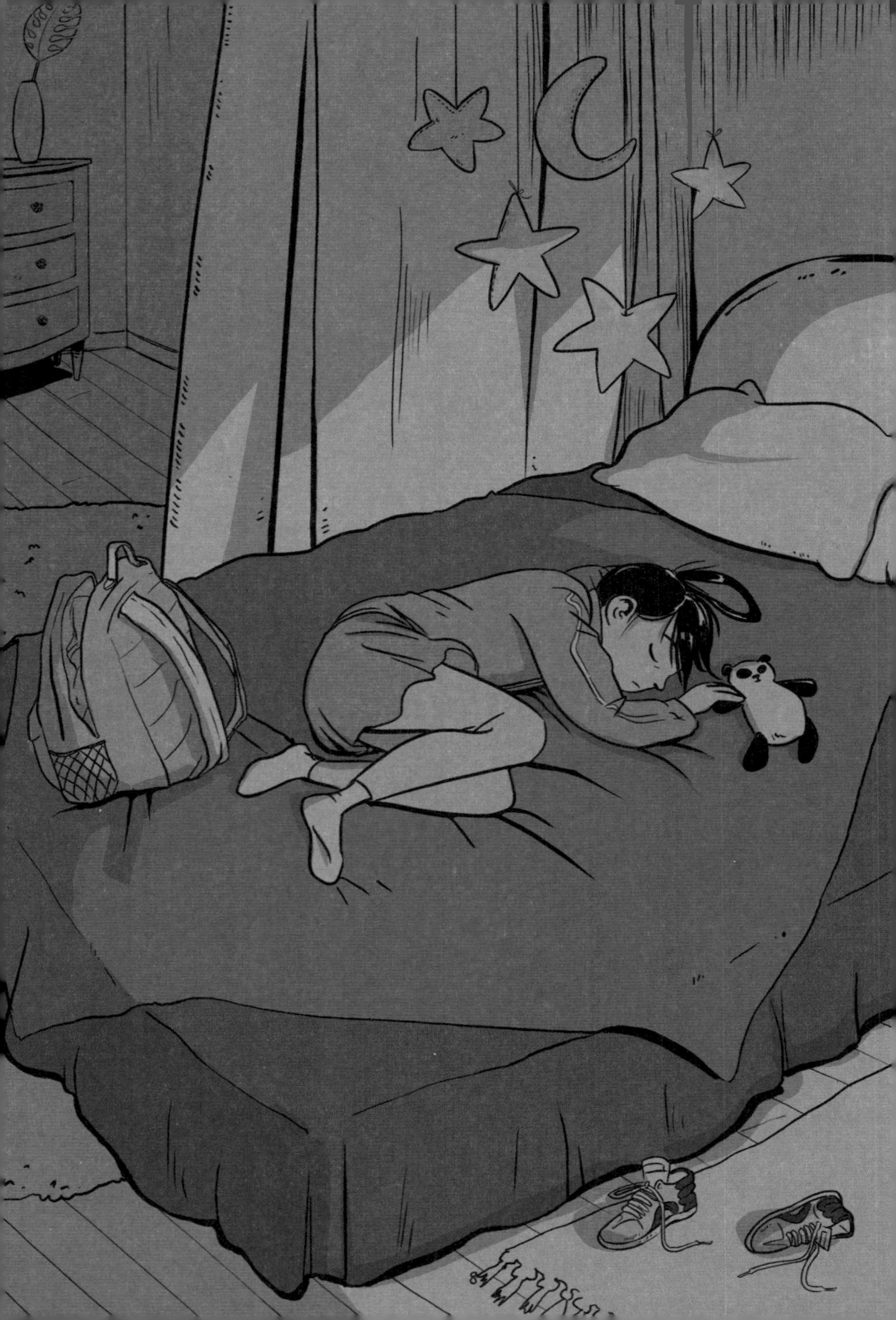

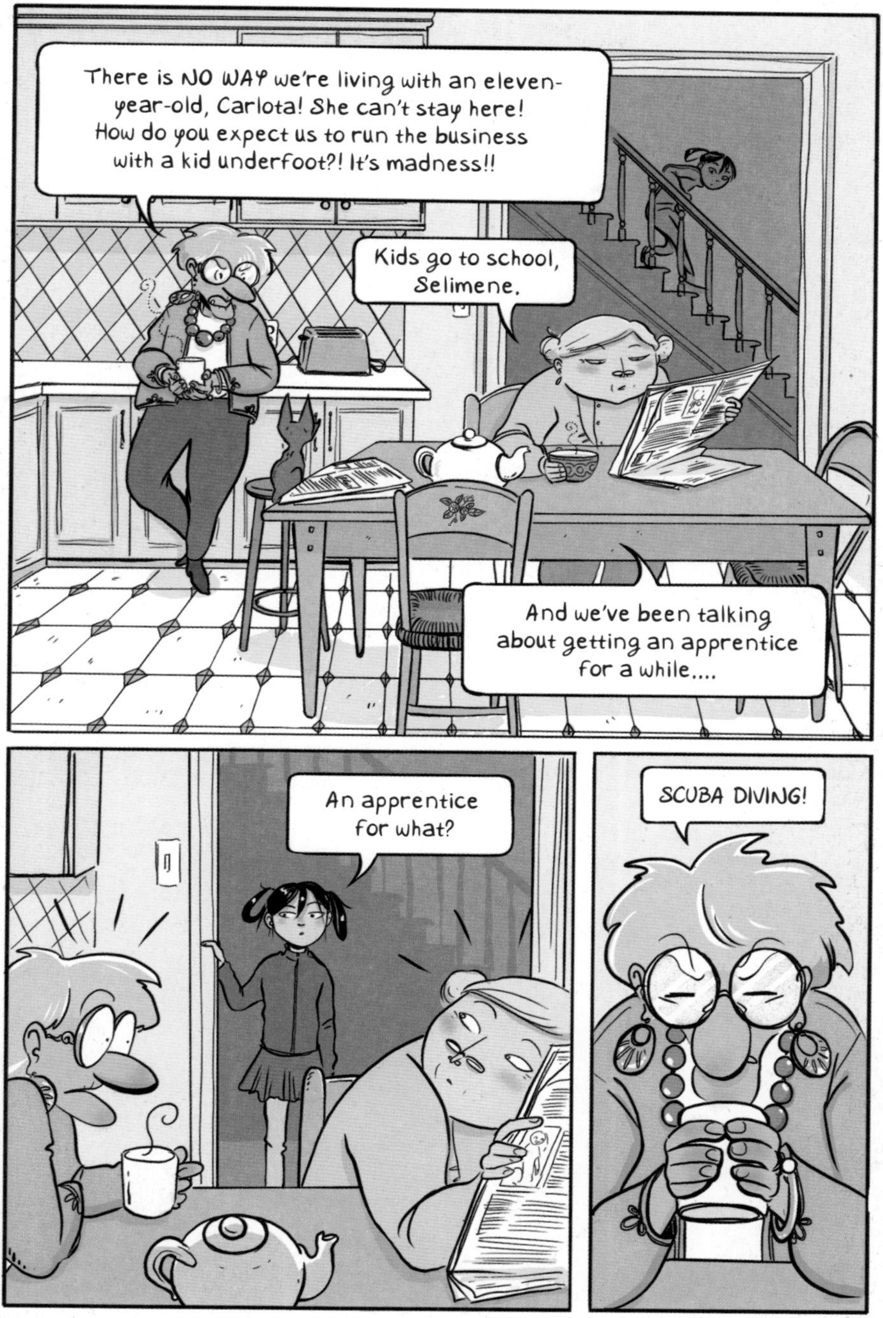
There is NO WAY we're living with an eleven-year-old, Carlota! She can't stay here! How do you expect us to run the business with a kid underfoot?! It's madness!!
Kids go to school, Selimene.
And we've been talking about getting an apprentice for a while....
An apprentice for what?
SCUBA DIVING!

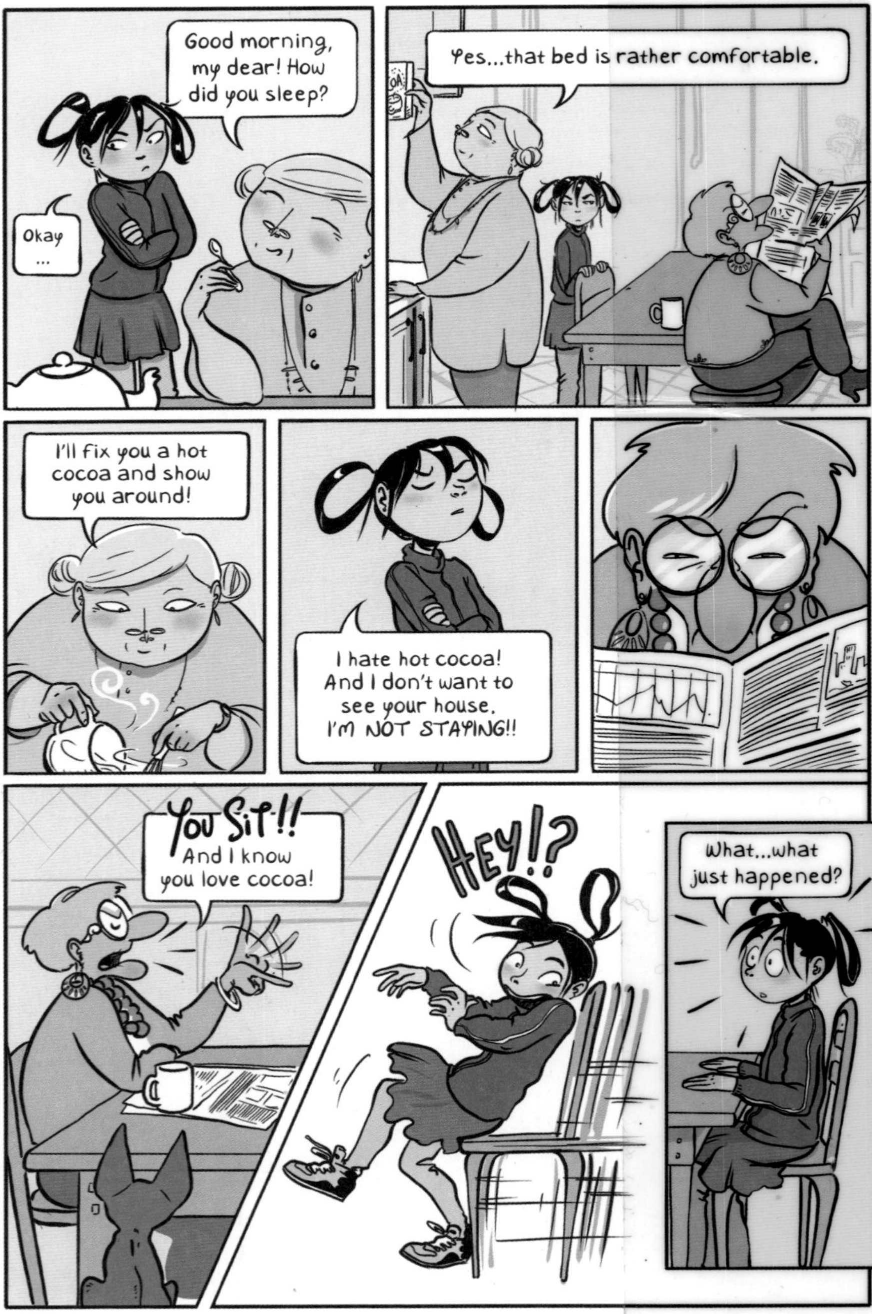
Good morning, my dear! How did you sleep?
Okay ...
Yes...that bed is rather comfortable.
I'll fix you a hot cocoa and show you around!
I hate hot cocoa! And I don't want to see your house. I'M NOT STAYING!!
YOU SIT!! And I know you love cocoa!
HEY!?
What...what just happened?

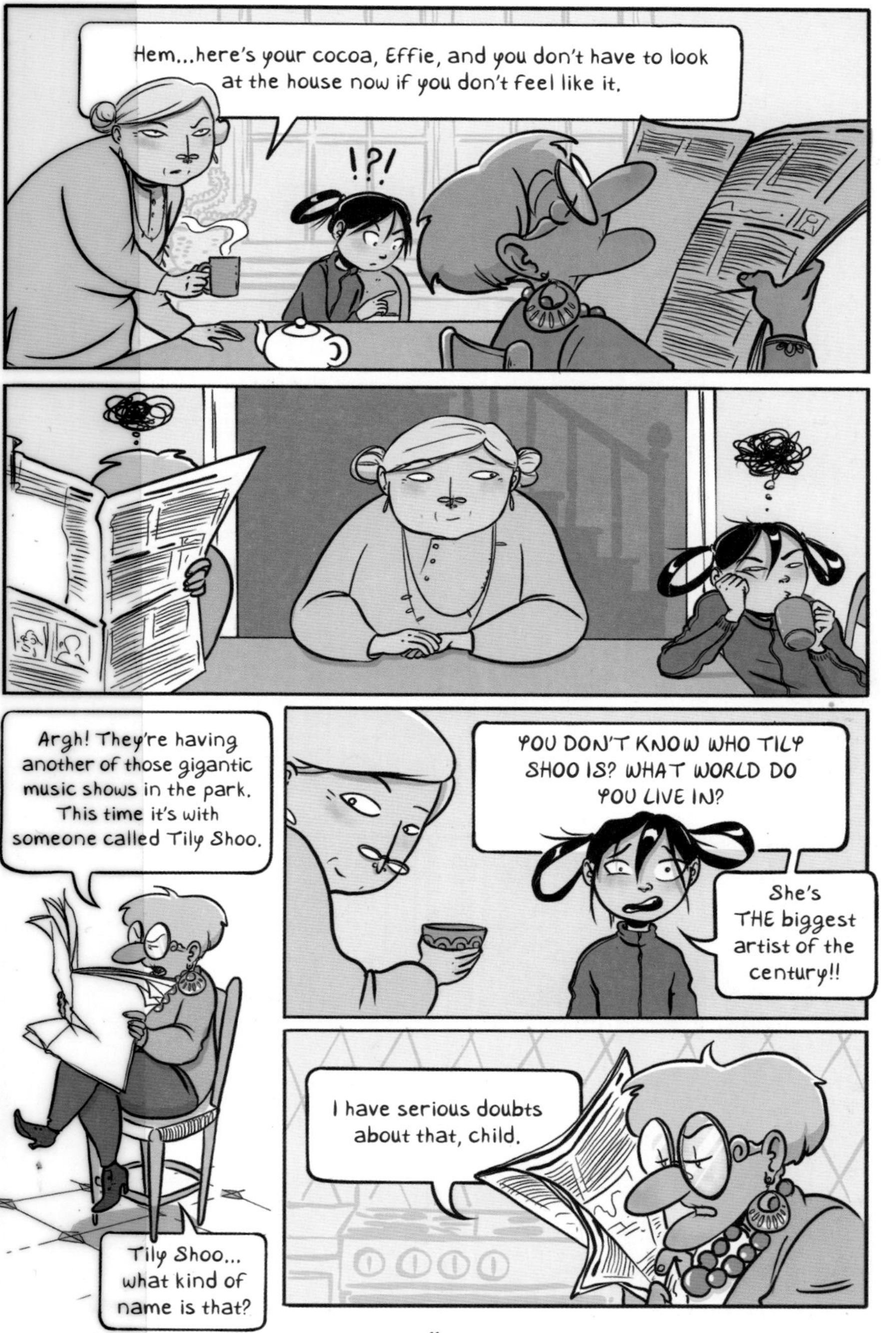
Hem...here's your cocoa, Effie, and you don't have to look at the house now if you don't feel like it.
!?!
Argh! They're having another of those gigantic music shows in the park. This time it's with someone called Tily Shoo.
Tily Shoo... what kind of name is that?
YOU DON'T KNOW WHO TILY SHOO IS? WHAT WORLD DO YOU LIVE IN?
She's THE biggest artist of the century!!
I have serious doubts about that, child.

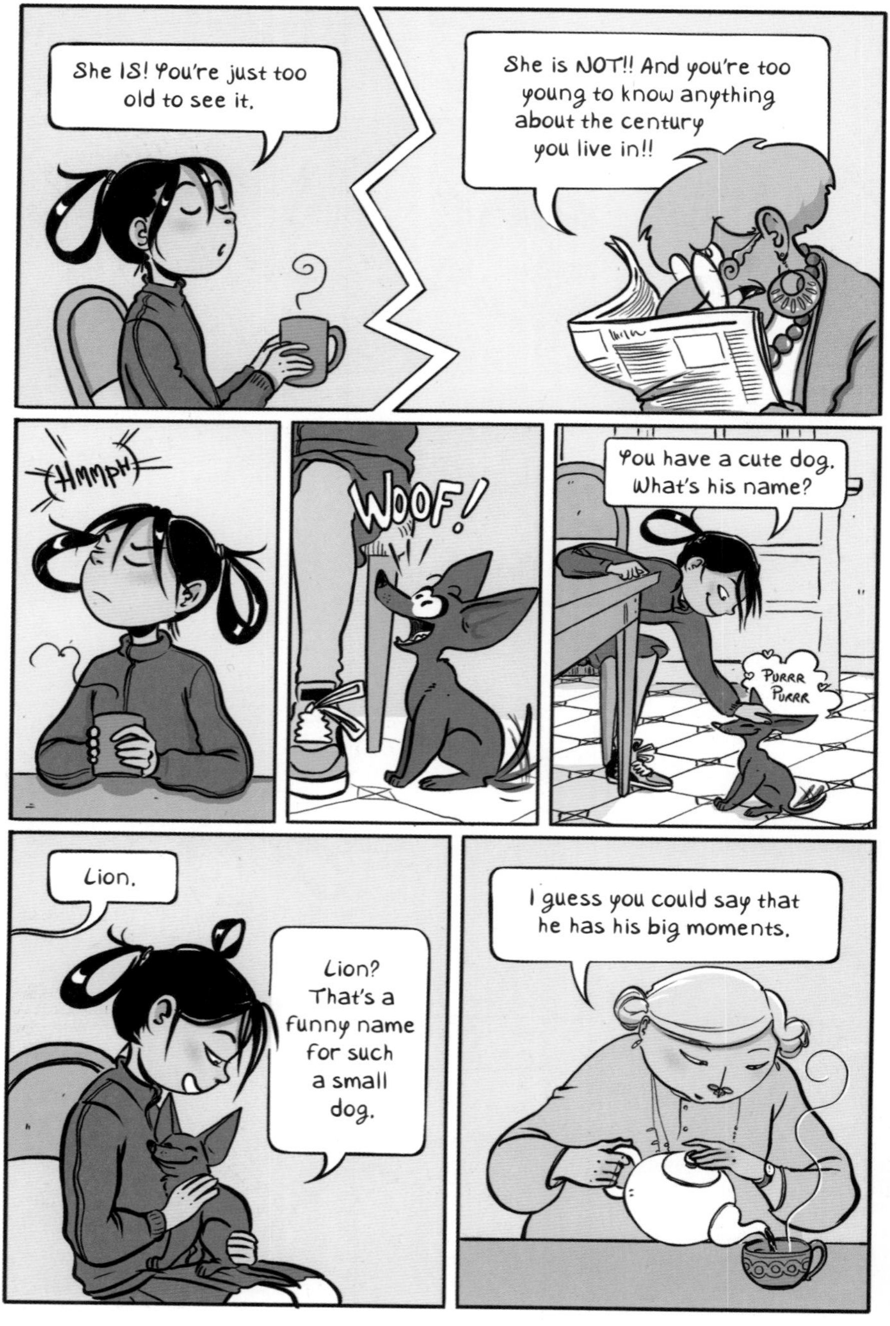
She IS! You're just too old to see it.
She is NOT!! And you're too young to know anything about the century you live in!!
HMMPH
WOOF!
You have a cute dog. What's his name?
PURRR PURRR
Lion.
Lion? That's a funny name for such a small dog.
I guess you could say that he has his big moments.

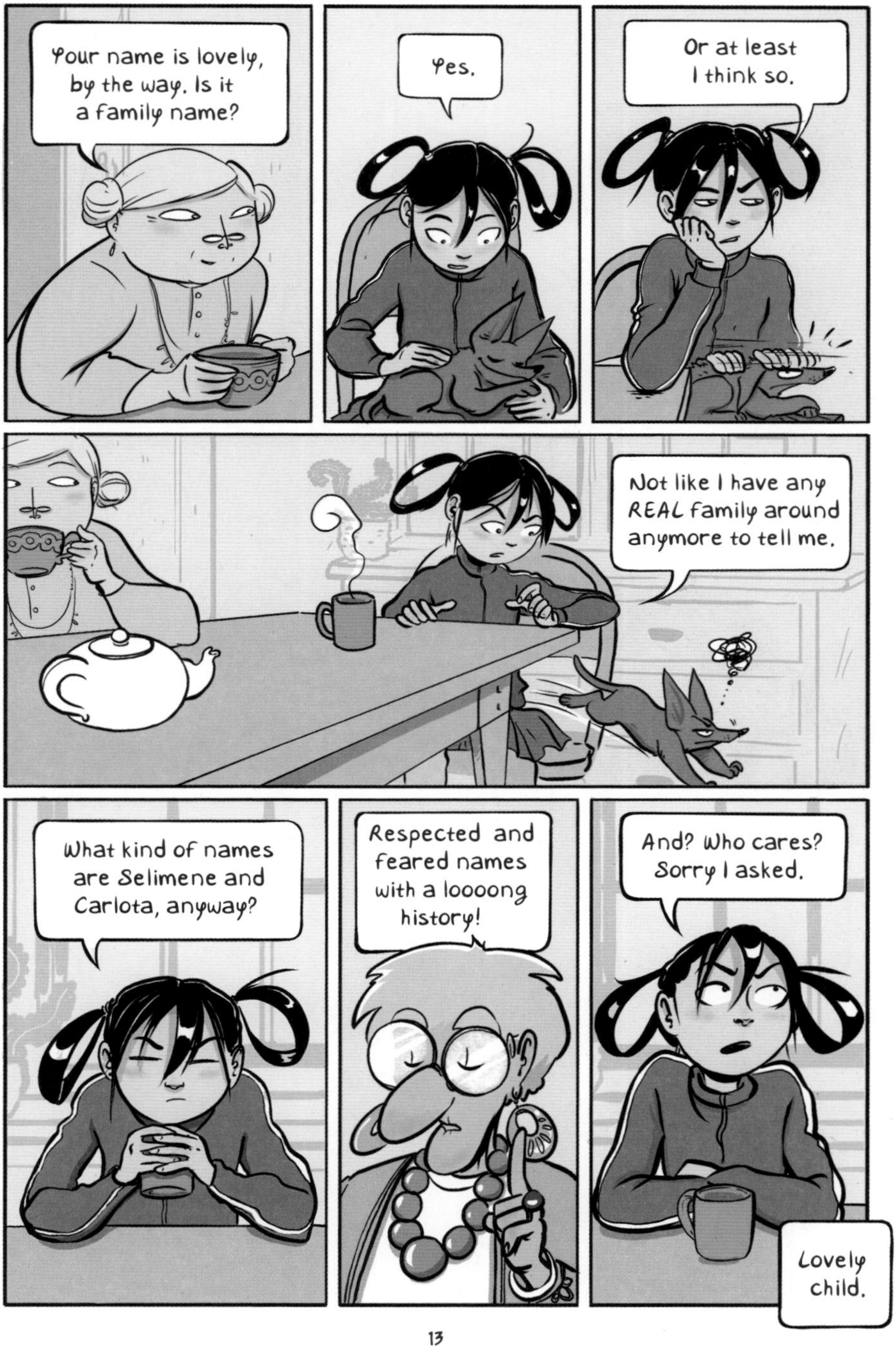

Your name is lovely, by the way. Is it a family name?
Yes.
Or at least I think so.
Not like I have any *REAL* family around anymore to tell me.
What kind of names are Selimene and Carlota, anyway?
Respected and feared names with a loooong history!
And? Who cares? Sorry I asked.
Lovely child.

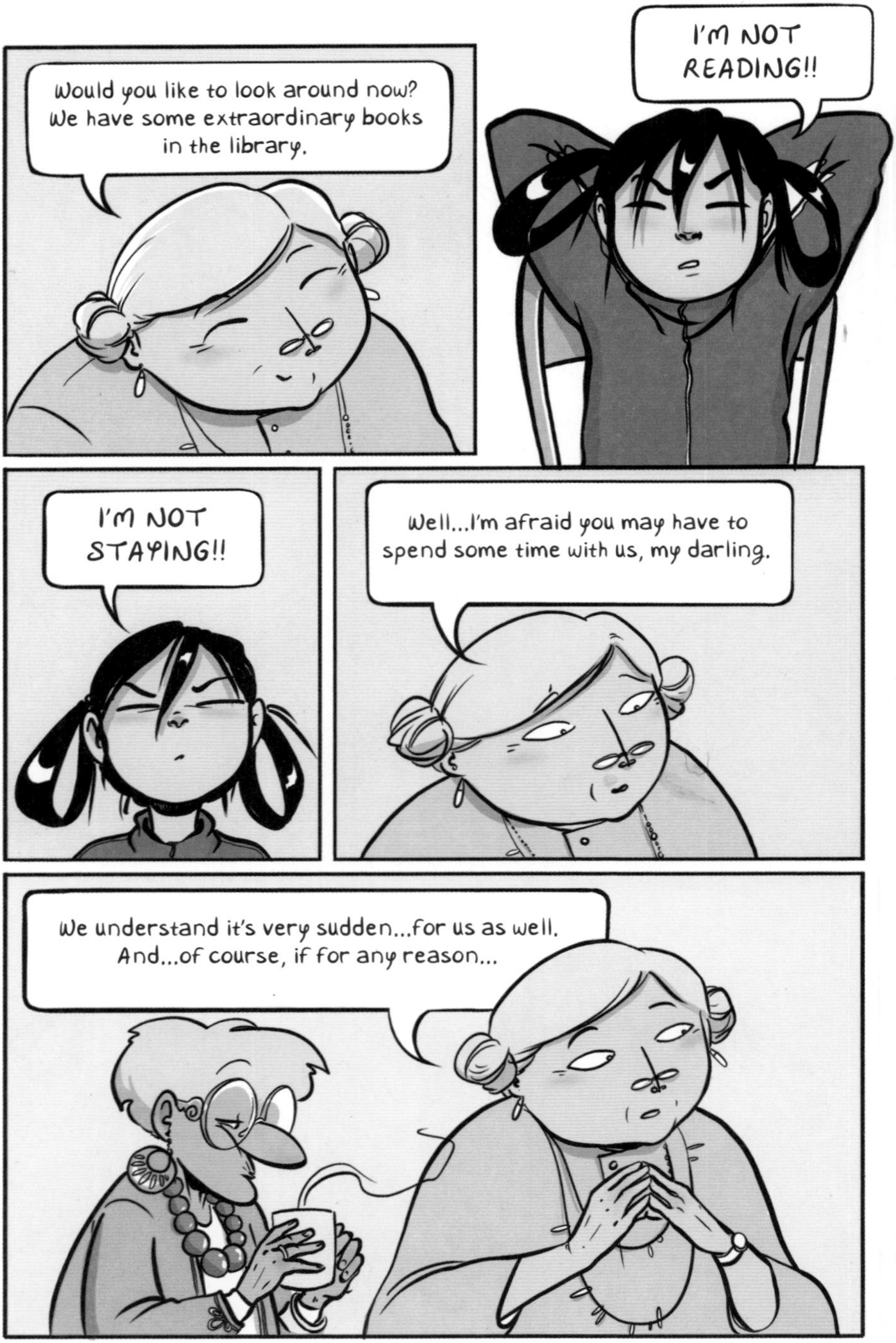
Would you like to look around now? We have some extraordinary books in the library.
I'M NOT READING!!
I'M NOT STAYING!!
Well...I'm afraid you may have to spend some time with us, my darling.
We understand it's very sudden...for us as well. And...of course, if for any reason...

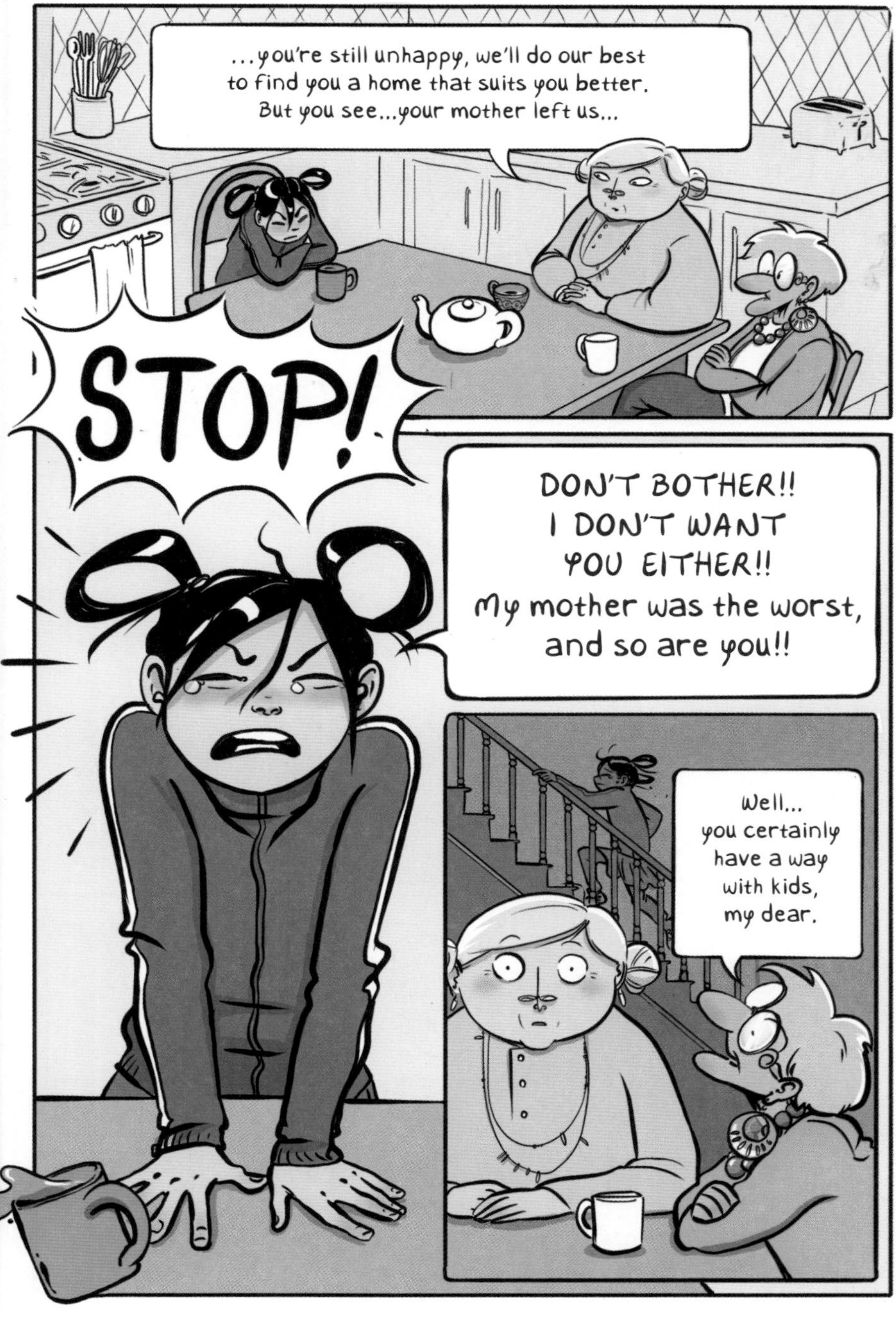
...you're still unhappy, we'll do our best to find you a home that suits you better. But you see...your mother left us...
STOP!
DON'T BOTHER!! I DON'T WANT YOU EITHER!! My mother was the worst, and so are you!!
Well... you certainly have a way with kids, my dear.

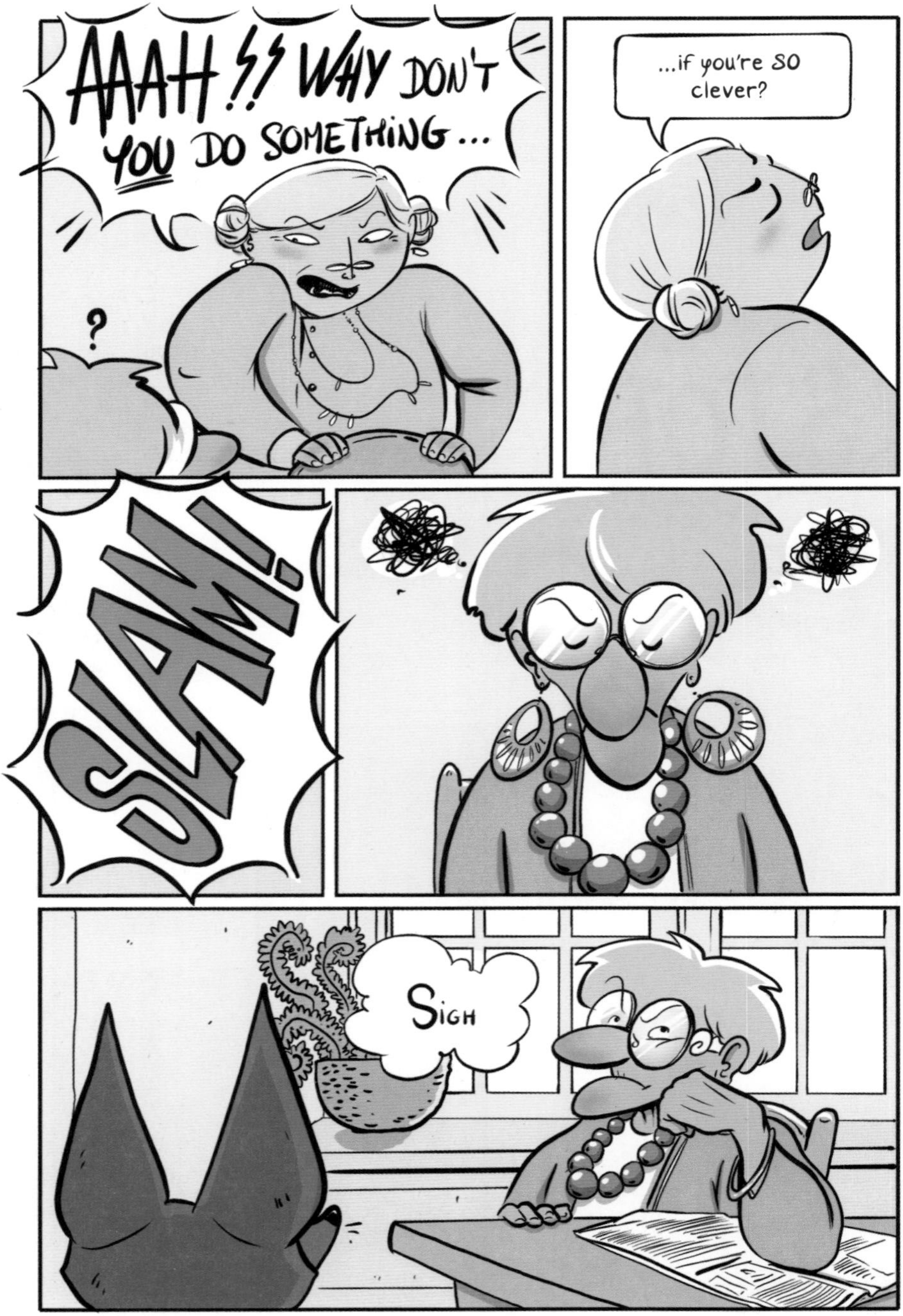
AAAH!! WHY DON'T YOU DO SOMETHING...
?
...if you're SO clever?
SLAM!
SIGH

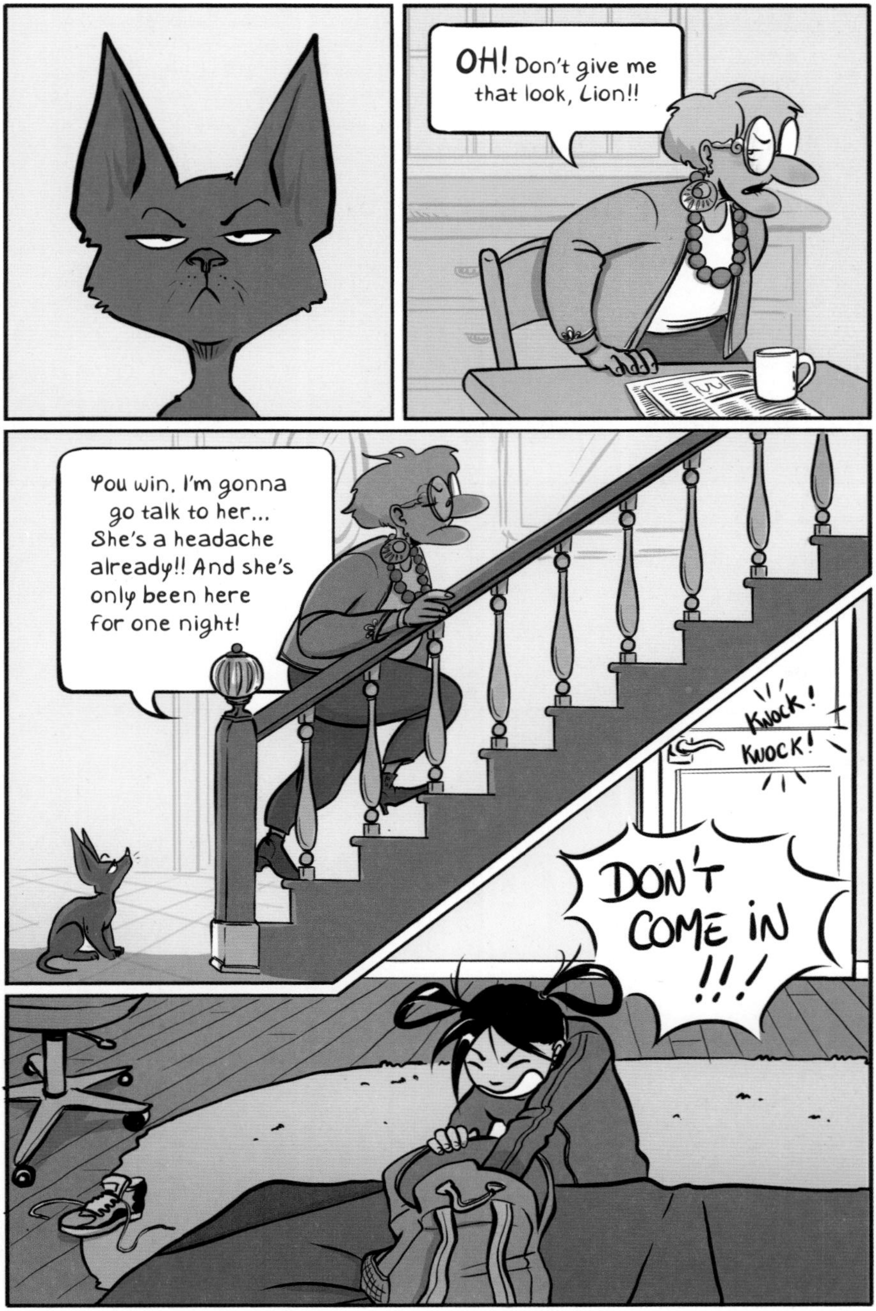
OH! Don't give me that look, Lion!!
You win. I'm gonna go talk to her... She's a headache already!! And she's only been here for one night!
KNOCK! KNOCK!
DON'T COME IN !!!

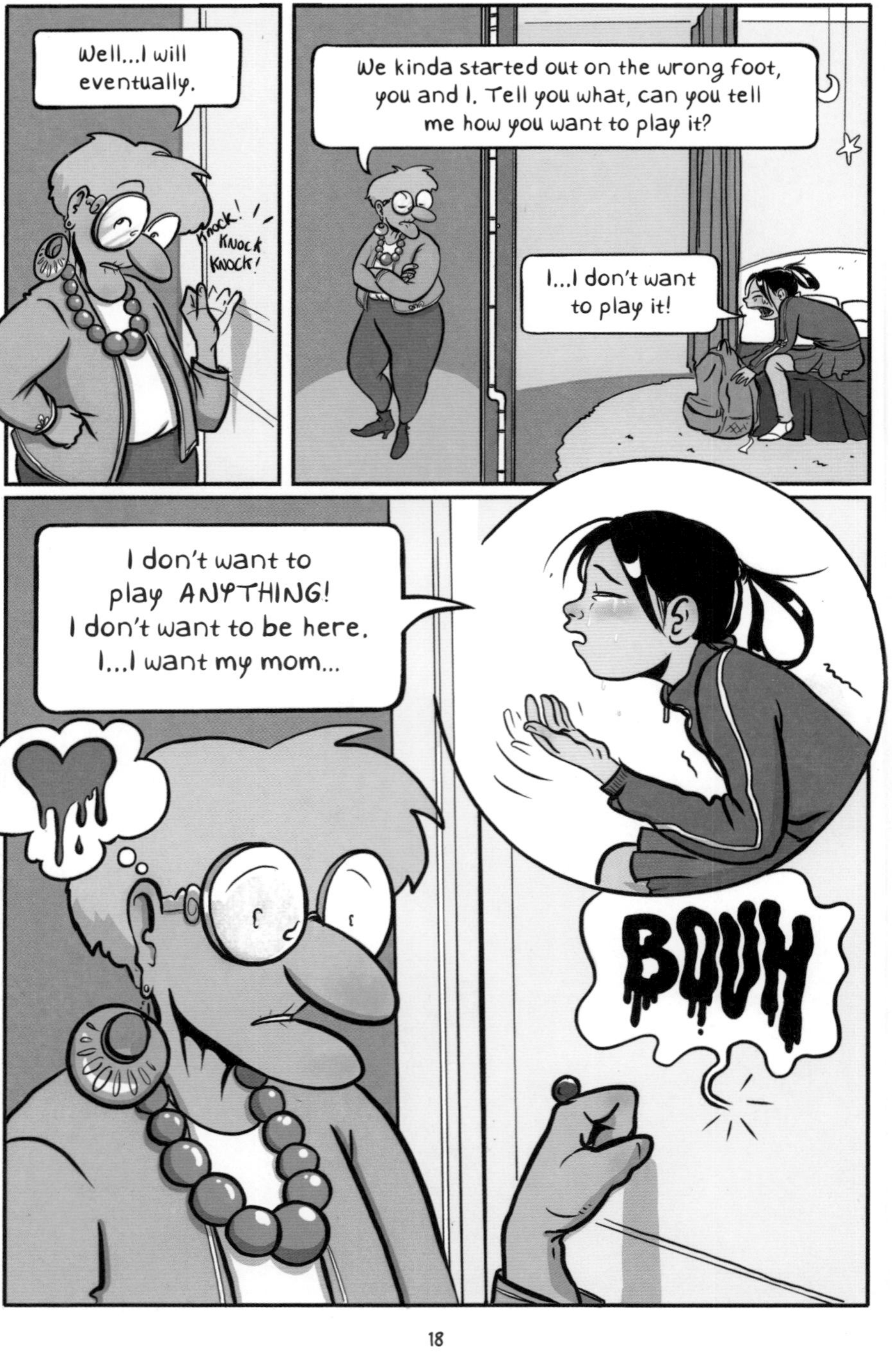
Well...I will eventually.
KNOCK! KNOCK KNOCK!
We kinda started out on the wrong foot, you and I. Tell you what, can you tell me how you want to play it?
I...I don't want to play it!
I don't want to play ANYTHING! I don't want to be here. I...I want my mom...
BOUH

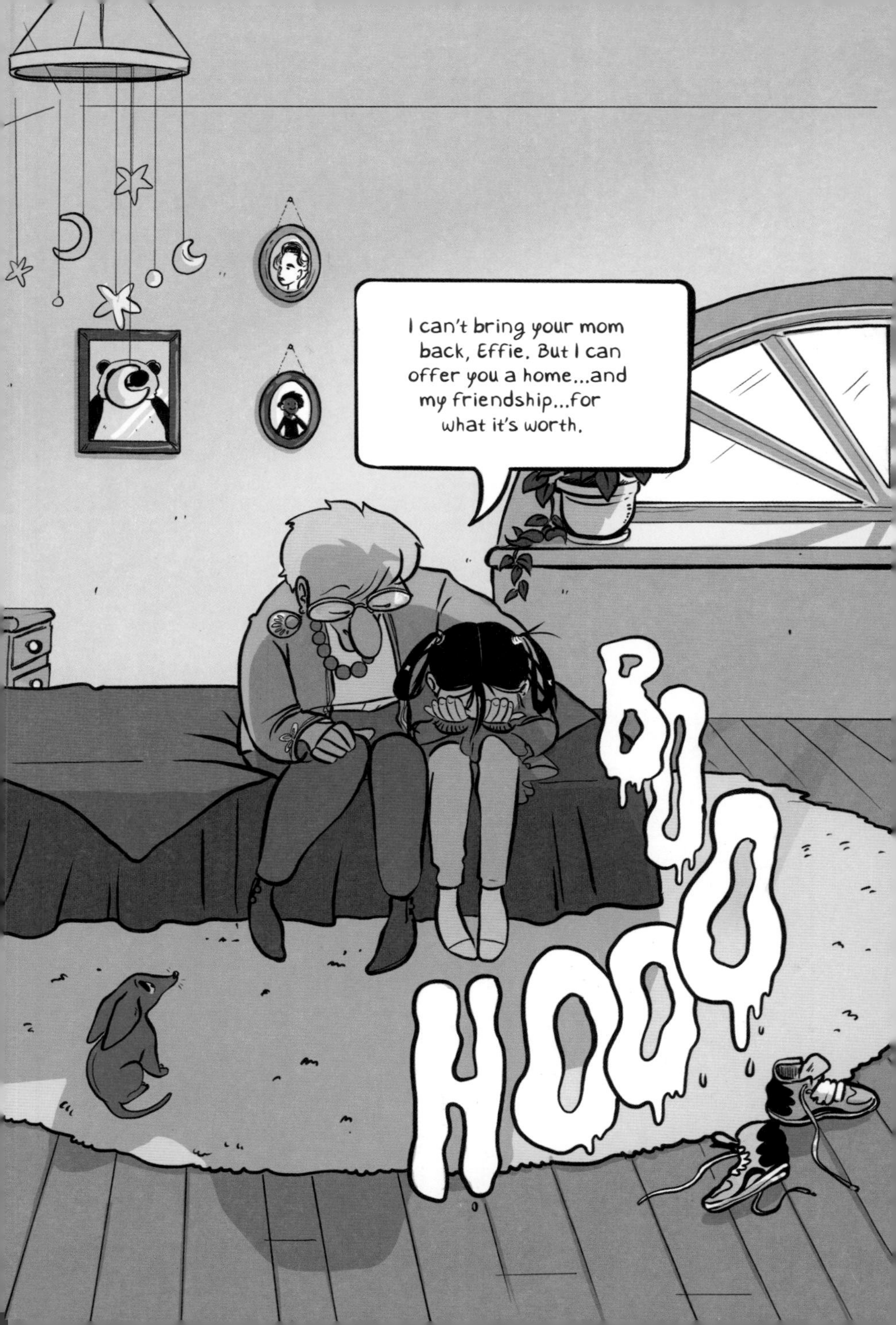
I can't bring your mom back, Effie. But I can offer you a home...and my friendship...for what it's worth.
BOO HOOO

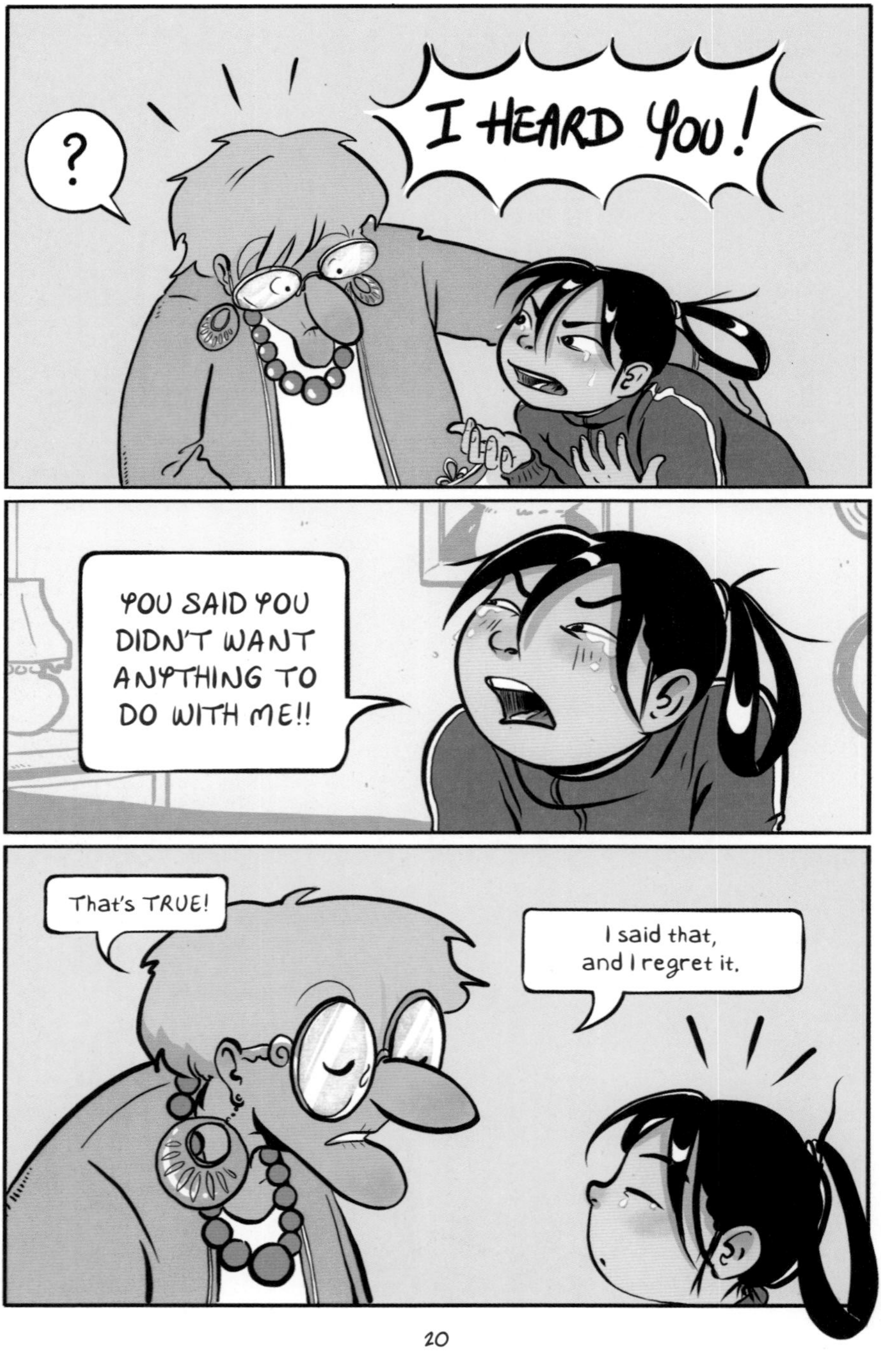

?
I HEARD YOU!
YOU SAID YOU DIDN'T WANT ANYTHING TO DO WITH ME!!
That's TRUE!
I said that, and I regret it.

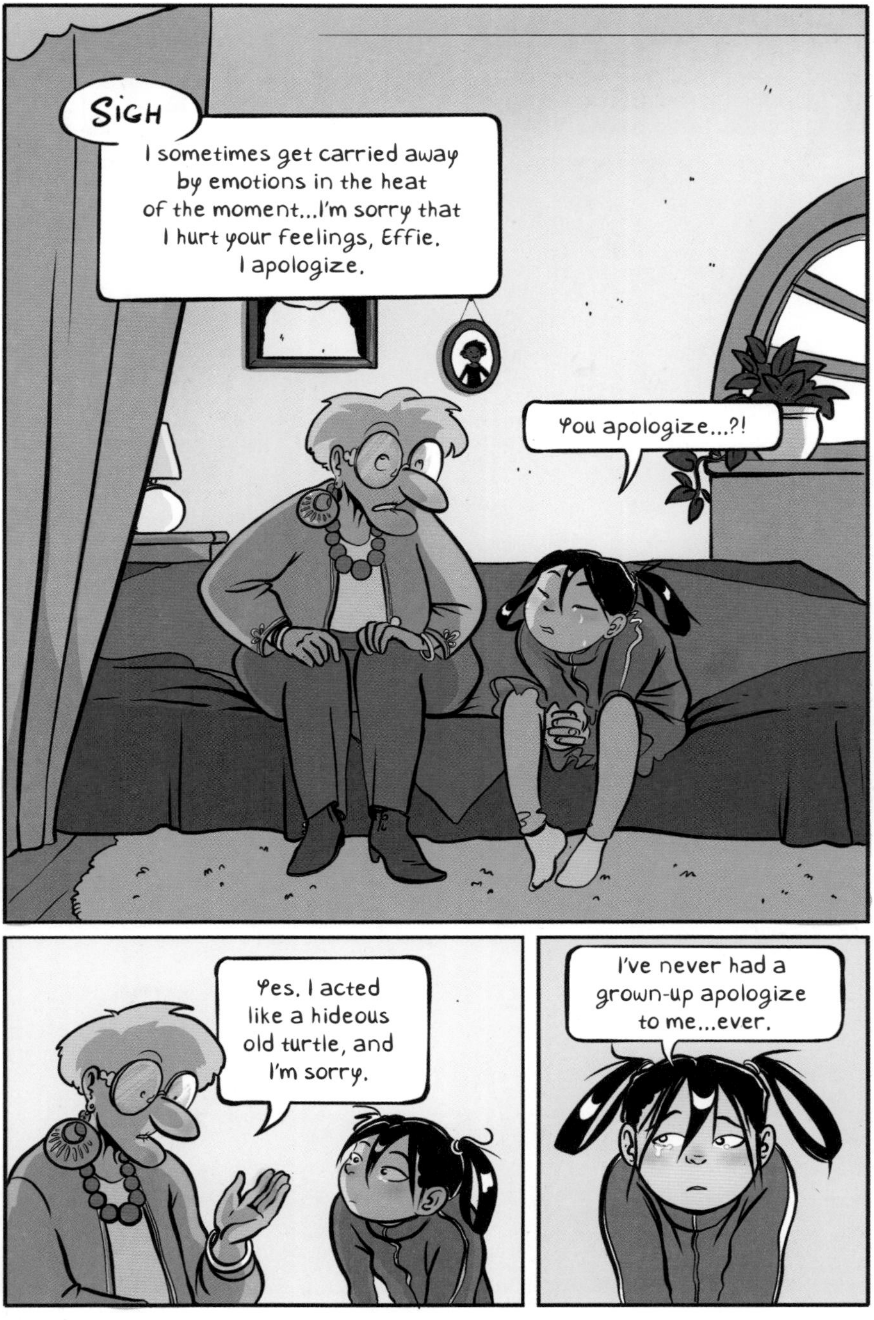
SIGH
I sometimes get carried away by emotions in the heat of the moment...I'm sorry that I hurt your feelings, Effie. I apologize.
You apologize...?!
Yes. I acted like a hideous old turtle, and I'm sorry.
I've never had a grown-up apologize to me...ever.

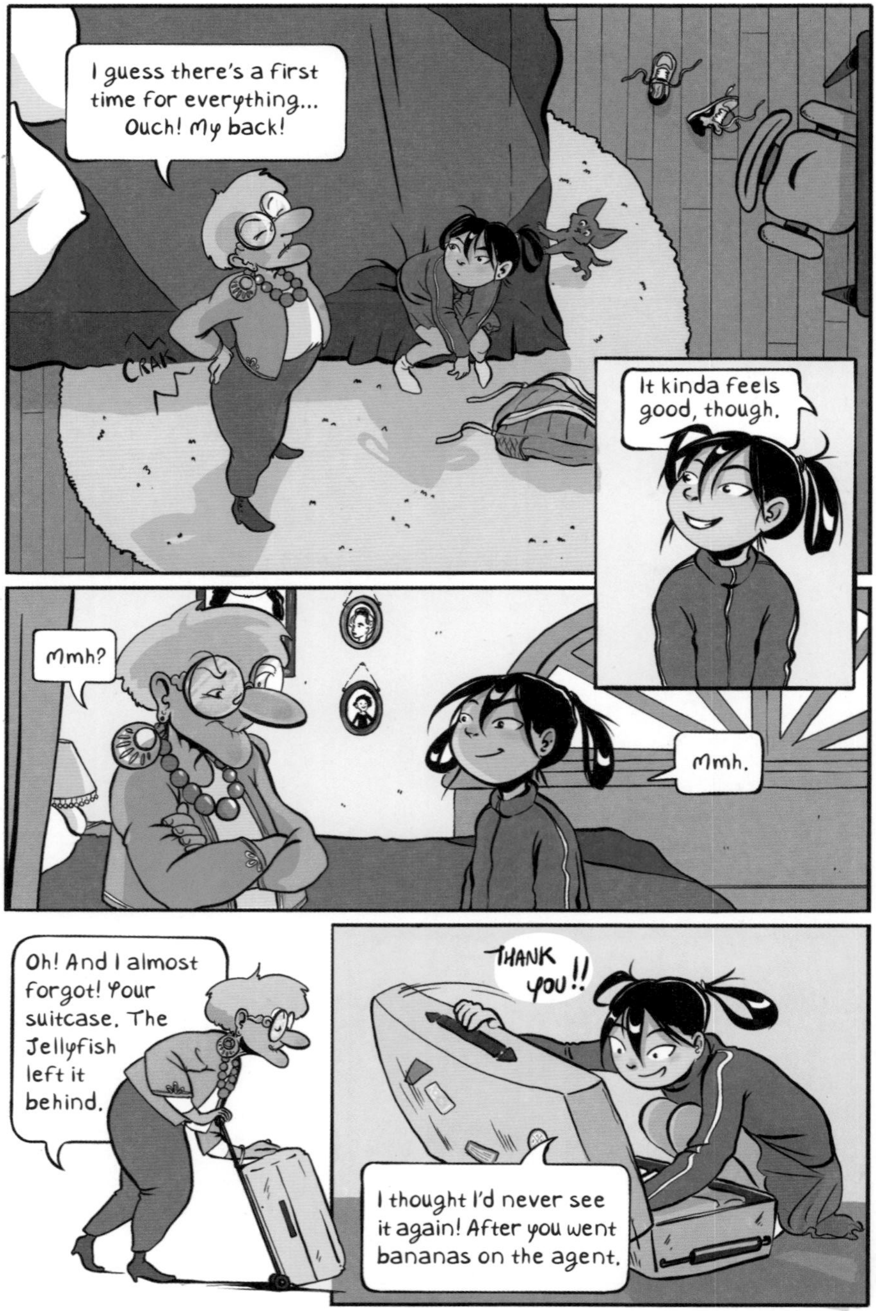
I guess there's a first time for everything... Ouch! My back!
CRAK
It kinda feels good, though.
Mmh?
Mmh.
Oh! And I almost forgot! Your suitcase. The Jellyfish left it behind.
THANK YOU!!
I thought I'd never see it again! After you went bananas on the agent.

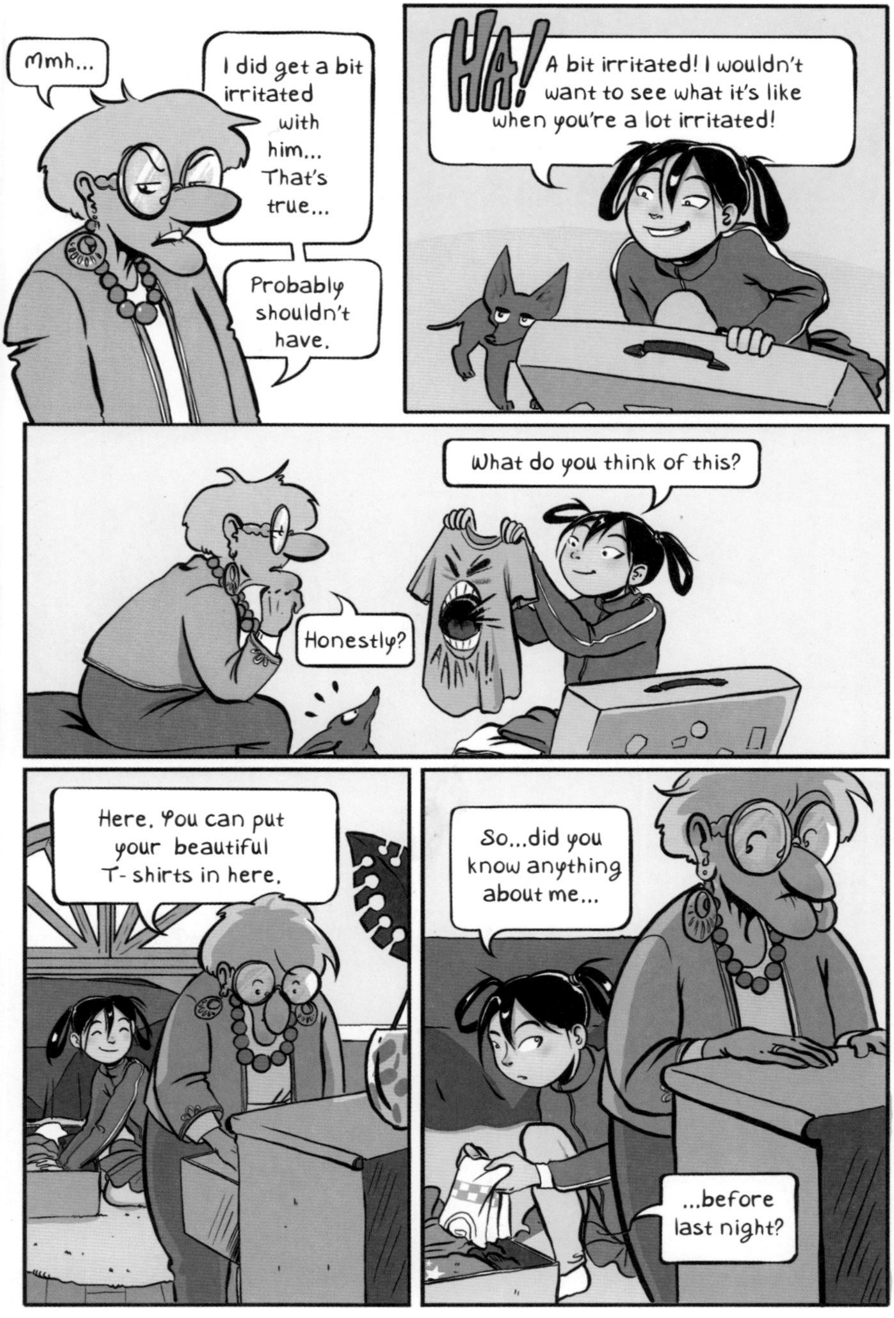
Mmh...
I did get a bit irritated with him... That's true...
Probably shouldn't have.
HA!
A bit irritated! I wouldn't want to see what it's like when you're a lot irritated!
What do you think of this?
Honestly?
Here. You can put your beautiful T-shirts in here.
So...did you know anything about me...
...before last night?

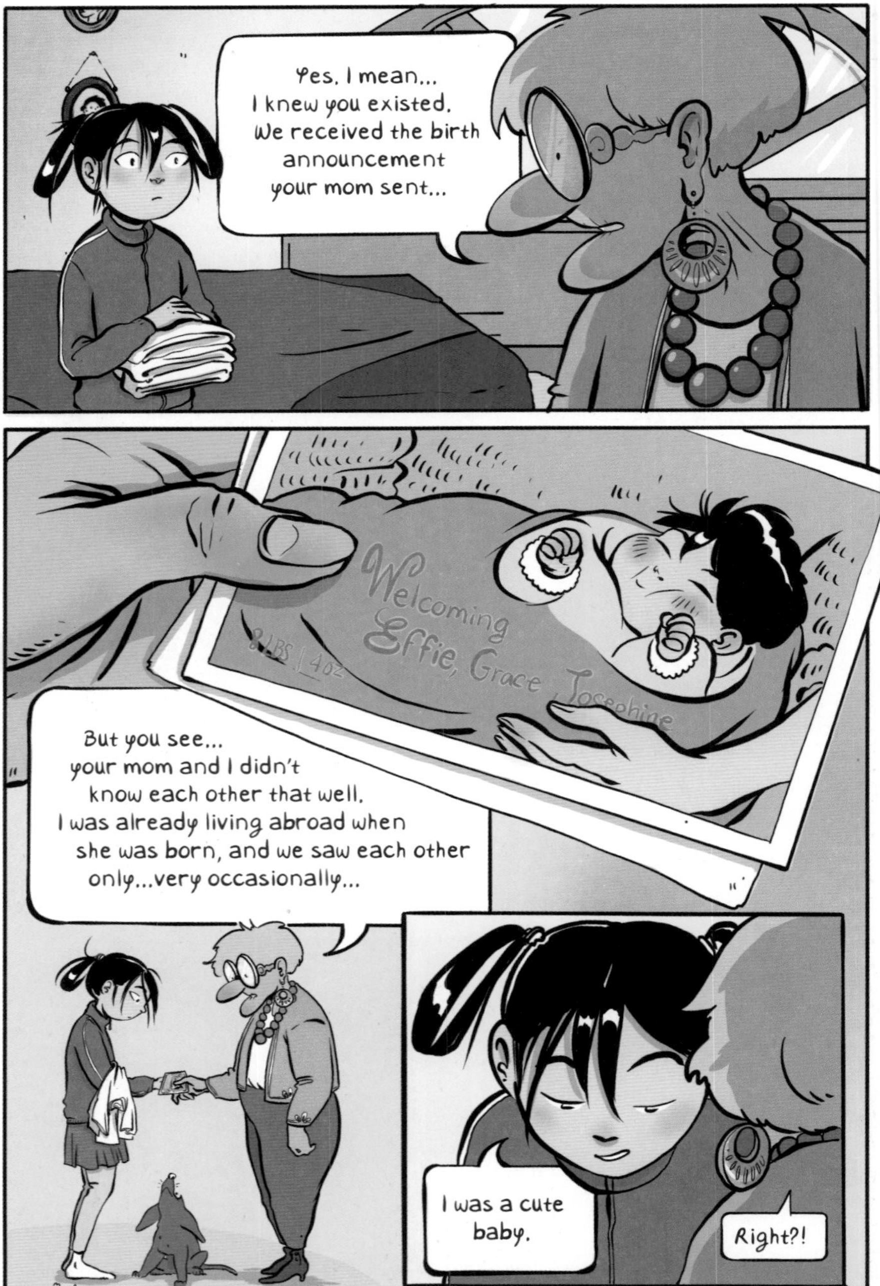
Yes. I mean...
I knew you existed.
We received the birth announcement your mom sent...
Welcoming
Effie, Grace, Josephine
But you see...
your mom and I didn't know each other that well.
I was already living abroad when she was born, and we saw each other only...very occasionally...
I was a cute baby.
Right?!

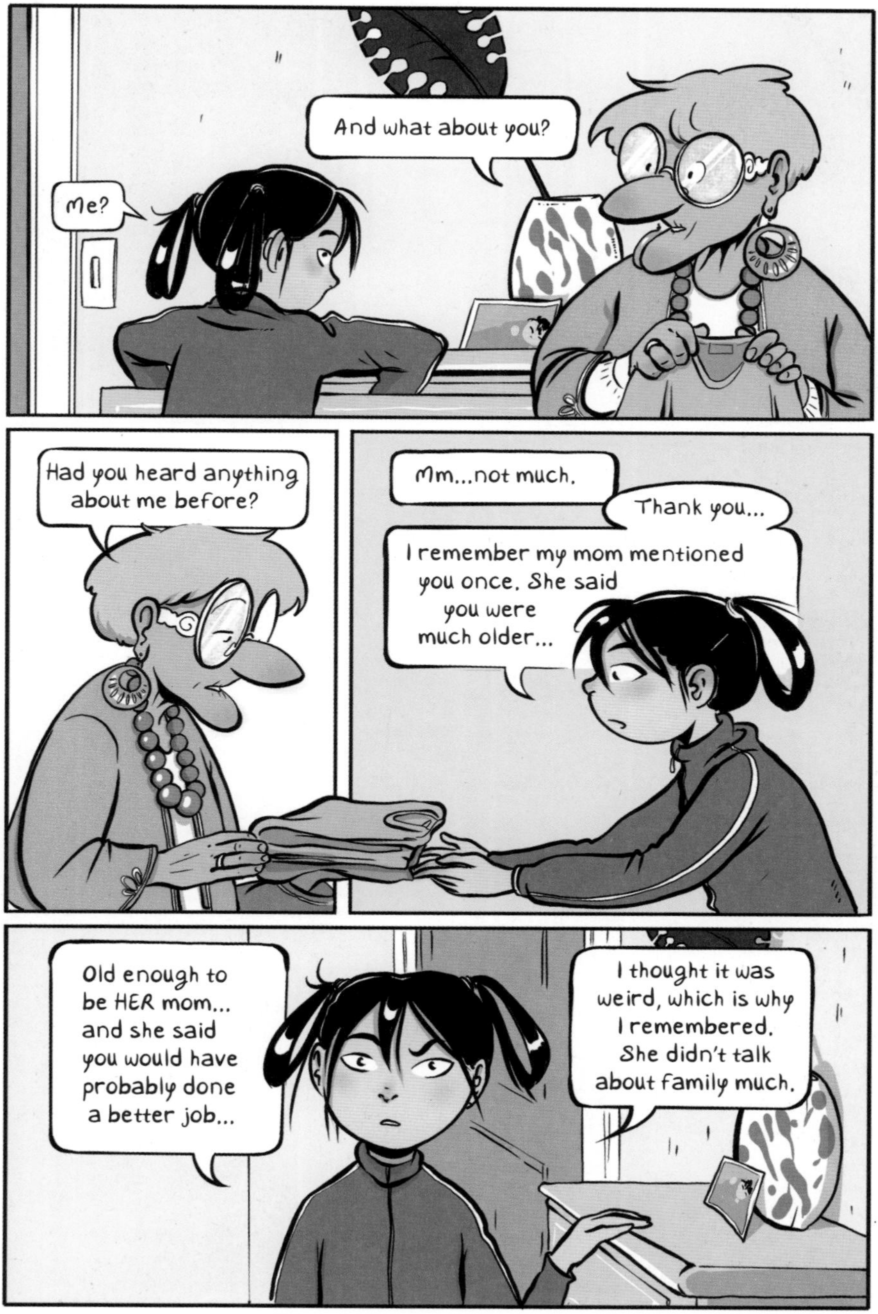
And what about you?
Me?
Had you heard anything about me before?
Mm...not much.
Thank you...
I remember my mom mentioned you once. She said you were much older...
Old enough to be HER mom... and she said you would have probably done a better job...
I thought it was weird, which is why I remembered. She didn't talk about family much.

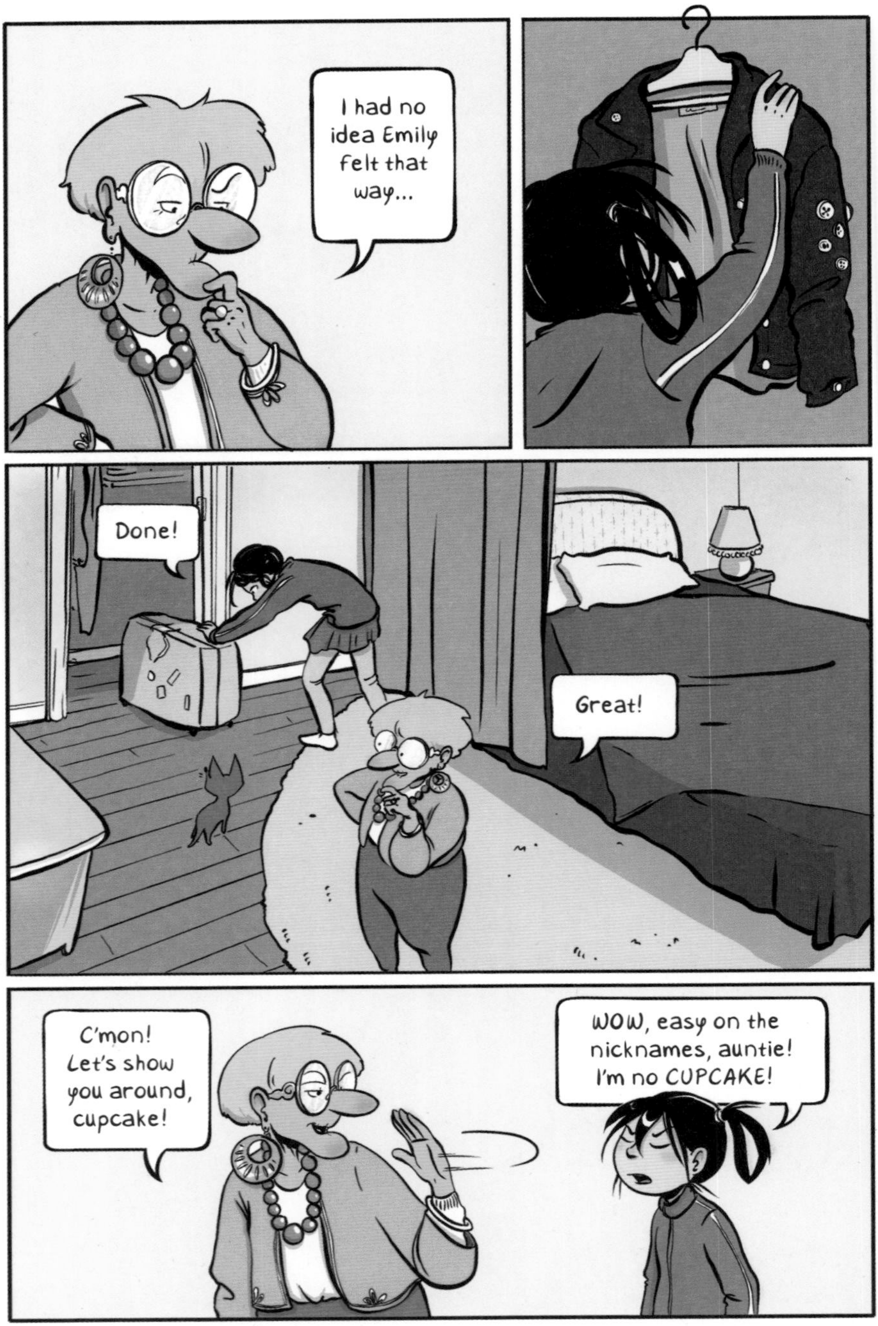
I had no idea Emily felt that way...
Done!
Great!
C'mon! Let's show you around, cupcake!
WOW, easy on the nicknames, auntie! I'm no CUPCAKE!

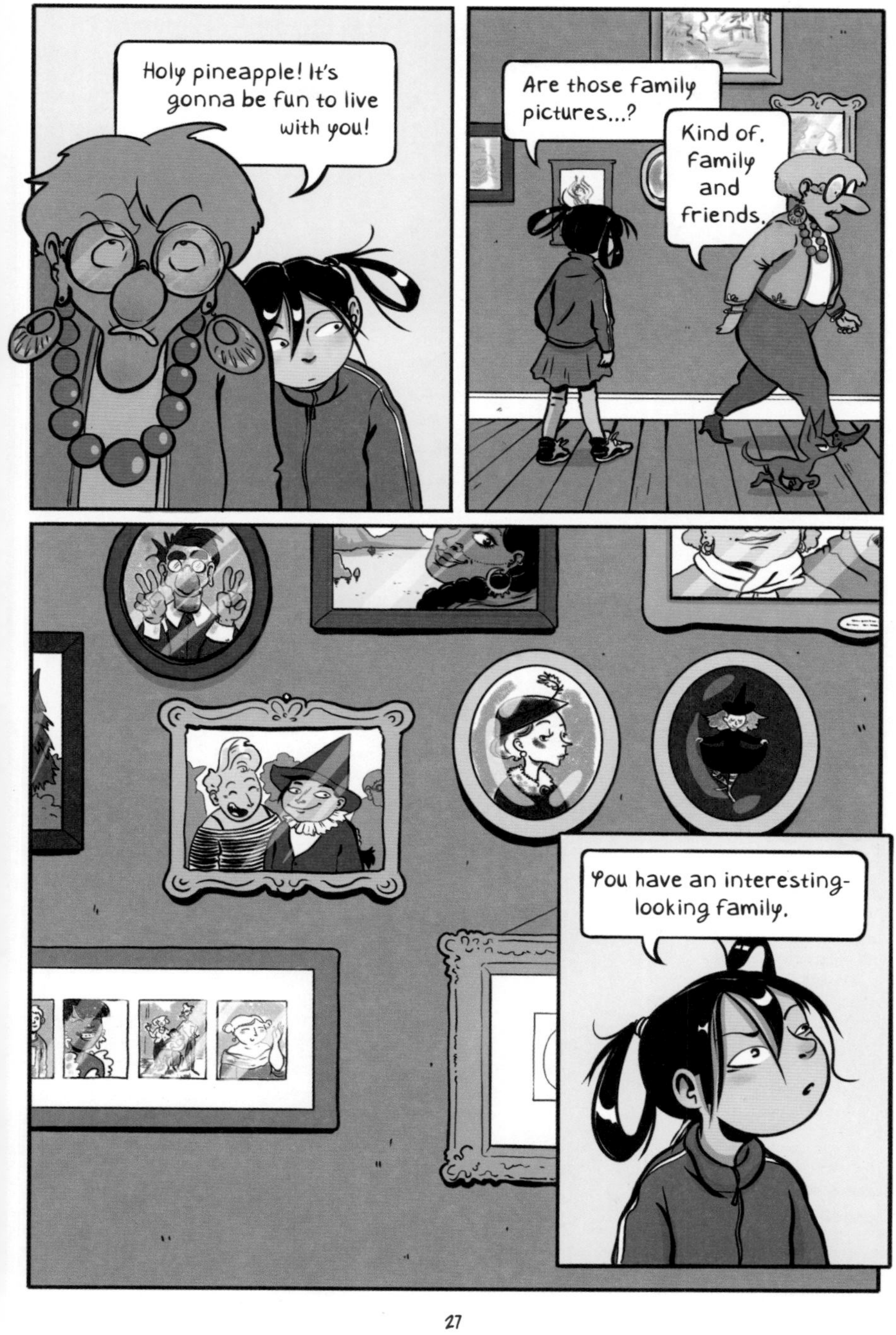
Holy pineapple! It's gonna be fun to live with you!
Are those family pictures...?
Kind of. Family and friends.
You have an interesting-looking family.

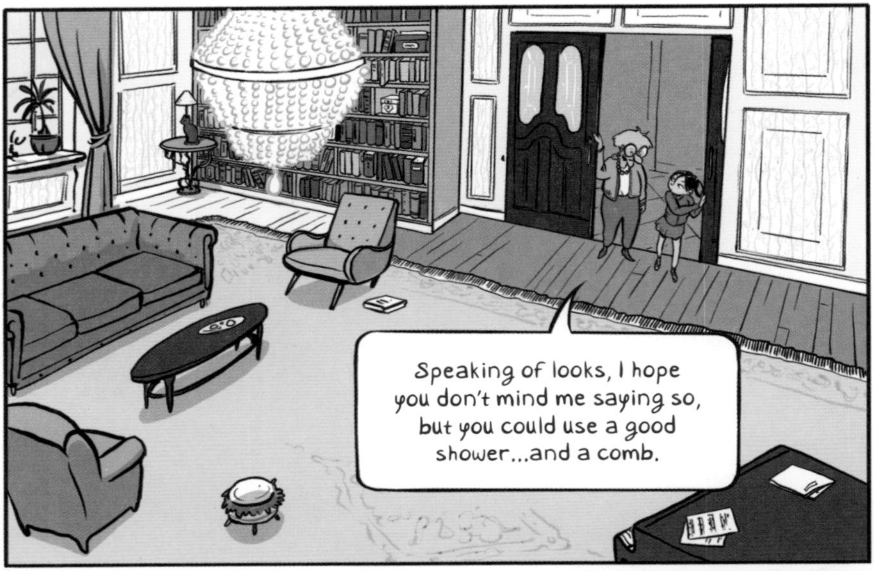
Speaking of looks, I hope you don't mind me saying so, but you could use a good shower...and a comb.

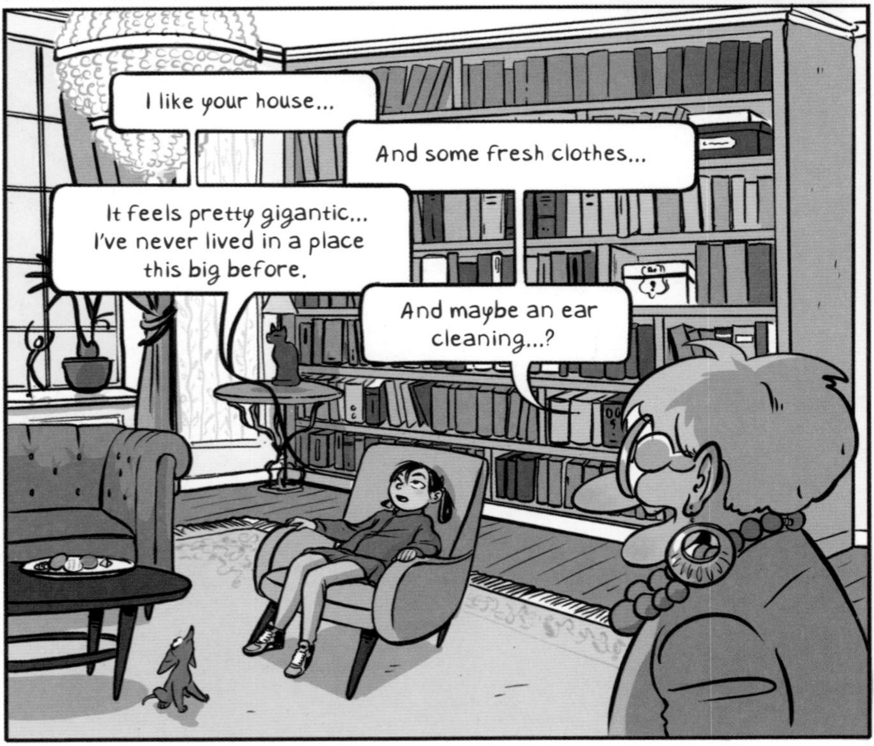
I like your house...
And some fresh clothes...
It feels pretty gigantic... I've never lived in a place this big before.
And maybe an ear cleaning...?

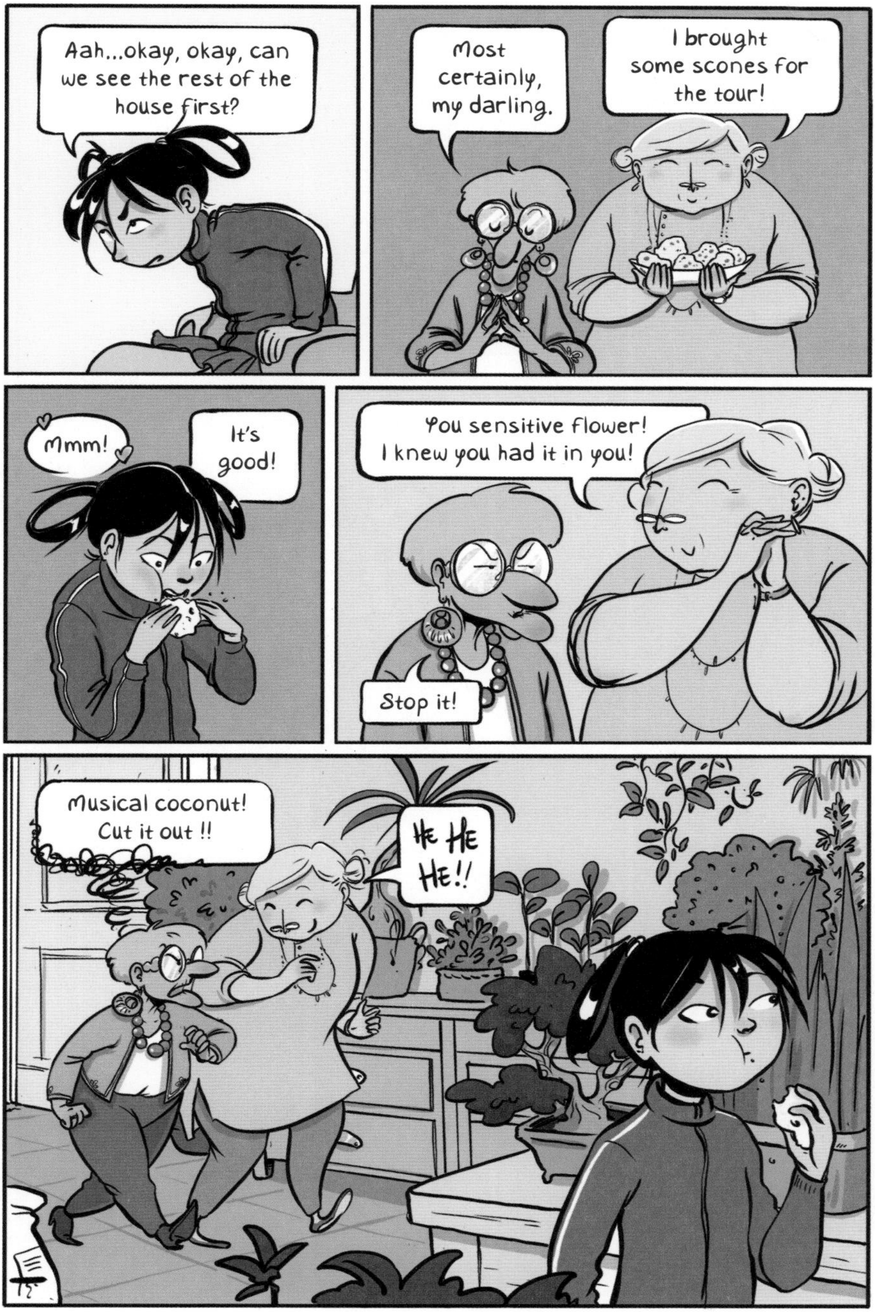

Aah...okay, okay, can we see the rest of the house first?
Most certainly, my darling.
I brought some scones for the tour!
Mmm!
It's good!
You sensitive flower! I knew you had it in you!
Stop it!
Musical coconut! Cut it out !!
HE HE HE!!

Ground Floor

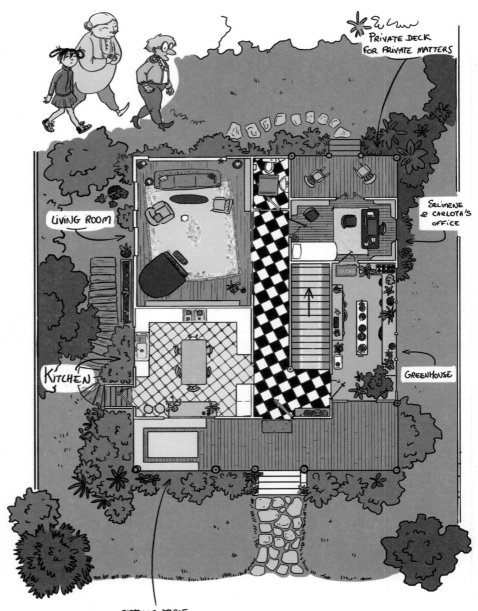

PRIVATE DECK
FOR PRIVATE MATTERS

LIVING ROOM

SELIMENE
& CARLOTA'S
OFFICE

KITCHEN

GREENHOUSE

OUTDOOR TABLE
FOR SUMMER DINNER
AND GAMES

2nd FLOOR

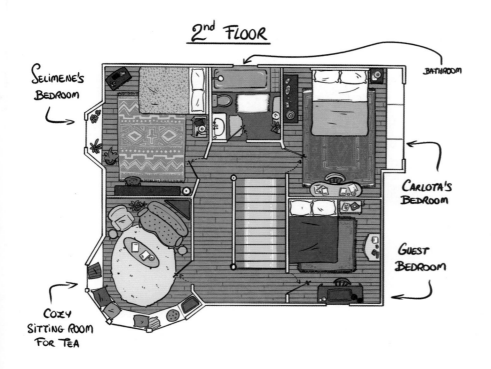

SELIMENE'S BEDROOM

BATHROOM

CARLOTA'S BEDROOM

GUEST BEDROOM

COZY SITTING ROOM FOR TEA

3rd FLOOR

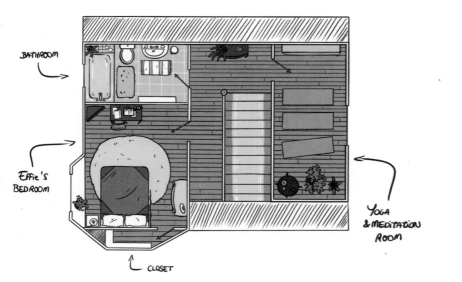

BATHROOM

EFFIE'S BEDROOM

YOGA & MEDITATION ROOM

CLOSET

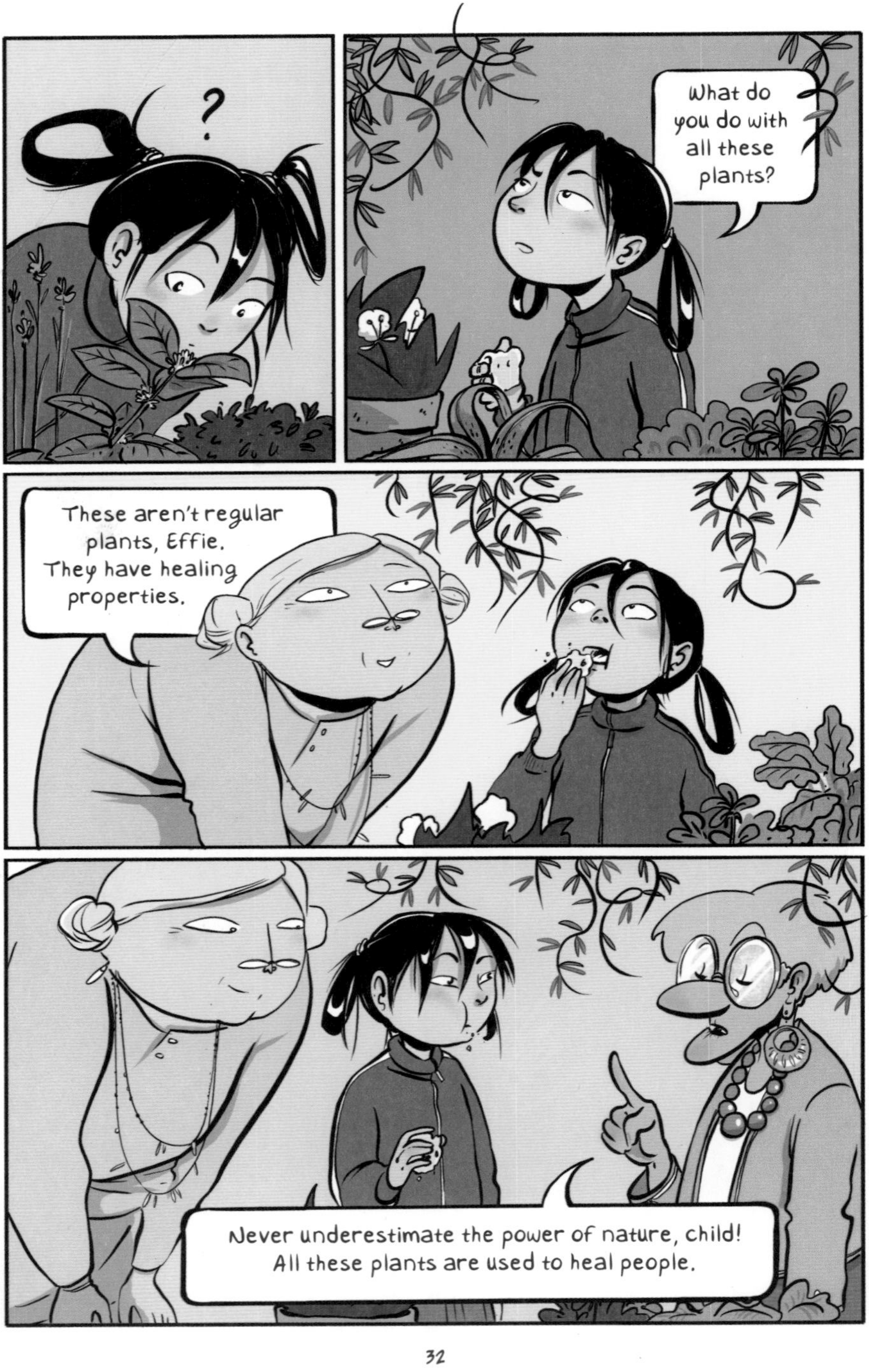
?
What do you do with all these plants?
These aren't regular plants, Effie. They have healing properties.
Never underestimate the power of nature, child! All these plants are used to heal people.

Wait a second. Does that mean you are doctors?

Sort of . . .

We are HERBALISTS, my dear.

. . . ?

You see, everyday aches and pains don't require heavy chemicals. For centuries, people have used plants to heal them!

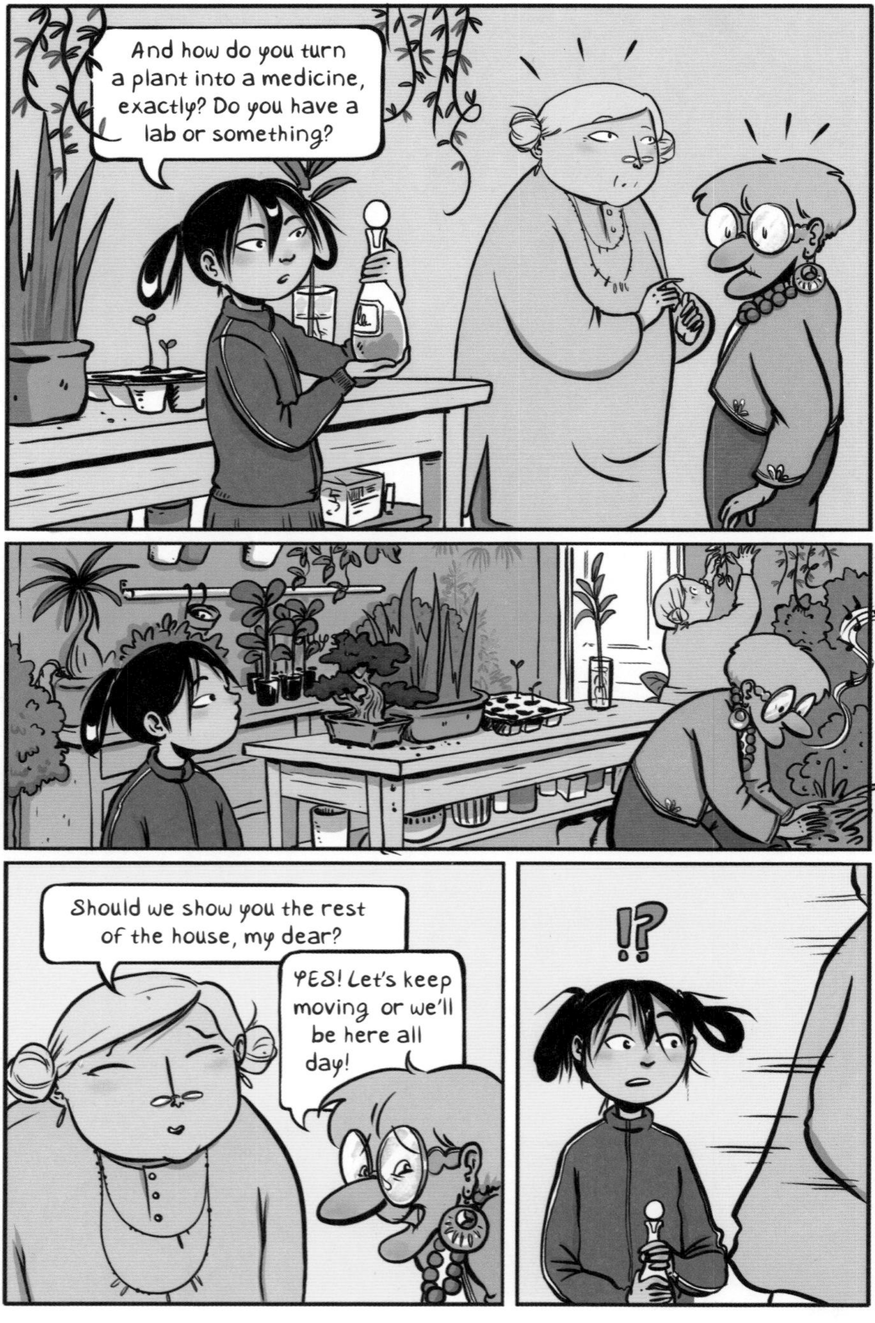
And how do you turn a plant into a medicine, exactly? Do you have a lab or something?
Should we show you the rest of the house, my dear?
YES! Let's keep moving or we'll be here all day!
!?

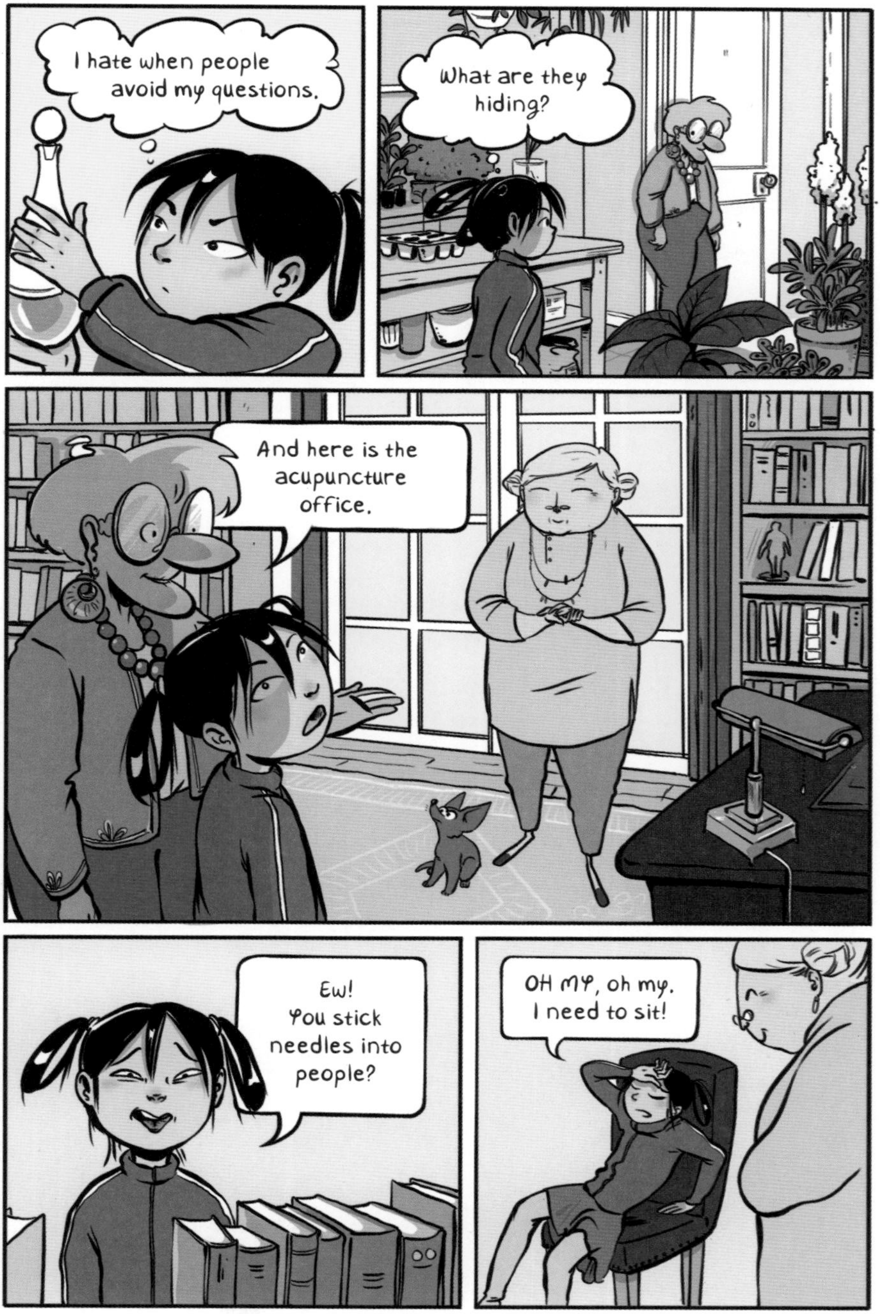
I hate when people avoid my questions.
What are they hiding?
And here is the acupuncture office.
Ew! You stick needles into people?
OH MY, oh my. I need to sit!

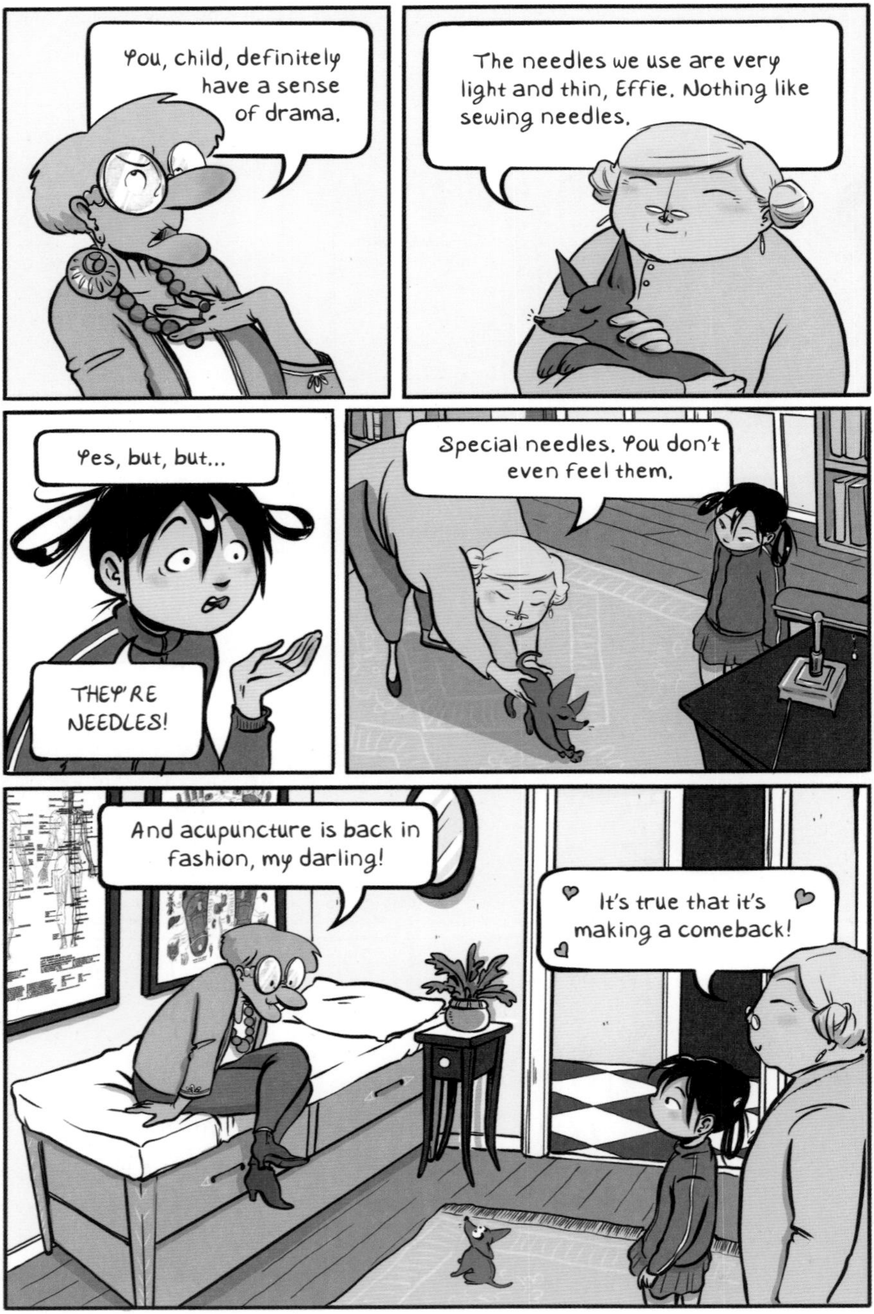
You, child, definitely have a sense of drama.
The needles we use are very light and thin, Effie. Nothing like sewing needles.
Yes, but, but...
THEY'RE NEEDLES!
Special needles. You don't even feel them.
And acupuncture is back in fashion, my darling!
It's true that it's making a comeback!

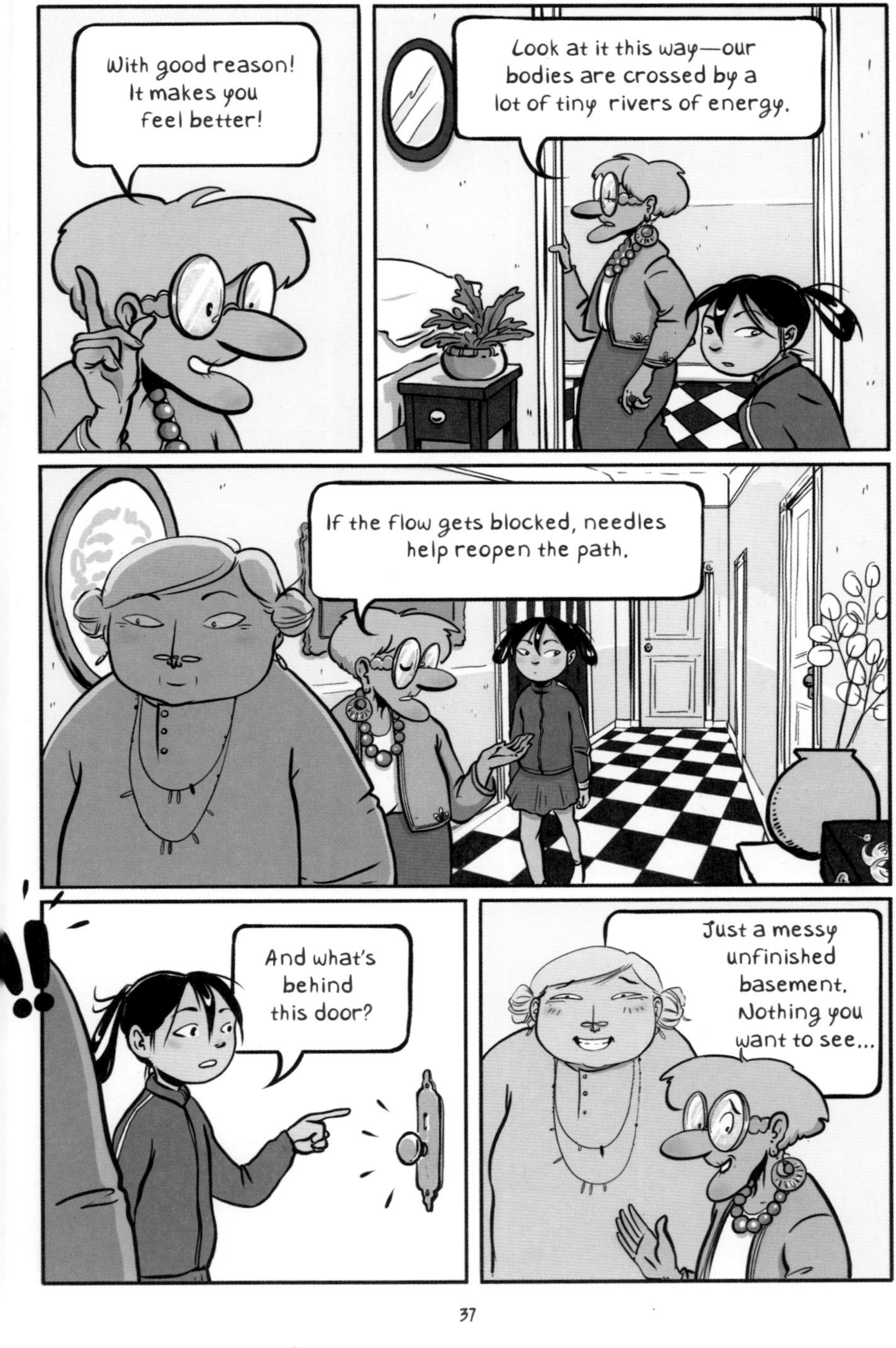
With good reason! It makes you feel better!
Look at it this way—our bodies are crossed by a lot of tiny rivers of energy.
If the flow gets blocked, needles help reopen the path.
!!
And what's behind this door?
Just a messy unfinished basement. Nothing you want to see...

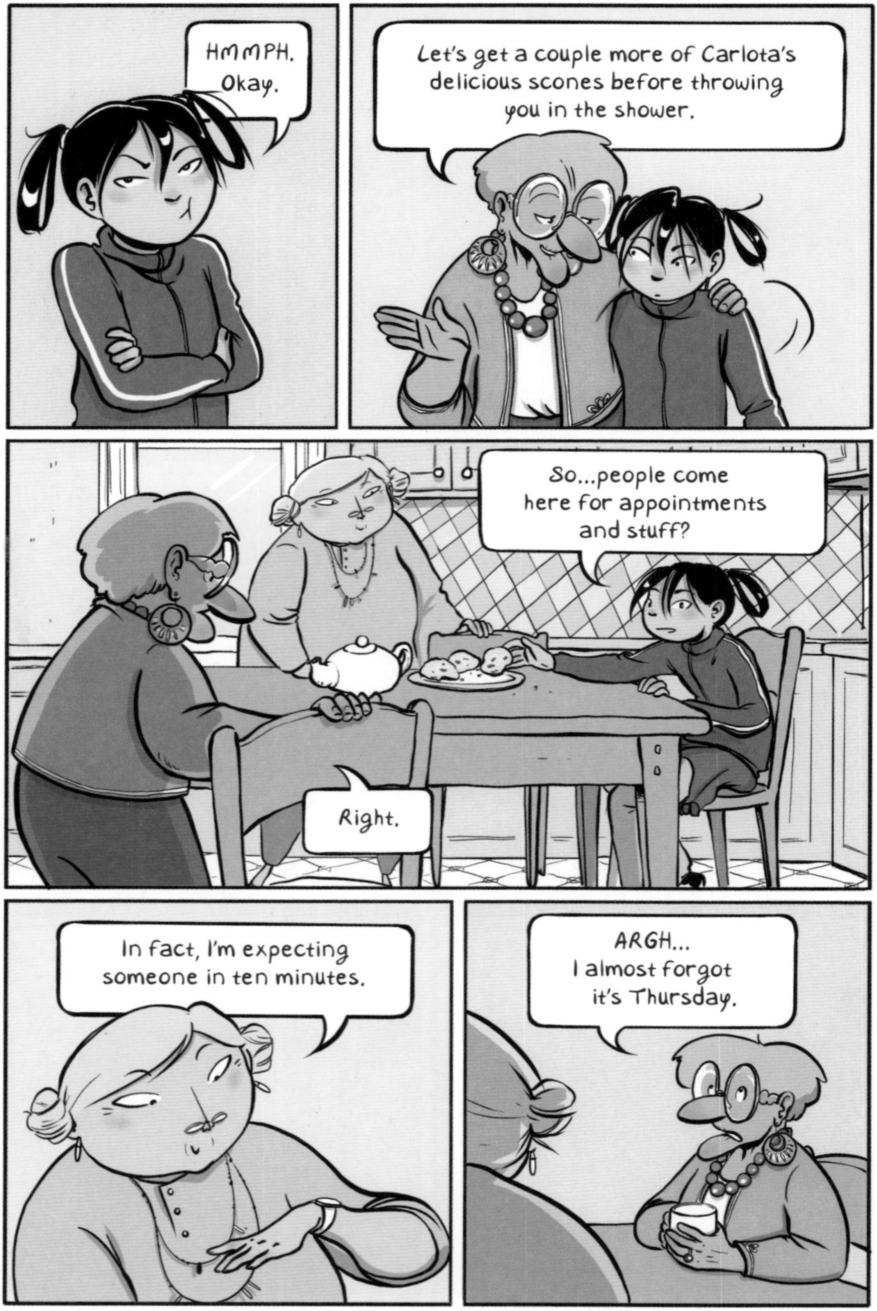
HMMPH. Okay.
Let's get a couple more of Carlota's delicious scones before throwing you in the shower.
So...people come here for appointments and stuff?
Right.
In fact, I'm expecting someone in ten minutes.
ARGH... I almost forgot it's Thursday.

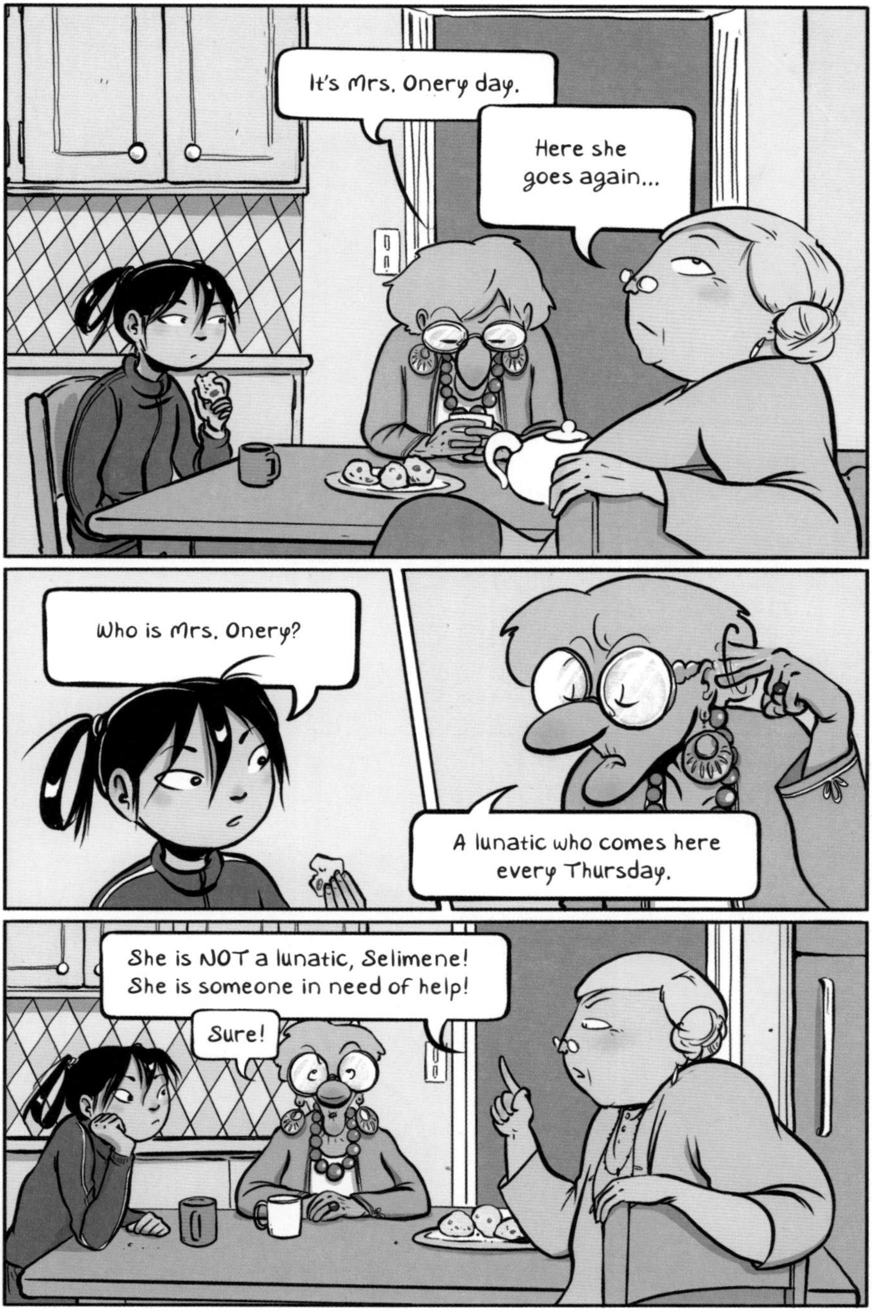
It's Mrs. Onery day.
Here she goes again...
Who is Mrs. Onery?
A lunatic who comes here every Thursday.
She is NOT a lunatic, Selimene! She is someone in need of help!
Sure!

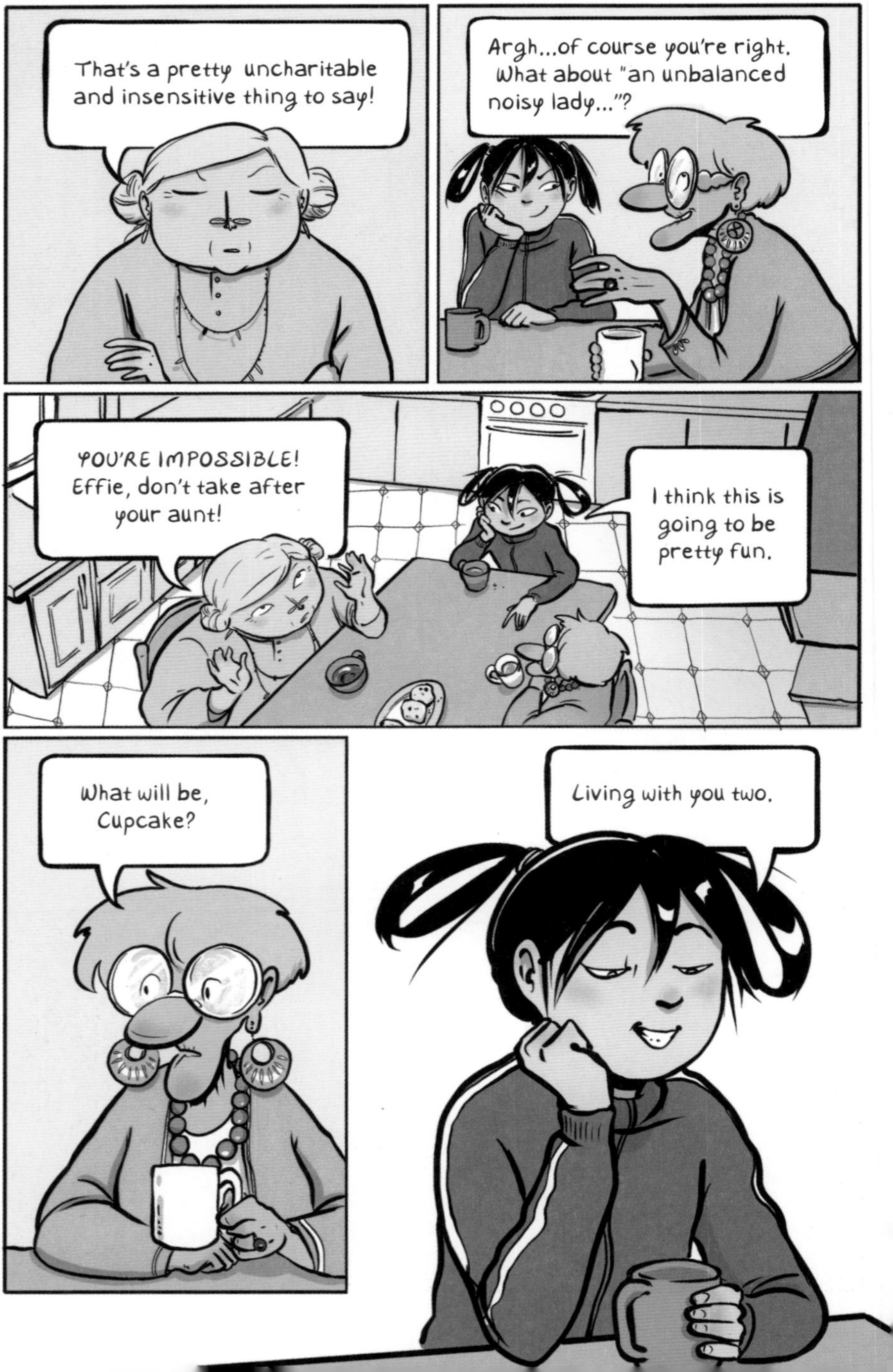
That's a pretty uncharitable and insensitive thing to say!
Argh...of course you're right. What about "an unbalanced noisy lady..."?
YOU'RE IMPOSSIBLE! Effie, don't take after your aunt!
I think this is going to be pretty fun.
What will be, Cupcake?
Living with you two.

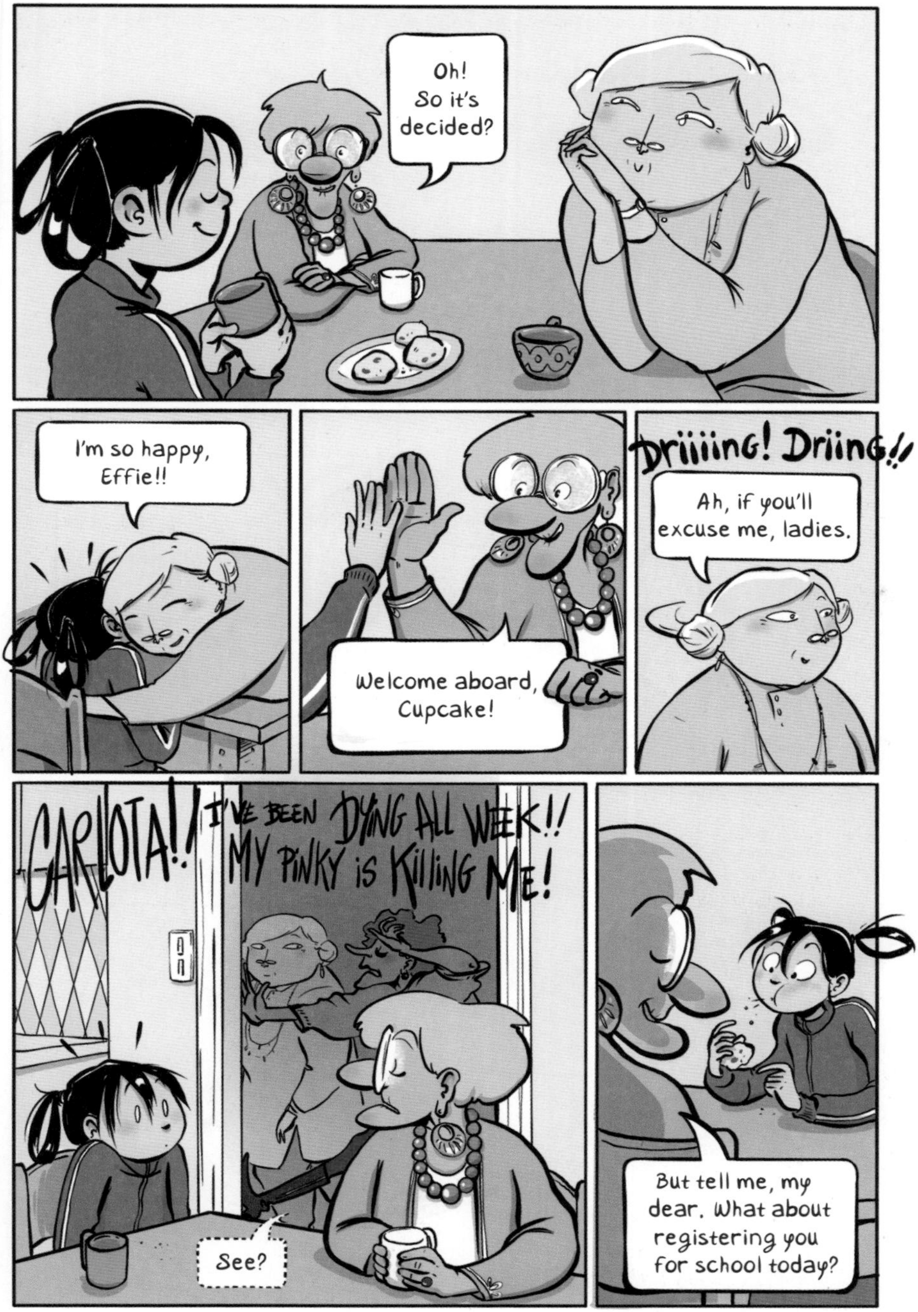
Oh!
So it's decided?
I'm so happy, Effie!!
Welcome aboard, Cupcake!
Driiiing! Driing!!
Ah, if you'll excuse me, ladies.
CARLOTA!! I'VE BEEN DYING ALL WEEK!! MY PINKY IS KILLING ME!
See?
But tell me, my dear. What about registering you for school today?

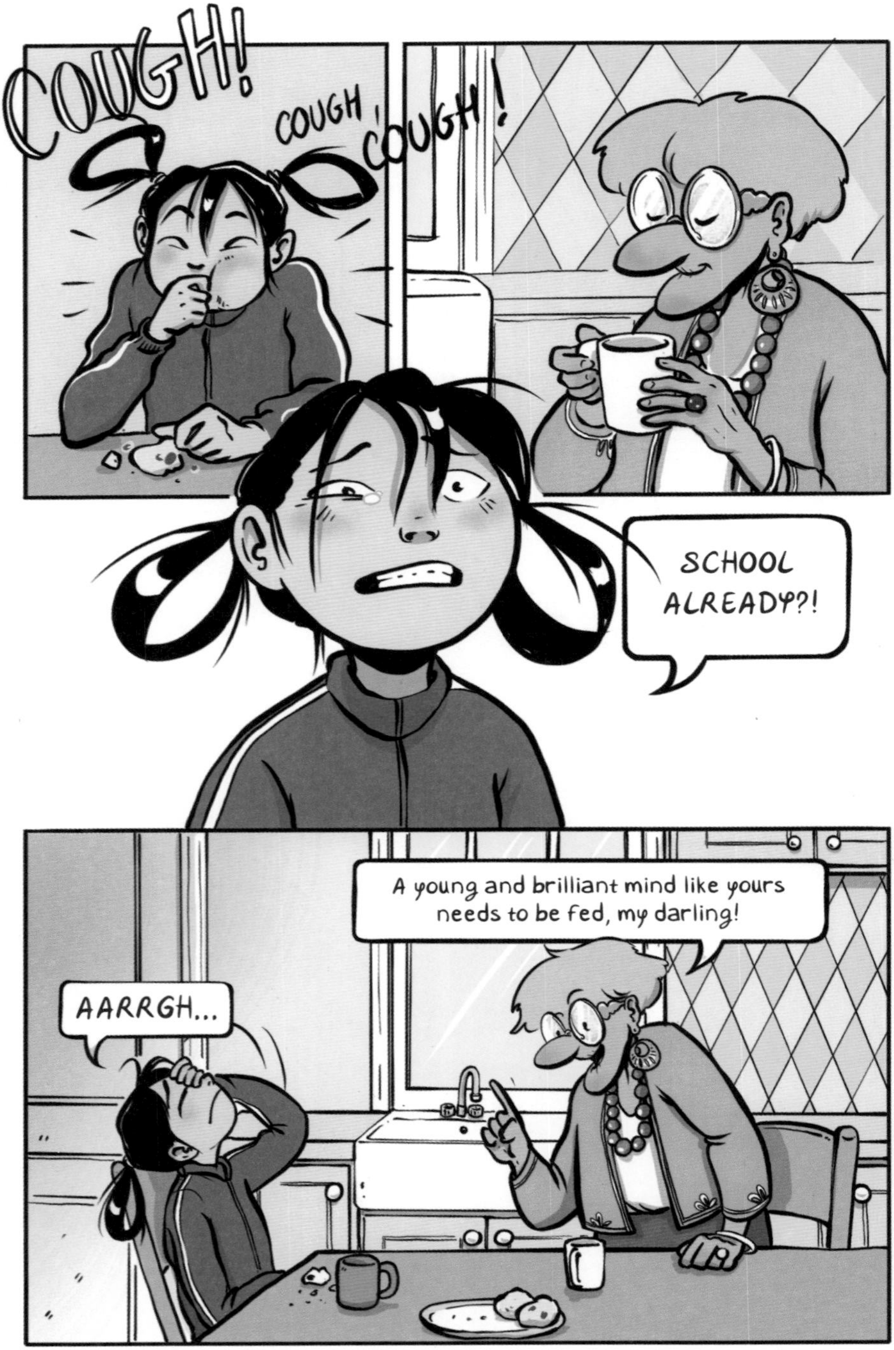
COUGH!
COUGH, COUGH!
SCHOOL ALREADY?!
A young and brilliant mind like yours needs to be fed, my darling!
AARRGH...

Are there even schools in this neighborhood?!
Oh, you'd be surprised how many things there are in this neighborhood!

Chapter 2

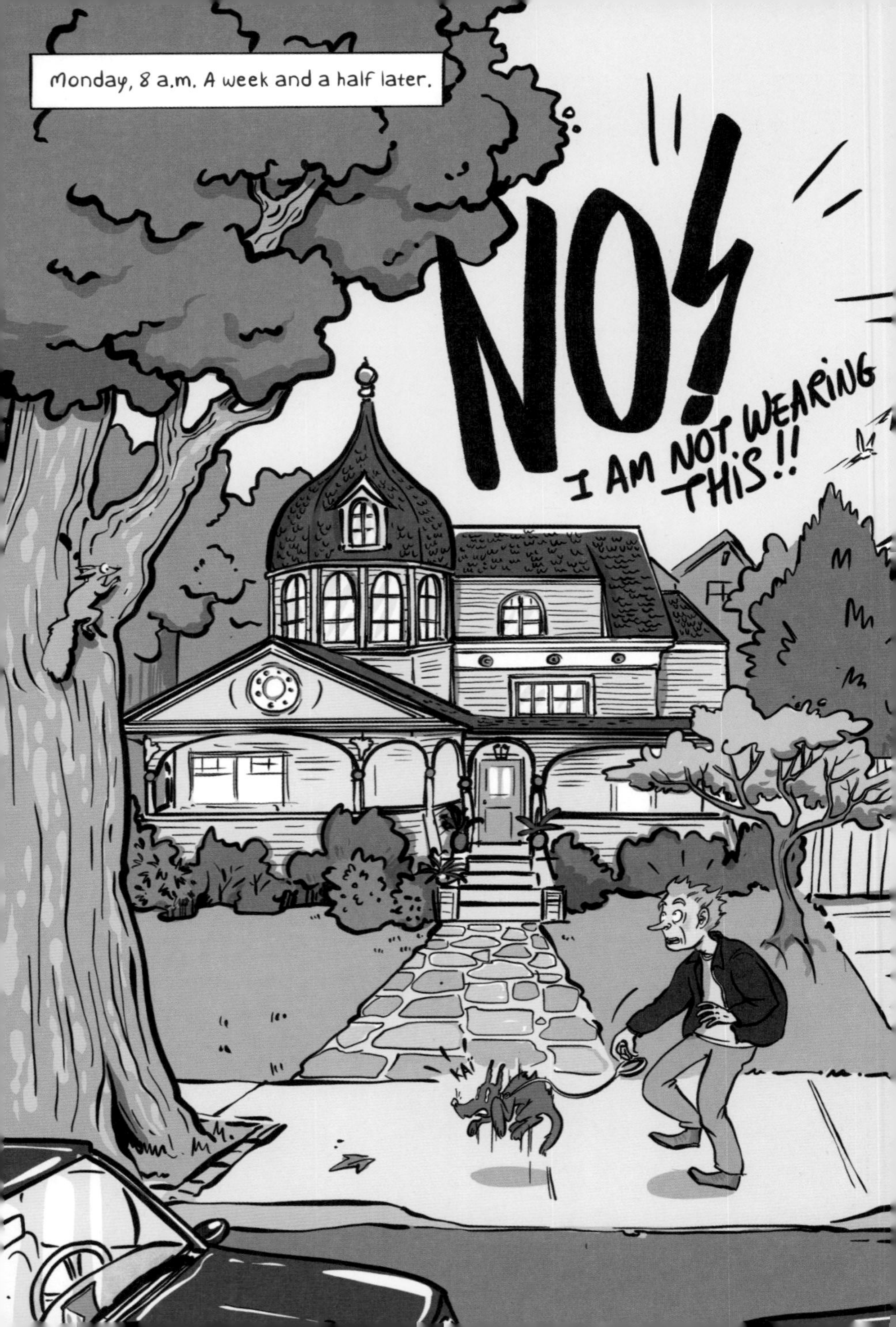
Monday, 8 a.m. A week and a half later.
NO!
I AM NOT WEARING THIS!!
KAI

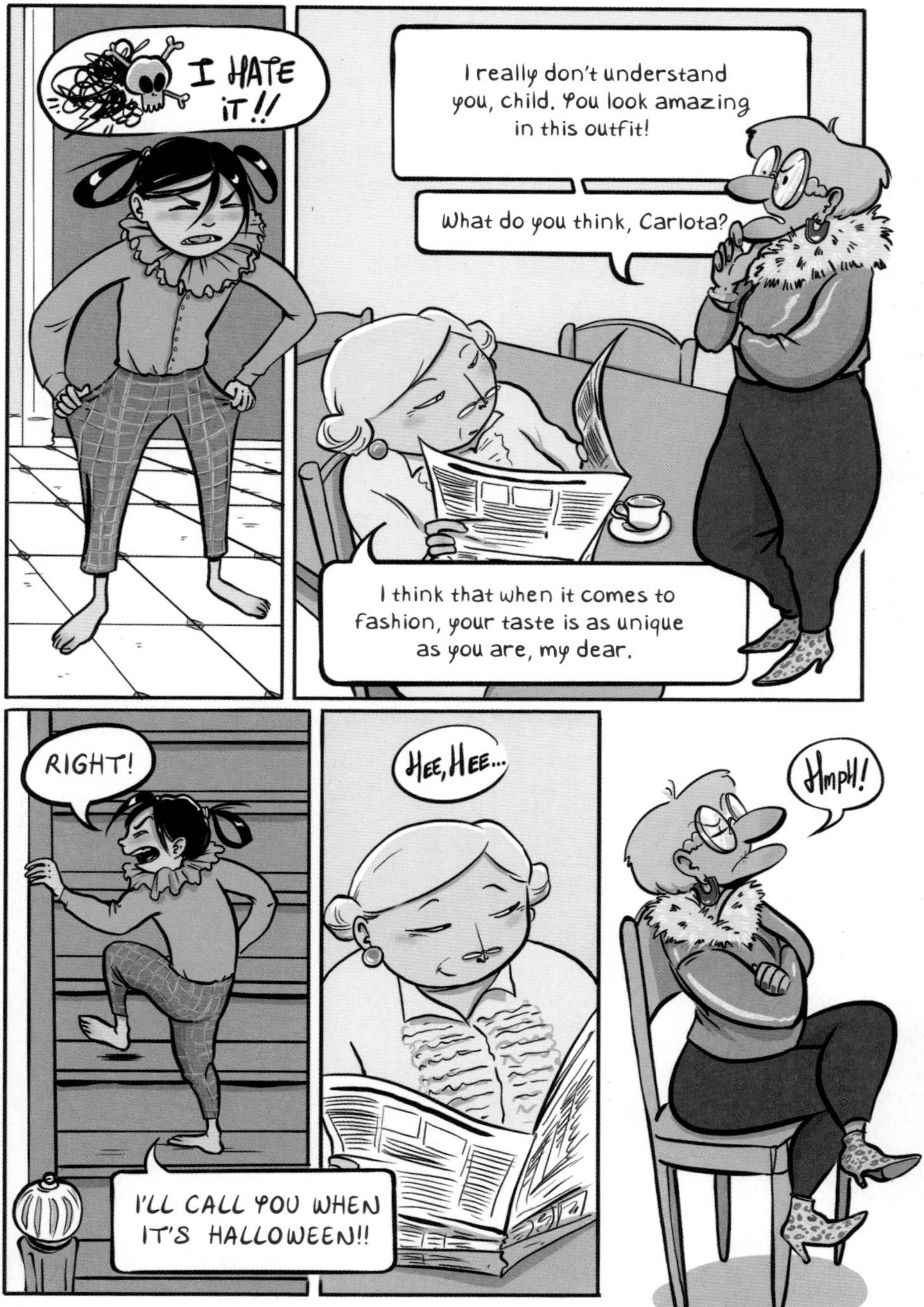
I HATE IT!!
I really don't understand you, child. You look amazing in this outfit!
What do you think, Carlota?
I think that when it comes to fashion, your taste is as unique as you are, my dear.
RIGHT!
I'LL CALL YOU WHEN IT'S HALLOWEEN!!
HEE, HEE...
HMPH!

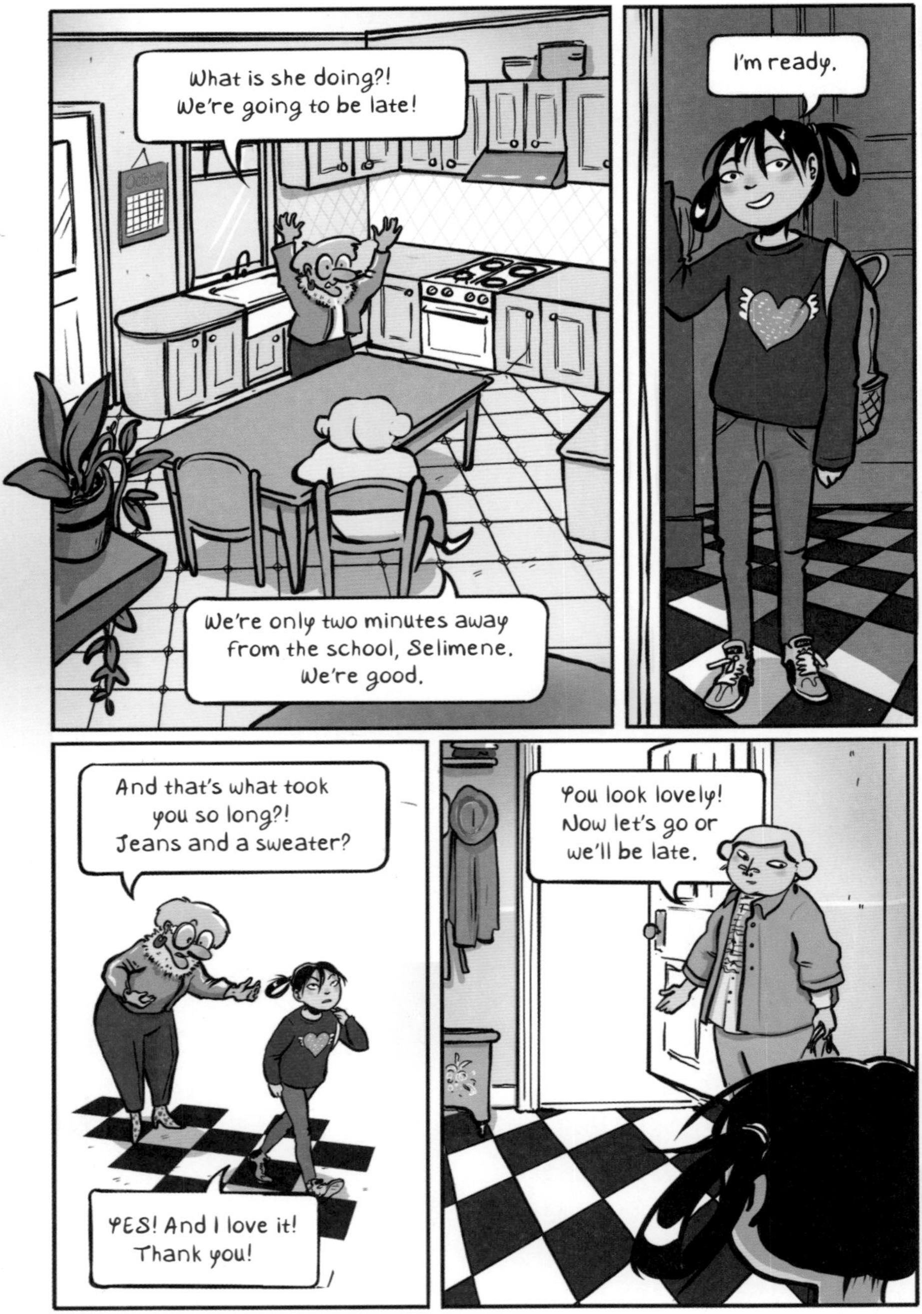
What is she doing?! We're going to be late!
We're only two minutes away from the school, Selimene. We're good.
I'm ready.
And that's what took you so long?! Jeans and a sweater?
YES! And I love it! Thank you!
You look lovely! Now let's go or we'll be late.

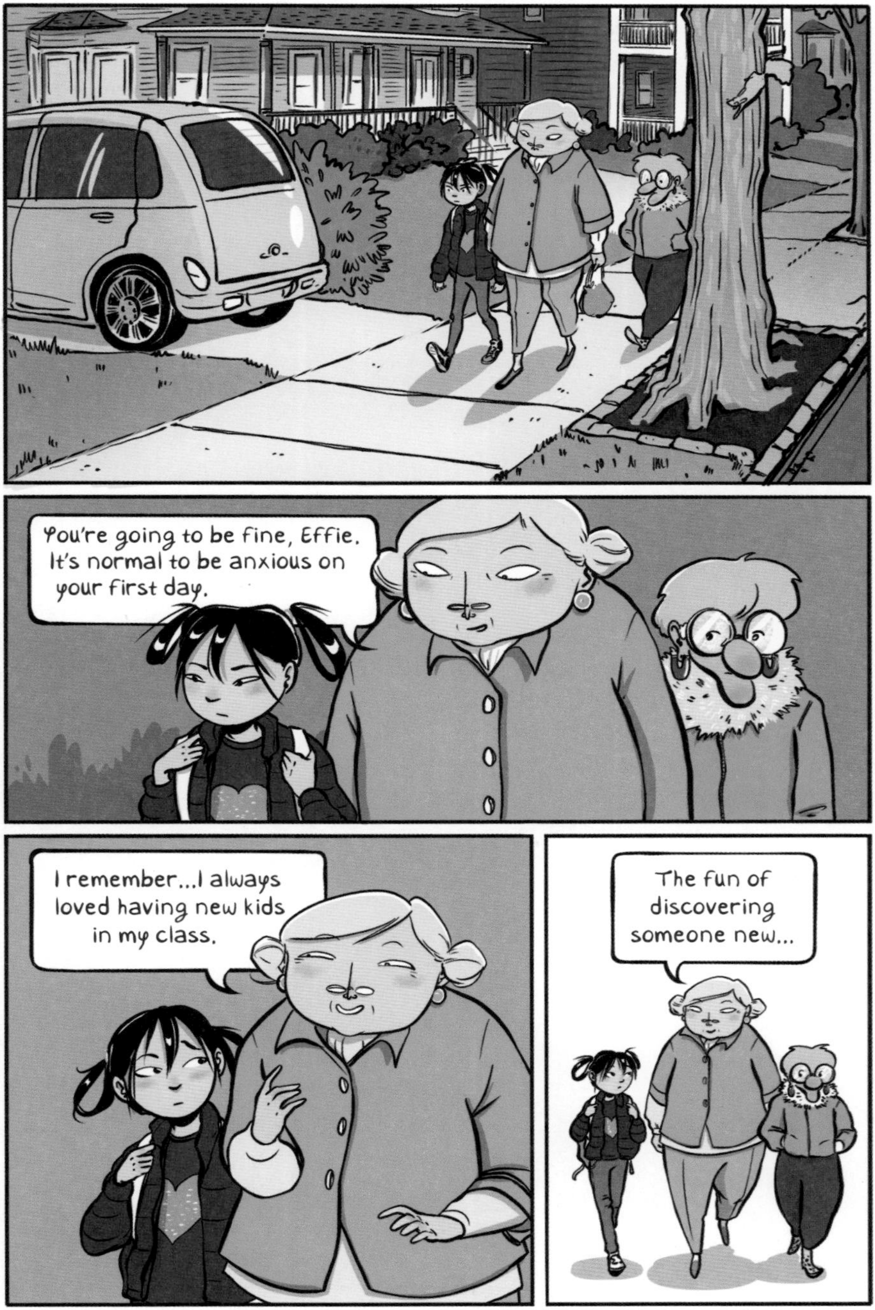
You're going to be fine, Effie. It's normal to be anxious on your first day.
I remember...I always loved having new kids in my class.
The fun of discovering someone new...

Seeing if the book's cover matches the inside...

?

Right. And if some kids aren't nice, just punch them in the nose!

HA HA HA HA!

SELIMENE!! HOW CAN YOU SAY THINGS LIKE THAT?!

I'm only joking, Carlota.

I wanted to see if I could get her to smile.

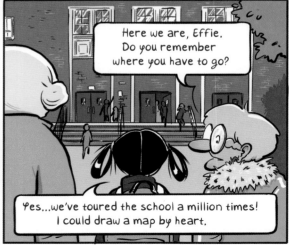

Here we are, Effie. Do you remember where you have to go?

Yes...we've toured the school a million times! I could draw a map by heart.

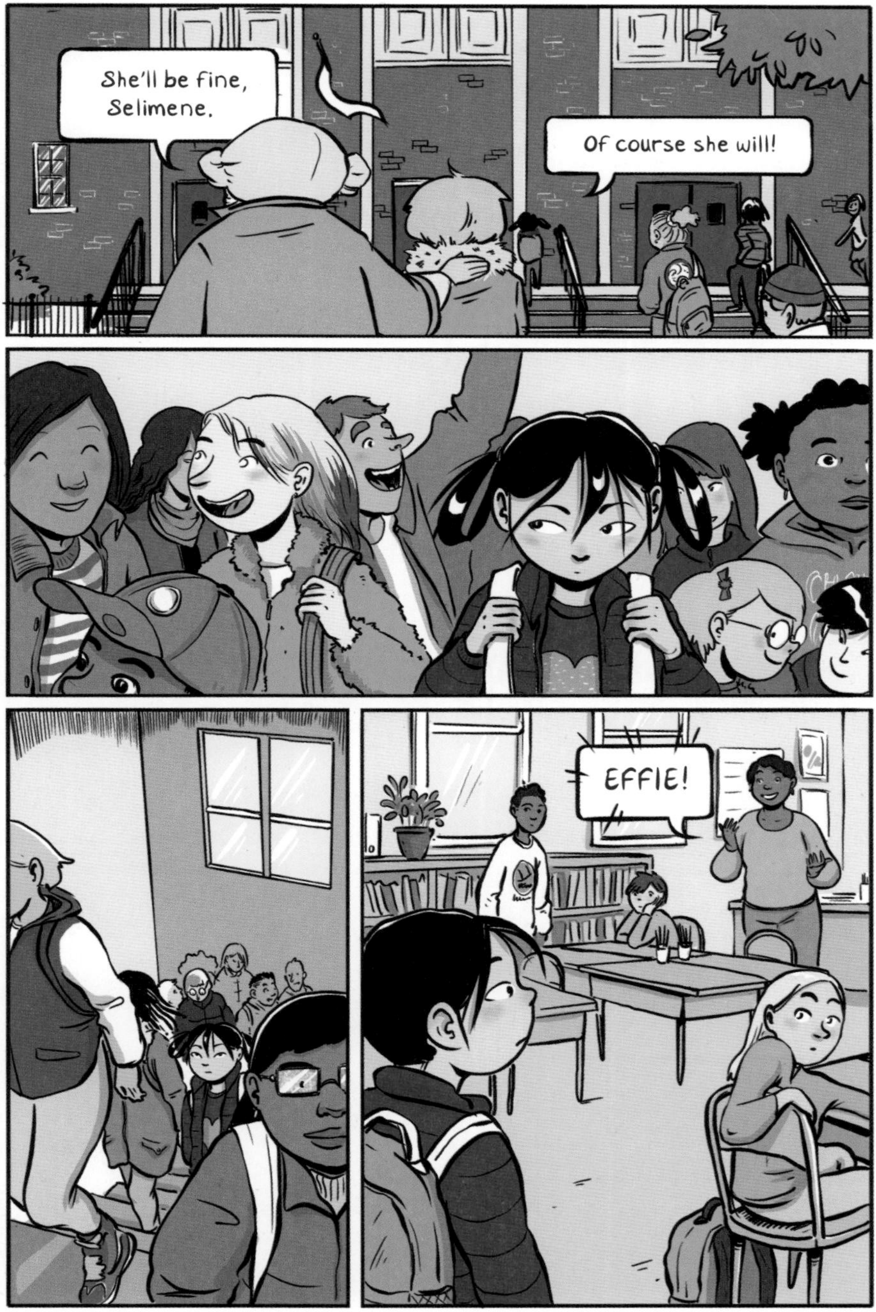
She'll be fine, Selimene.
Of course she will!
EFFIE!

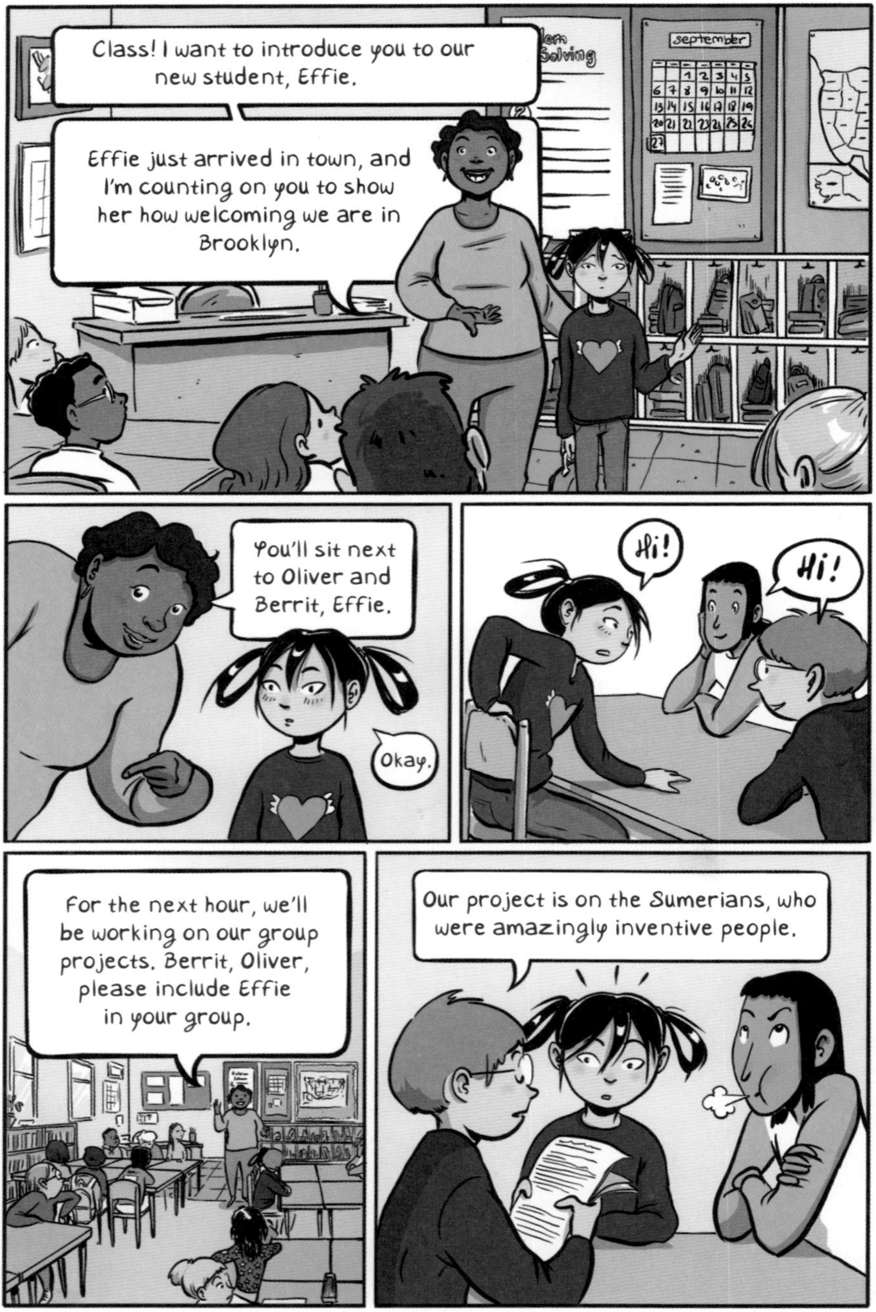
Class! I want to introduce you to our new student, Effie.
Effie just arrived in town, and I'm counting on you to show her how welcoming we are in Brooklyn.
september
You'll sit next to Oliver and Berrit, Effie.
Okay.
Hi!
Hi!
For the next hour, we'll be working on our group projects. Berrit, Oliver, please include Effie in your group.
Our project is on the Sumerians, who were amazingly inventive people.

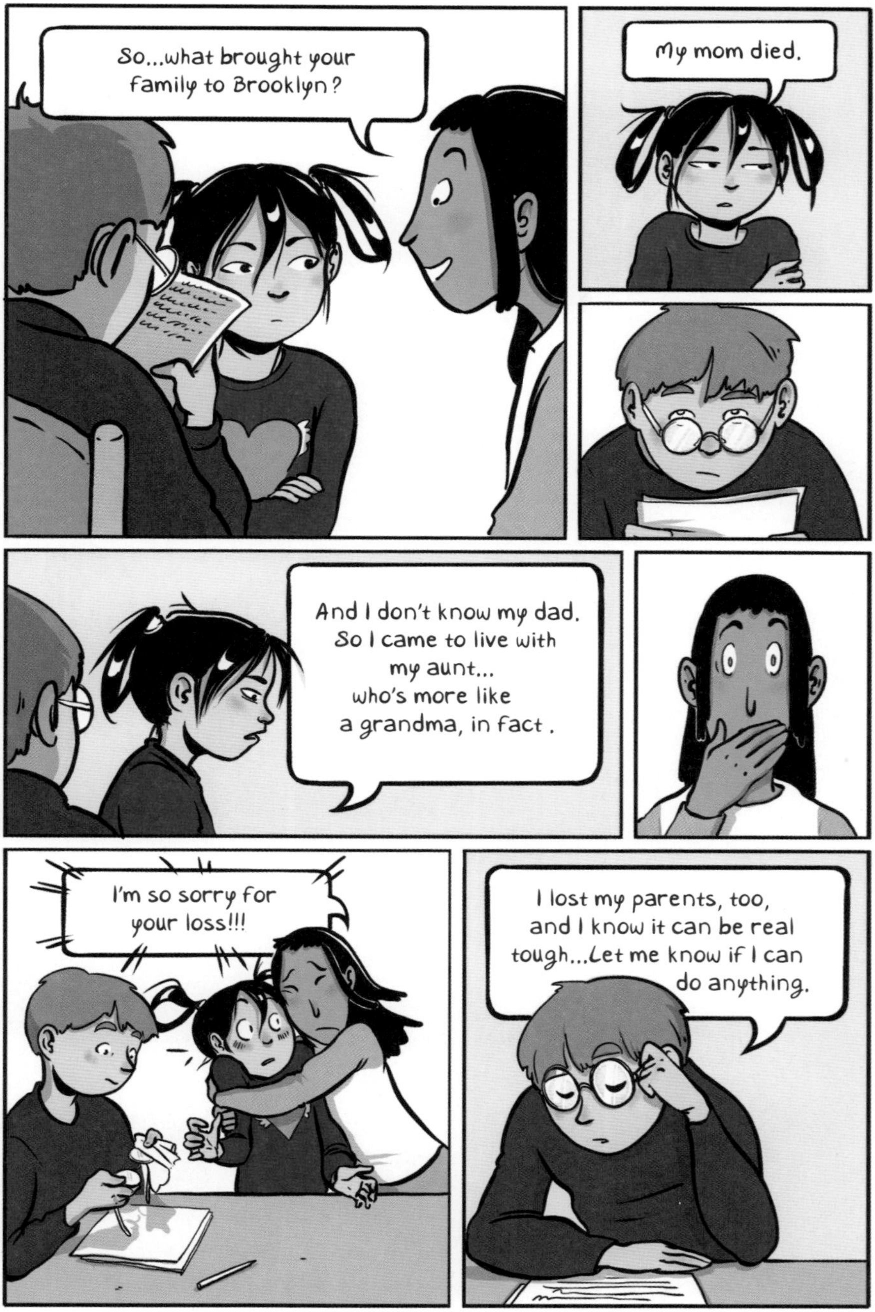
So...what brought your family to Brooklyn?
My mom died.
And I don't know my dad. So I came to live with my aunt... who's more like a grandma, in fact.
I'm so sorry for your loss!!!
I lost my parents, too, and I know it can be real tough...Let me know if I can do anything.

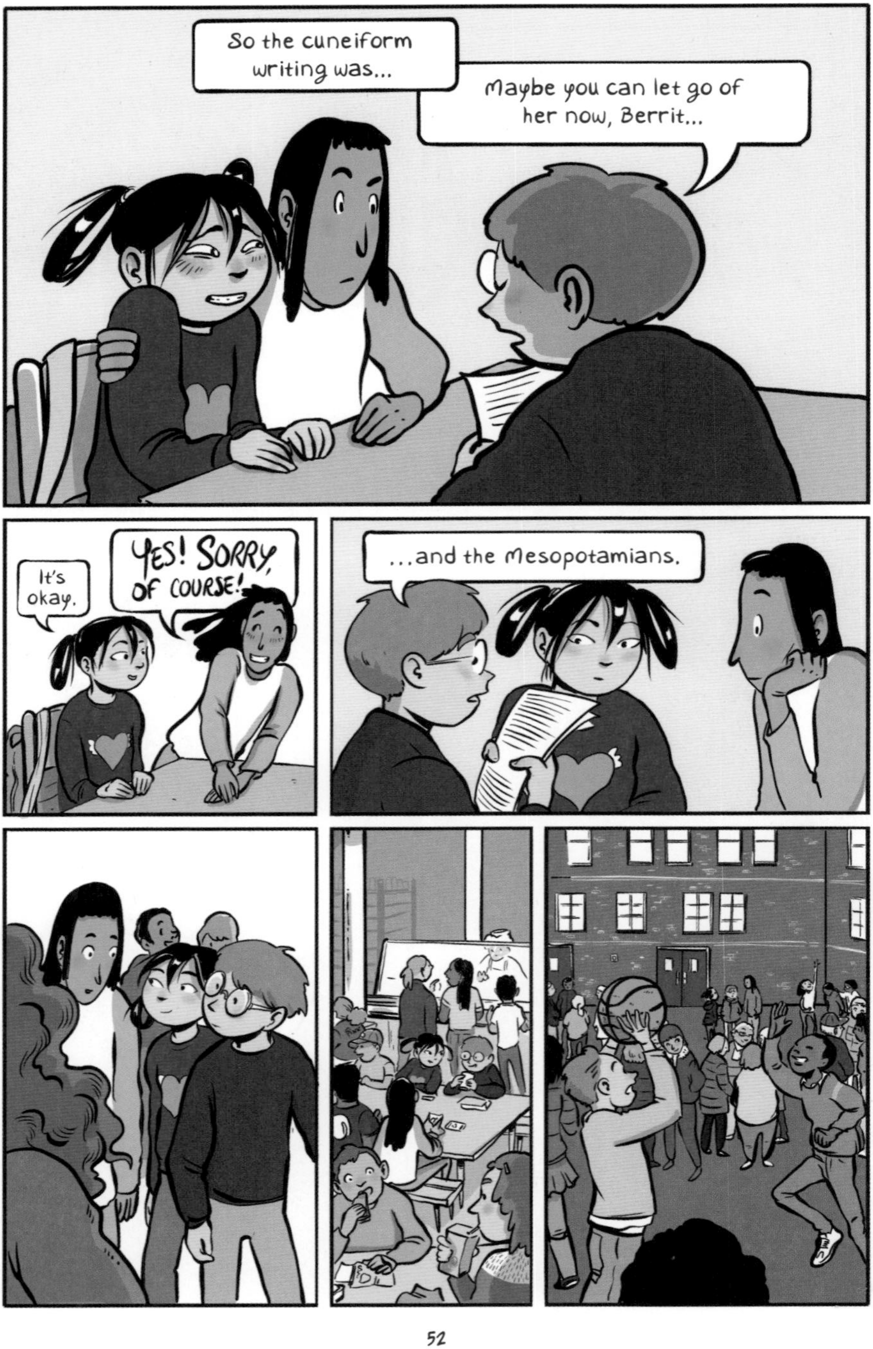
So the cuneiform writing was...
Maybe you can let go of her now, Berrit...
It's okay.
YES! SORRY, OF COURSE!
...and the Mesopotamians.

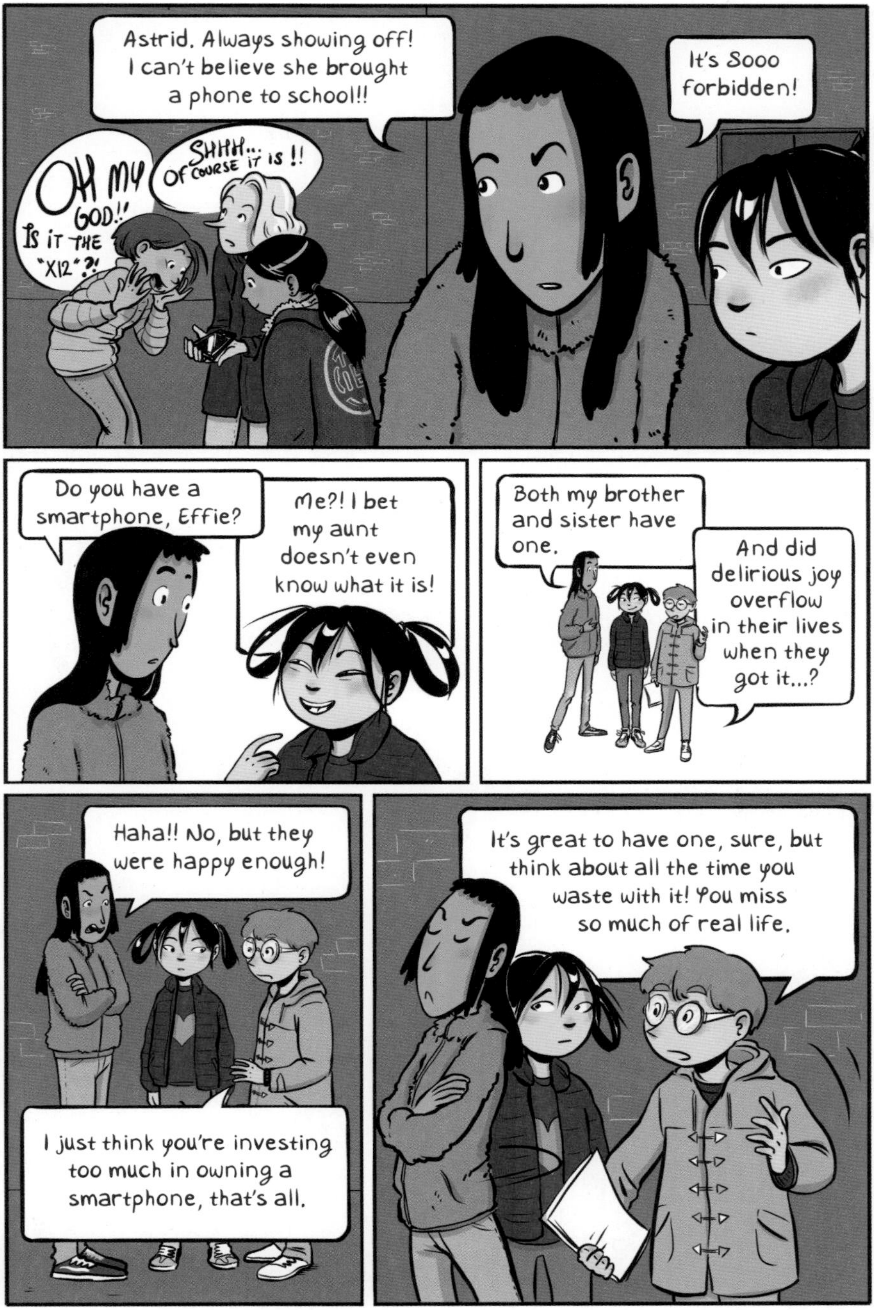
Astrid. Always showing off! I can't believe she brought a phone to school!!
It's Sooo forbidden!
OH MY GOD!! IS IT THE "X12"?!
SHHH... OF COURSE IT IS !!
Do you have a smartphone, Effie?
Me?! I bet my aunt doesn't even know what it is!
Both my brother and sister have one.
And did delirious joy overflow in their lives when they got it...?
Haha!! No, but they were happy enough!
I just think you're investing too much in owning a smartphone, that's all.
It's great to have one, sure, but think about all the time you waste with it! You miss so much of real life.

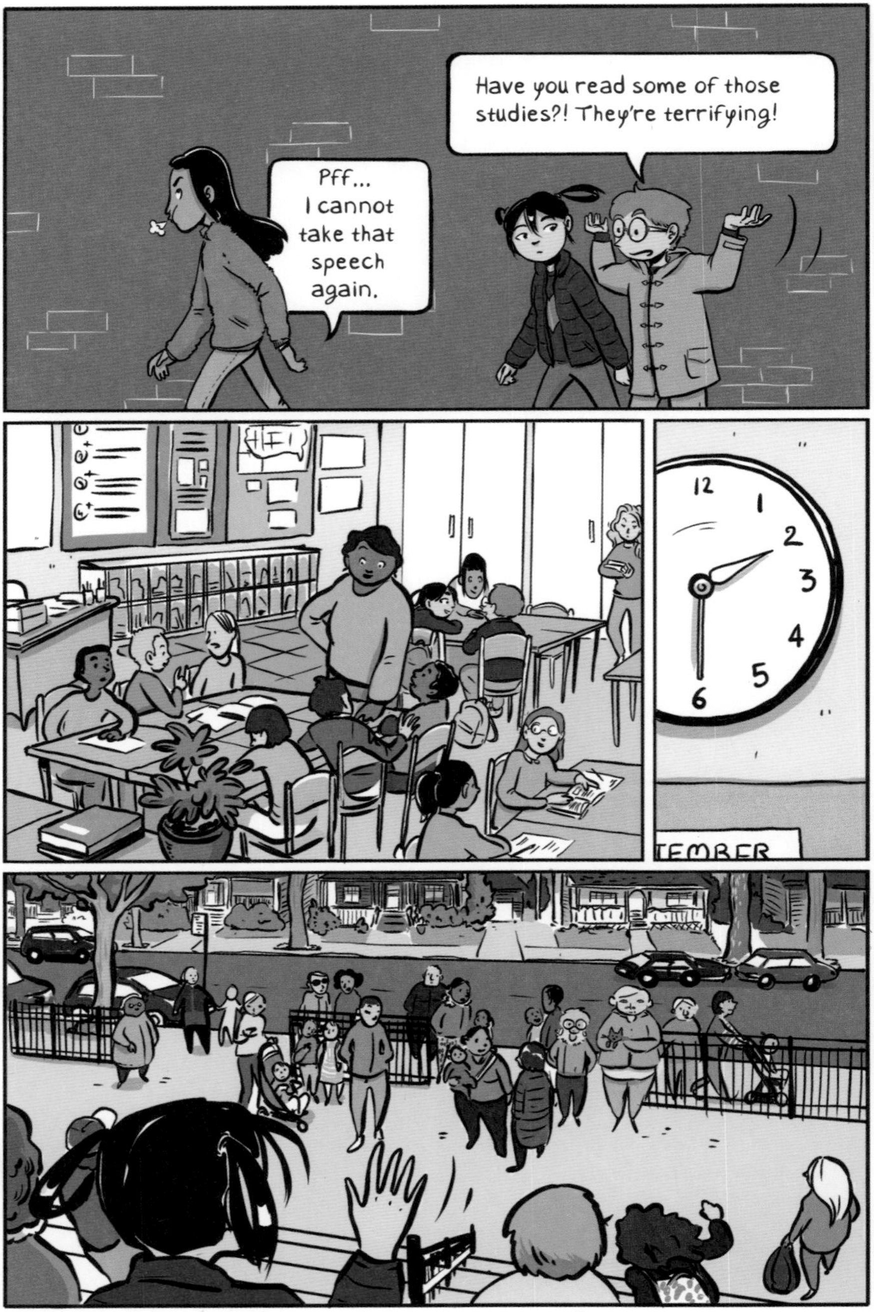

Pff... I cannot take that speech again.
Have you read some of those studies?! They're terrifying!
HI!
12
1
2
3
4
5
6
TEMBER

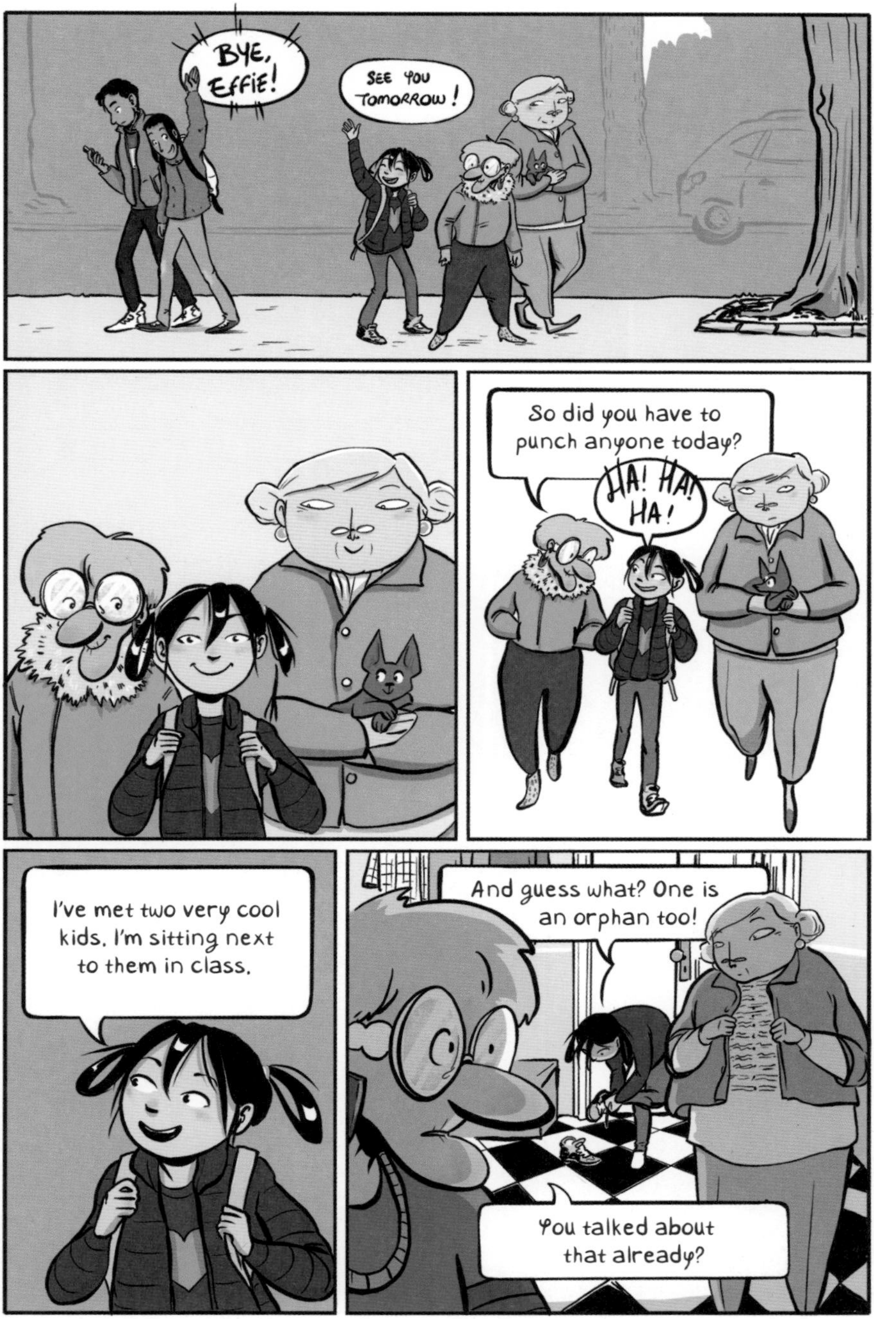

BYE, EFFIE!
SEE YOU TOMORROW!
So did you have to punch anyone today?
HA! HA! HA!
I've met two very cool kids. I'm sitting next to them in class.
And guess what? One is an orphan too!
You talked about that already?

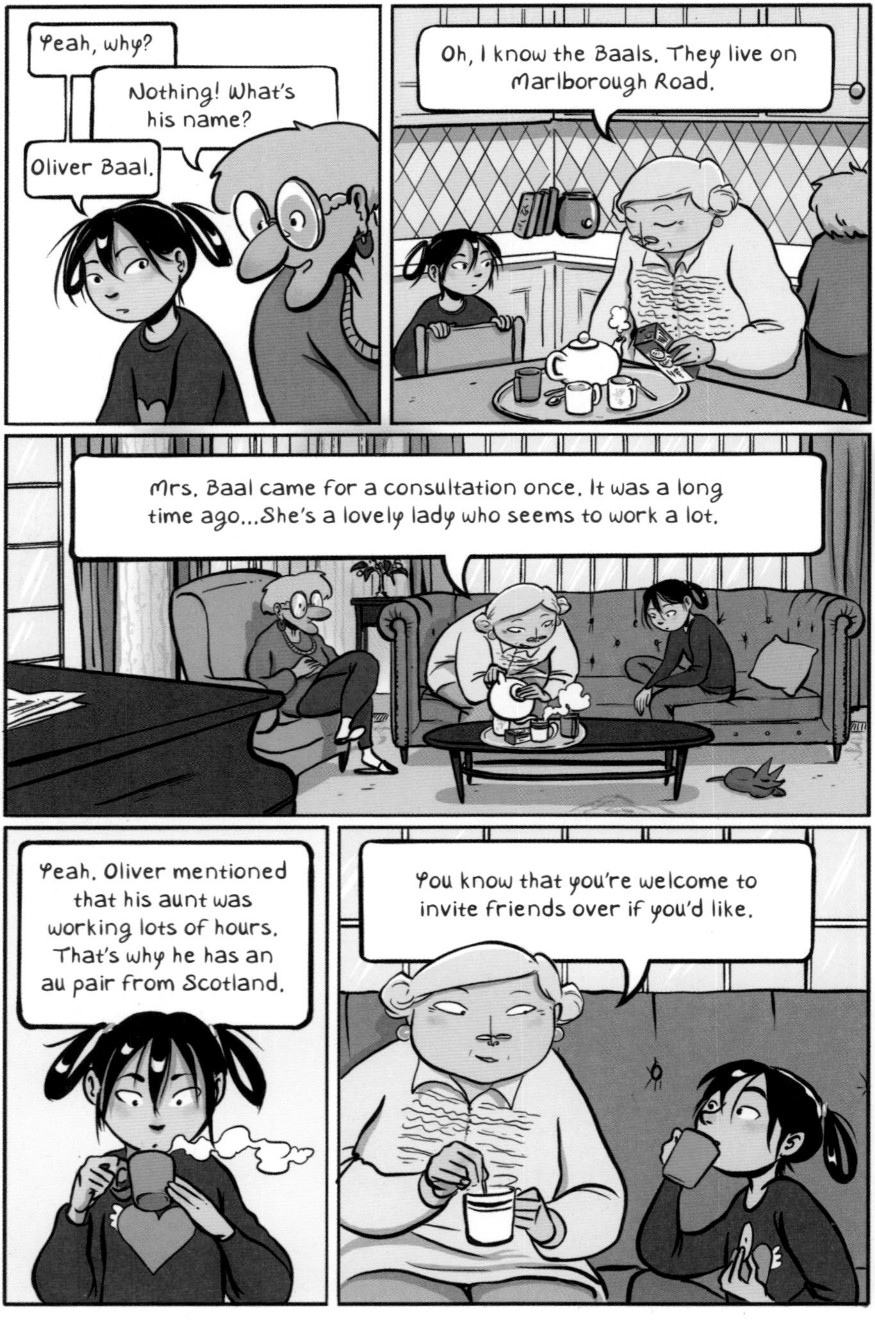
Yeah, why?
Nothing! What's his name?
Oliver Baal.
Oh, I know the Baals. They live on Marlborough Road.
Mrs. Baal came for a consultation once. It was a long time ago...She's a lovely lady who seems to work a lot.
Yeah. Oliver mentioned that his aunt was working lots of hours. That's why he has an au pair from Scotland.
You know that you're welcome to invite friends over if you'd like.

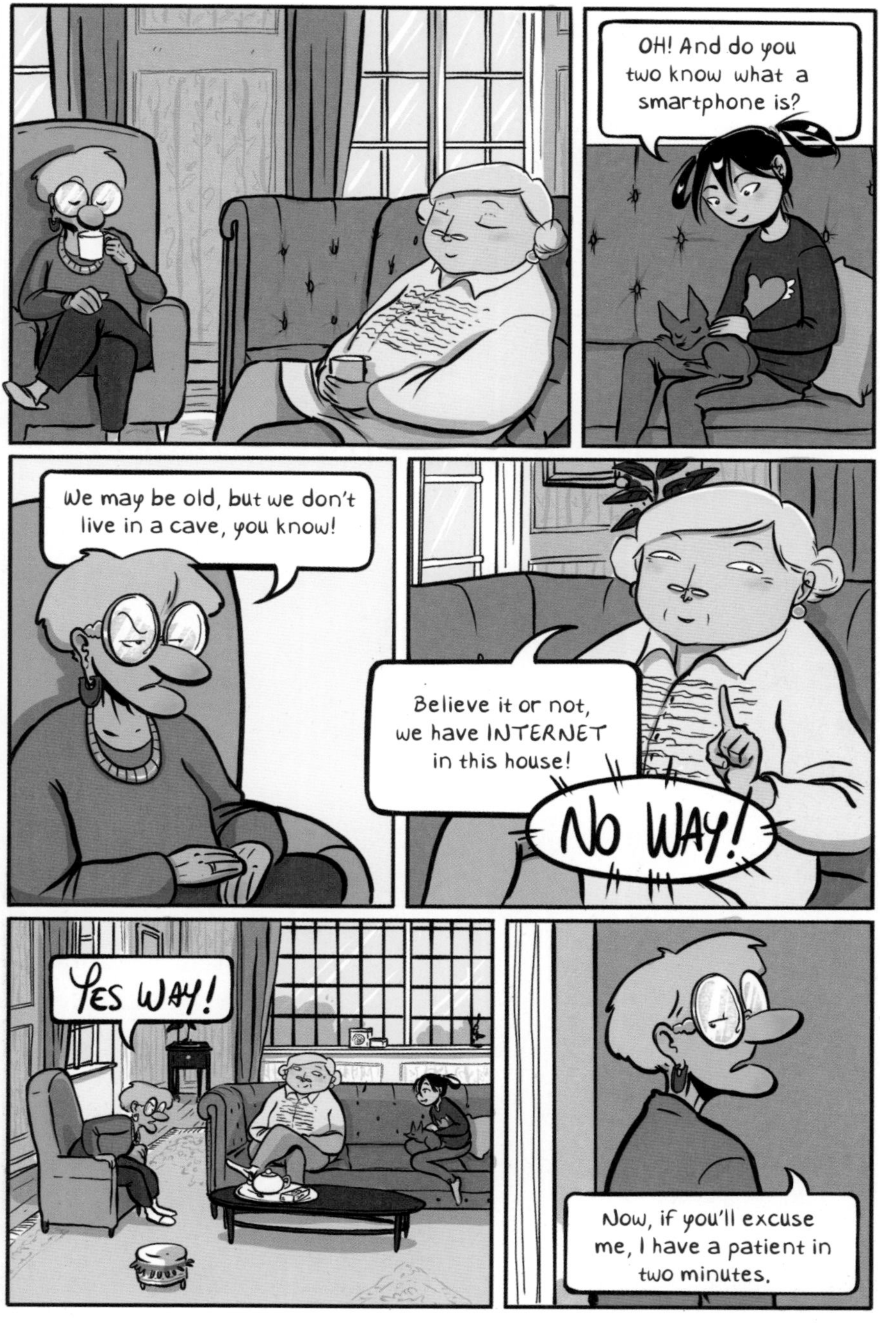
OH! And do you two know what a smartphone is?
We may be old, but we don't live in a cave, you know!
Believe it or not, we have INTERNET in this house!
NO WAY!
YES WAY!
Now, if you'll excuse me, I have a patient in two minutes.

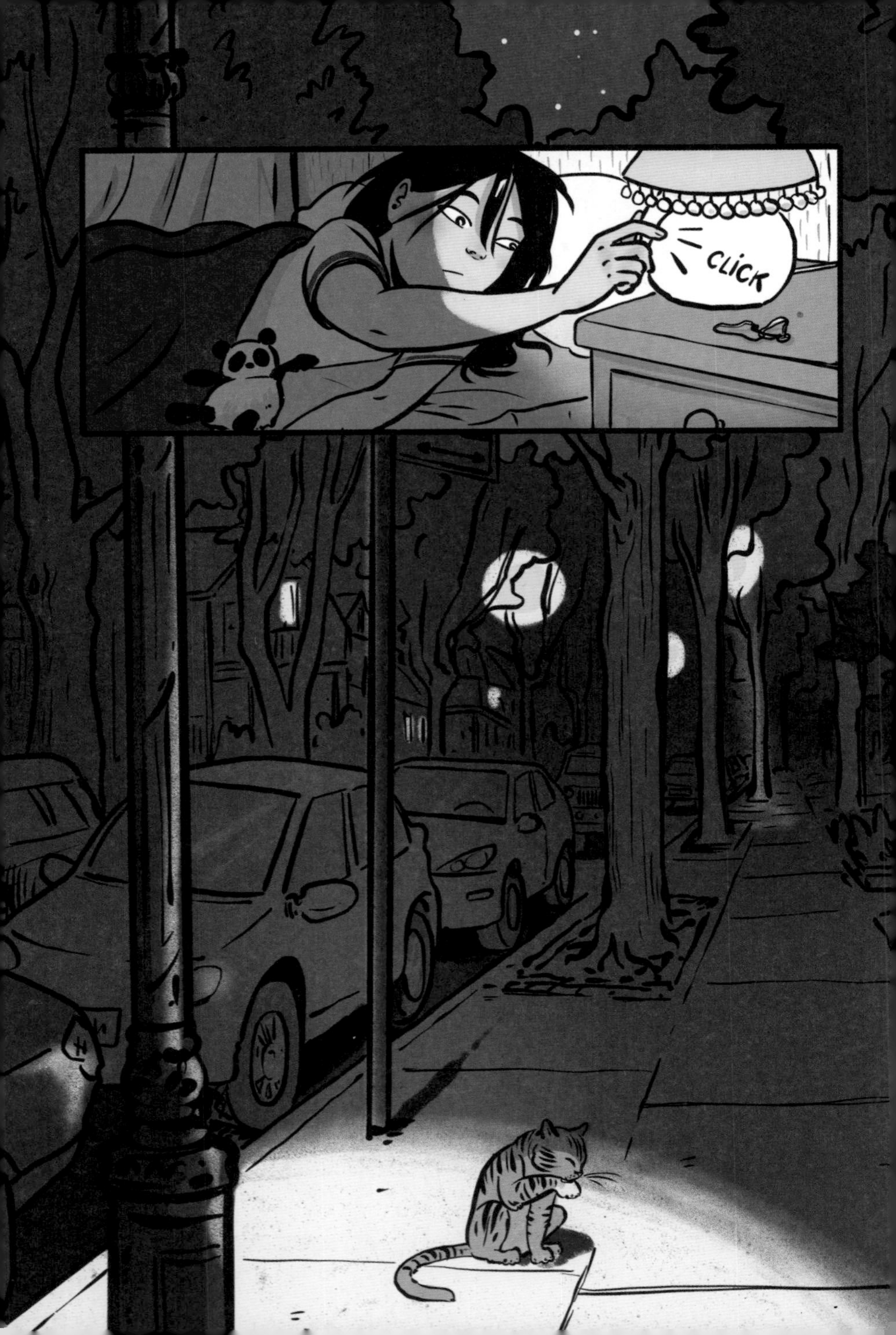
CLICK

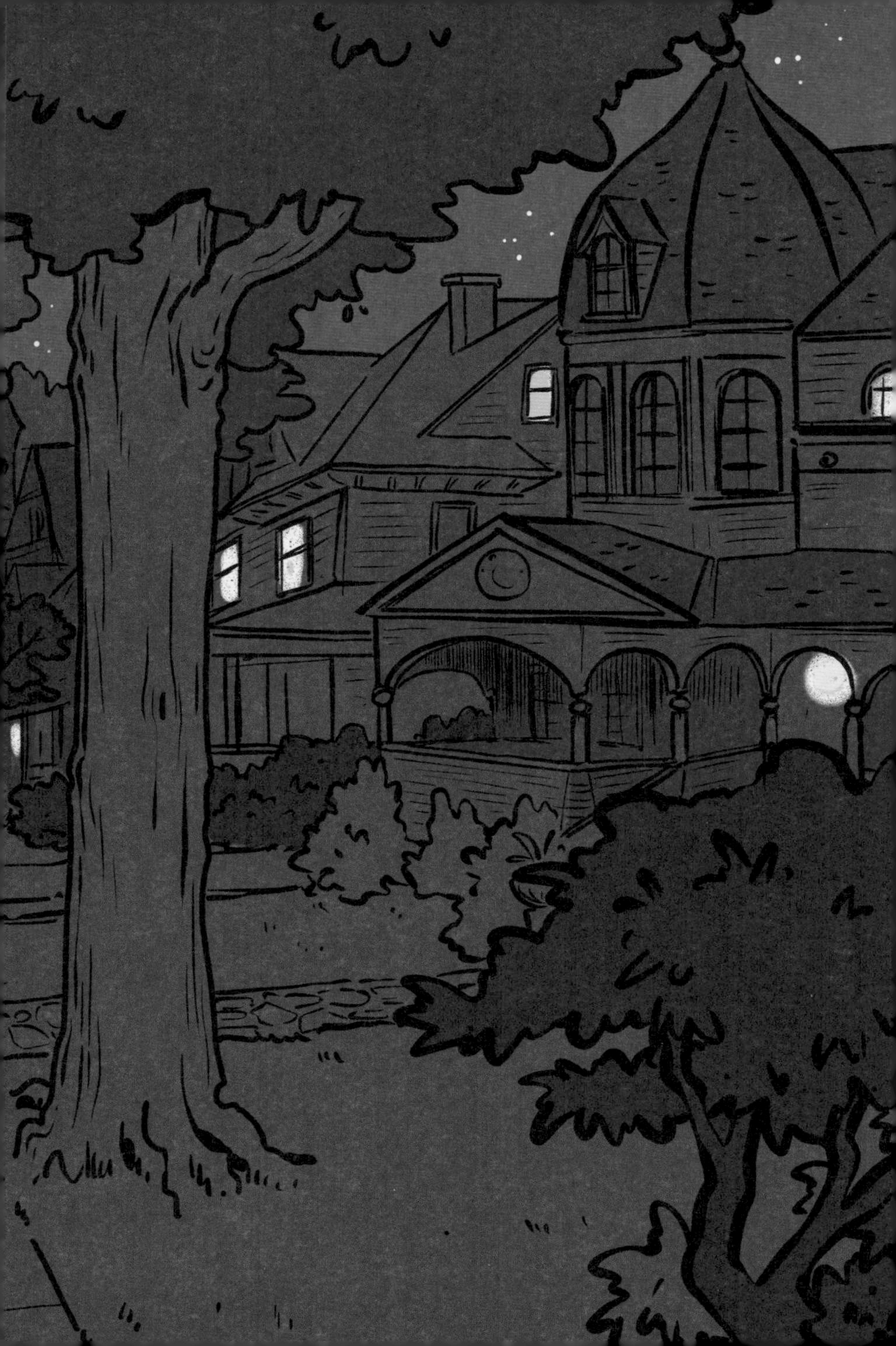

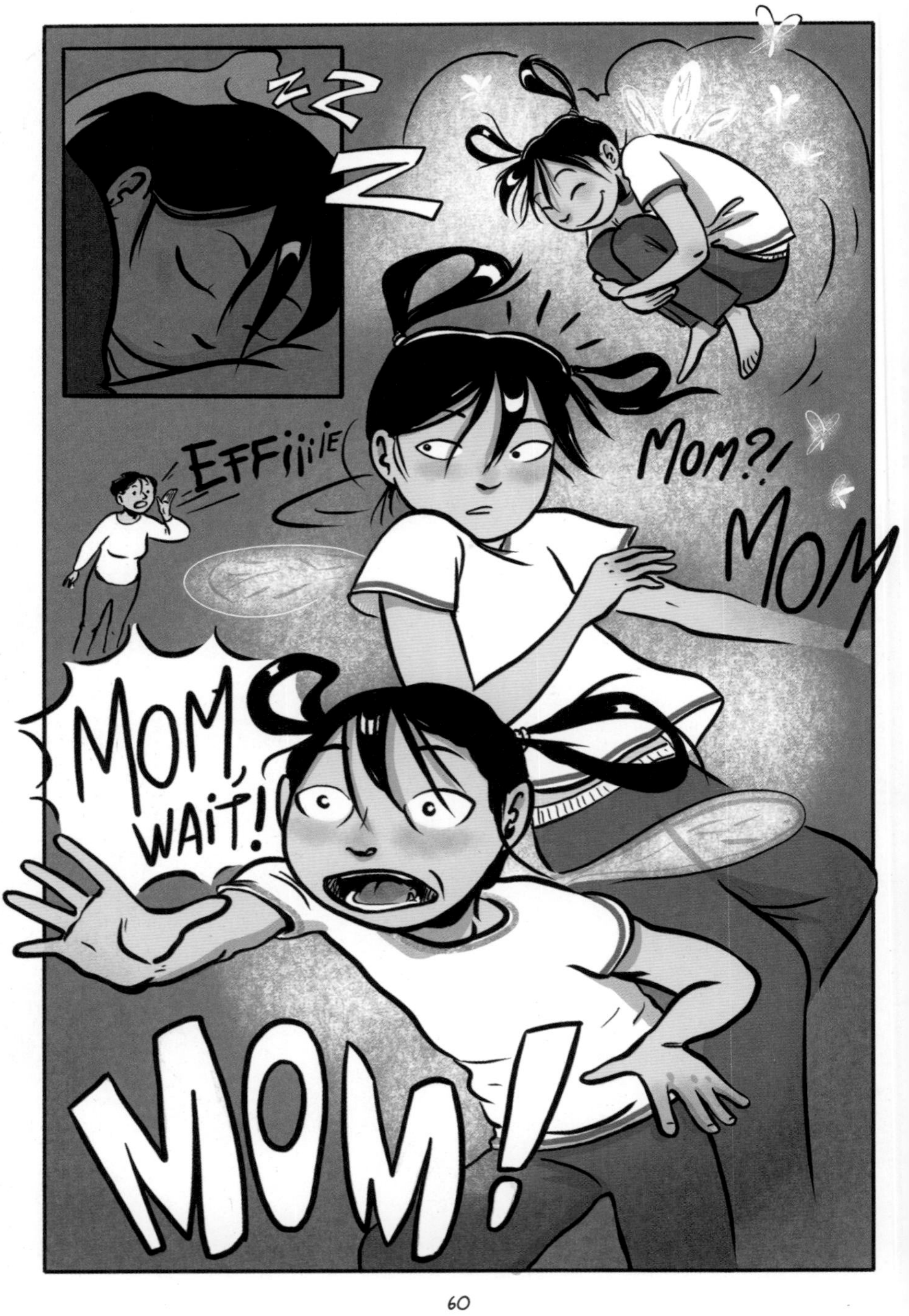
Z Z
Z
EFFiiiiIE
Mom?!
MOM
MOM, WAIT!
MOM!

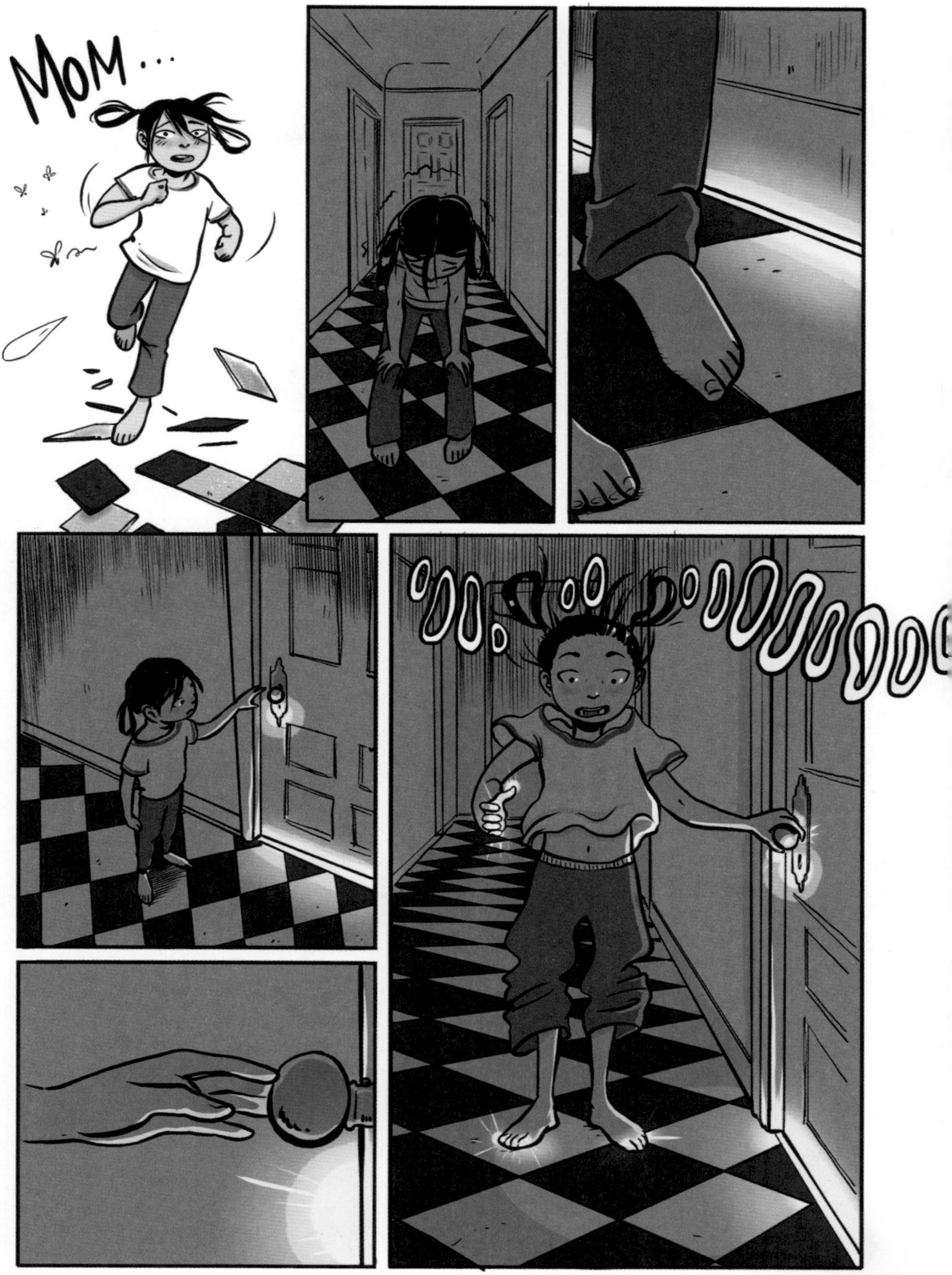
MOM ...

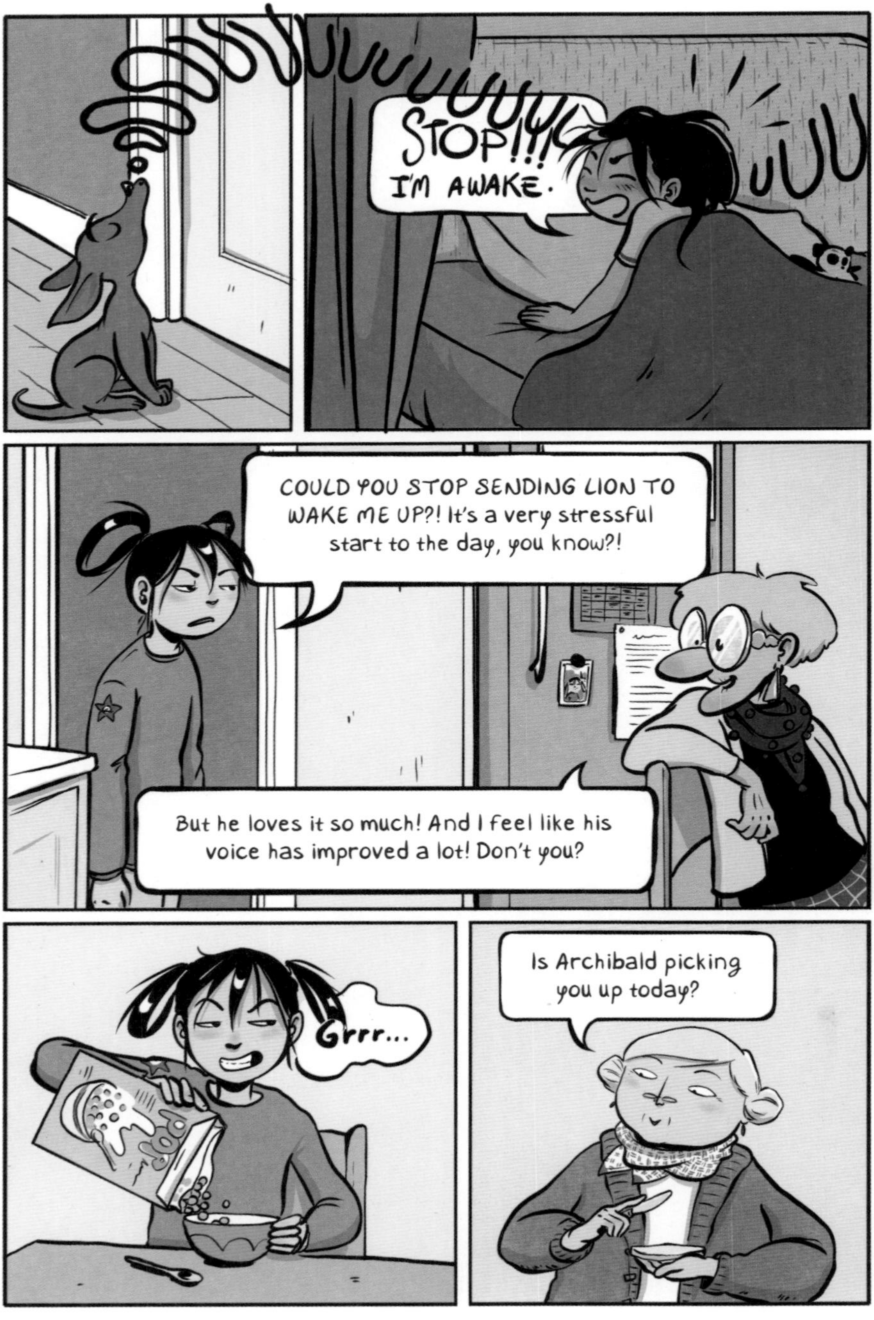

UUUUUUUUUUUU
STOP!!!
I'M AWAKE.
UUU
COULD YOU STOP SENDING LION TO WAKE ME UP?! It's a very stressful start to the day, you know?!
But he loves it so much! And I feel like his voice has improved a lot! Don't you?
Grrr...
Is Archibald picking you up today?

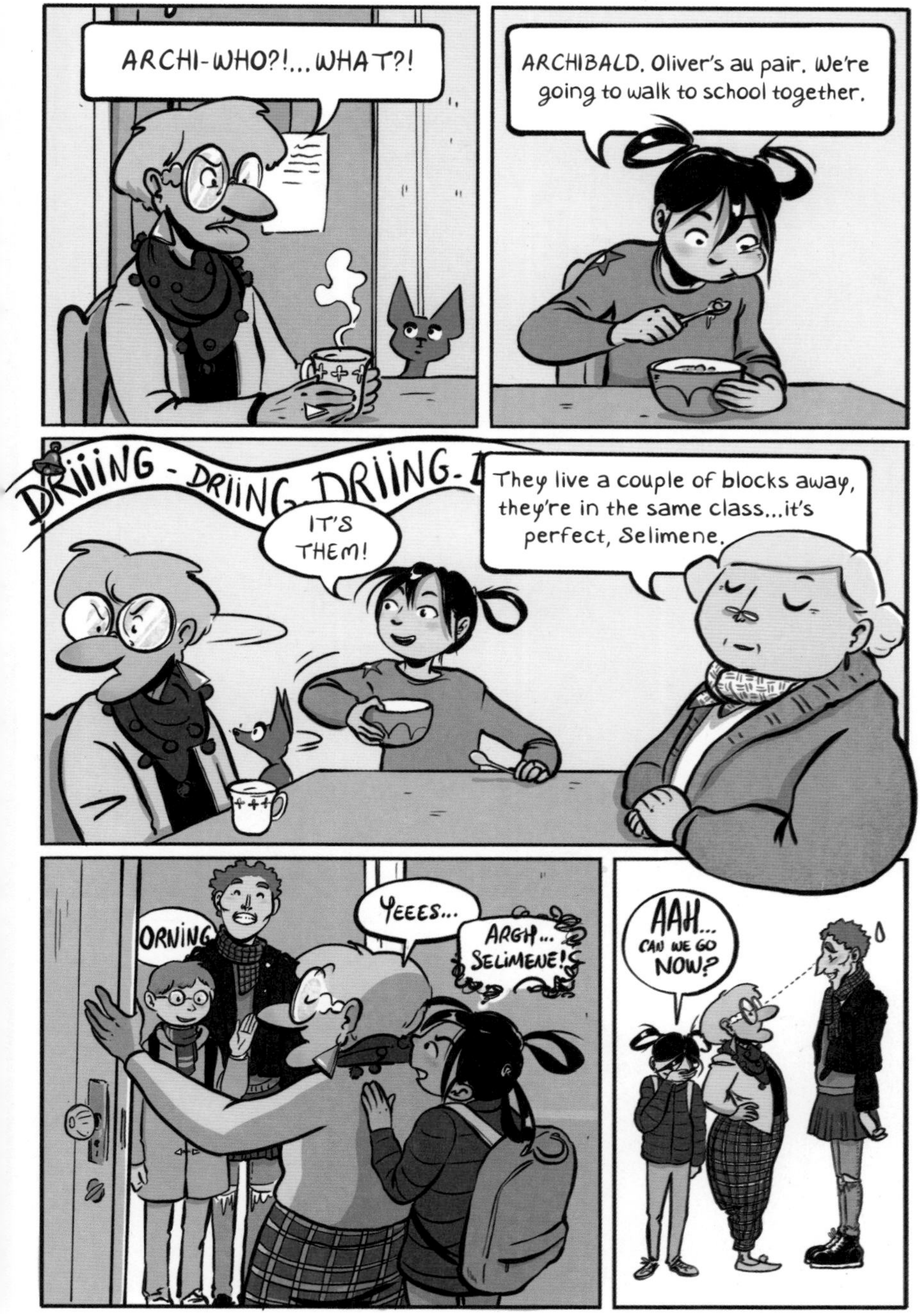
ARCHI-WHO?!...WHAT?!
ARCHIBALD. Oliver's au pair. We're going to walk to school together.
DRIIING - DRIING - DRIING -
IT'S THEM!
They live a couple of blocks away, they're in the same class...it's perfect, Selimene.
ORNING
YEEES...
ARGH... SELIMENE!
AAH... CAN WE GO NOW?

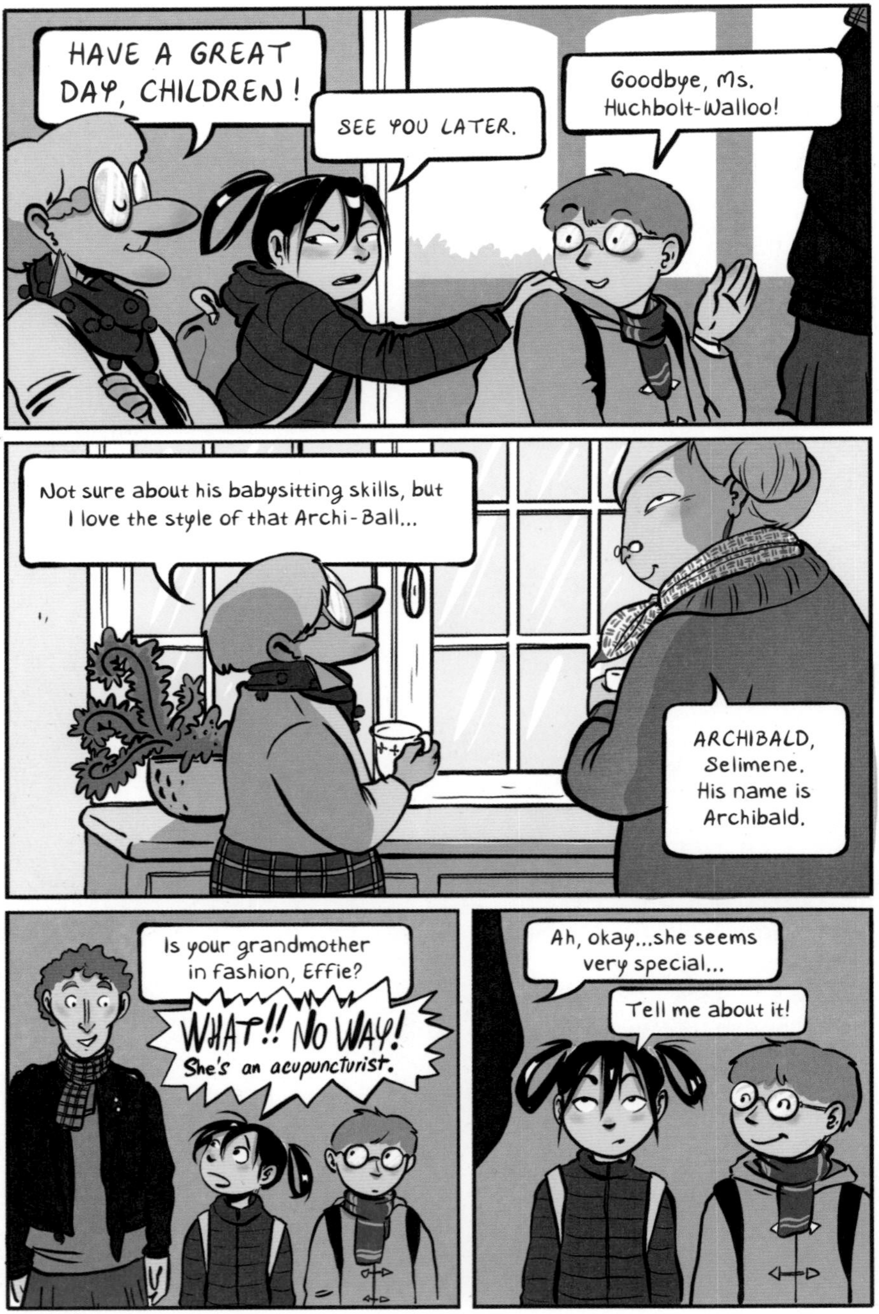
HAVE A GREAT DAY, CHILDREN!
SEE YOU LATER.
Goodbye, Ms. Huchbolt-Walloo!
Not sure about his babysitting skills, but I love the style of that Archi-Ball...
ARCHIBALD, Selimene. His name is Archibald.
Is your grandmother in fashion, Effie?
WHAT!! NO WAY! She's an acupuncturist.
Ah, okay...she seems very special...
Tell me about it!

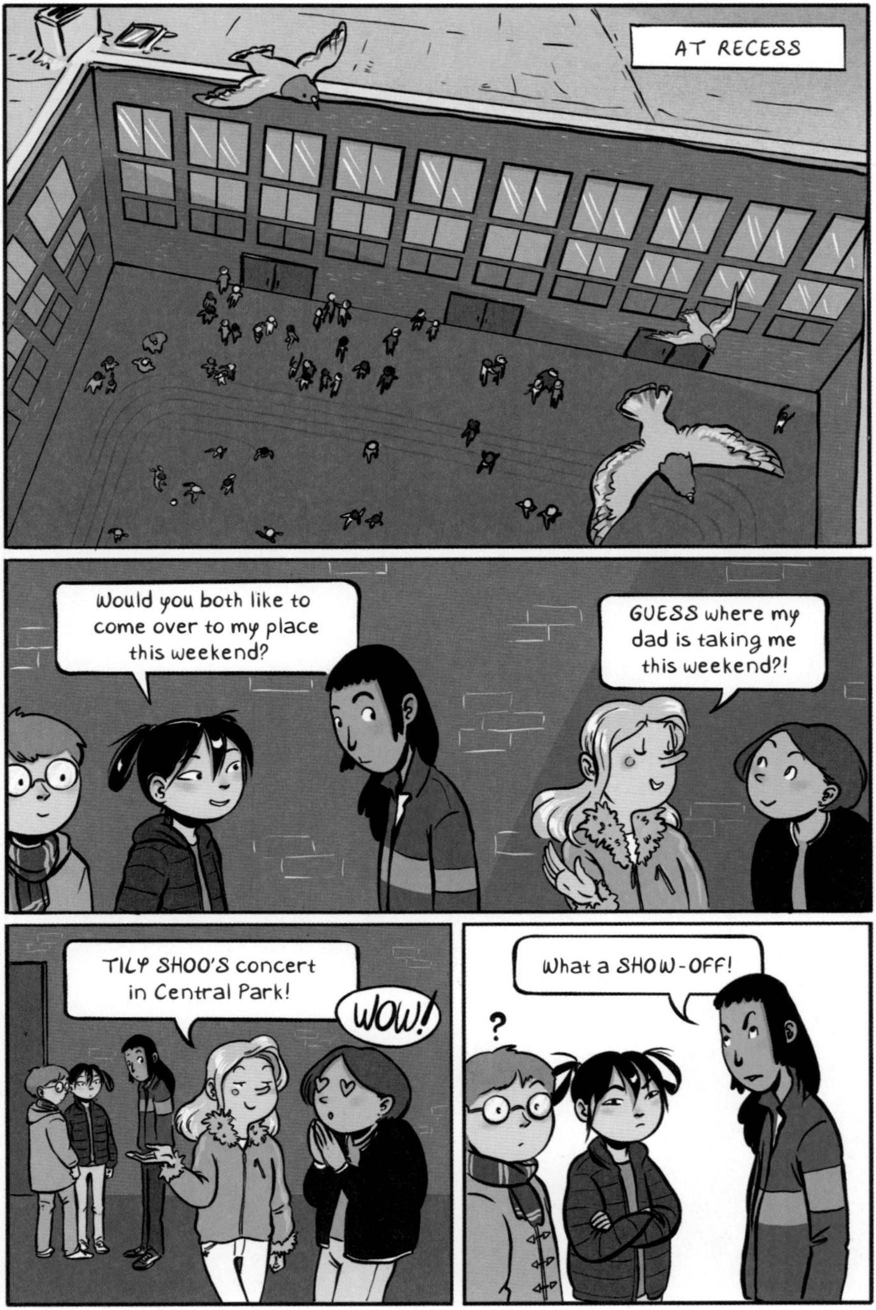
AT RECESS
Would you both like to come over to my place this weekend?
GUESS where my dad is taking me this weekend?!
TILY SHOO'S concert in Central Park!
WOW!
?
What a SHOW-OFF!

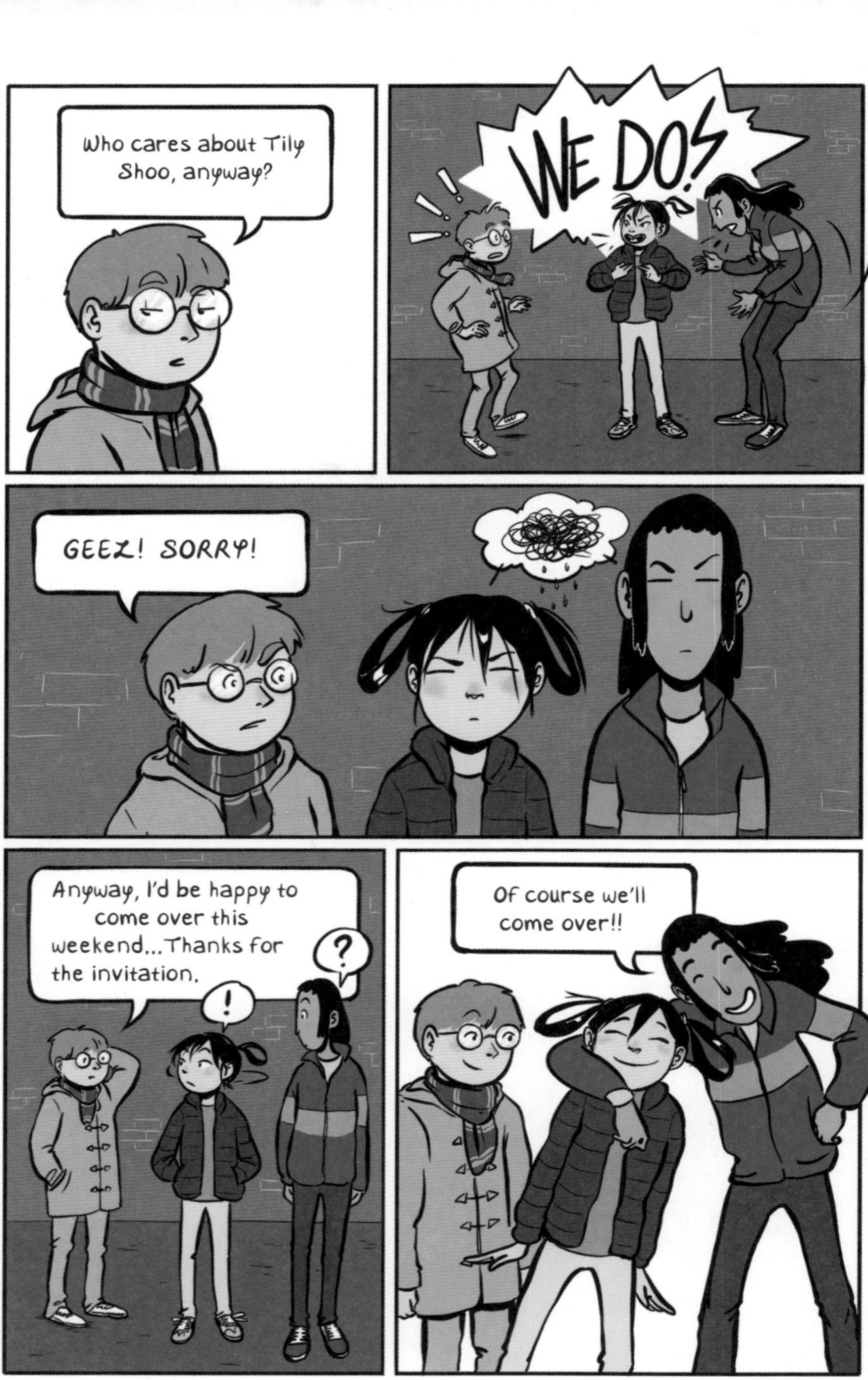
Who cares about Tily Shoo, anyway?
WE DO!
GEEZ! SORRY!
Anyway, I'd be happy to come over this weekend... Thanks for the invitation.
!
?
Of course we'll come over!!

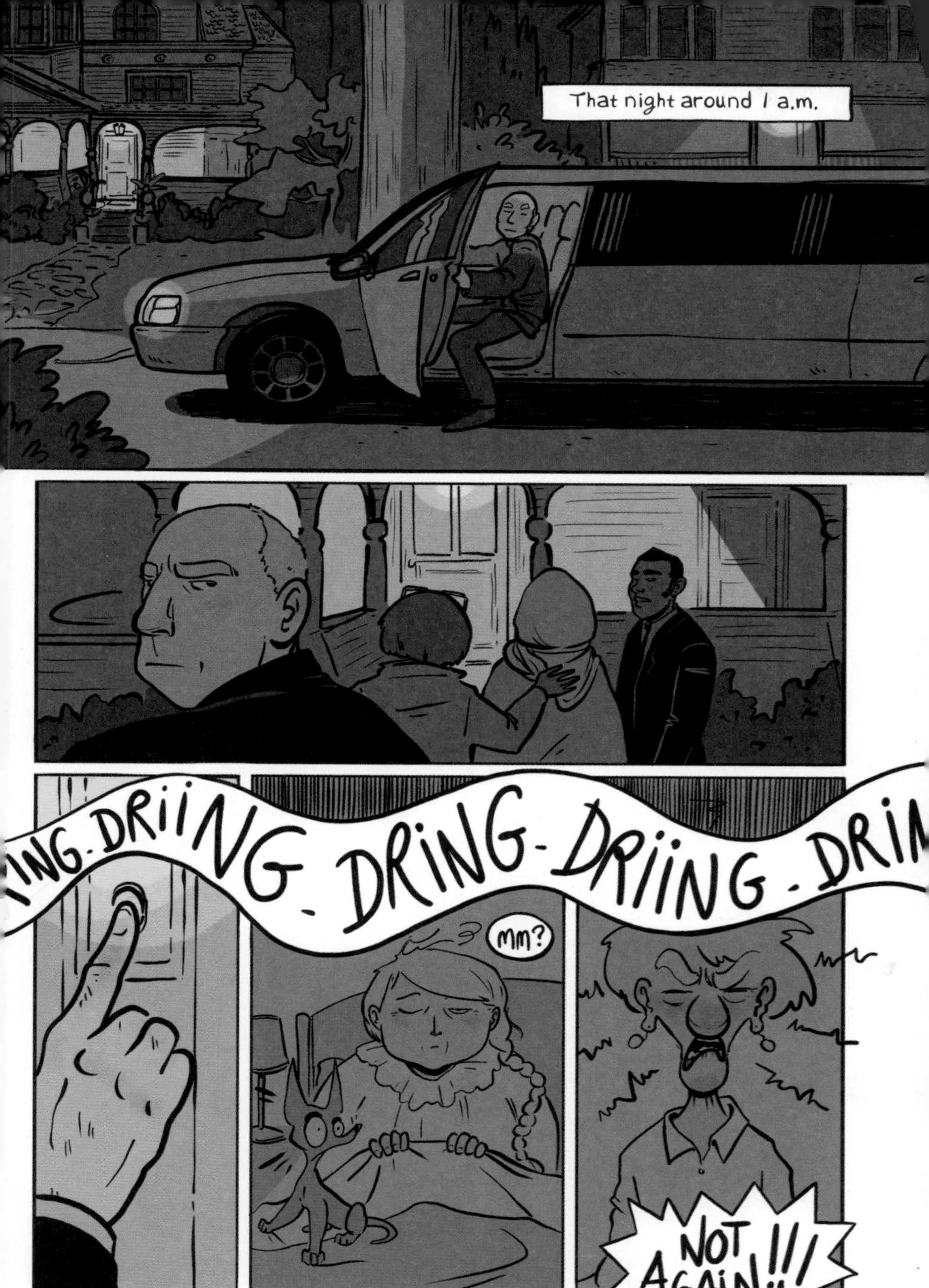
That night around 1 a.m.
ING-DRIING-DRING-DRIING-DRI
mm?
NOT AGAIN!!!

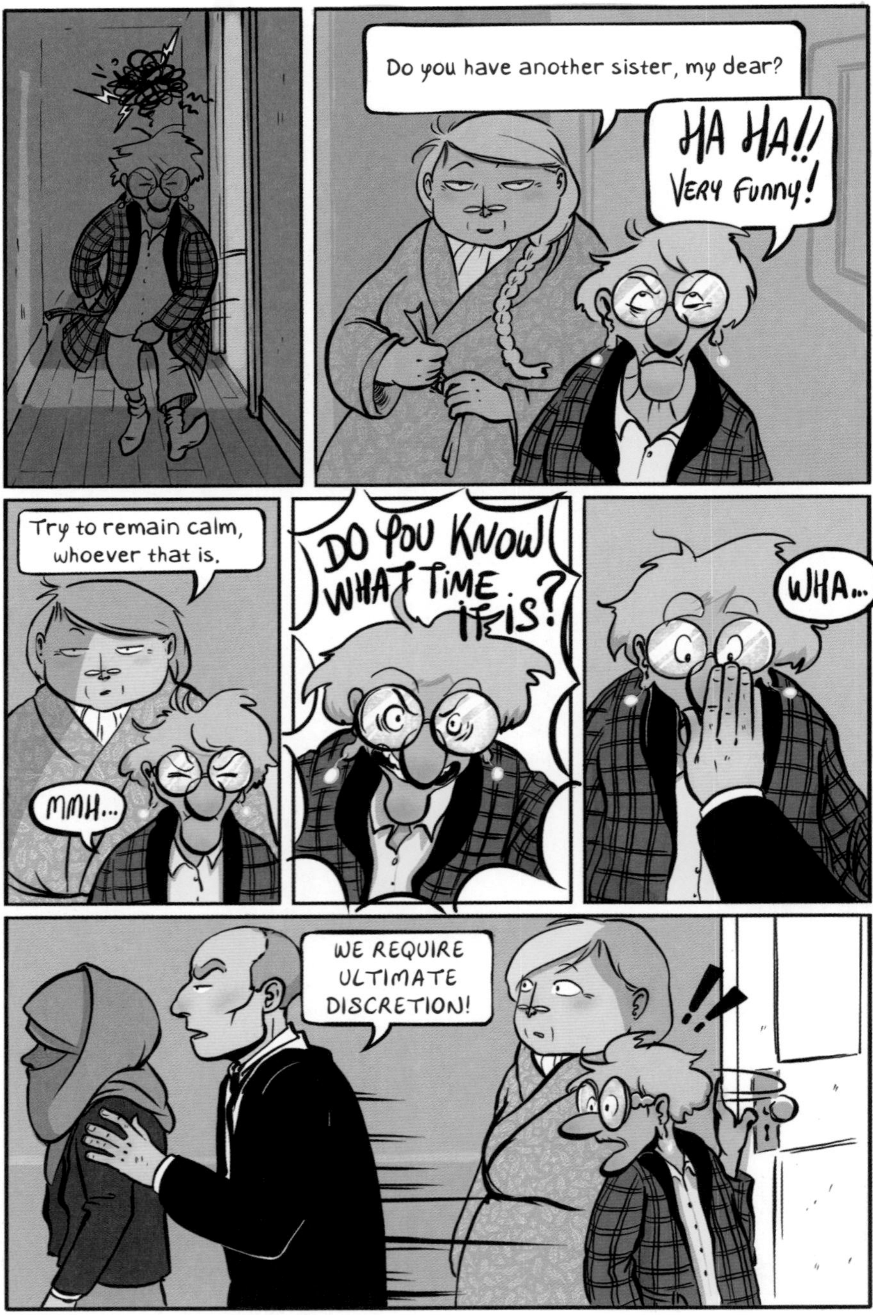
Do you have another sister, my dear?
HA HA!! VERY FUNNY!
Try to remain calm, whoever that is.
MMH...
DO YOU KNOW WHAT TIME IT IS?
WHA...
WE REQUIRE ULTIMATE DISCRETION!

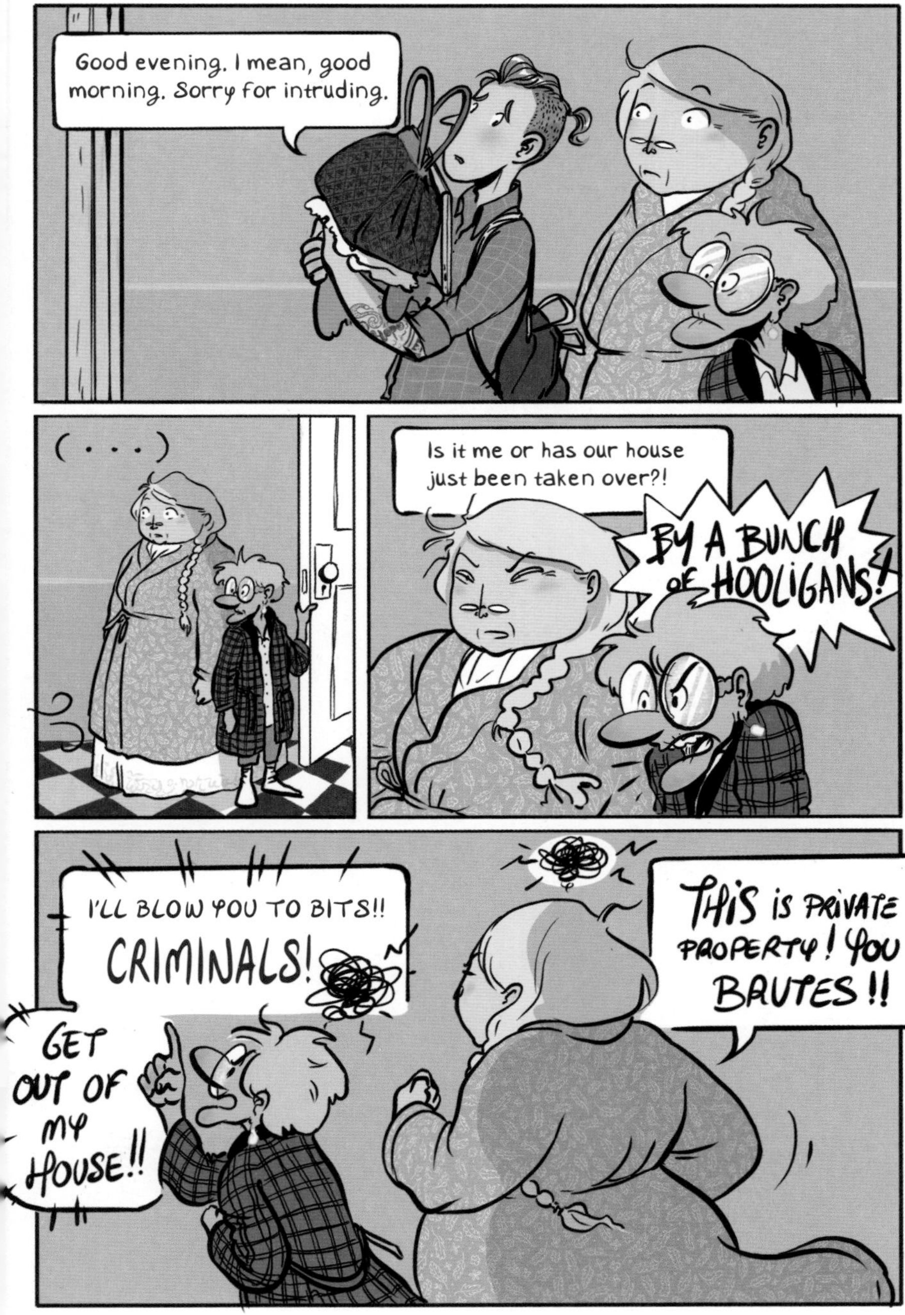
Good evening. I mean, good morning. Sorry for intruding.
(. . .)
Is it me or has our house just been taken over?!
BY A BUNCH OF HOOLIGANS!
I'LL BLOW YOU TO BITS!! CRIMINALS!
THIS IS PRIVATE PROPERTY! YOU BRUTES!!
GET OUT OF MY HOUSE!!

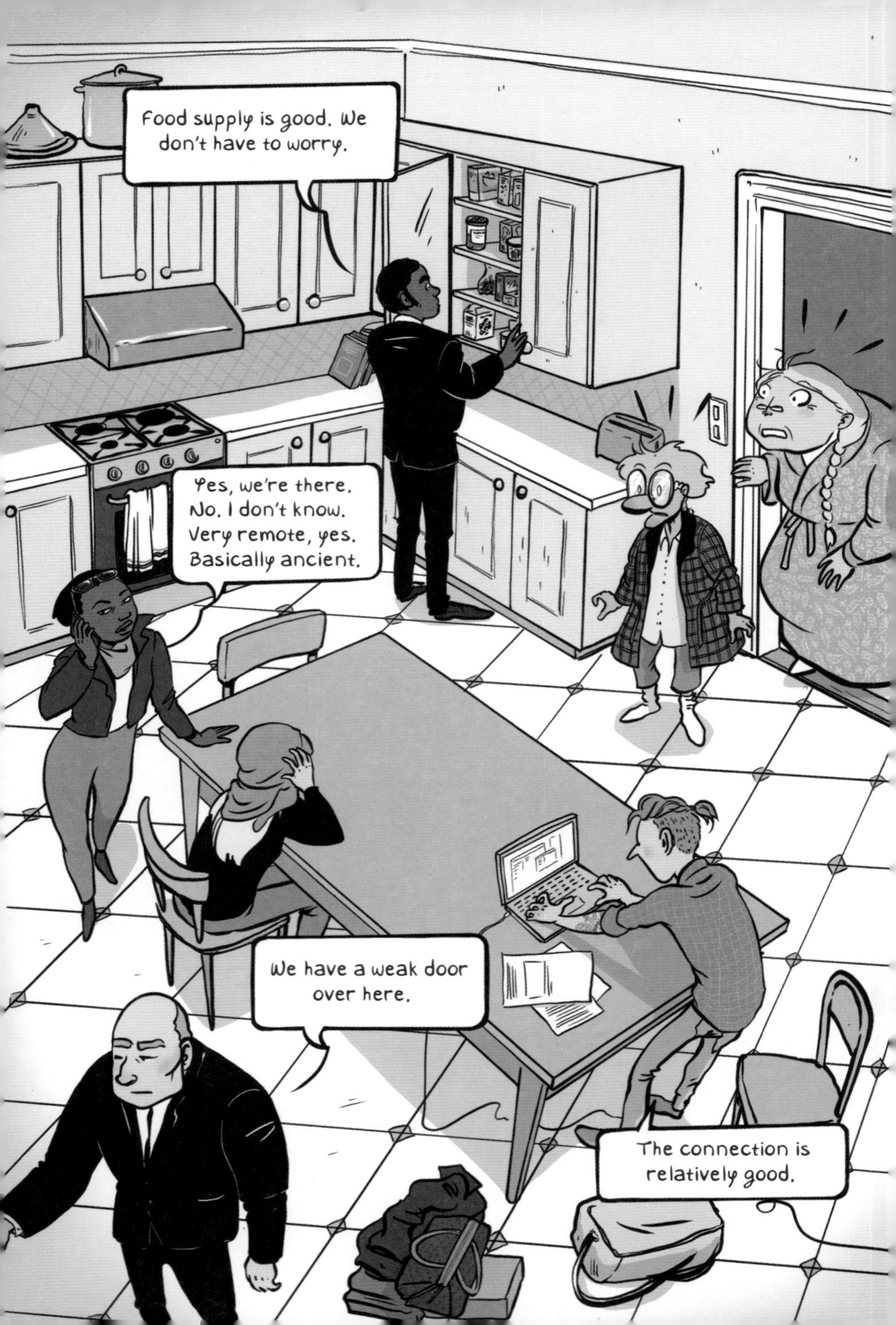
Food supply is good. We don't have to worry.
Yes, we're there. No. I don't know. Very remote, yes. Basically ancient.
We have a weak door over here.
The connection is relatively good.

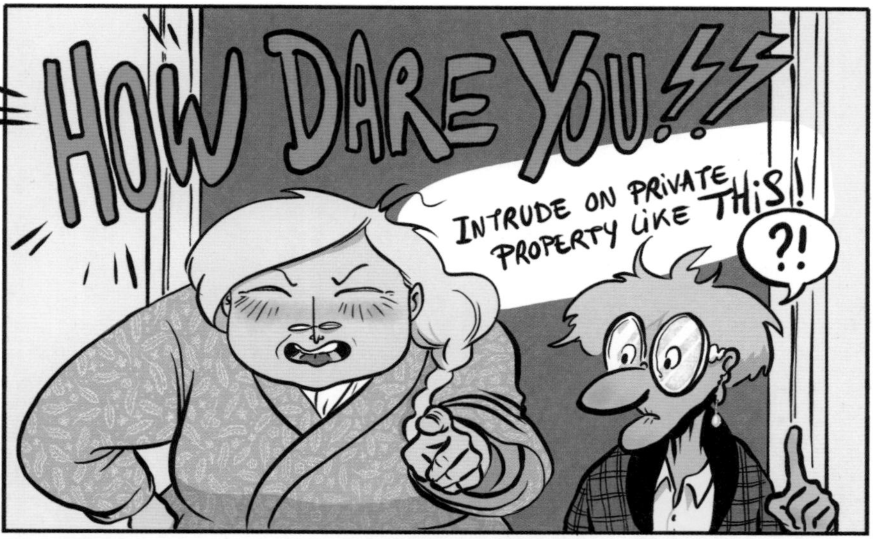
HOW DARE YOU!!
INTRUDE ON PRIVATE PROPERTY LIKE THIS!
?!

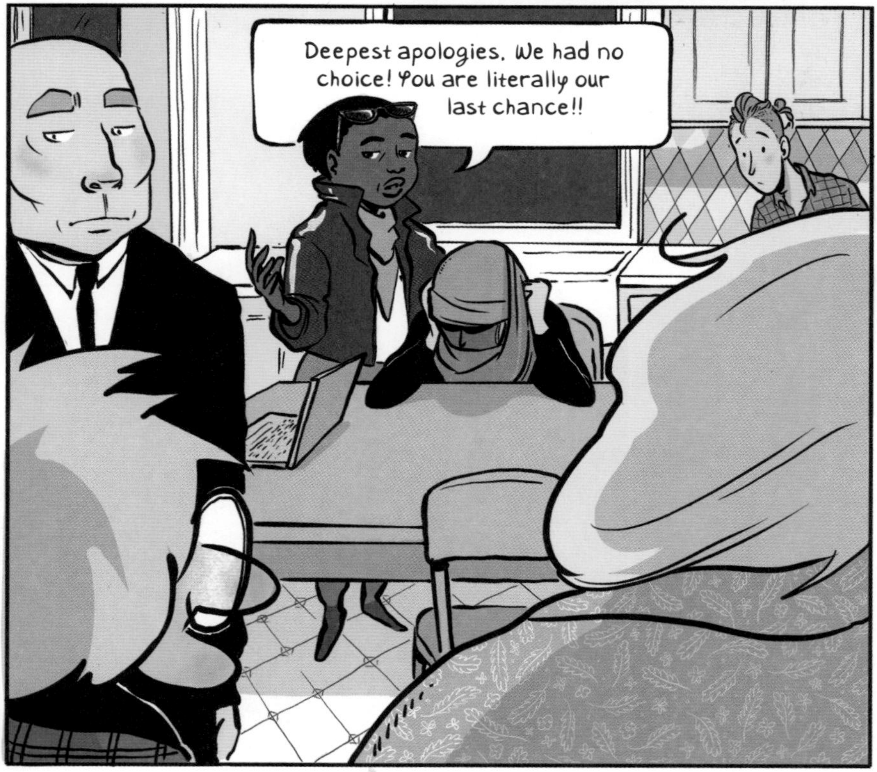
Deepest apologies. We had no choice! You are literally our last chance!!

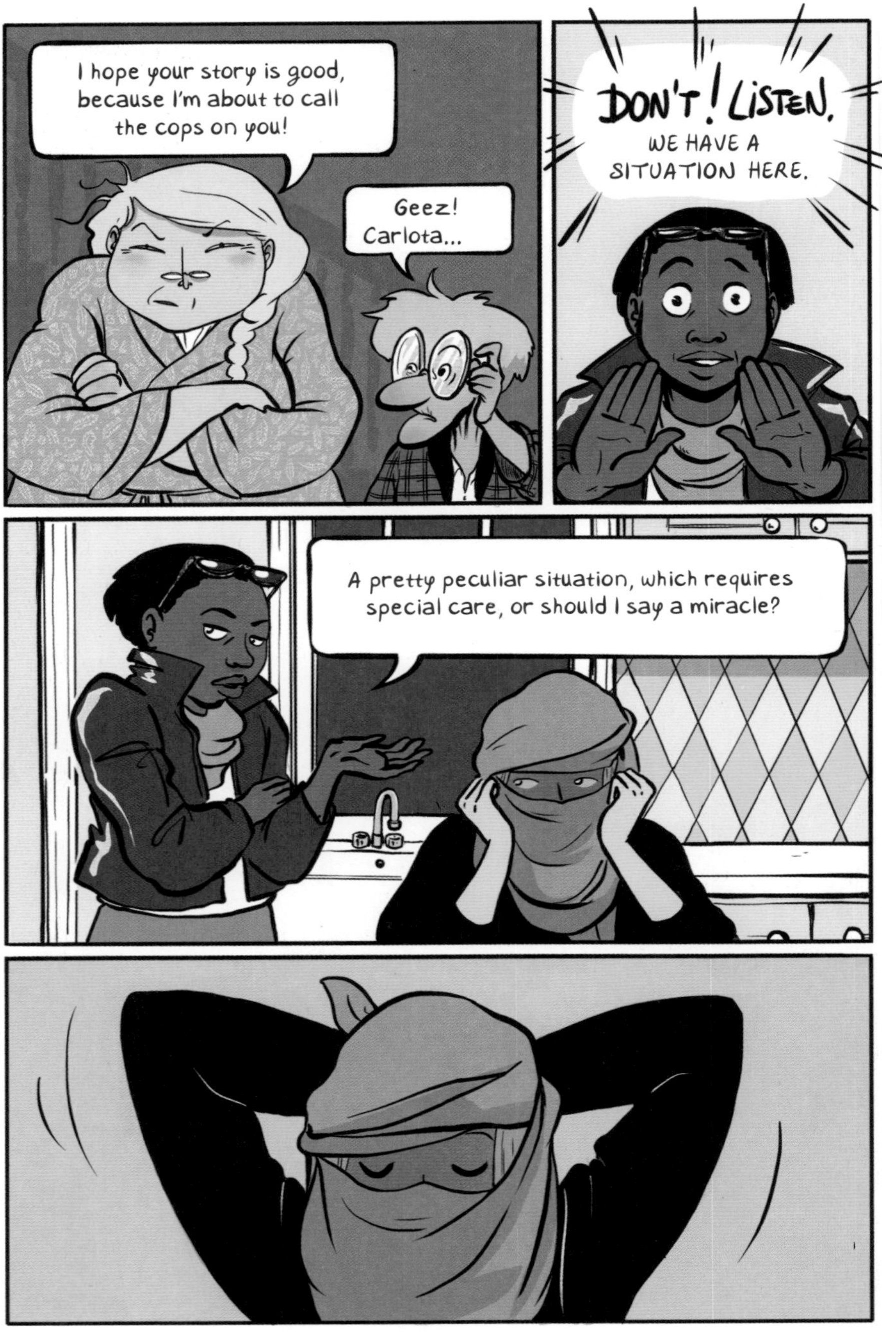
I hope your story is good, because I'm about to call the cops on you!
Geez! Carlota...
DON'T! LISTEN.
WE HAVE A SITUATION HERE.
A pretty peculiar situation, which requires special care, or should I say a miracle?

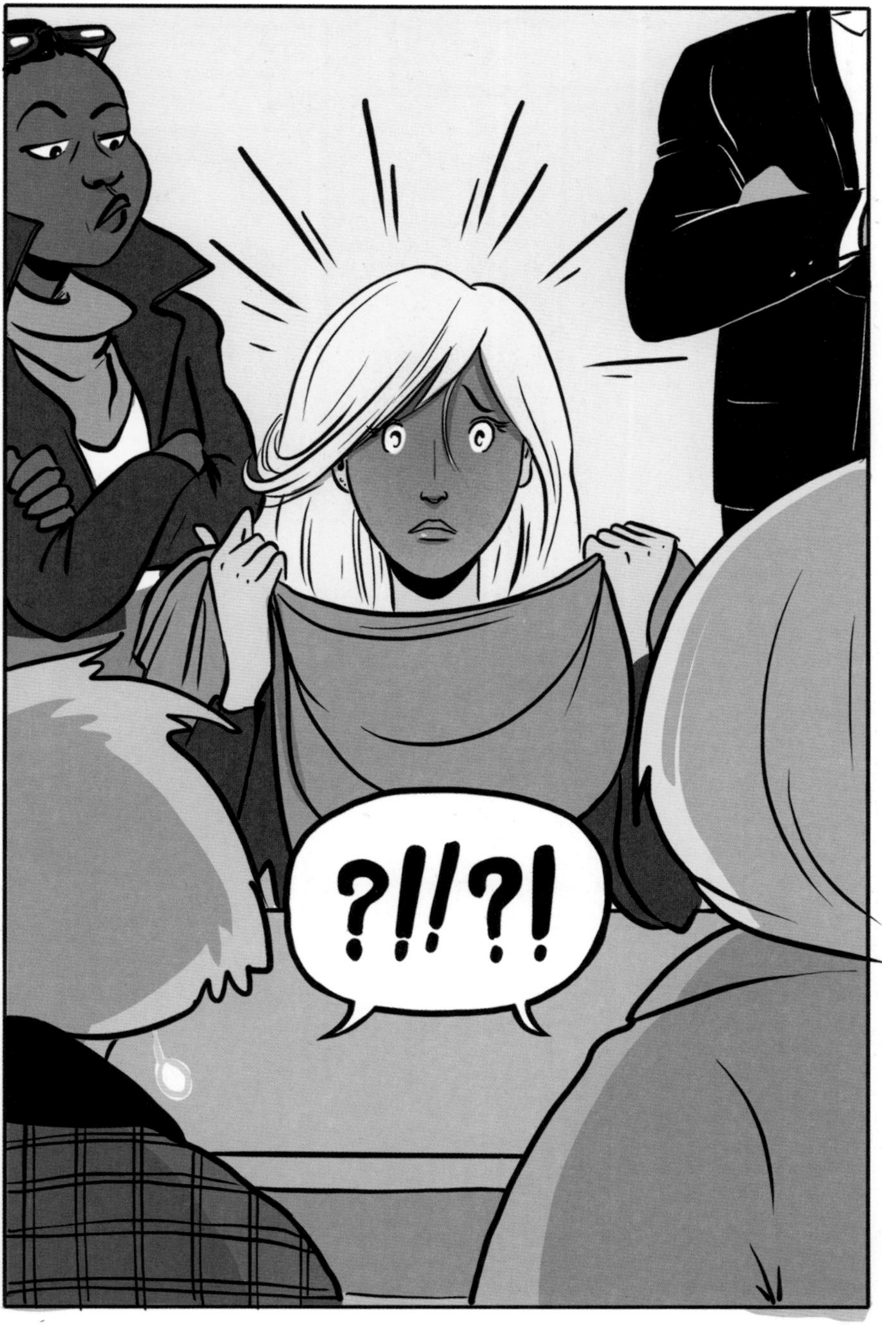
?!!?!

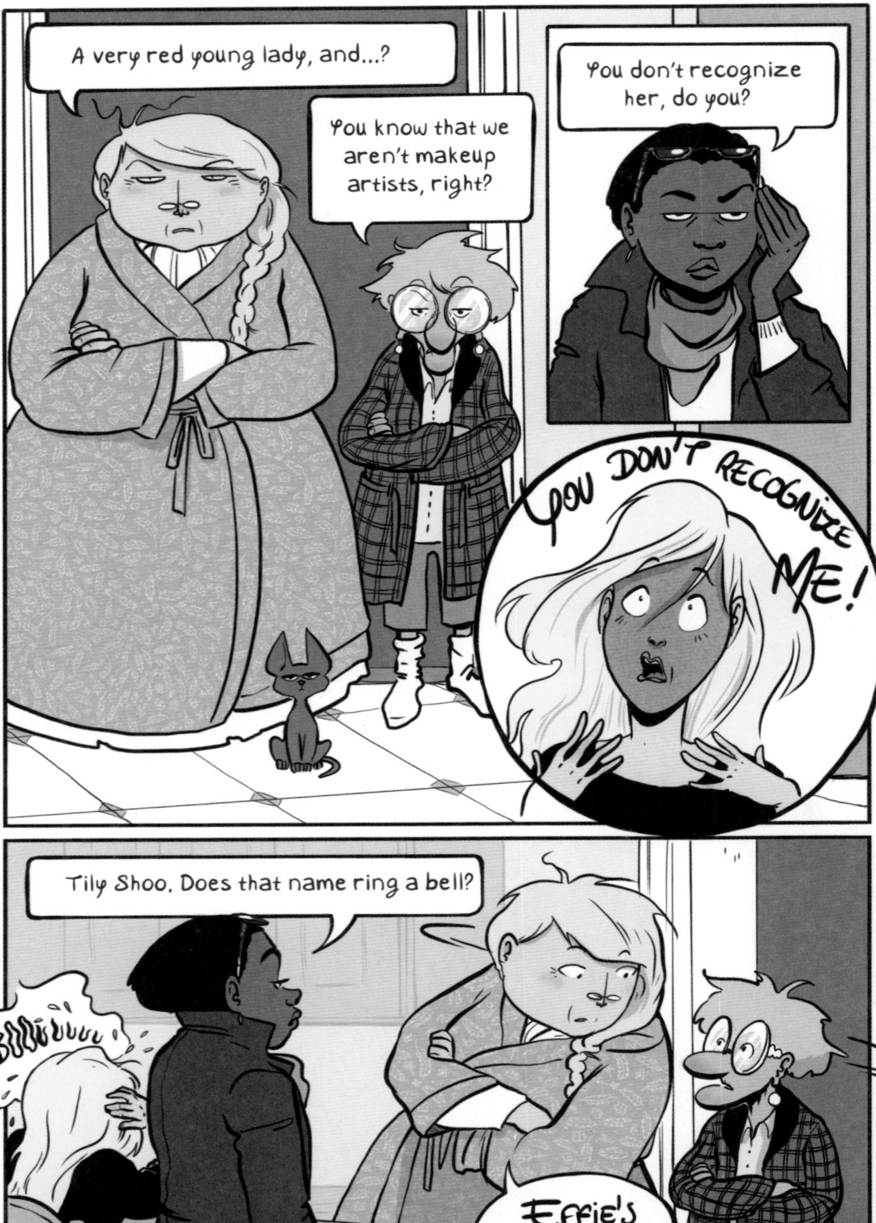
A very red young lady, and...?
You know that we aren't makeup artists, right?
You don't recognize her, do you?
YOU DON'T RECOGNIZE ME!
Tily Shoo. Does that name ring a bell?
BWUUUUU
EFFIE'S SINGER!

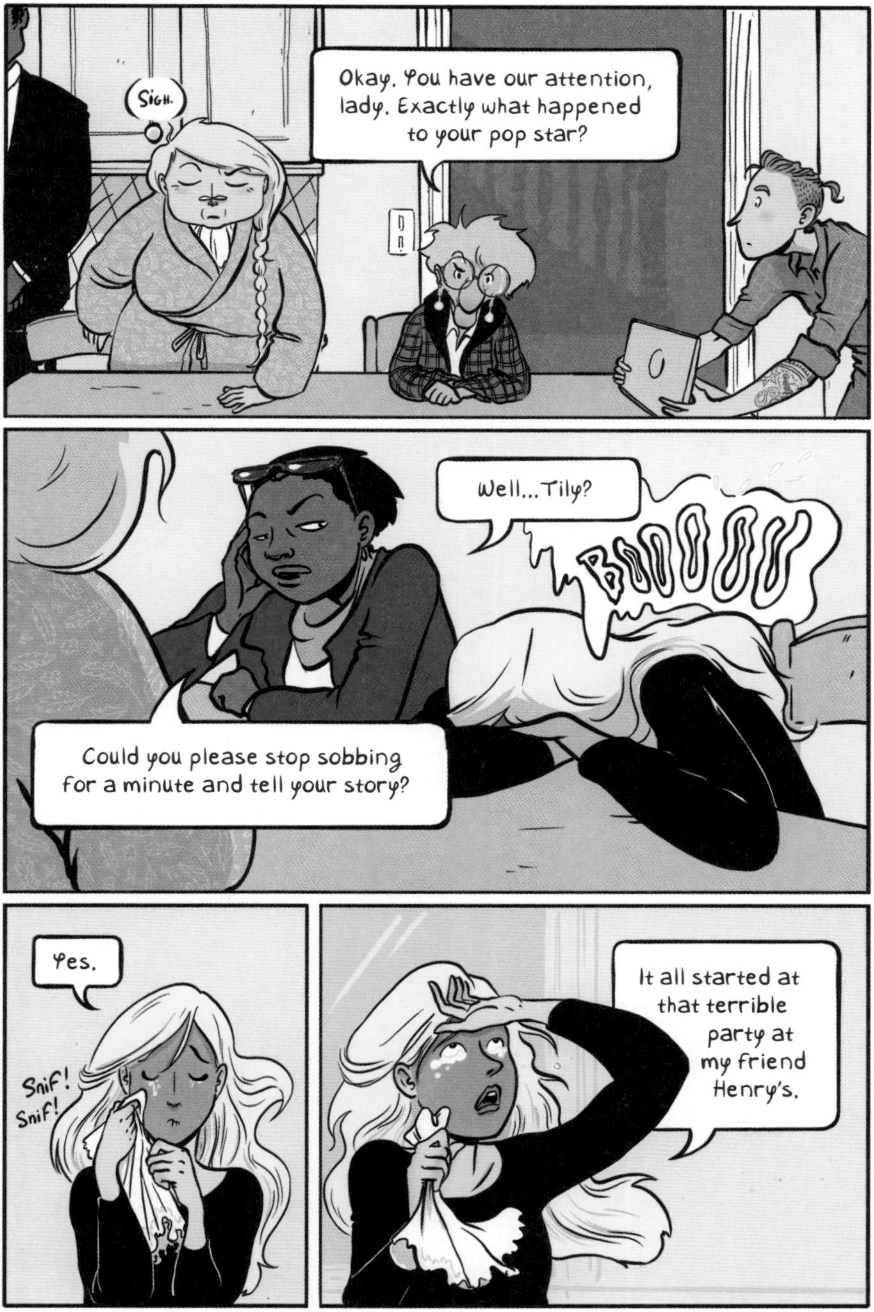
Sigh.
Okay. You have our attention, lady. Exactly what happened to your pop star?
Well... Tily?
Could you please stop sobbing for a minute and tell your story?
BOOOOU
Yes.
Snif! Snif!
It all started at that terrible party at my friend Henry's.

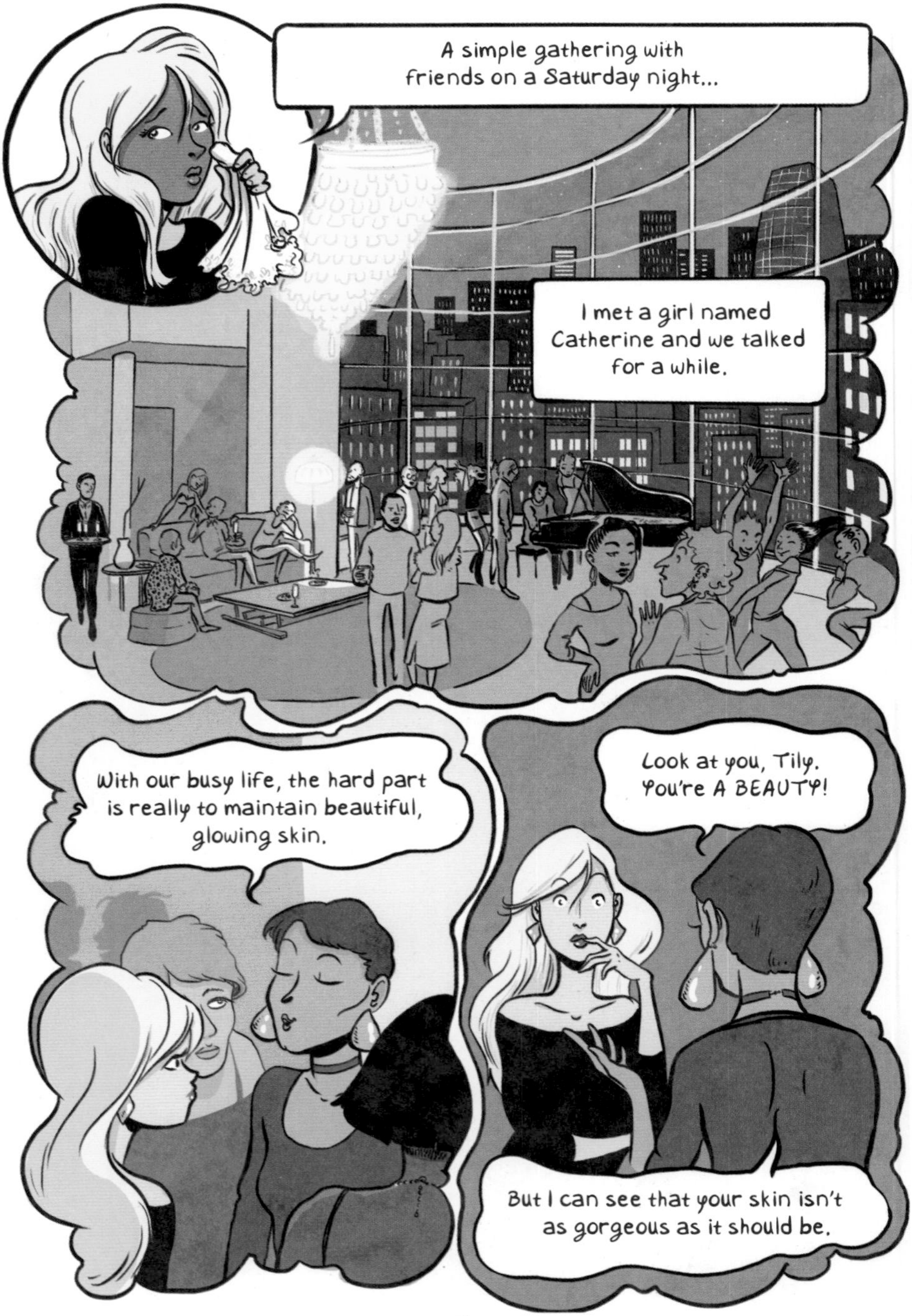
A simple gathering with friends on a Saturday night...
I met a girl named Catherine and we talked for a while.
With our busy life, the hard part is really to maintain beautiful, glowing skin.
Look at you, Tily. You're A BEAUTY!
But I can see that your skin isn't as gorgeous as it should be.

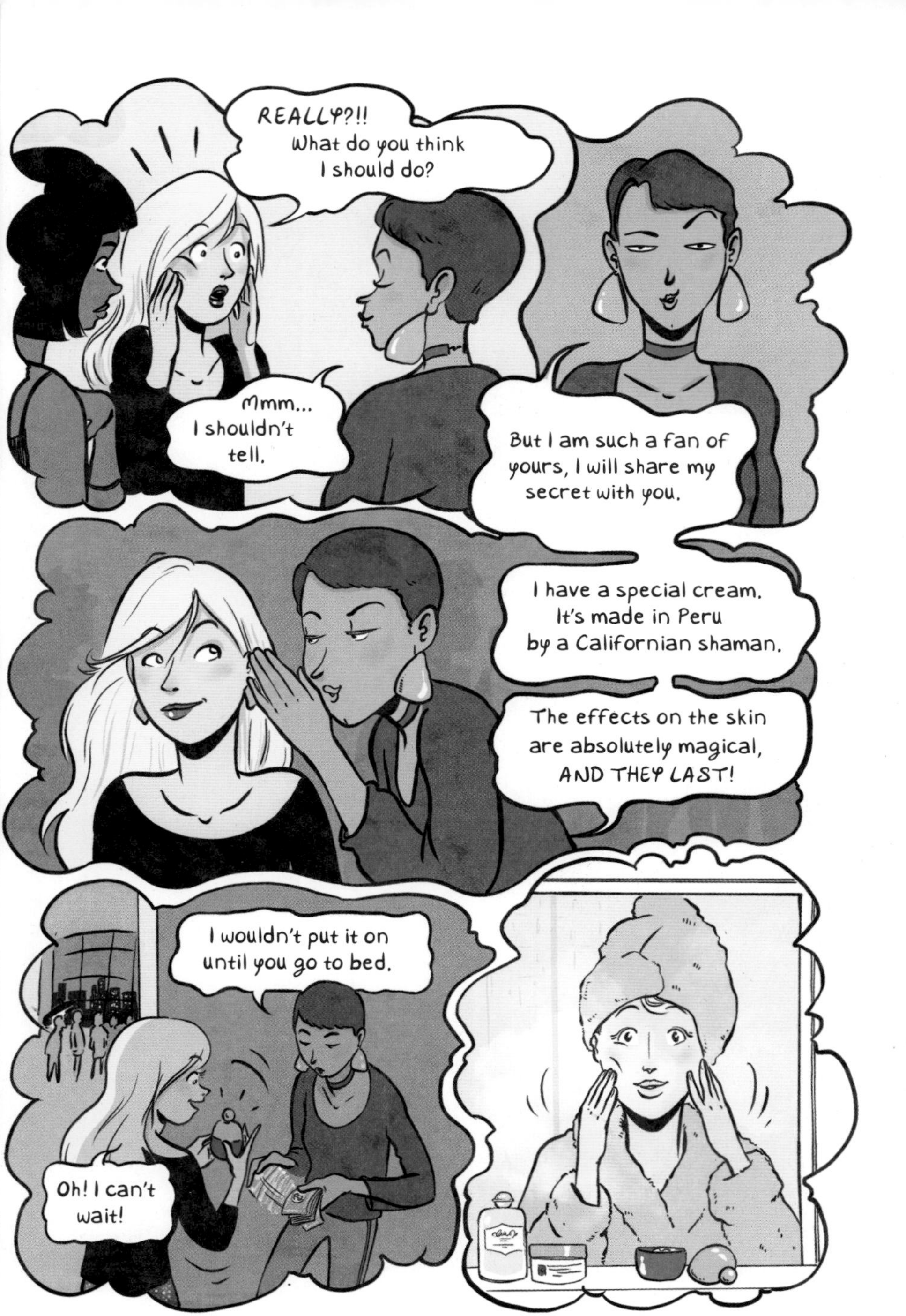
REALLY?!!
What do you think I should do?
Mmm... I shouldn't tell.
But I am such a fan of yours, I will share my secret with you.
I have a special cream. It's made in Peru by a Californian shaman.
The effects on the skin are absolutely magical, AND THEY LAST!
I wouldn't put it on until you go to bed.
Oh! I can't wait!

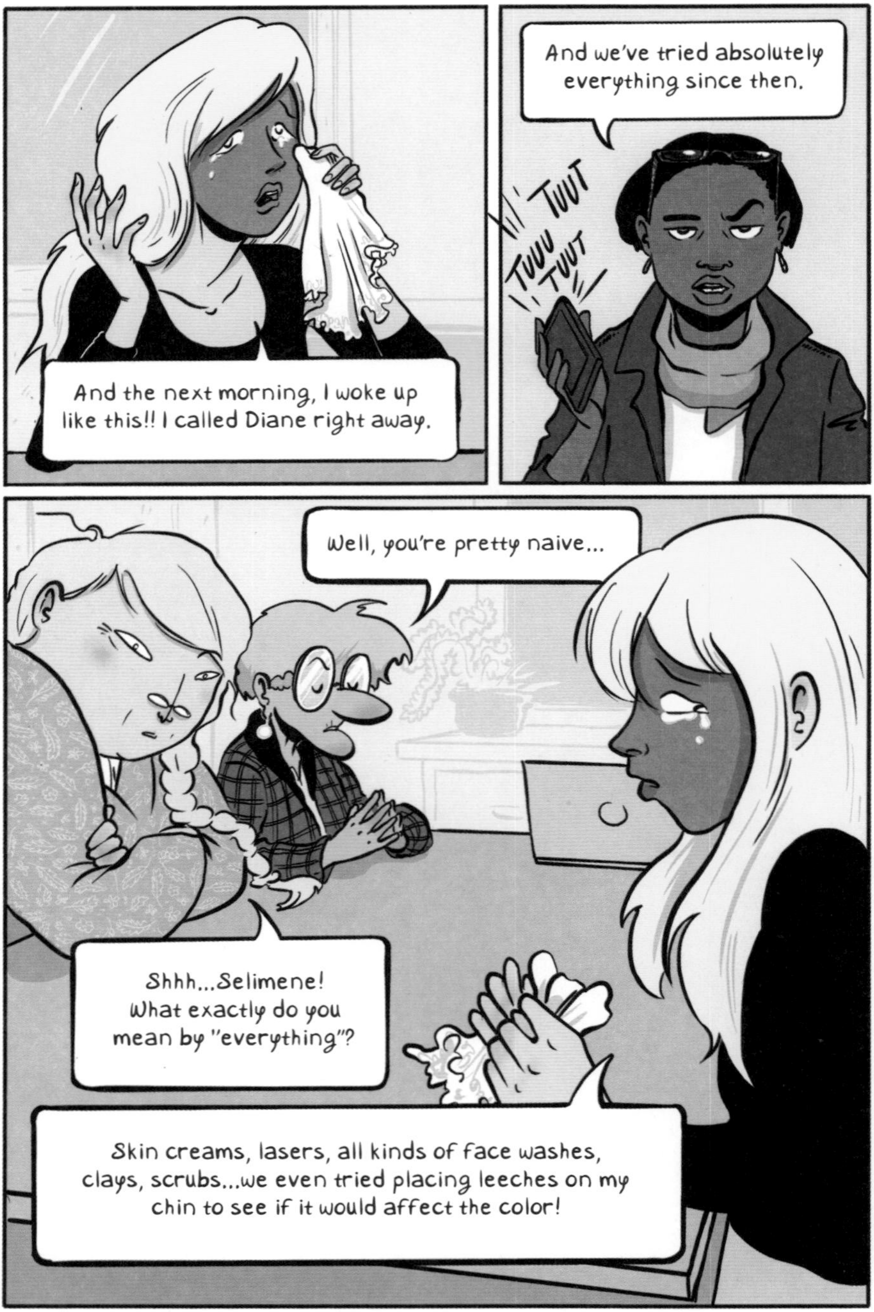
And the next morning, I woke up like this!! I called Diane right away.
And we've tried absolutely everything since then.
TUUT
TUUU
TUUT
Well, you're pretty naive...
Shhh...Selimene! What exactly do you mean by "everything"?
Skin creams, lasers, all kinds of face washes, clays, scrubs...we even tried placing leeches on my chin to see if it would affect the color!

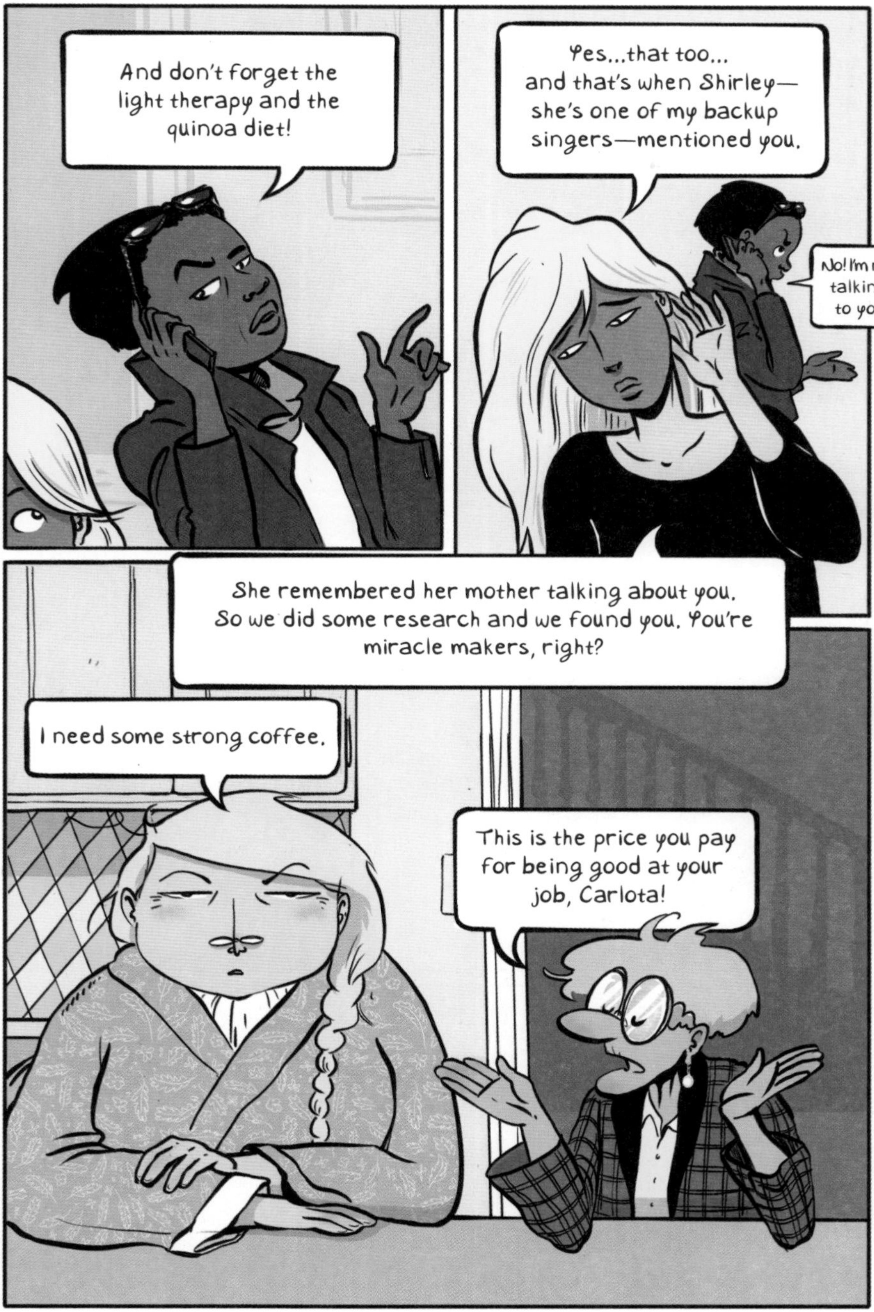
And don't forget the light therapy and the quinoa diet!
Yes...that too... and that's when Shirley—she's one of my backup singers—mentioned you.
No! I'm not talking to you.
She remembered her mother talking about you. So we did some research and we found you. You're miracle makers, right?
I need some strong coffee.
This is the price you pay for being good at your job, Carlota!

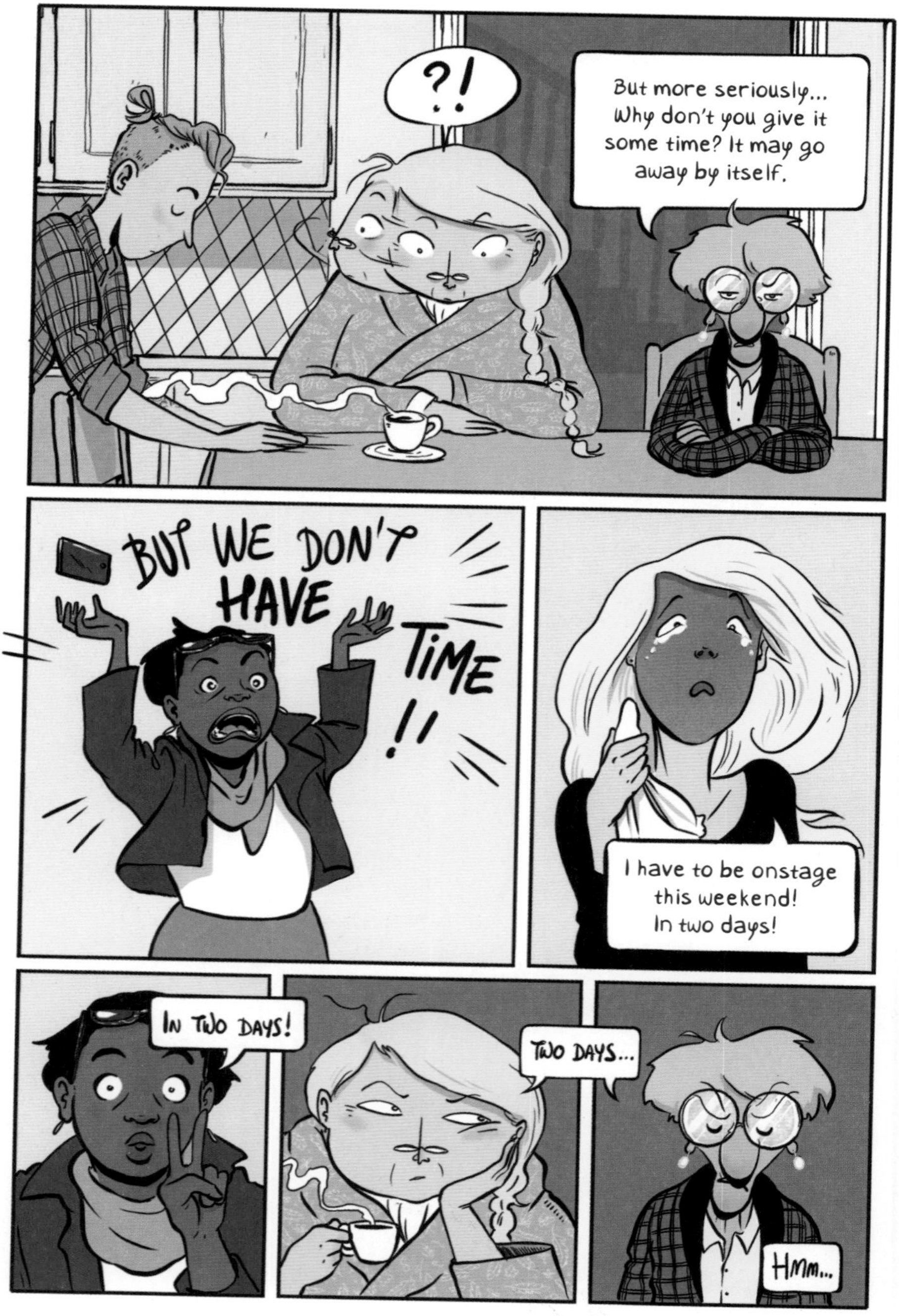

?!
But more seriously... Why don't you give it some time? It may go away by itself.
BUT WE DON'T HAVE TIME!!
I have to be onstage this weekend! In two days!
IN TWO DAYS!
TWO DAYS...
HMM...

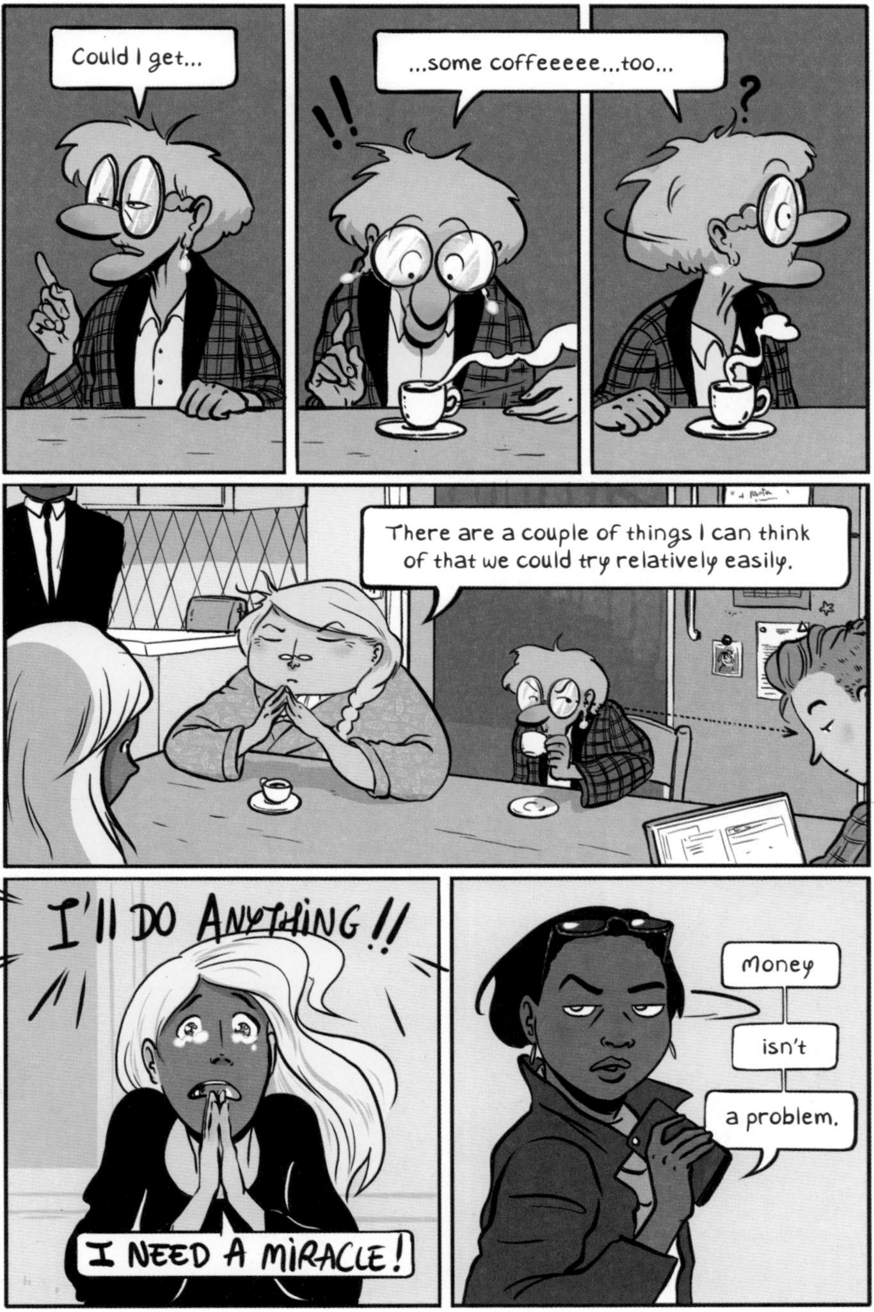
Could I get...
!!
...some coffeeeee...too...
?
There are a couple of things I can think of that we could try relatively easily.
I'll DO ANYTHING!!
I NEED A MIRACLE!
Money
isn't
a problem.

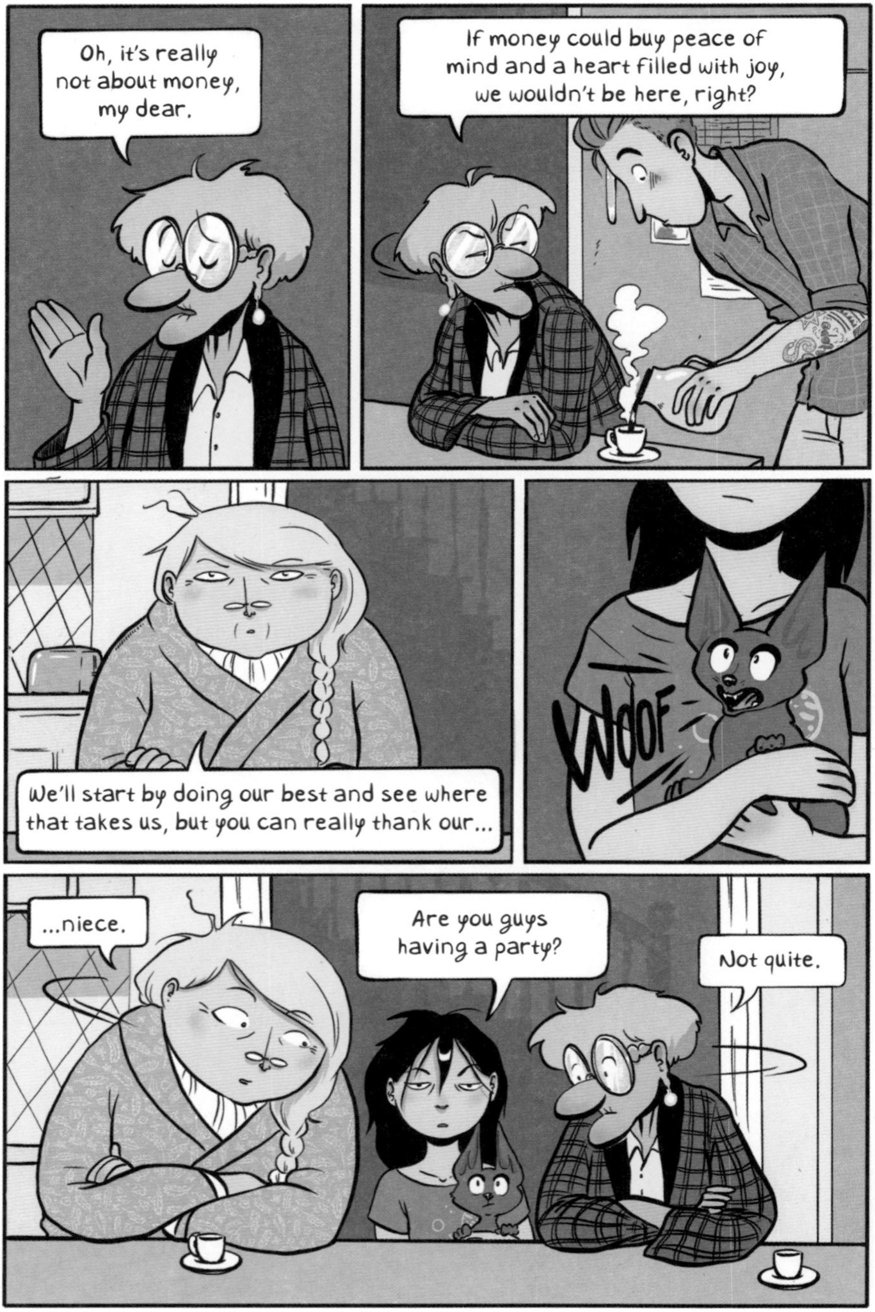

Oh, it's really not about money, my dear.
If money could buy peace of mind and a heart filled with joy, we wouldn't be here, right?
We'll start by doing our best and see where that takes us, but you can really thank our...
WOOF
...niece.
Are you guys having a party?
Not quite.

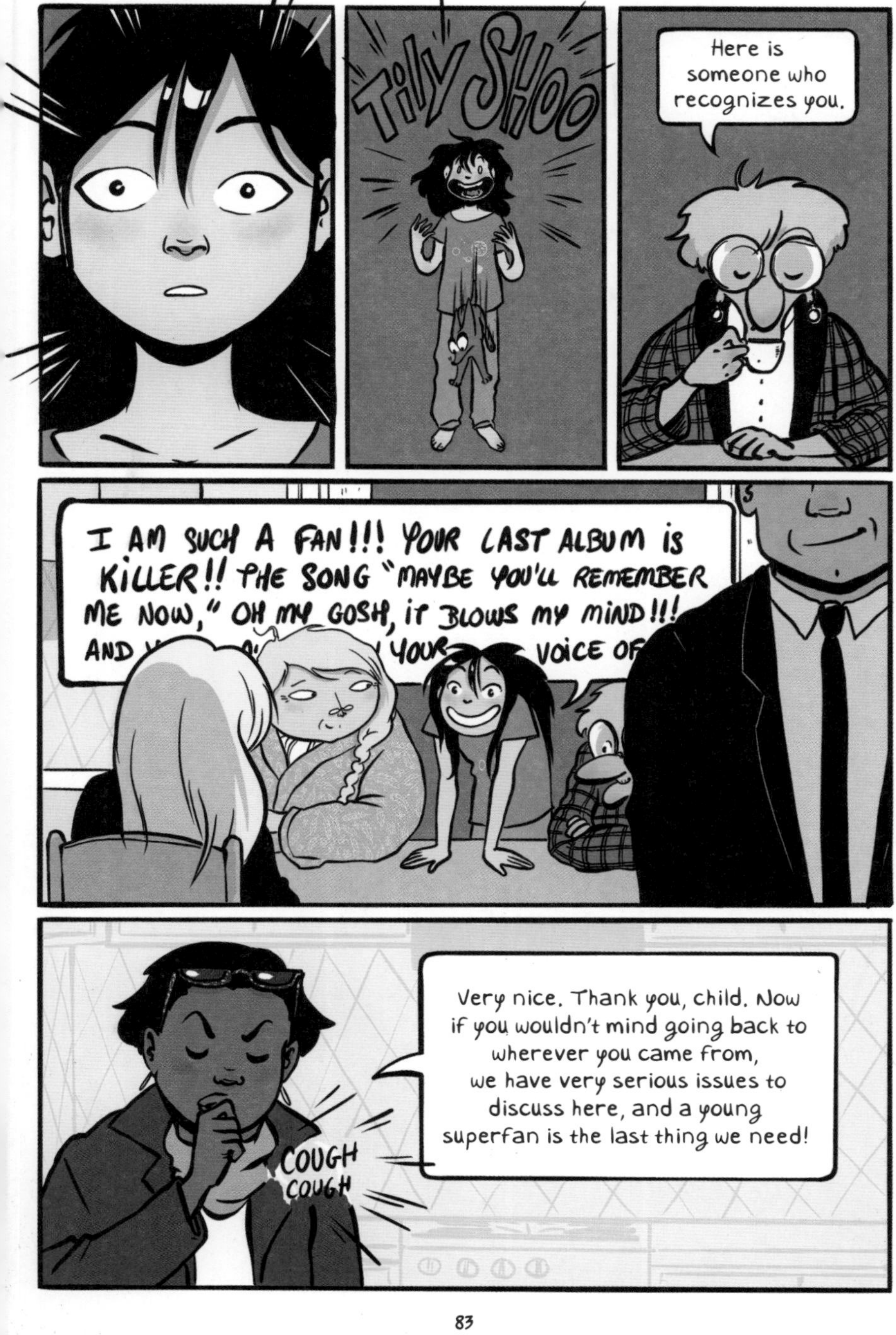
TILLY SHOO
Here is someone who recognizes you.
I AM SUCH A FAN!!! YOUR LAST ALBUM IS KILLER!! THE SONG "MAYBE YOU'LL REMEMBER ME NOW," OH MY GOSH, IT BLOWS MY MIND!!! AND
YOUR
VOICE OF
Very nice. Thank you, child. Now if you wouldn't mind going back to wherever you came from, we have very serious issues to discuss here, and a young superfan is the last thing we need!
COUGH COUGH

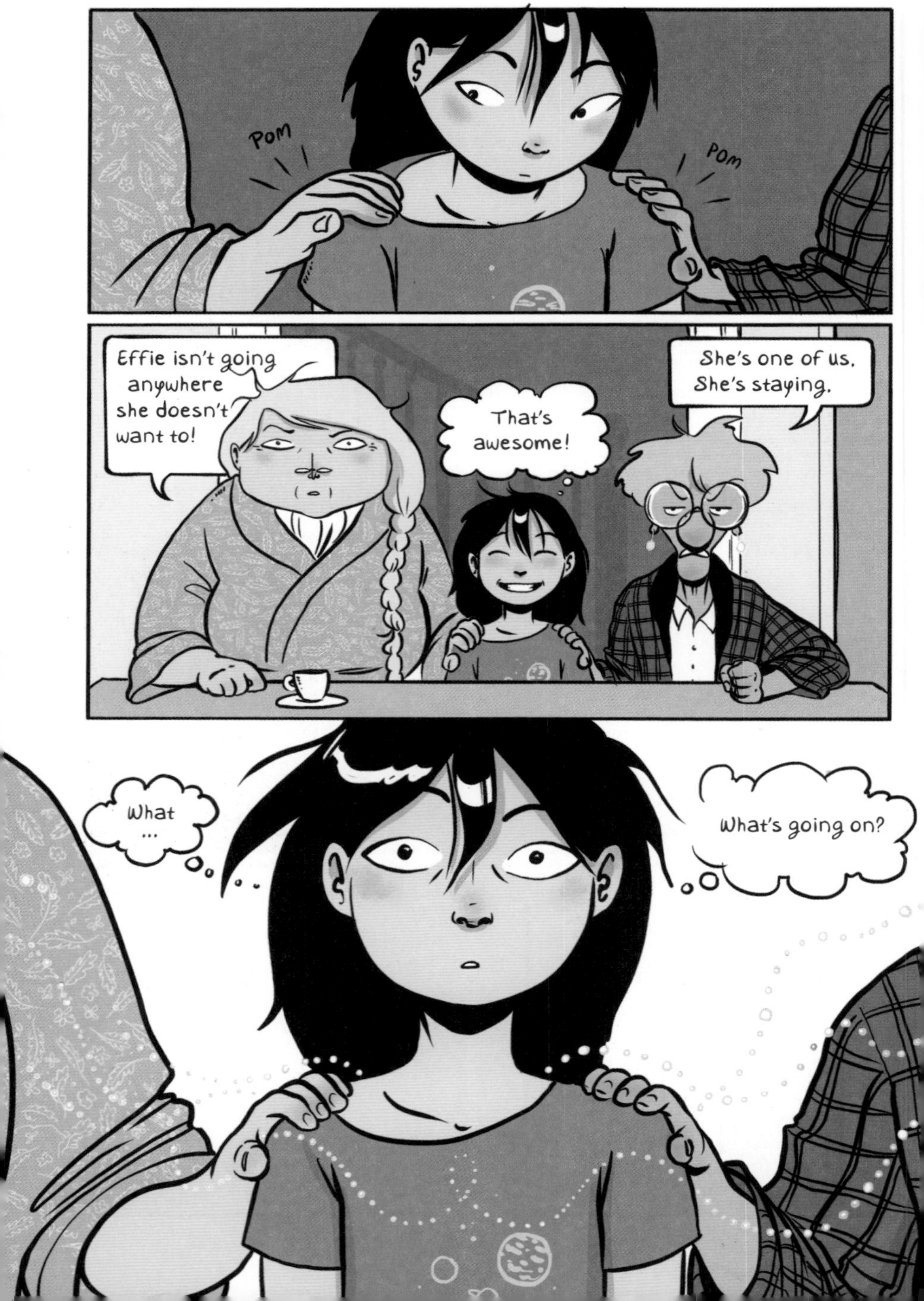
POM
POM
Effie isn't going anywhere she doesn't want to!
That's awesome!
She's one of us. She's staying.
What ...
What's going on?

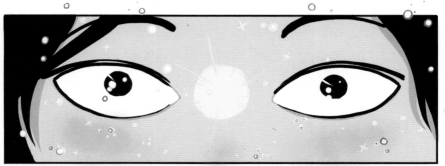

Am I coming down with something?

Dizzy...

Oh no! I think I'm gonna be sick!

?!

EXCUSE ME!

?!

In front of Tily Shoo! That's so embarrassing!

CLICK

What's wrong with me?!

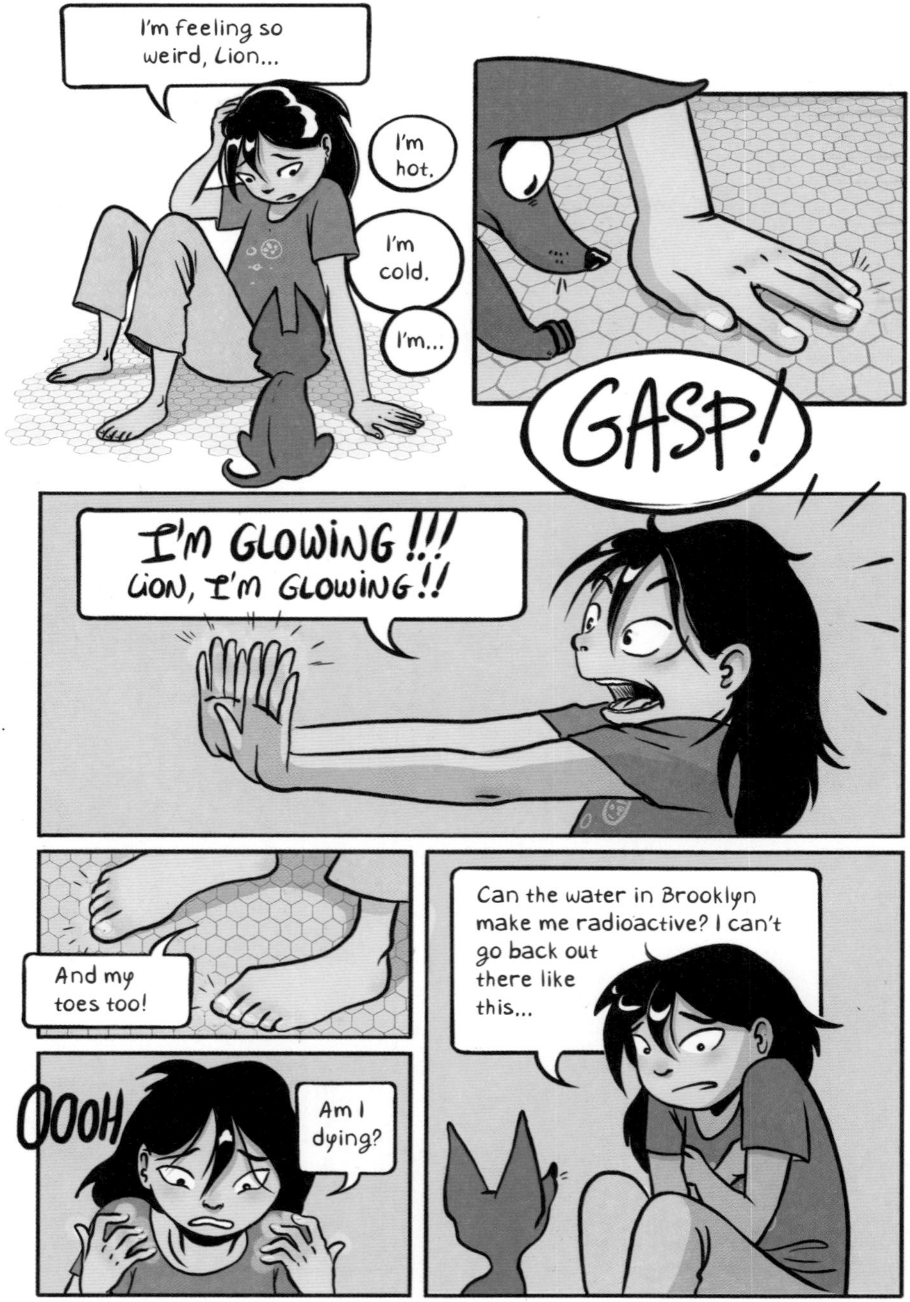

I'm feeling so weird, Lion...
I'm hot.
I'm cold.
I'm...
GASP!
I'M GLOWING!!!
LION, I'M GLOWING!!
And my toes too!
OOOH
Am I dying?
Can the water in Brooklyn make me radioactive? I can't go back out there like this...

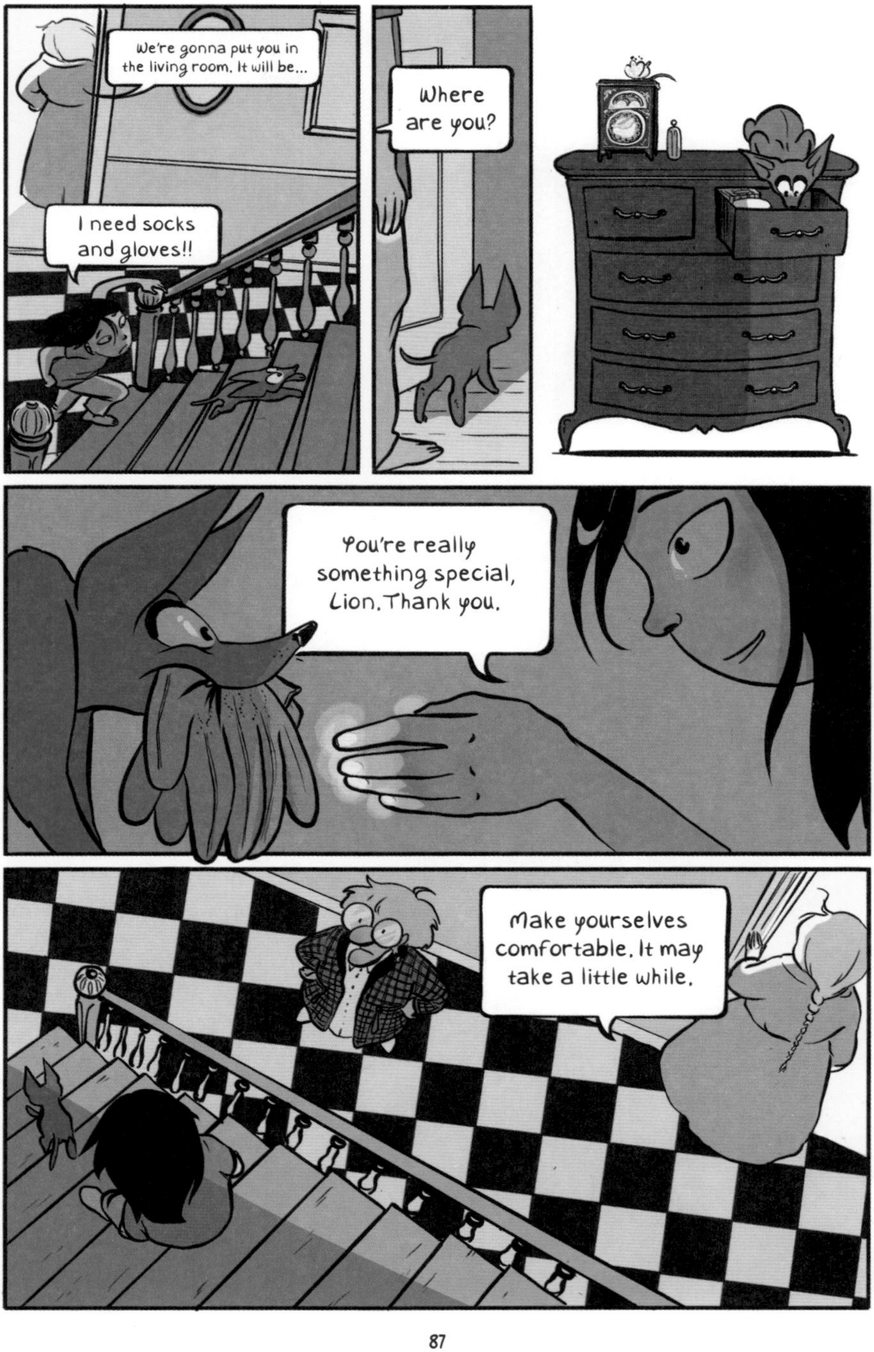
We're gonna put you in the living room. It will be...
I need socks and gloves!!
Where are you?
You're really something special, Lion. Thank you.
Make yourselves comfortable. It may take a little while.

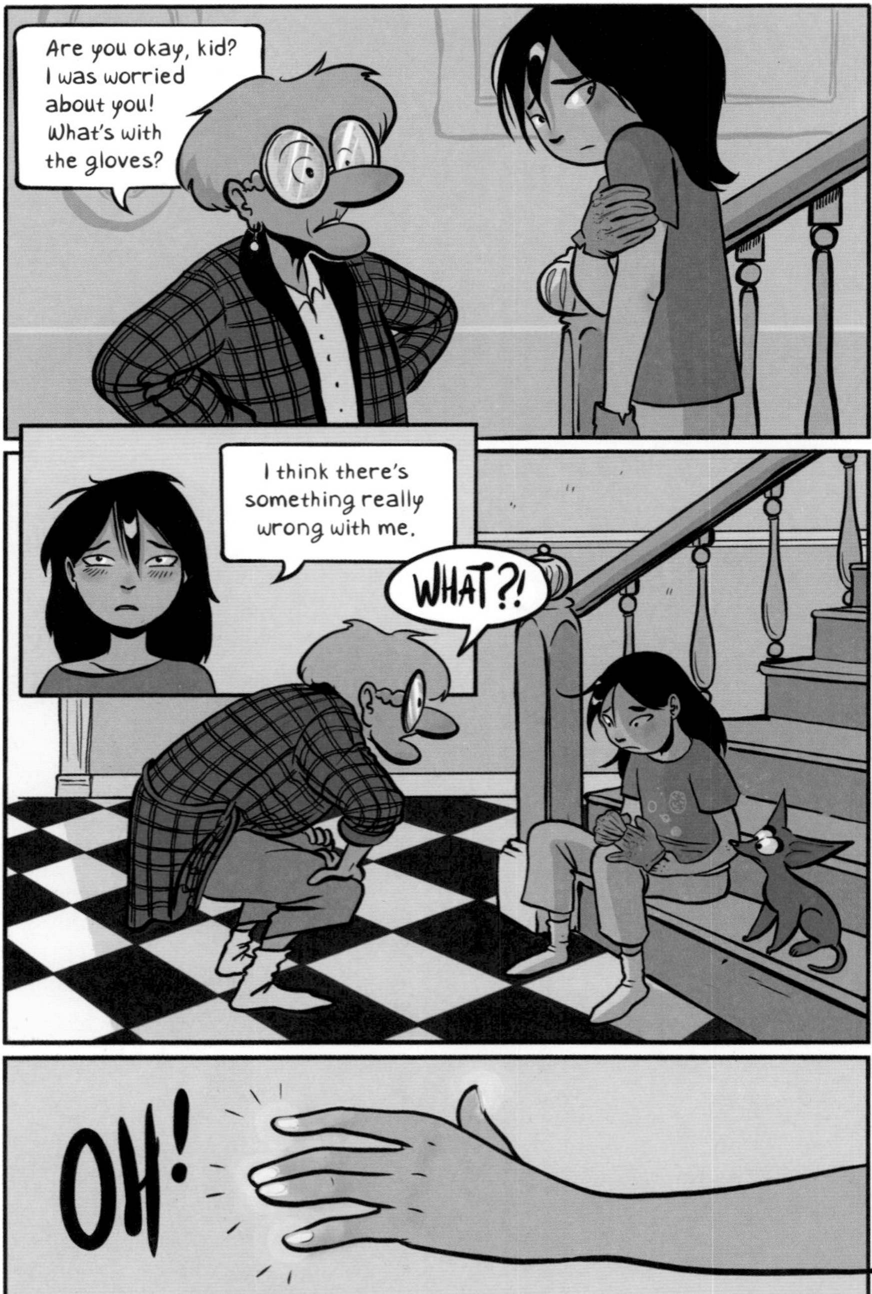
Are you okay, kid? I was worried about you! What's with the gloves?
I think there's something really wrong with me.
WHAT?!
OH!

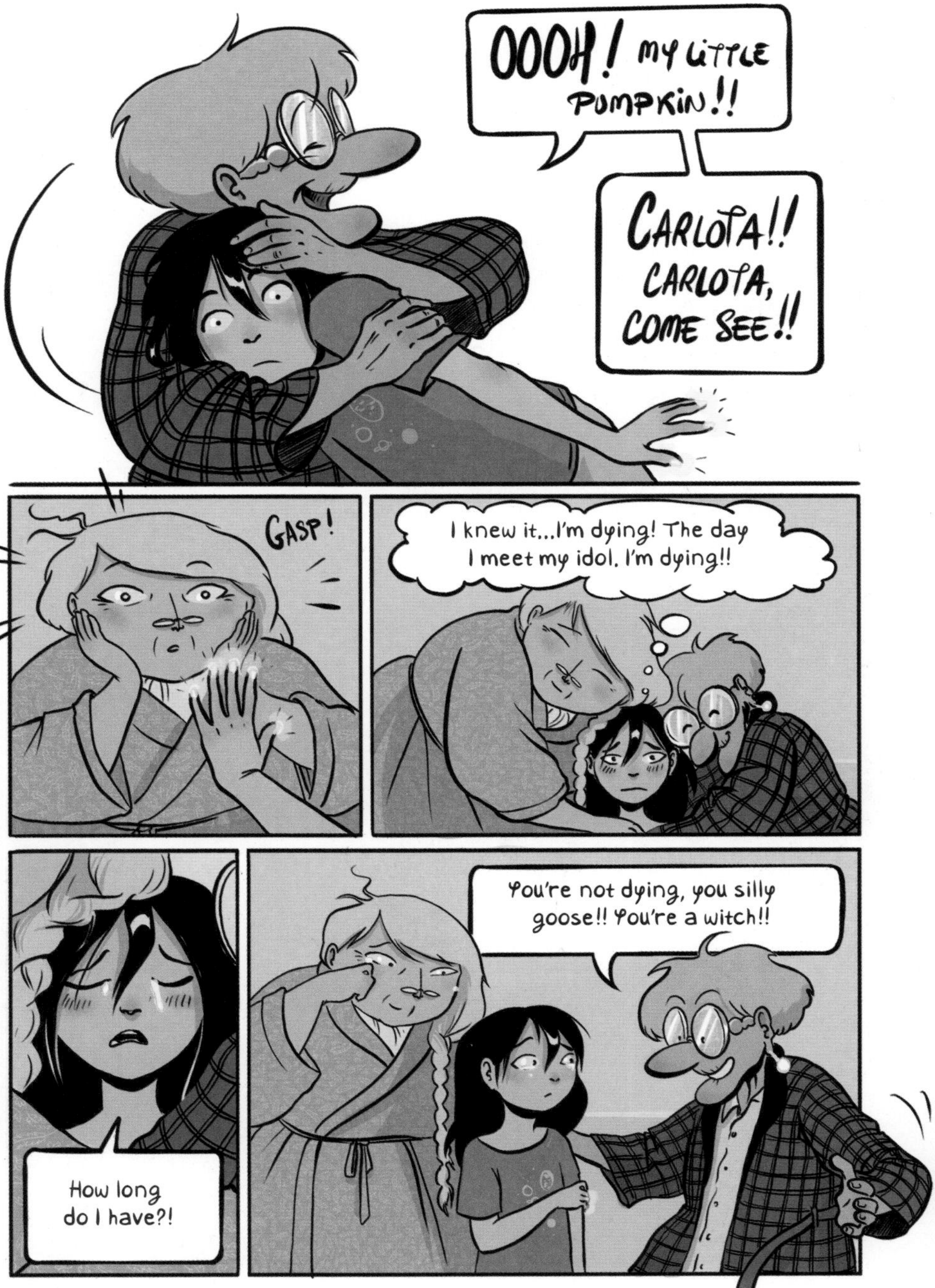
OOOH! MY LITTLE PUMPKIN!!
CARLOTA!! CARLOTA, COME SEE!!
GASP!
I knew it...I'm dying! The day I meet my idol. I'm dying!!
How long do I have?!
You're not dying, you silly goose!! You're a witch!!

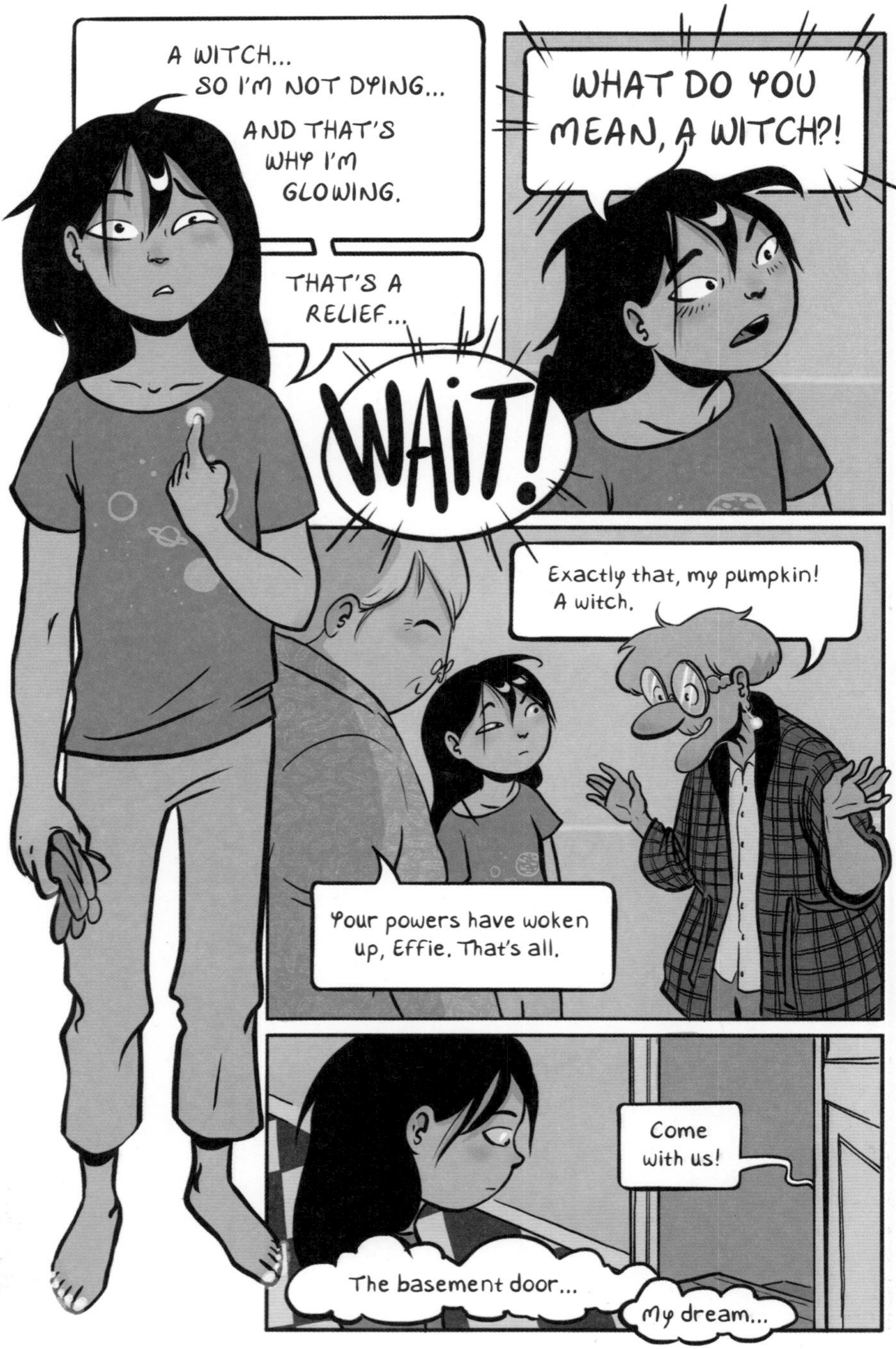
A WITCH... SO I'M NOT DYING... AND THAT'S WHY I'M GLOWING.
THAT'S A RELIEF...
WAIT!
WHAT DO YOU MEAN, A WITCH?!
Exactly that, my pumpkin! A witch.
Your powers have woken up, Effie. That's all.
Come with us!
The basement door...
My dream...

Chapter 3

click!

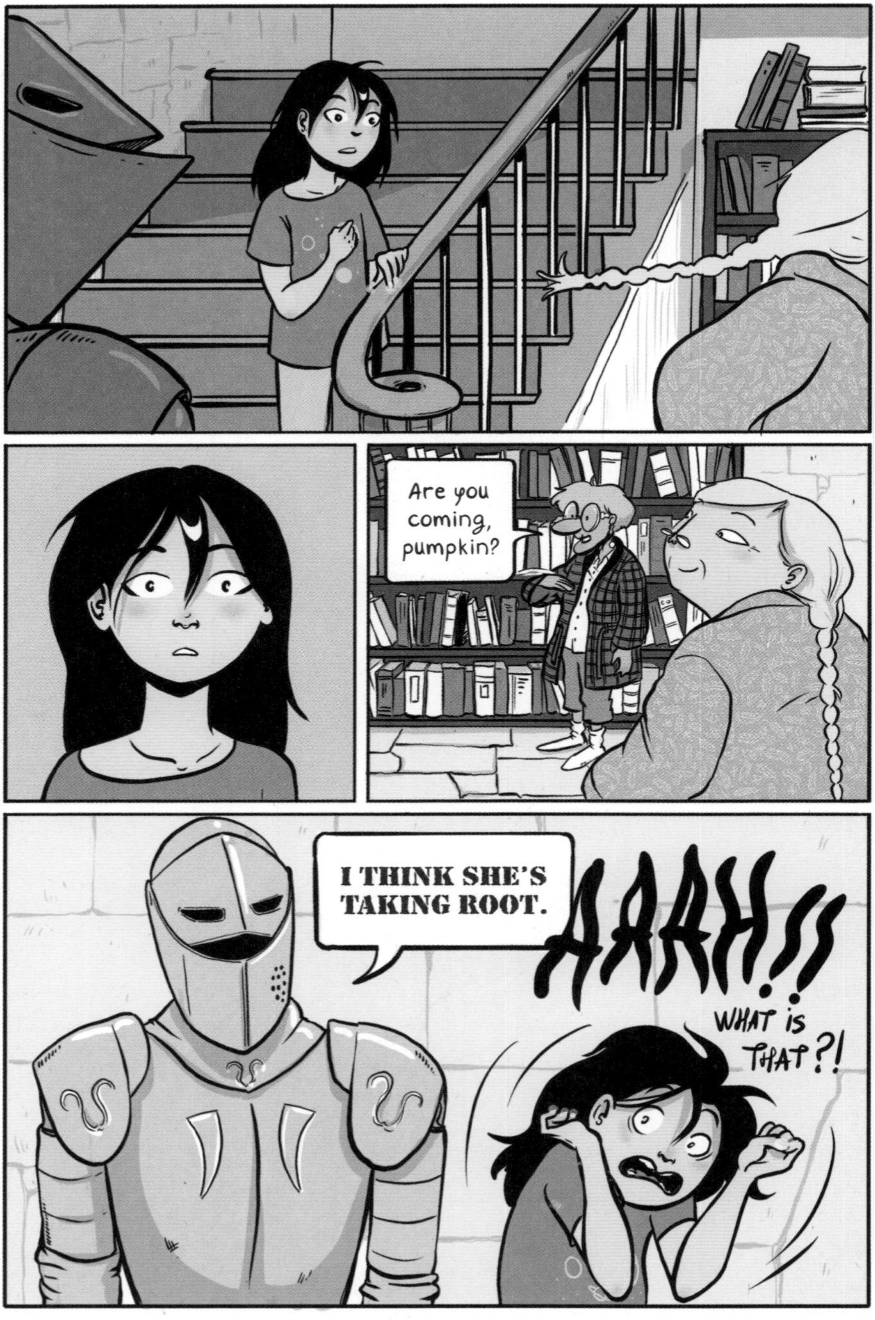
Are you coming, pumpkin?
I THINK SHE'S TAKING ROOT.
AAAH!!
WHAT IS THAT?!

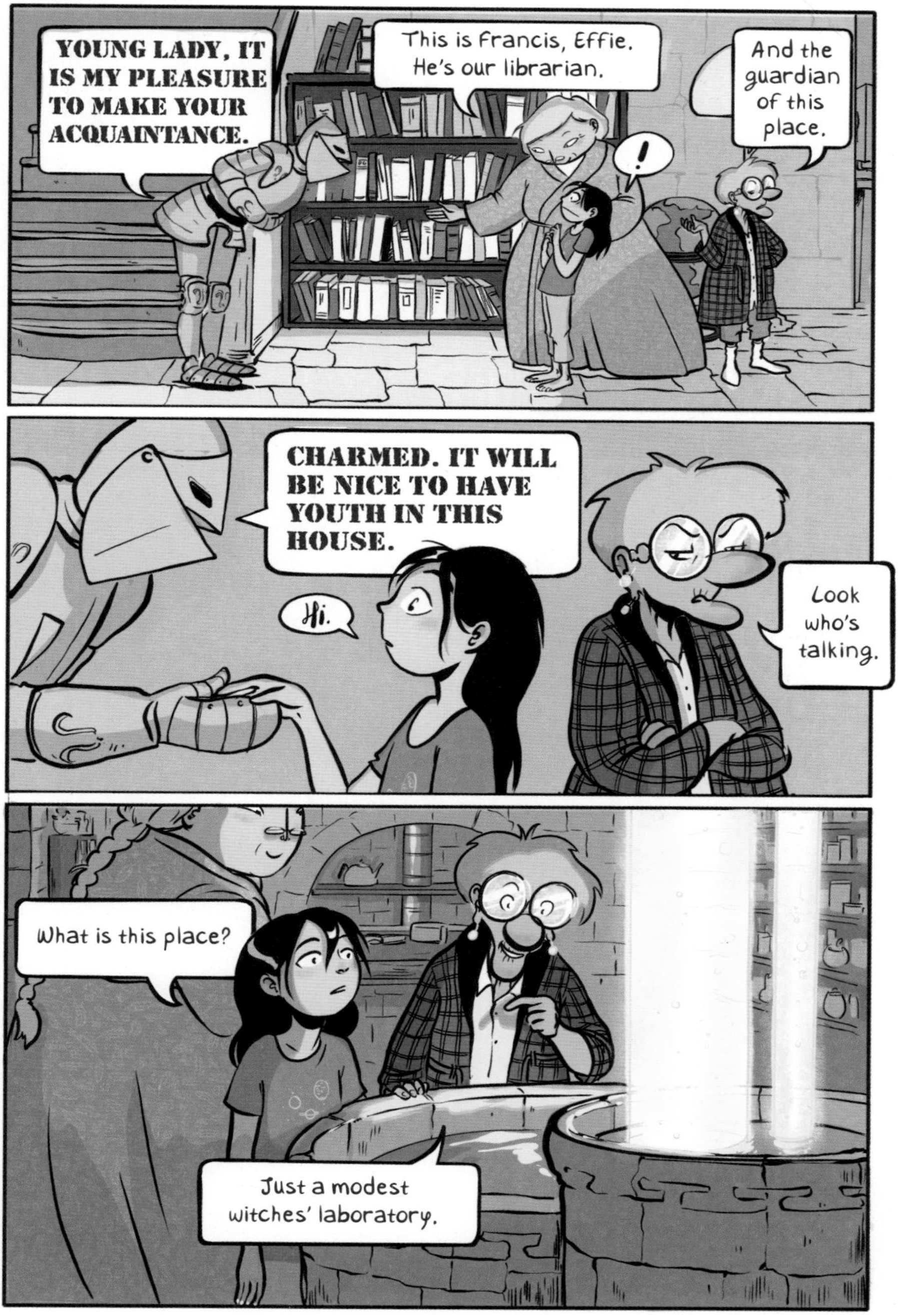
YOUNG LADY, IT IS MY PLEASURE TO MAKE YOUR ACQUAINTANCE.
This is Francis, Effie. He's our librarian.
!
And the guardian of this place.
CHARMED. IT WILL BE NICE TO HAVE YOUTH IN THIS HOUSE.
Hi.
Look who's talking.
What is this place?
Just a modest witches' laboratory.

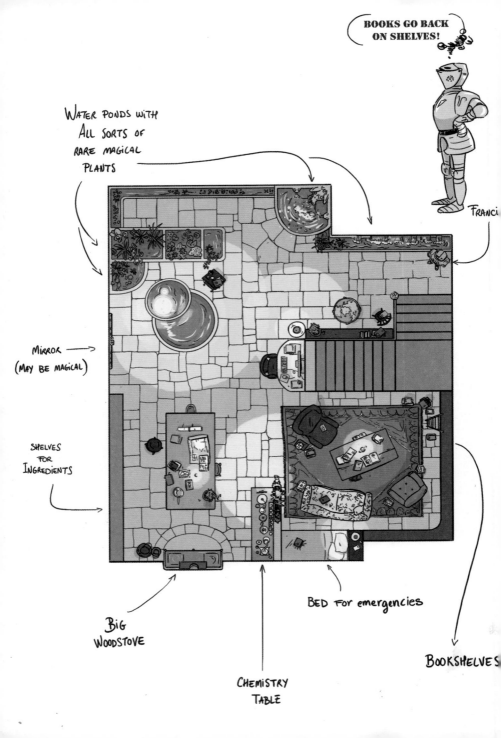

BOOKS GO BACK ON SHELVES!

WATER PONDS WITH ALL SORTS OF RARE MAGICAL PLANTS

Franci

MIRROR (MAY BE MAGICAL)

SHELVES FOR INGREDIENTS

BIG WOODSTOVE

CHEMISTRY TABLE

BED FOR emergencies

BOOKSHELVES

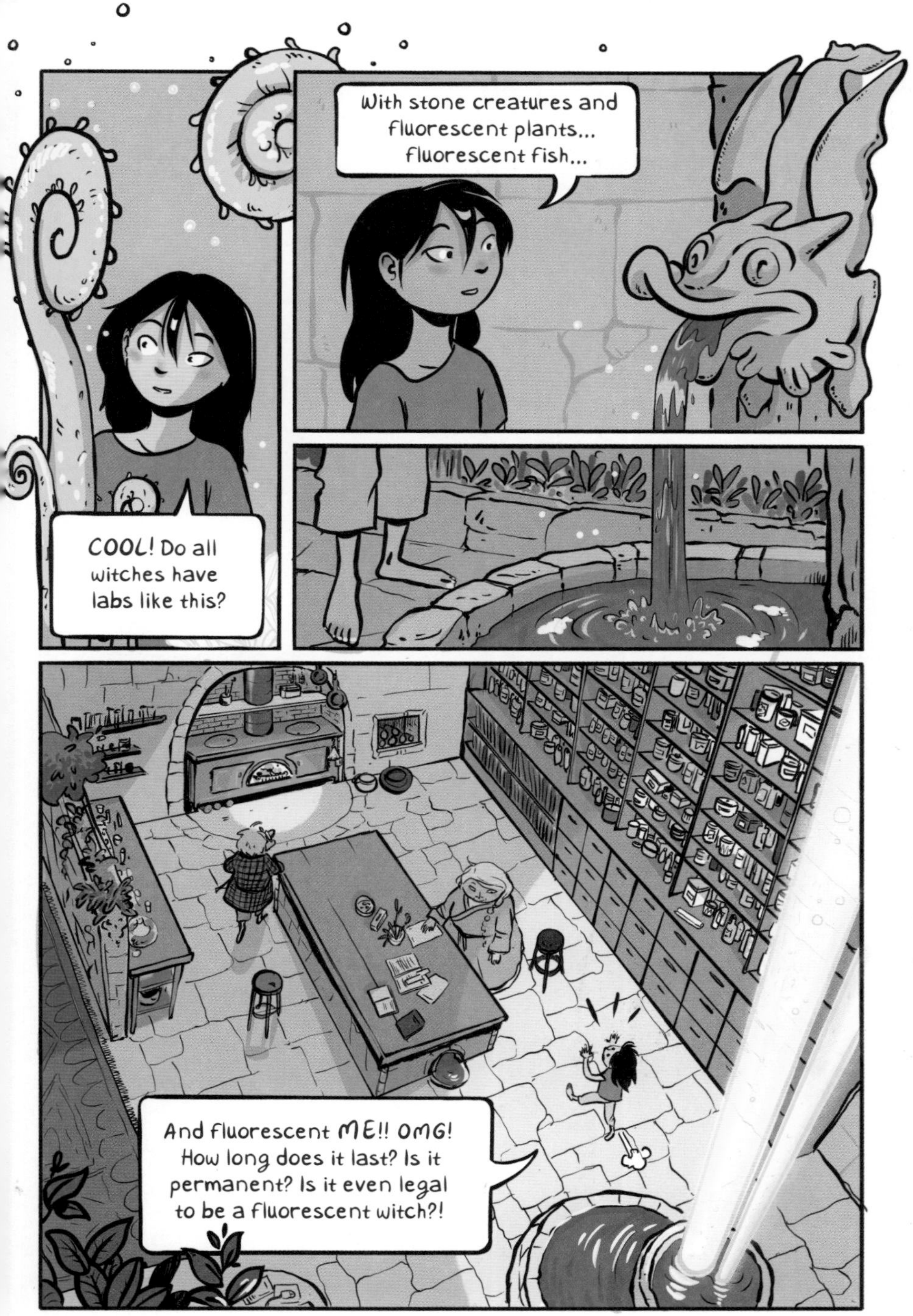
COOL! Do all witches have labs like this?
With stone creatures and fluorescent plants... fluorescent fish...
And fluorescent ME!! OMG! How long does it last? Is it permanent? Is it even legal to be a fluorescent witch?!

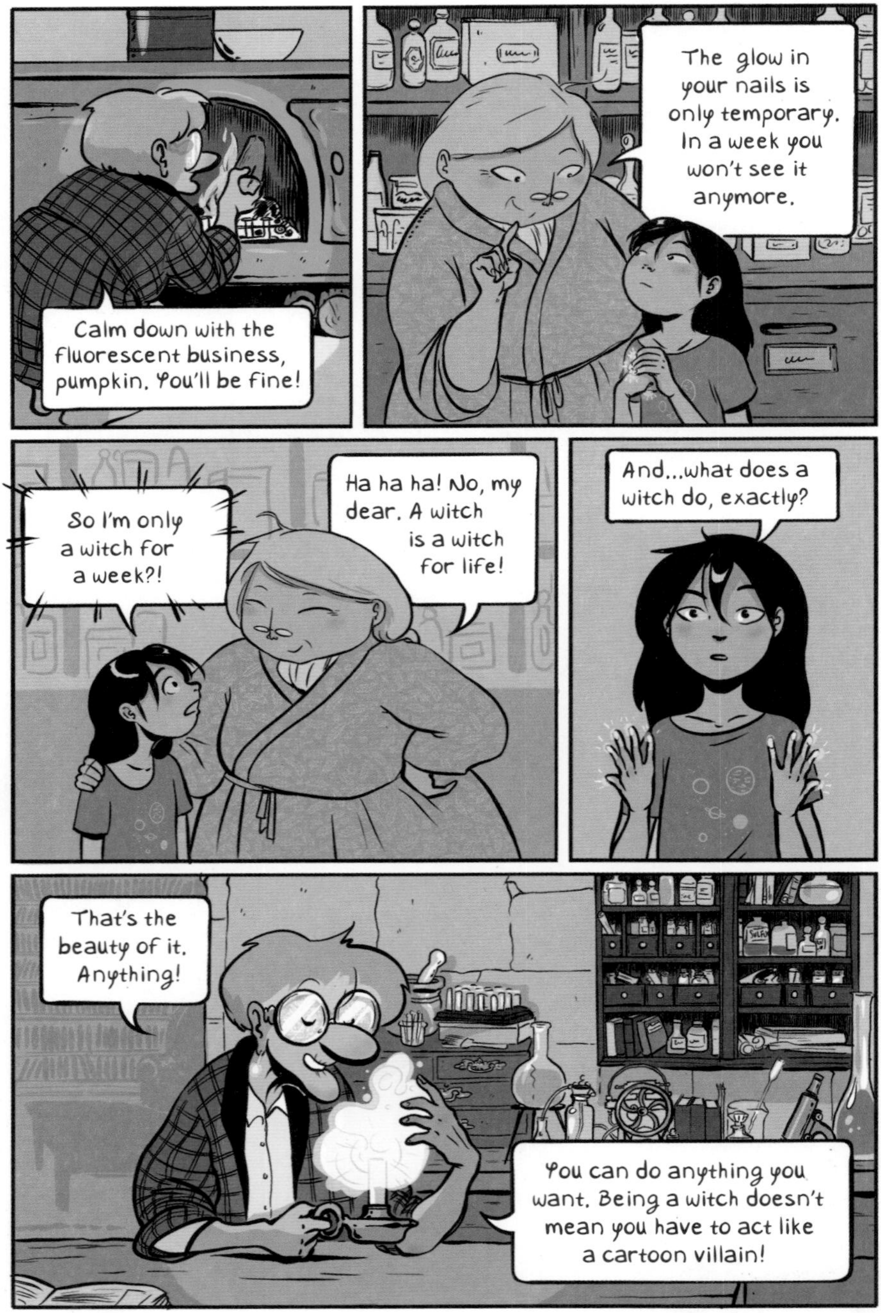
Calm down with the fluorescent business, pumpkin. You'll be fine!
The glow in your nails is only temporary. In a week you won't see it anymore.
So I'm only a witch for a week?!
Ha ha ha! No, my dear. A witch is a witch for life!
And...what does a witch do, exactly?
That's the beauty of it. Anything!
You can do anything you want. Being a witch doesn't mean you have to act like a cartoon villain!

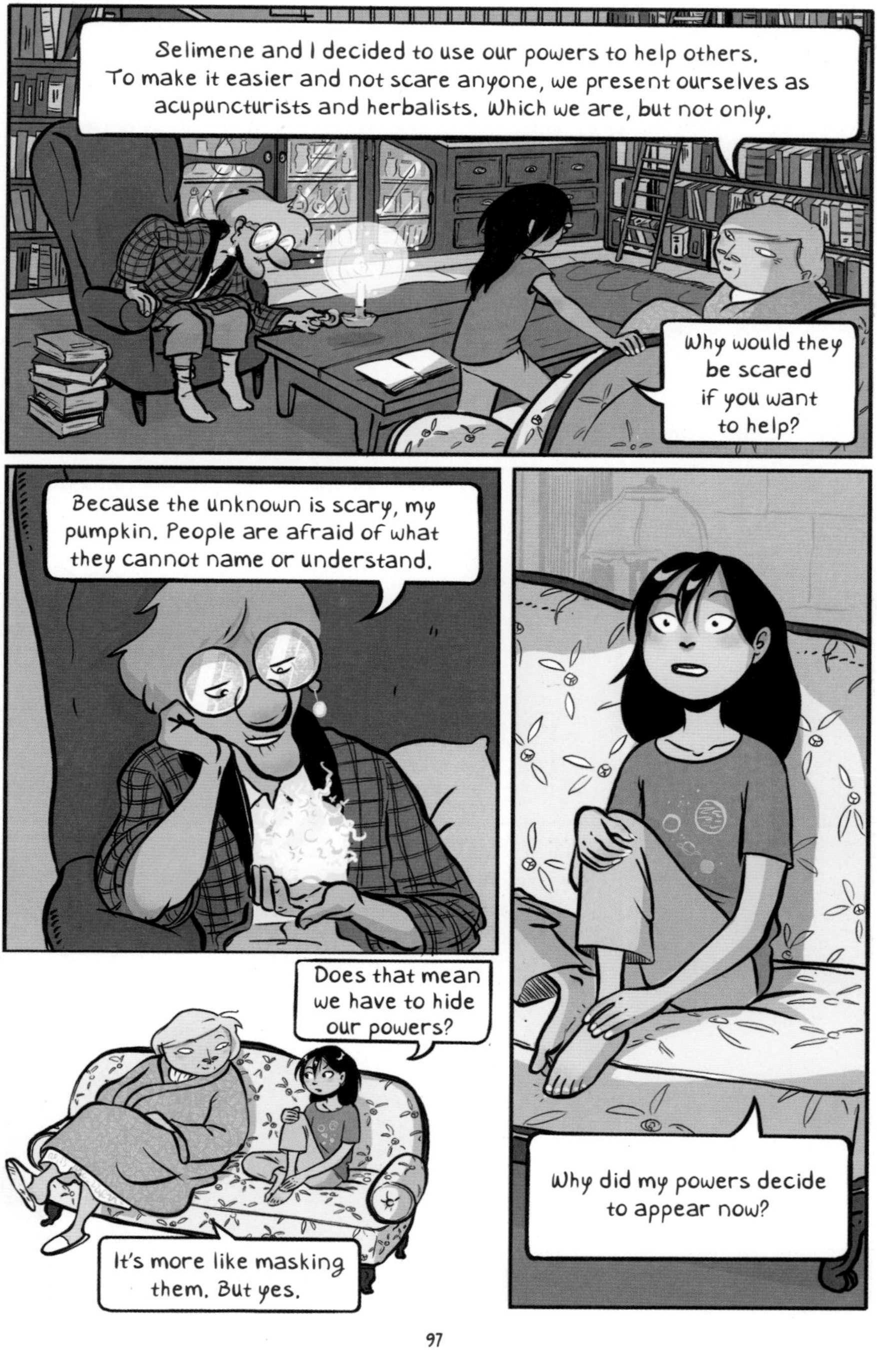
Selimene and I decided to use our powers to help others. To make it easier and not scare anyone, we present ourselves as acupuncturists and herbalists. Which we are, but not only.
Why would they be scared if you want to help?
Because the unknown is scary, my pumpkin. People are afraid of what they cannot name or understand.
Why did my powers decide to appear now?
Does that mean we have to hide our powers?
It's more like masking them. But yes.

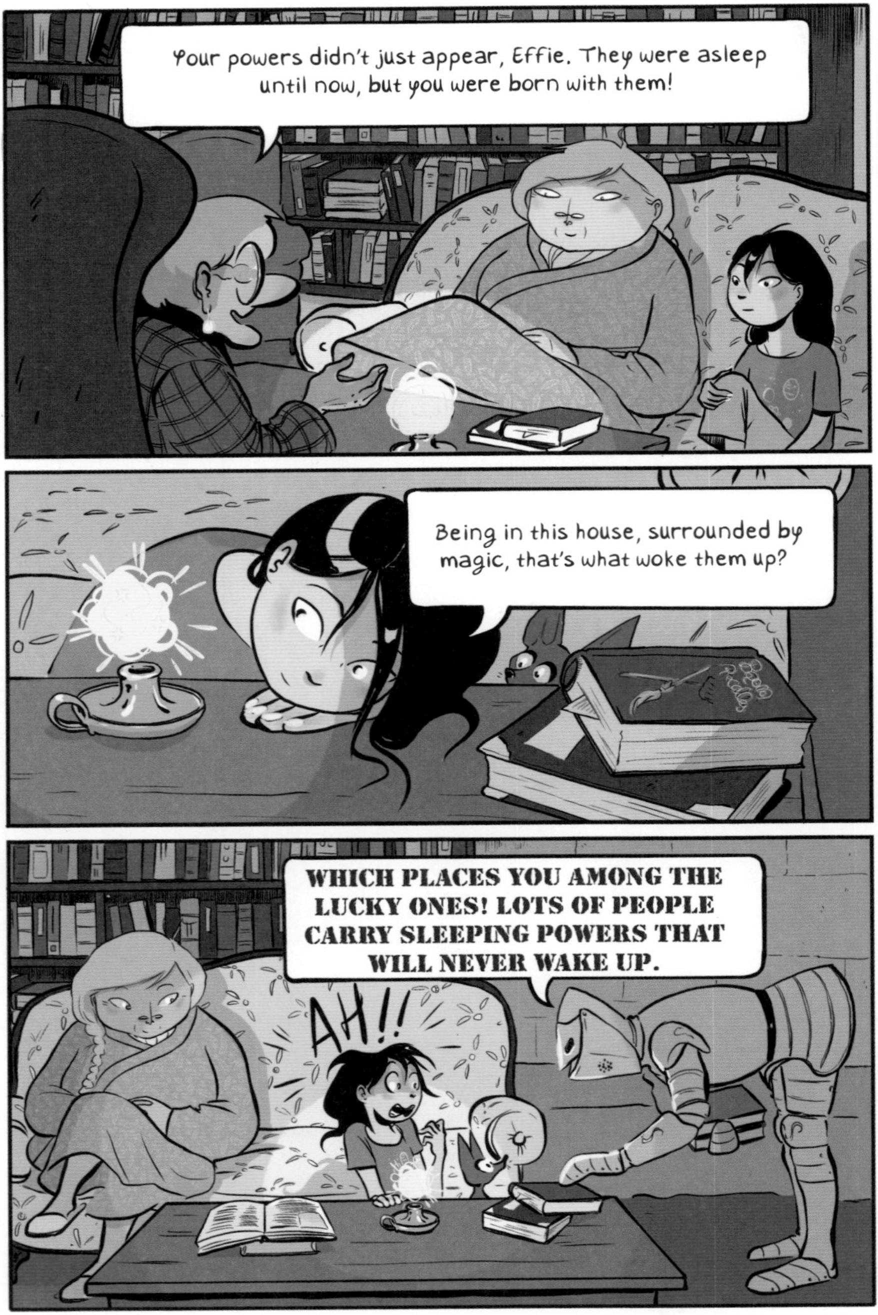
Your powers didn't just appear, Effie. They were asleep until now, but you were born with them!
Being in this house, surrounded by magic, that's what woke them up?
WHICH PLACES YOU AMONG THE LUCKY ONES! LOTS OF PEOPLE CARRY SLEEPING POWERS THAT WILL NEVER WAKE UP.
AH!!

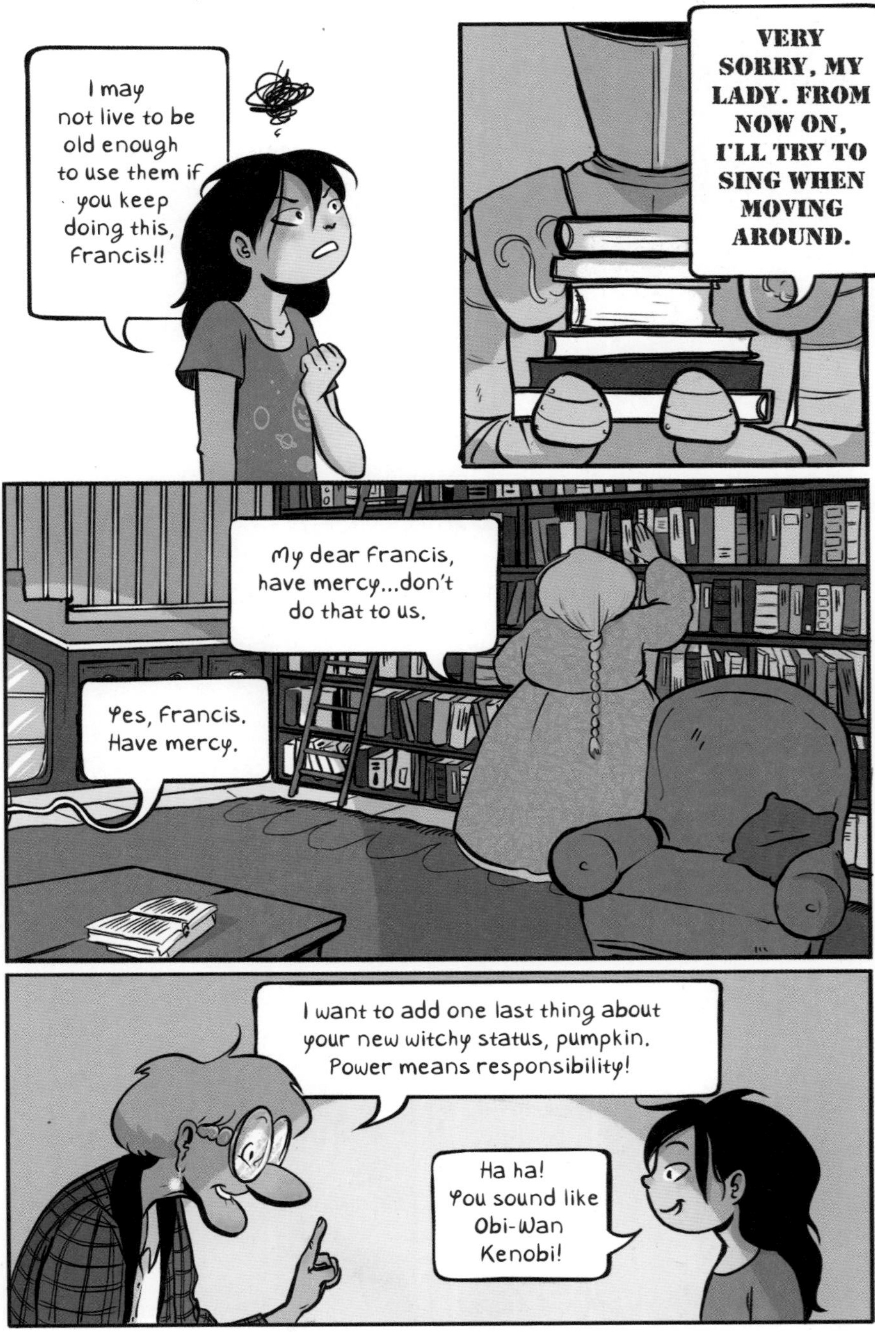
I may not live to be old enough to use them if you keep doing this, Francis!!
VERY SORRY, MY LADY. FROM NOW ON, I'LL TRY TO SING WHEN MOVING AROUND.
My dear Francis, have mercy...don't do that to us.
Yes, Francis. Have mercy.
I want to add one last thing about your new witchy status, pumpkin. Power means responsibility!
Ha ha! You sound like Obi-Wan Kenobi!

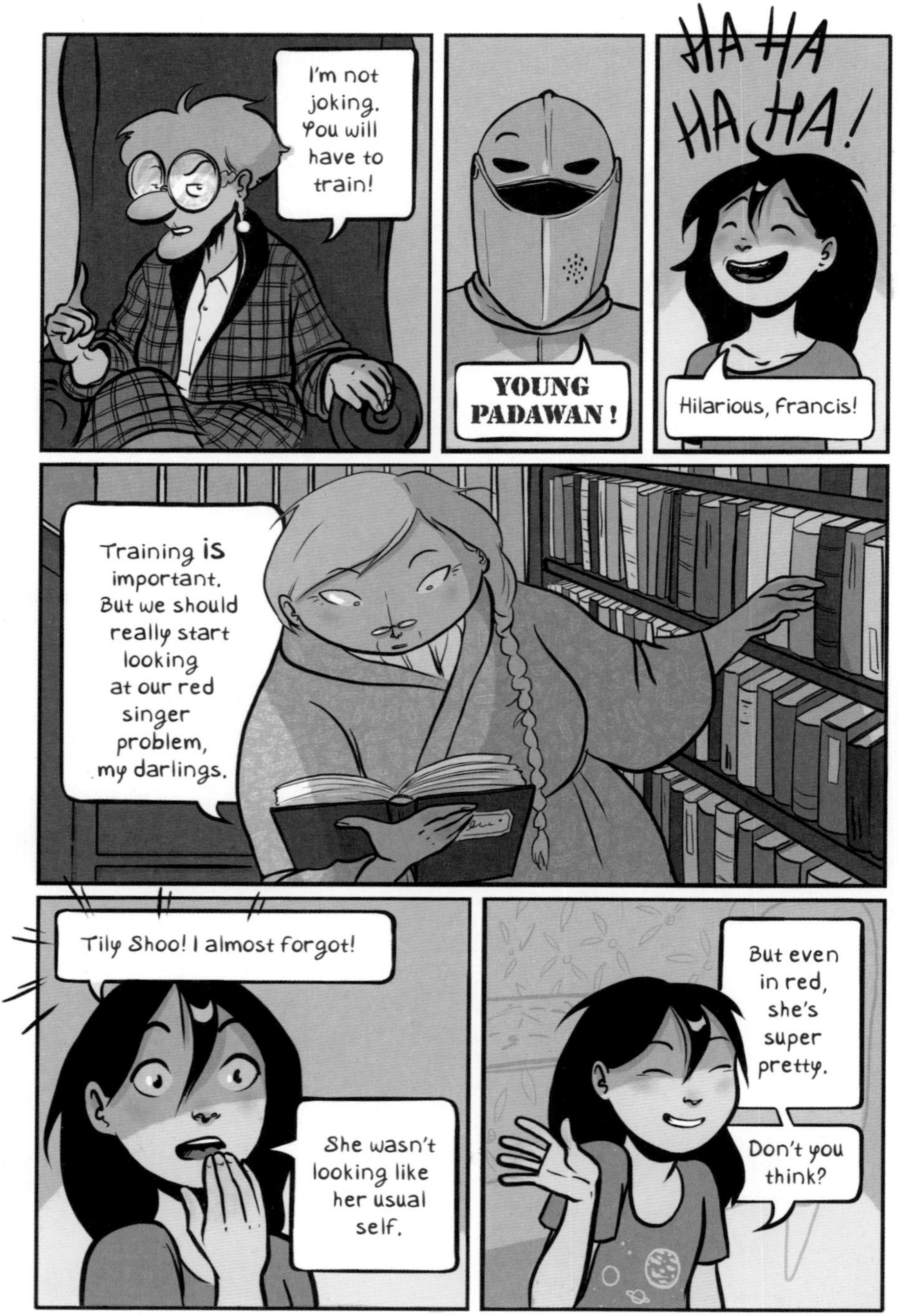
I'm not joking. You will have to train!
YOUNG PADAWAN!
HA HA HA HA!
Hilarious, Francis!
Training IS important. But we should really start looking at our red singer problem, my darlings.
Tily Shoo! I almost forgot!
She wasn't looking like her usual self.
But even in red, she's super pretty.
Don't you think?

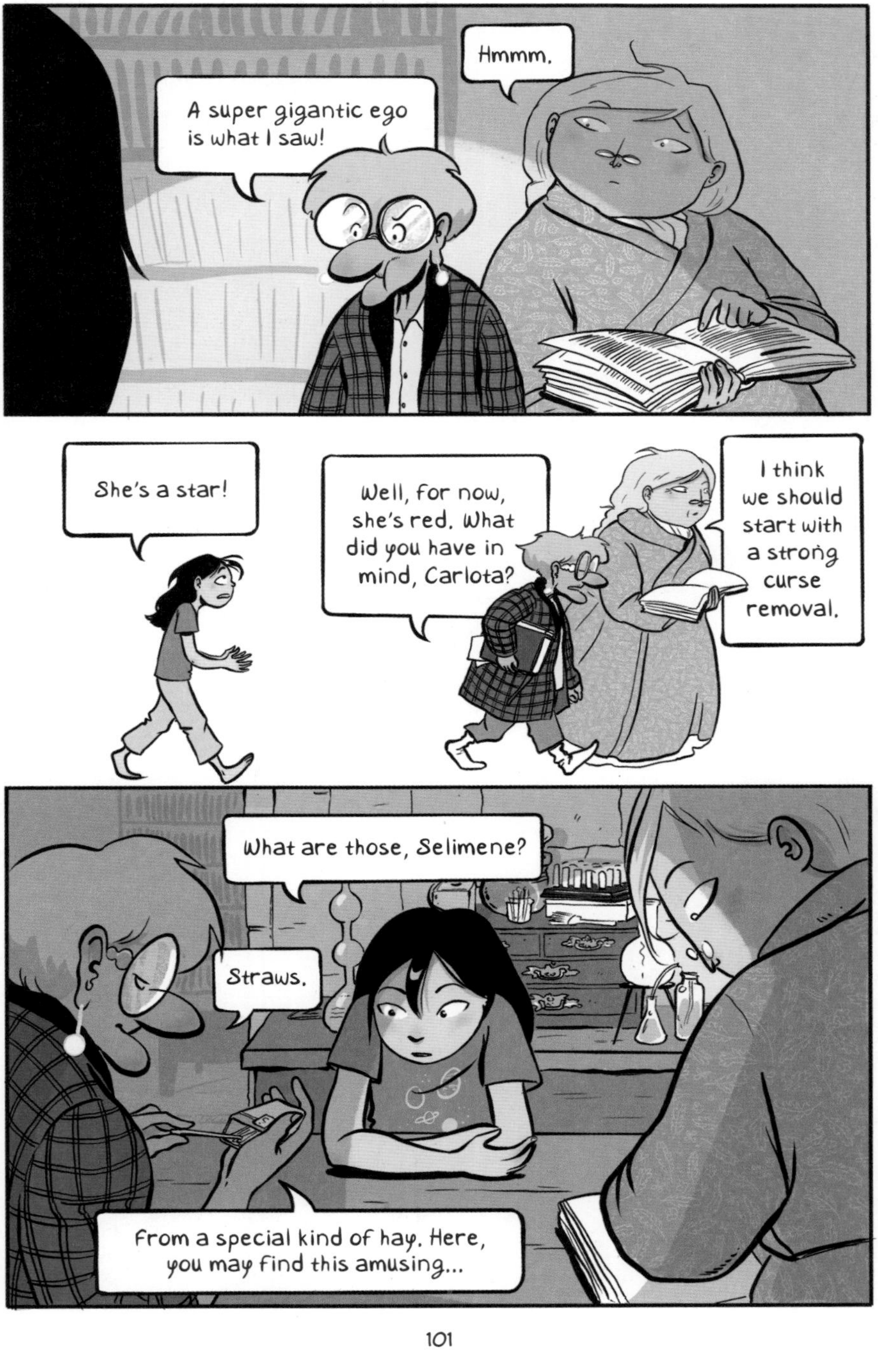
Hmmm.
A super gigantic ego is what I saw!
She's a star!
Well, for now, she's red. What did you have in mind, Carlota?
I think we should start with a strong curse removal.
What are those, Selimene?
Straws.
From a special kind of hay. Here, you may find this amusing...

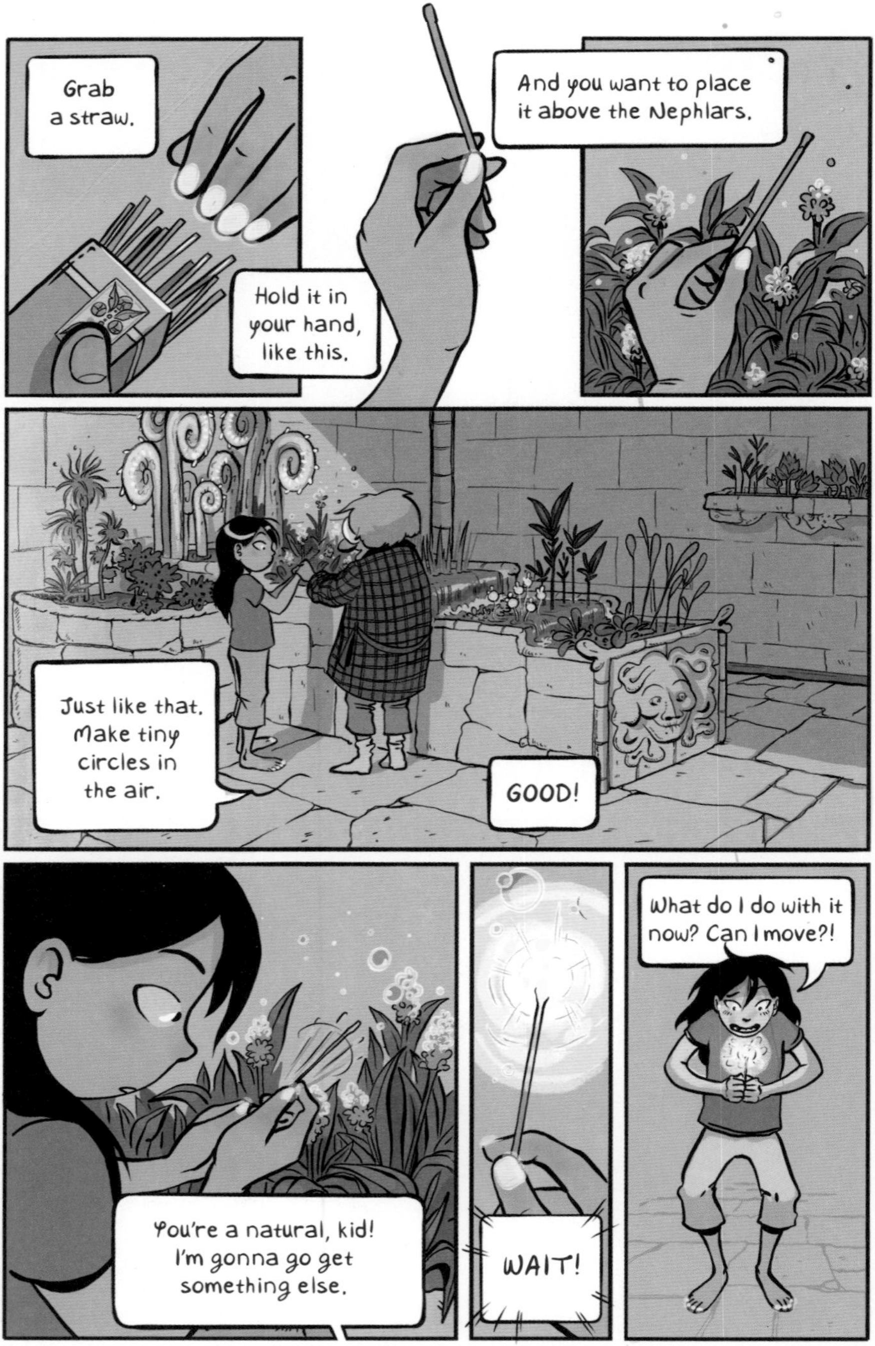
Grab a straw.
Hold it in your hand, like this.
And you want to place it above the Nephlars.
Just like that. Make tiny circles in the air.
GOOD!
You're a natural, kid! I'm gonna go get something else.
WAIT!
What do I do with it now? Can I move?!

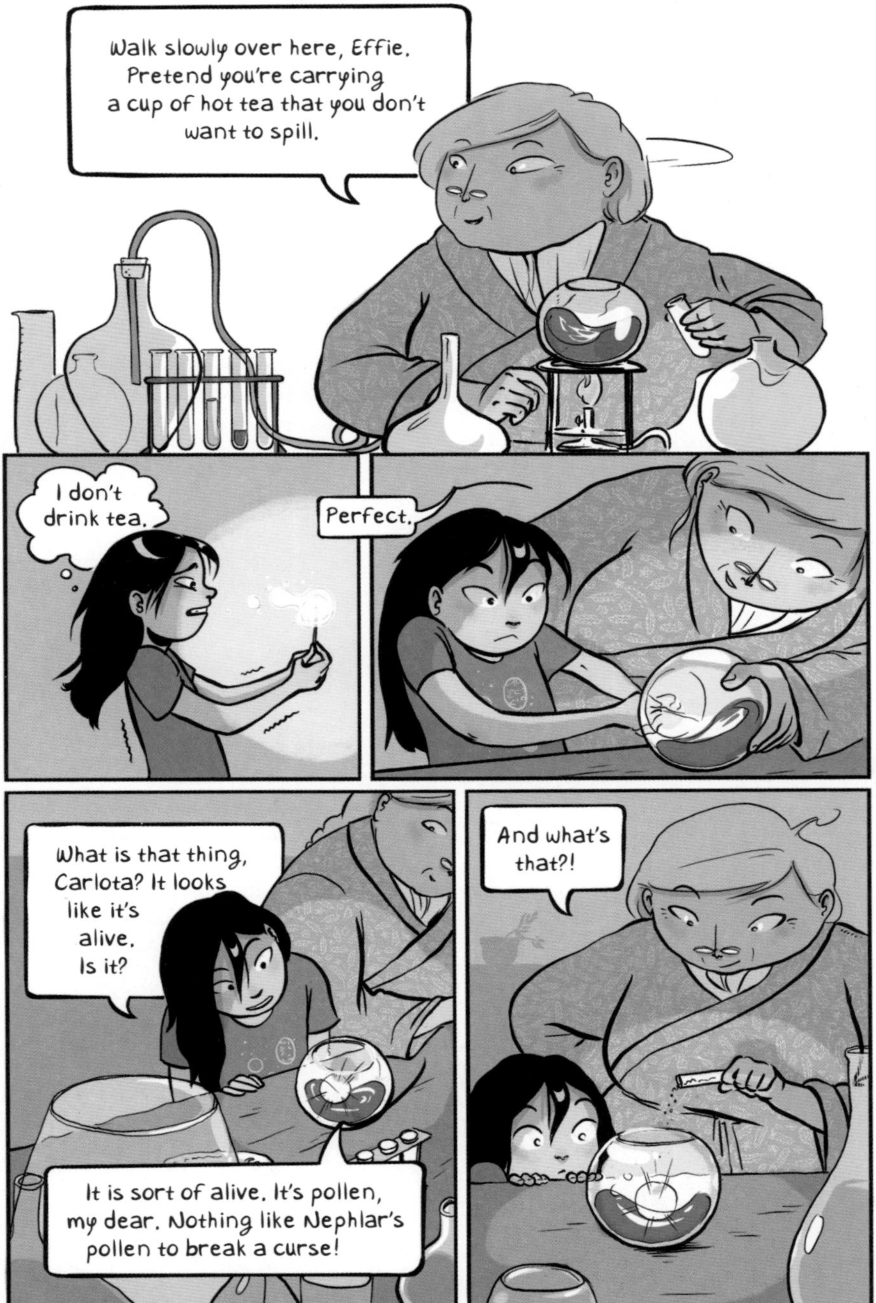

Walk slowly over here, Effie. Pretend you're carrying a cup of hot tea that you don't want to spill.
I don't drink tea.
Perfect.
What is that thing, Carlota? It looks like it's alive. Is it?
It is sort of alive. It's pollen, my dear. Nothing like Nephlar's pollen to break a curse!
And what's that?!

Humbint. It's rather unusual to put it in a curse removal potion.

But we've had great success with it. Just changed the composition slightly.

And what is this, Selimene?

GOOD LORD! YOU NEVER STOP ASKING QUESTIONS, DO YOU?!

How do you expect her to learn if she doesn't ask questions?

Asking questions is wonderful, Francis!

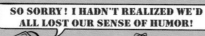

SO SORRY! I HADN'T REALIZED WE'D ALL LOST OUR SENSE OF HUMOR!

Here! We're almost ready to go!

So this is another kind of rarity that we grow down here, my dear. It's a fungus.

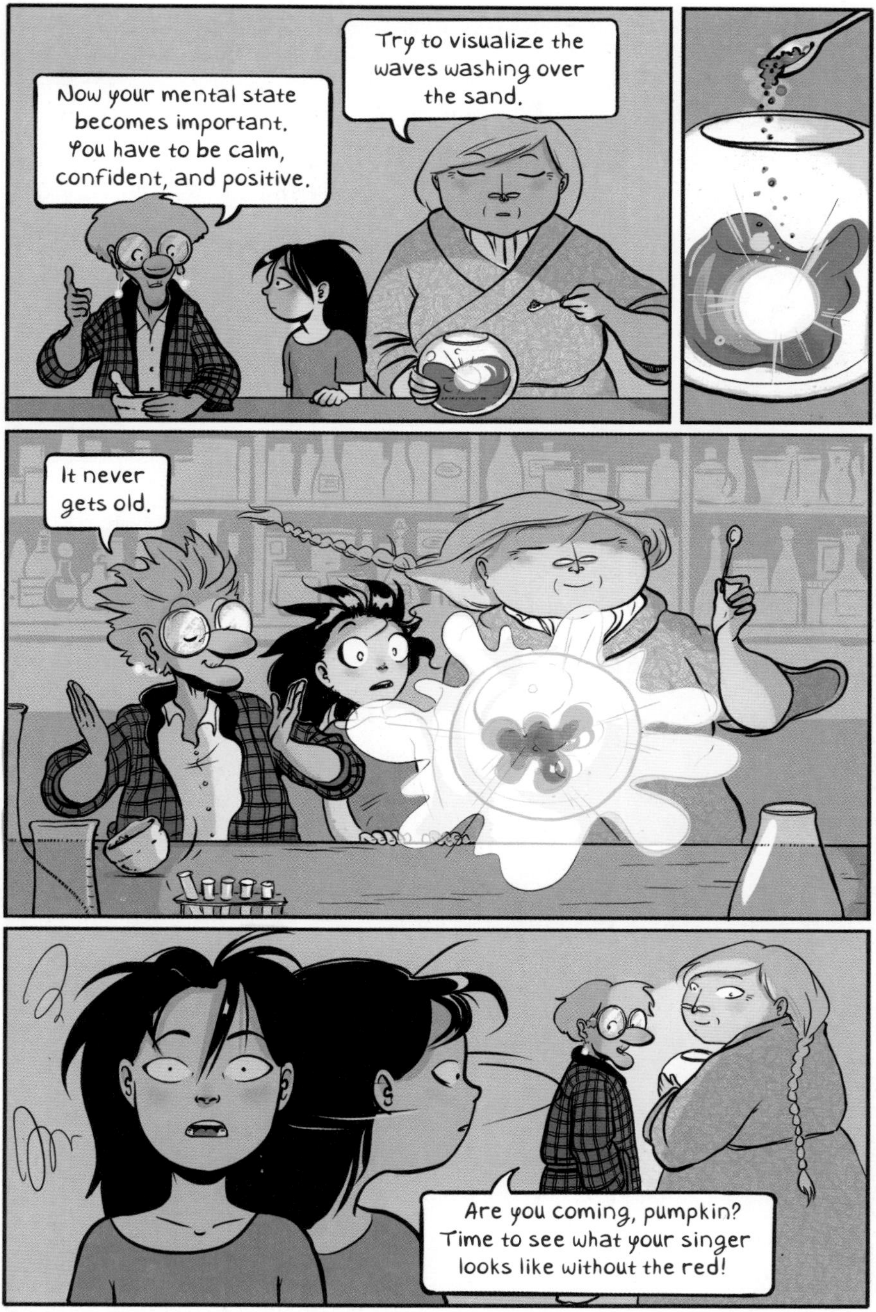
Now your mental state becomes important. You have to be calm, confident, and positive.
Try to visualize the waves washing over the sand.
It never gets old.
Are you coming, pumpkin? Time to see what your singer looks like without the red!

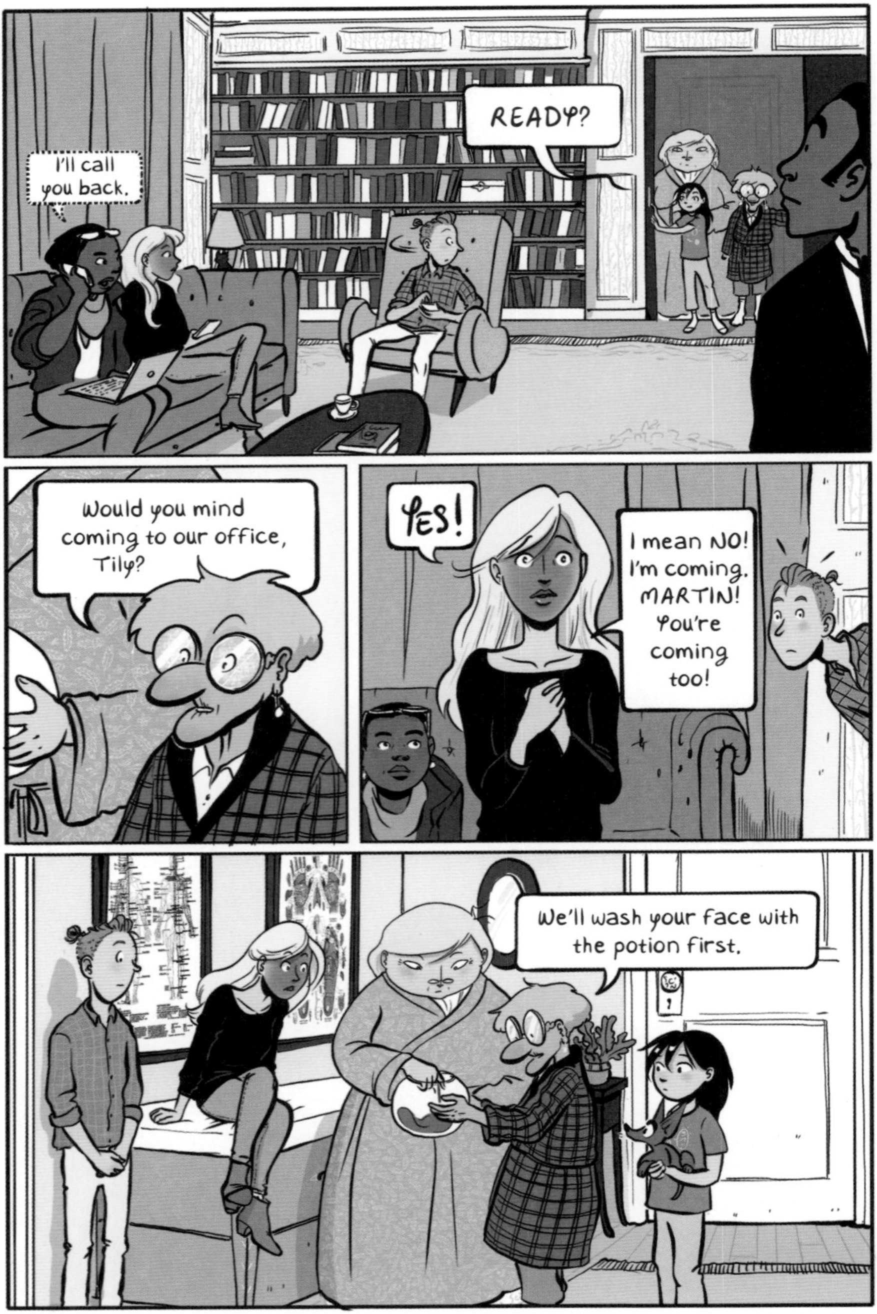
I'll call you back.
READY?
Would you mind coming to our office, Tily?
YES!
I mean NO! I'm coming. MARTIN! You're coming too!
We'll wash your face with the potion first.

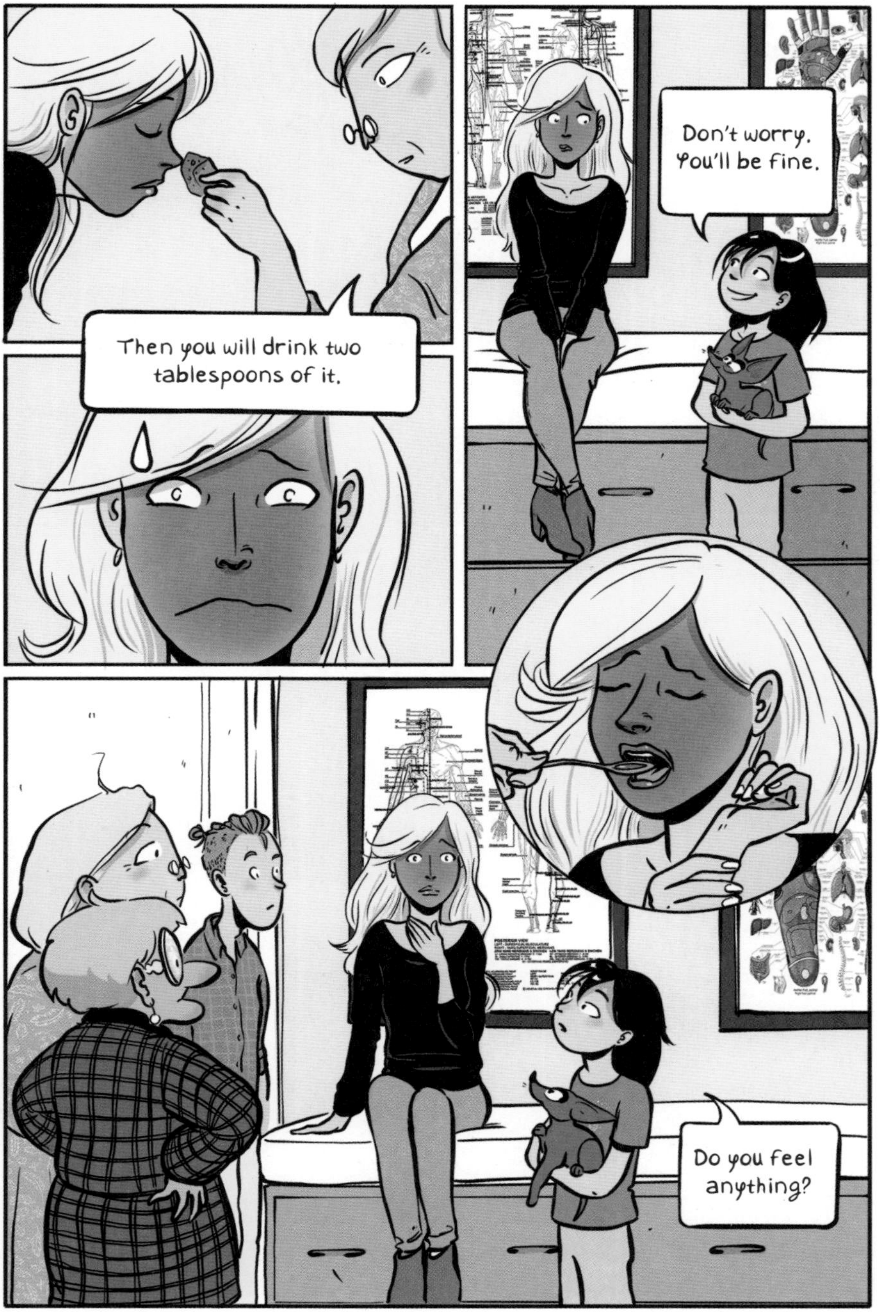
Then you will drink two tablespoons of it.
Don't worry. You'll be fine.
Do you feel anything?

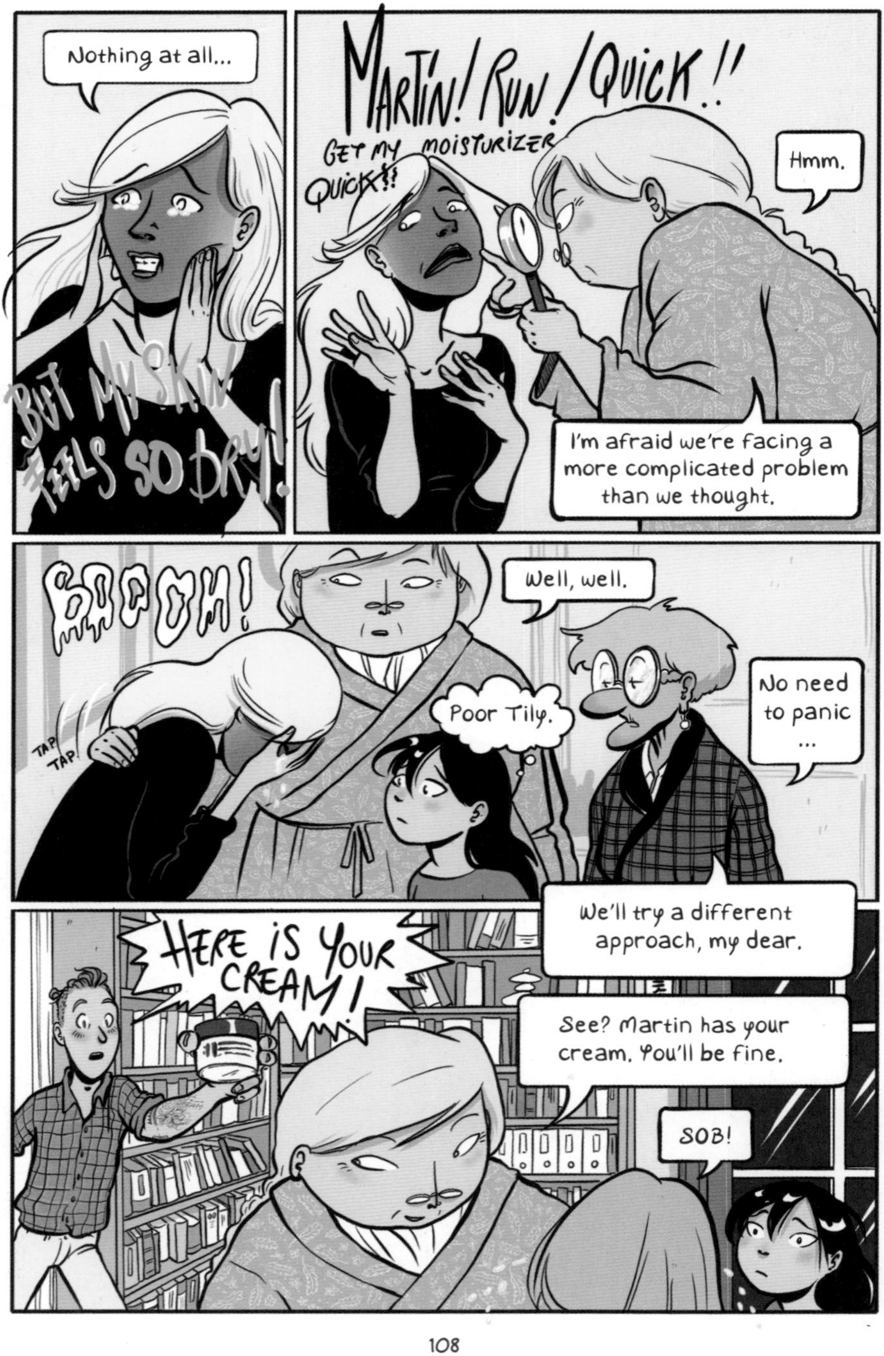
Nothing at all...
BUT MY SKIN FEELS SO DRY!
MARTIN! RUN! QUICK!!
GET MY MOISTURIZER QUICK!!!
Hmm.
I'm afraid we're facing a more complicated problem than we thought.
BOOOH!
TAP TAP
Well, well.
Poor Tily.
No need to panic ...
We'll try a different approach, my dear.
HERE IS YOUR CREAM!
See? Martin has your cream. You'll be fine.
SOB!

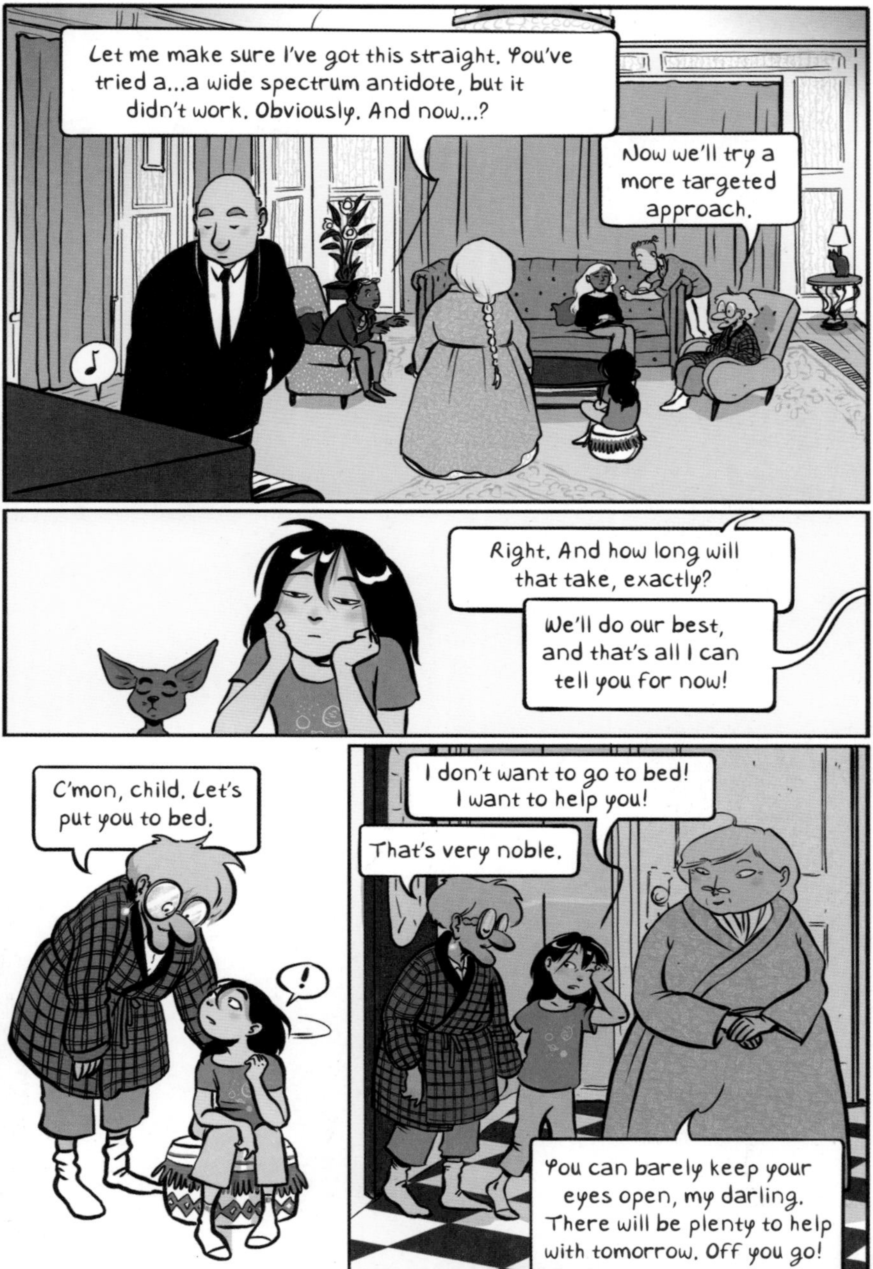
Let me make sure I've got this straight. You've tried a...a wide spectrum antidote, but it didn't work. Obviously. And now...?
Now we'll try a more targeted approach.
♪
Right. And how long will that take, exactly?
We'll do our best, and that's all I can tell you for now!
C'mon, child. Let's put you to bed.
!
I don't want to go to bed! I want to help you!
That's very noble.
You can barely keep your eyes open, my darling. There will be plenty to help with tomorrow. Off you go!

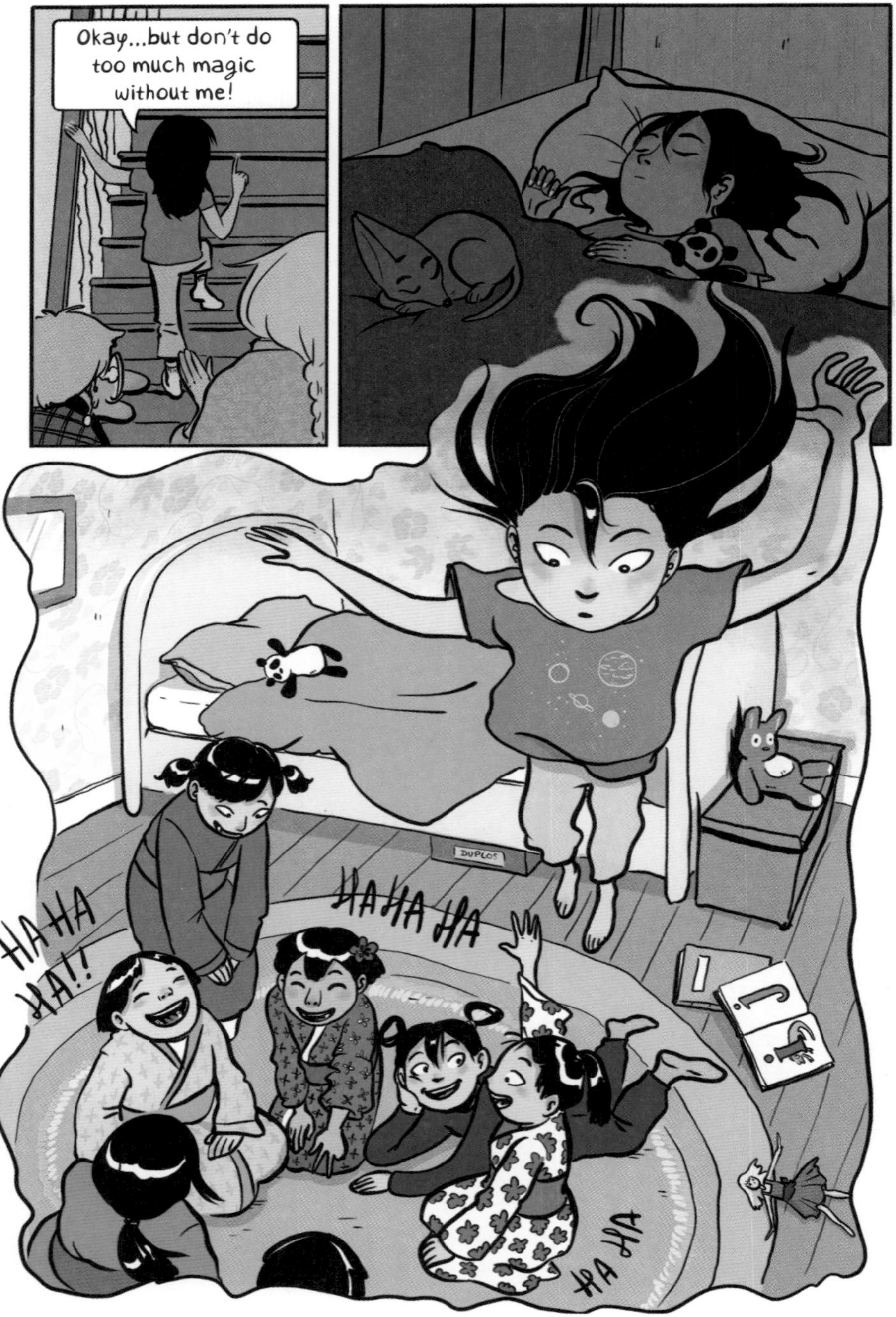
Okay...but don't do too much magic without me!
HA HA HA!!
HA HA HA HA
HA HA
DUPLOS

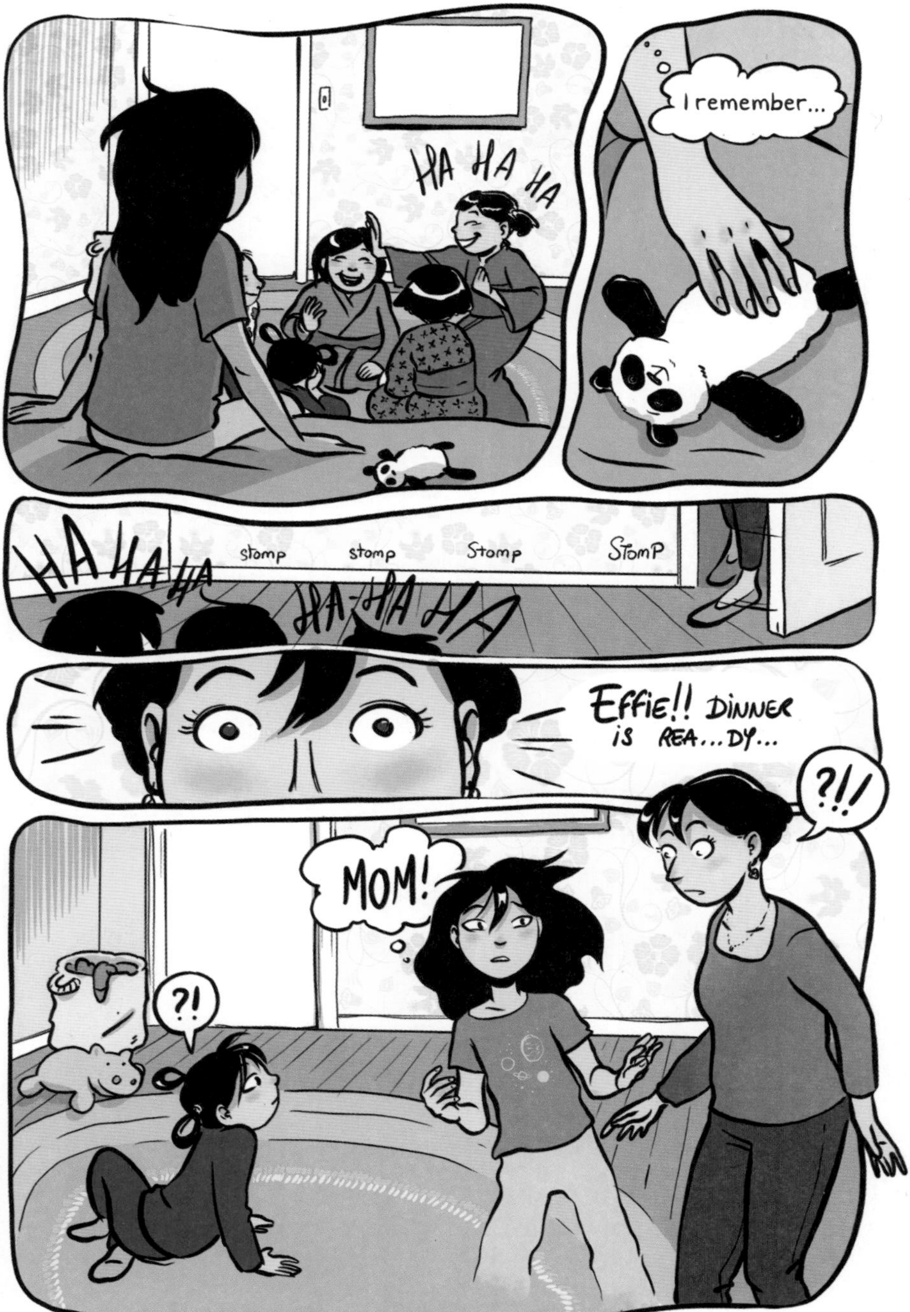
HA HA HA
I remember...
HA HA HA
stomp
stomp
Stomp
StomP
HA-HA HA HA
Effie!! DINNER IS REA...DY...
?!!
MOM!
?!

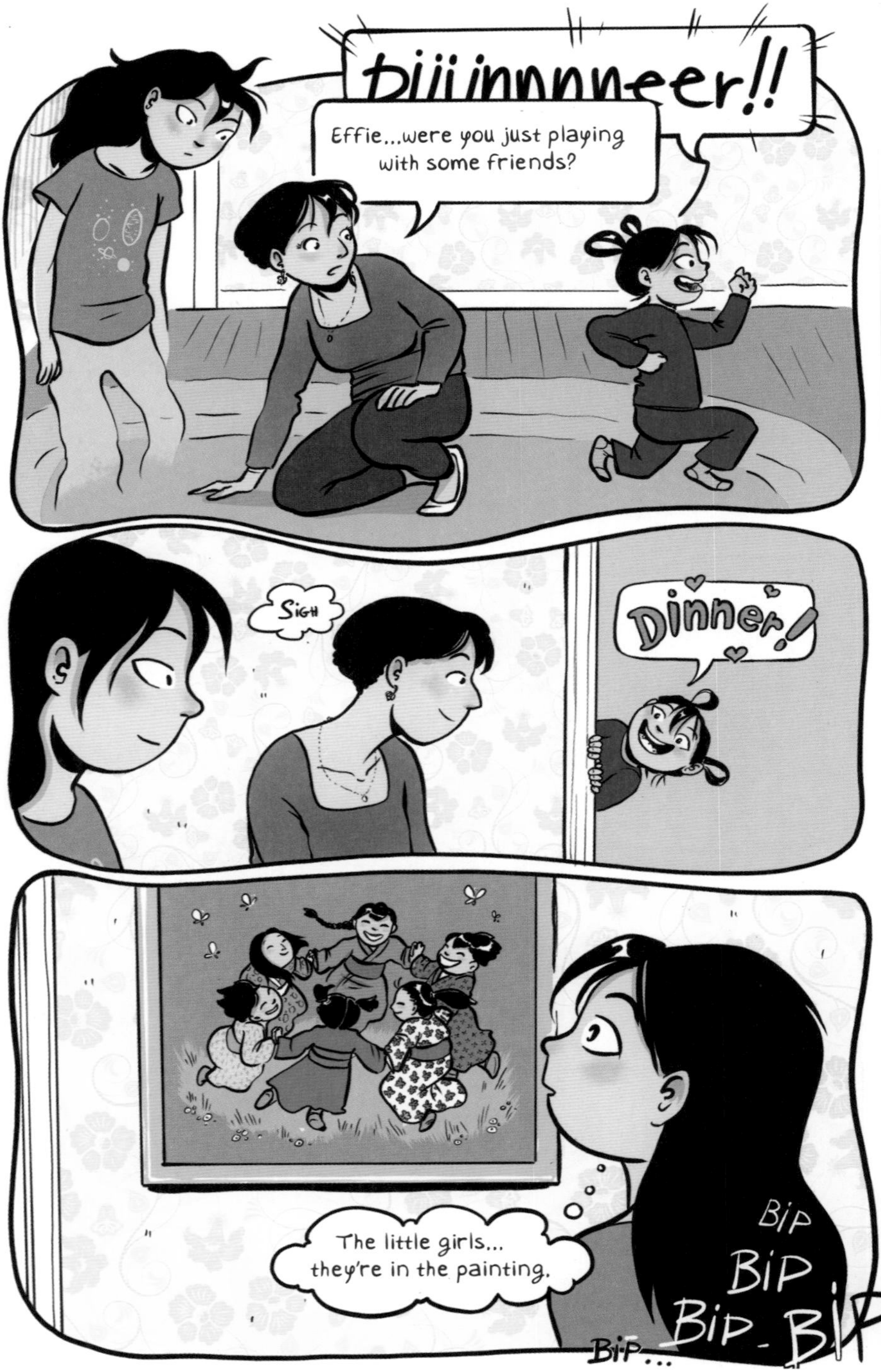
Diiiinnnneer!!
Effie...were you just playing with some friends?
Sigh
Dinner!
The little girls... they're in the painting.
Bip
Bip
Bip-Bip
Bi-p...

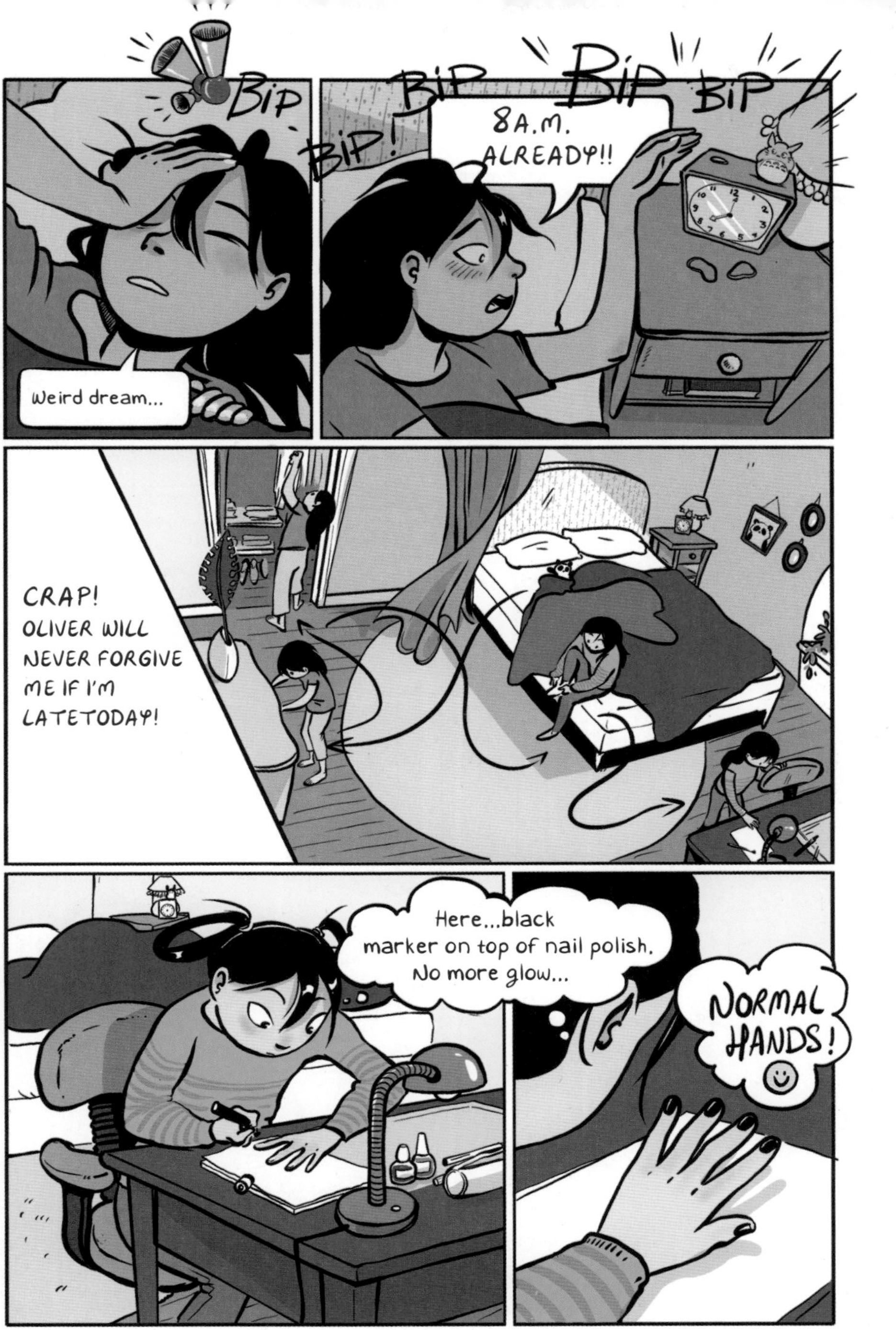
BIP
BIP!
BIP
BIP
BIP
BIP
8 A.M. ALREADY!!
Weird dream...
CRAP! OLIVER WILL NEVER FORGIVE ME IF I'M LATETODAY!
Here...black marker on top of nail polish. No more glow...
NORMAL HANDS!

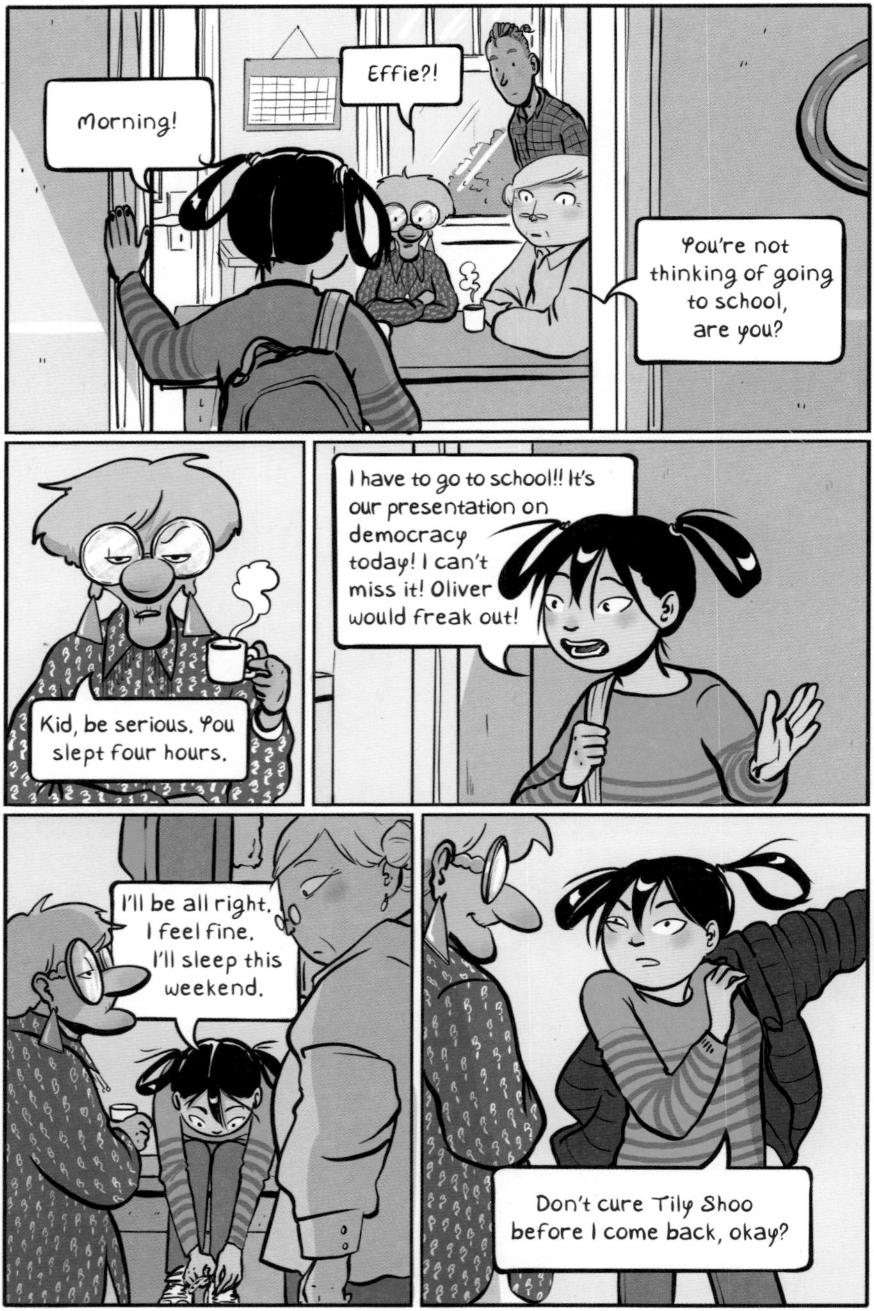
Morning!
Effie?!
You're not thinking of going to school, are you?
Kid, be serious. You slept four hours.
I have to go to school!! It's our presentation on democracy today! I can't miss it! Oliver would freak out!
I'll be all right. I feel fine. I'll sleep this weekend.
Don't cure Tily Shoo before I come back, okay?

DRIILIING

That's Oliver and Archibald!

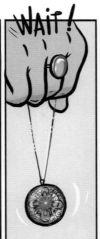

WAIT!

Not exactly your style. I know.

?

But you keep it! It's an order.

If anything happens, rub it twice on your nose.

Got it?

I rub the old thing on my nose twice.

Oookay...

See you!

Take care, kid.

Fingers crossed.

Fingers crossed.

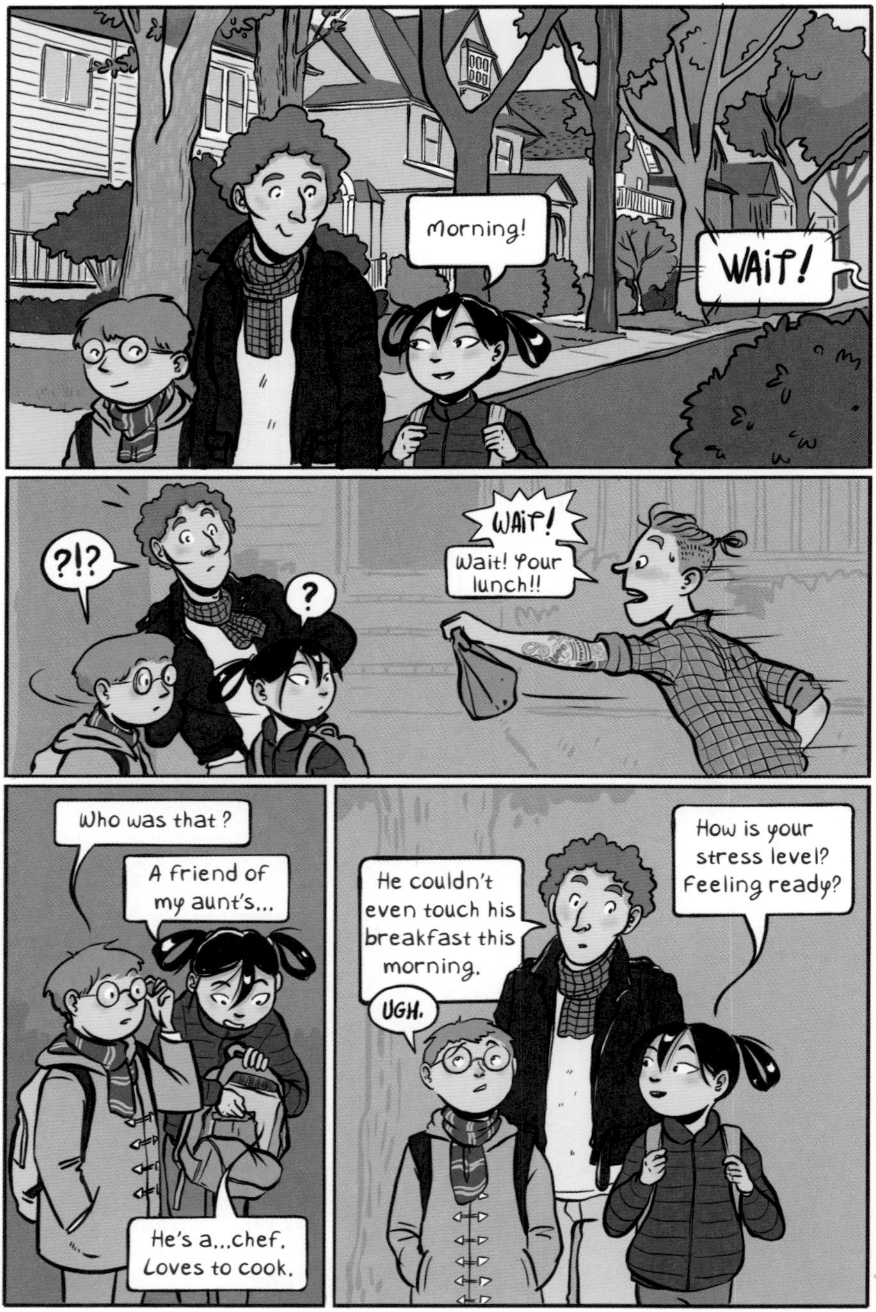

Morning!
WAIT!
?!?
?
WAIT!
Wait! Your lunch!!
Who was that?
A friend of my aunt's...
He's a...chef. Loves to cook.
He couldn't even touch his breakfast this morning.
UGH.
How is your stress level? Feeling ready?

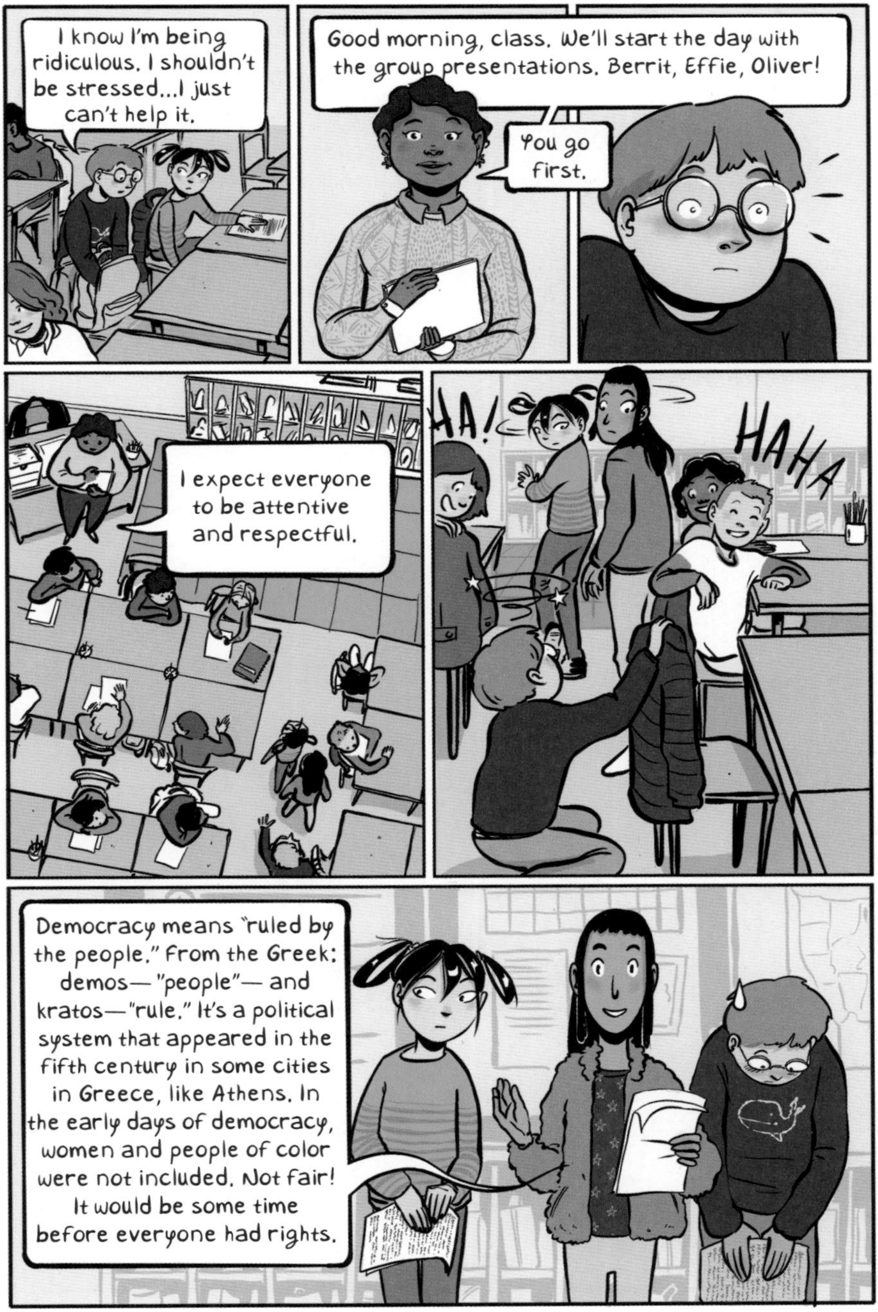
I know I'm being ridiculous. I shouldn't be stressed...I just can't help it.
Good morning, class. We'll start the day with the group presentations. Berrit, Effie, Oliver!
You go first.
I expect everyone to be attentive and respectful.
HA!
HAHA
Democracy means "ruled by the people." From the Greek: demos— "people"— and kratos—"rule." It's a political system that appeared in the fifth century in some cities in Greece, like Athens. In the early days of democracy, women and people of color were not included. Not fair! It would be some time before everyone had rights.

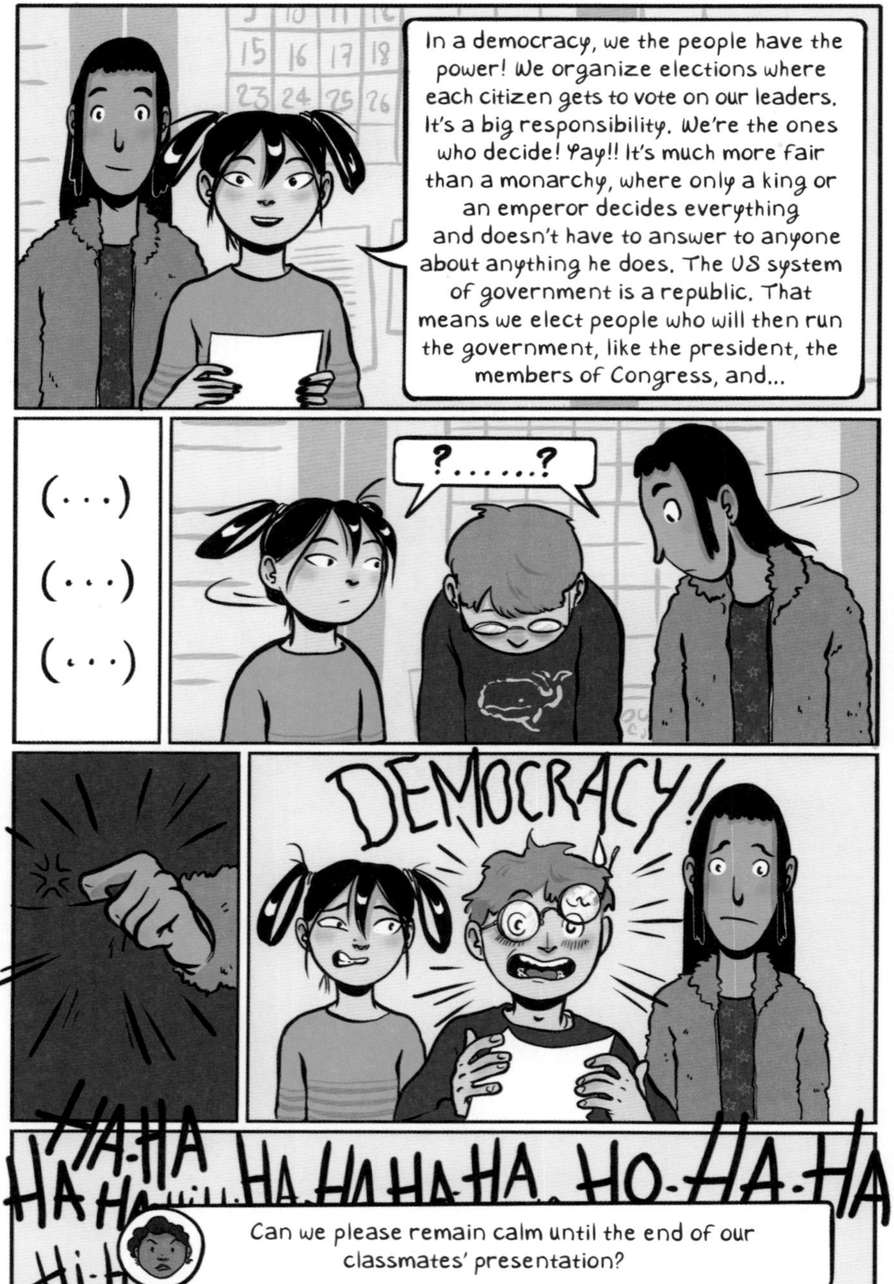
In a democracy, we the people have the power! We organize elections where each citizen gets to vote on our leaders. It's a big responsibility. We're the ones who decide! Yay!! It's much more fair than a monarchy, where only a king or an emperor decides everything and doesn't have to answer to anyone about anything he does. The US system of government is a republic. That means we elect people who will then run the government, like the president, the members of Congress, and...
(...)
(...)
(...)
?.....?
DEMOCRACY!
HA-HA
HA HA
HA HA HA HA HA. HO-HA-HA
Hi-
Can we please remain calm until the end of our classmates' presentation?

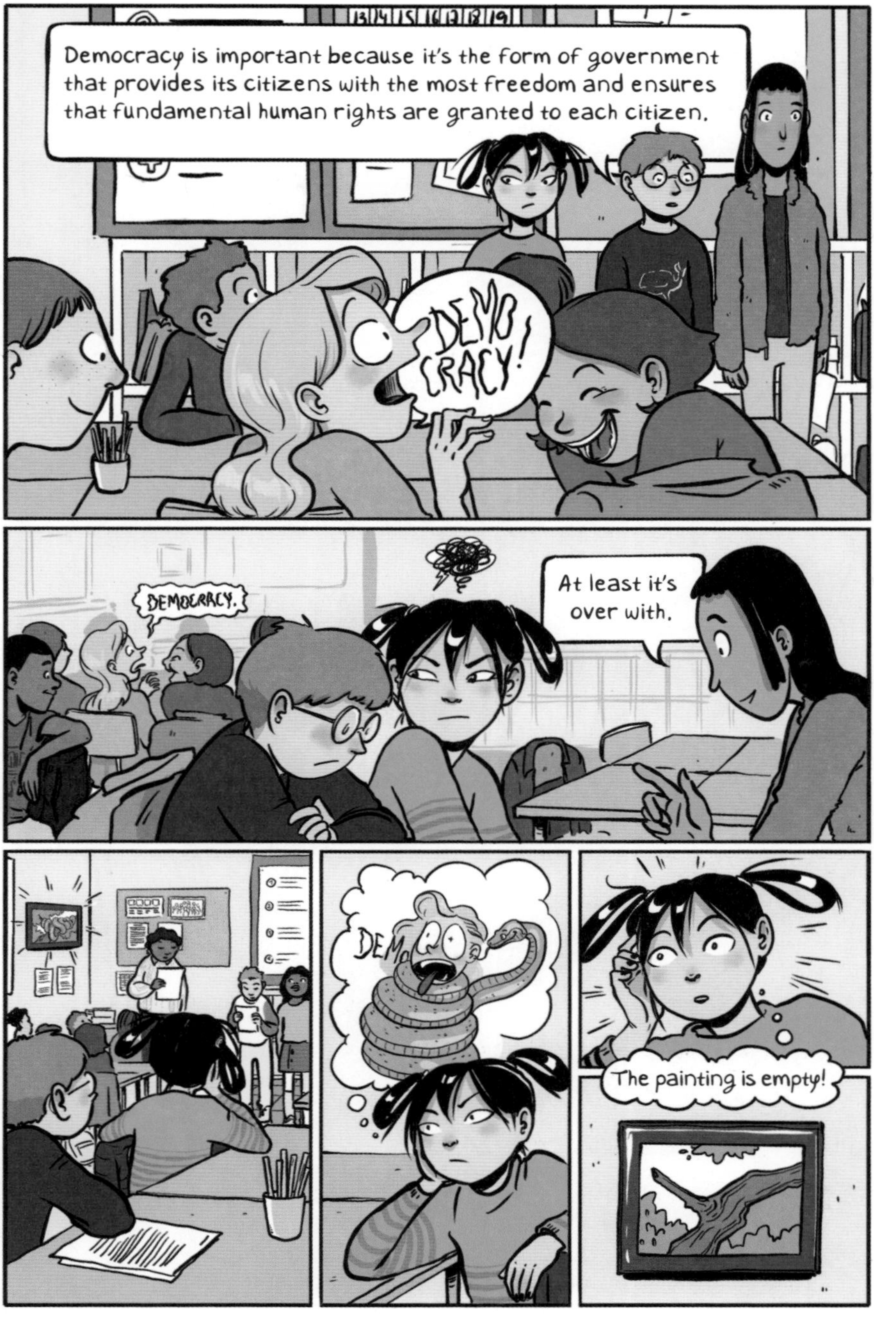
Democracy is important because it's the form of government that provides its citizens with the most freedom and ensures that fundamental human rights are granted to each citizen.
DEMO CRACY!
DEMOCRACY.
At least it's over with.
DEM...
The painting is empty!

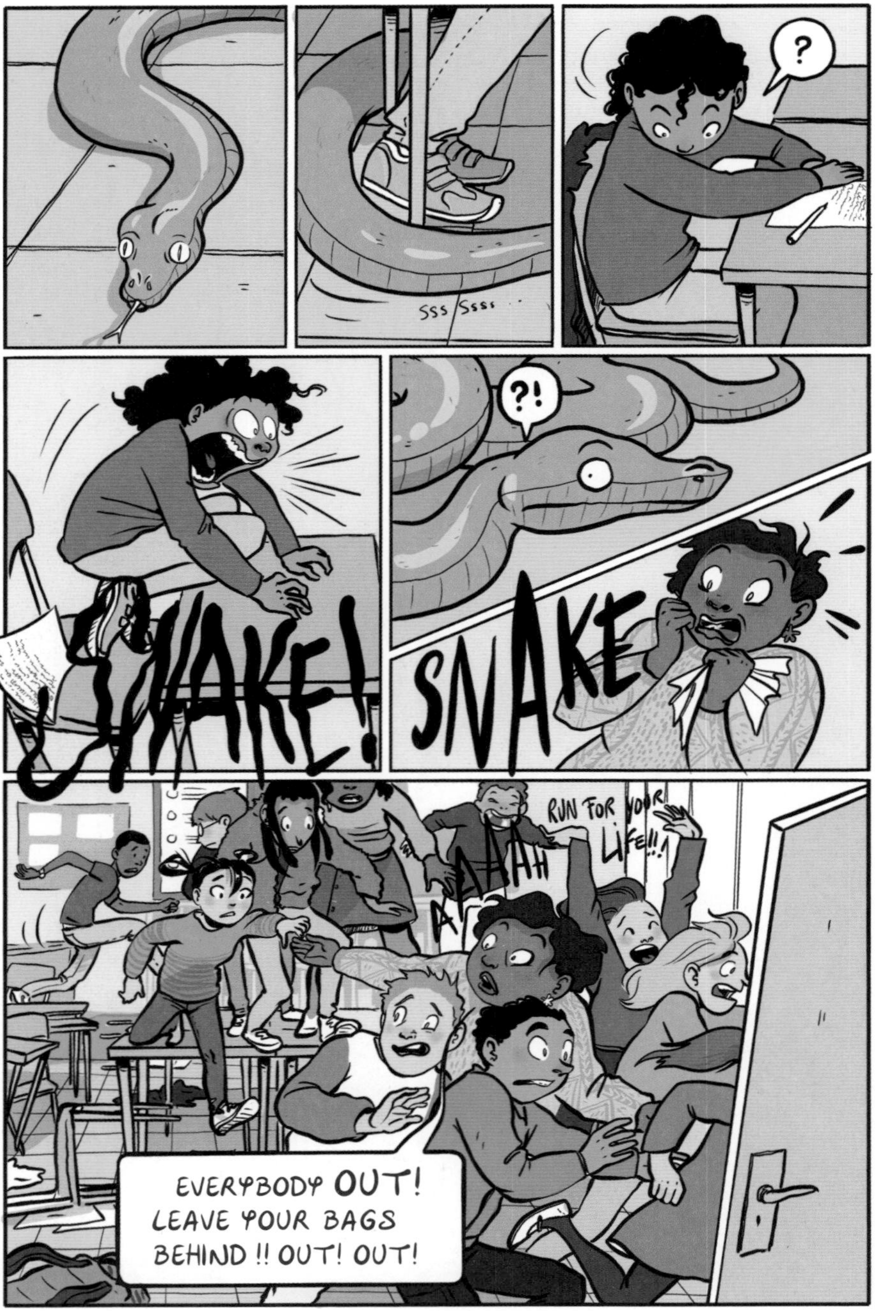
?
SSS SSSS . . .
?!
SNAKE!
SNAKE
RUN FOR YOUR LIFE!!!
AAAAH
EVERYBODY OUT! LEAVE YOUR BAGS BEHIND!! OUT! OUT!

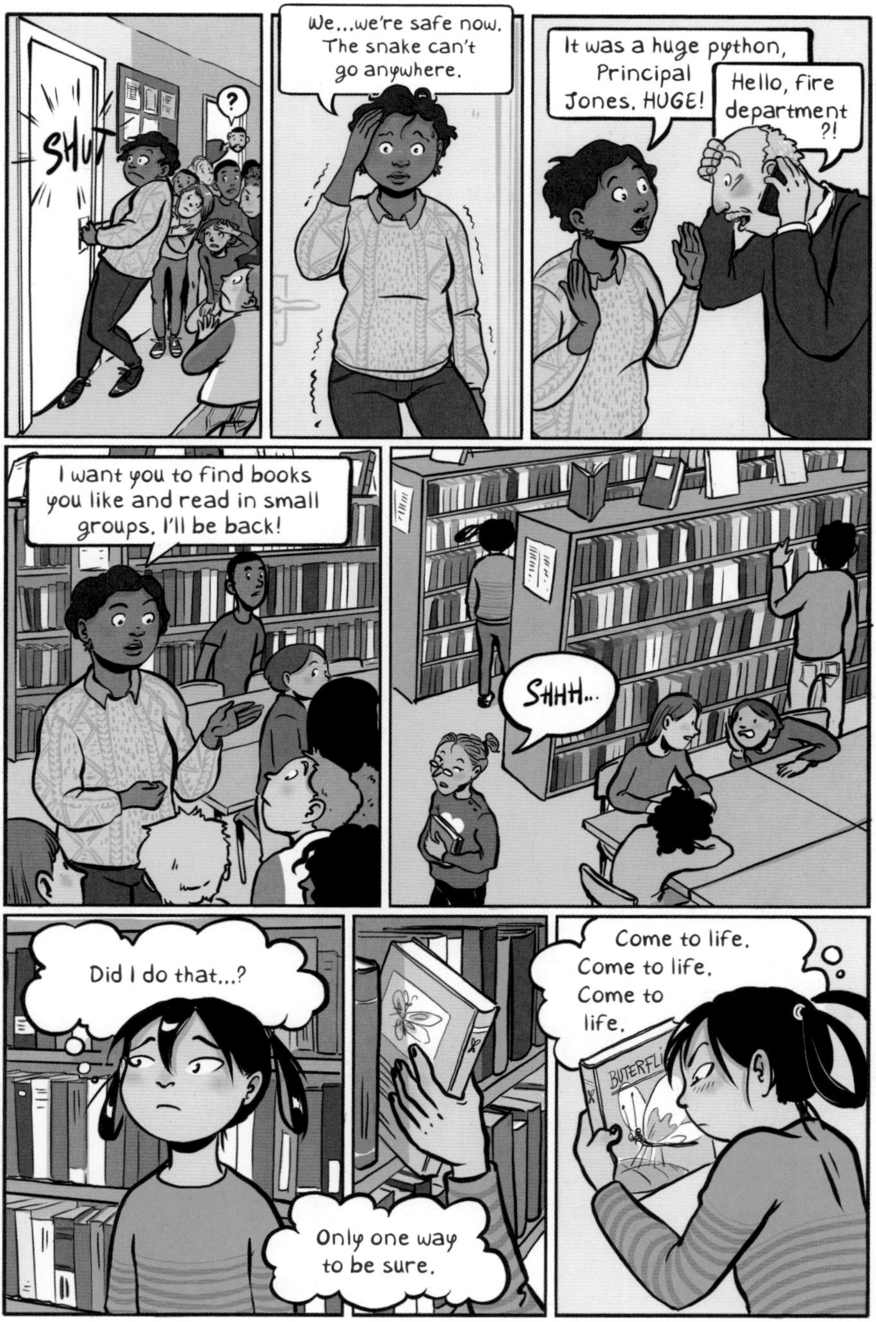
SHUT
?
We...we're safe now. The snake can't go anywhere.
It was a huge python, Principal Jones. HUGE!
Hello, fire department ?!
I want you to find books you like and read in small groups. I'll be back!
SHHH...
Did I do that...?
Only one way to be sure.
Come to life. Come to life. Come to life.
BUTERFLI

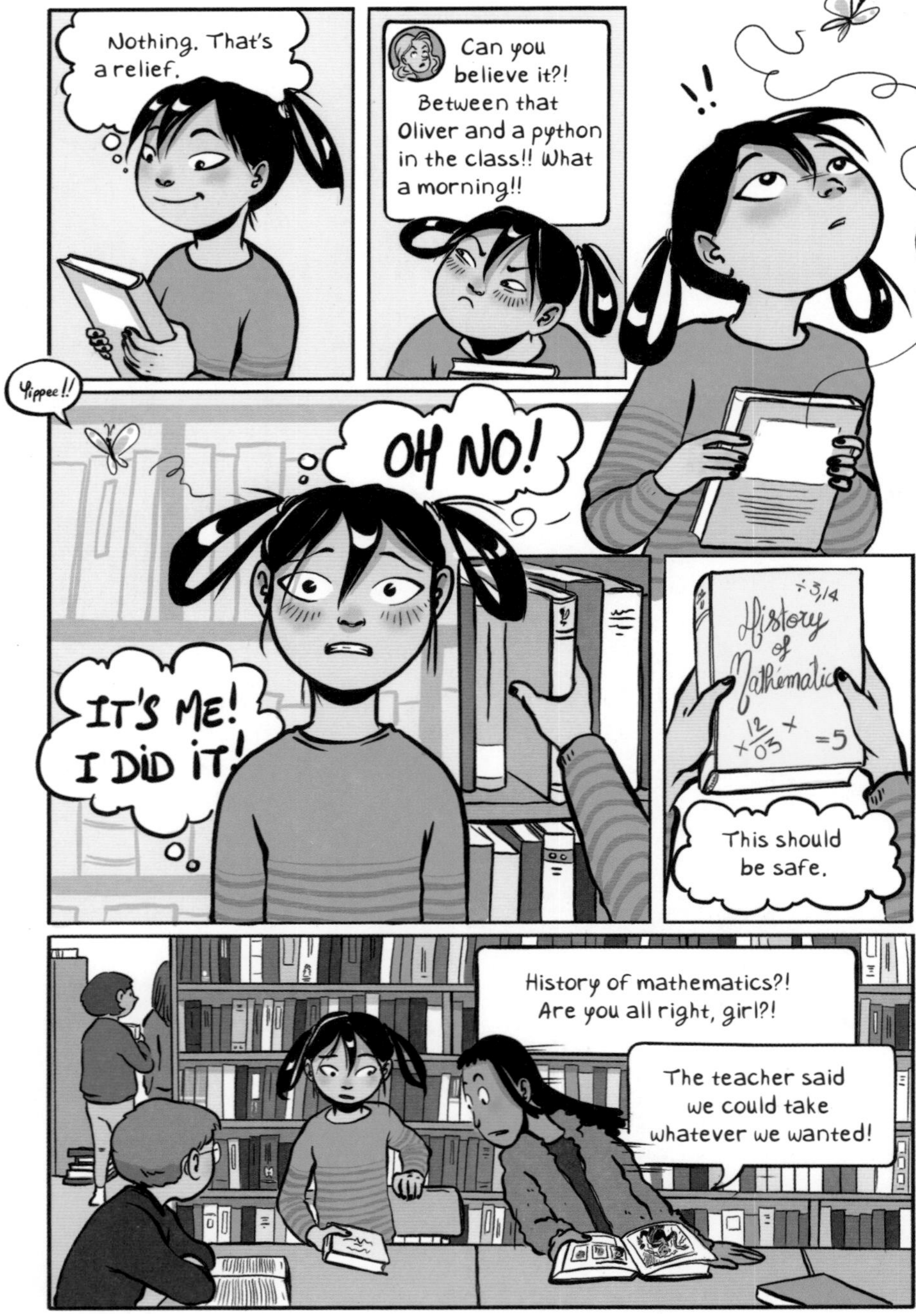

Nothing. That's a relief.
Can you believe it?! Between that Oliver and a python in the class!! What a morning!!
!!
Yippee!!
OH NO!
IT'S ME! I DID IT!
History of Mathematics
This should be safe.
History of mathematics?! Are you all right, girl?!
The teacher said we could take whatever we wanted!

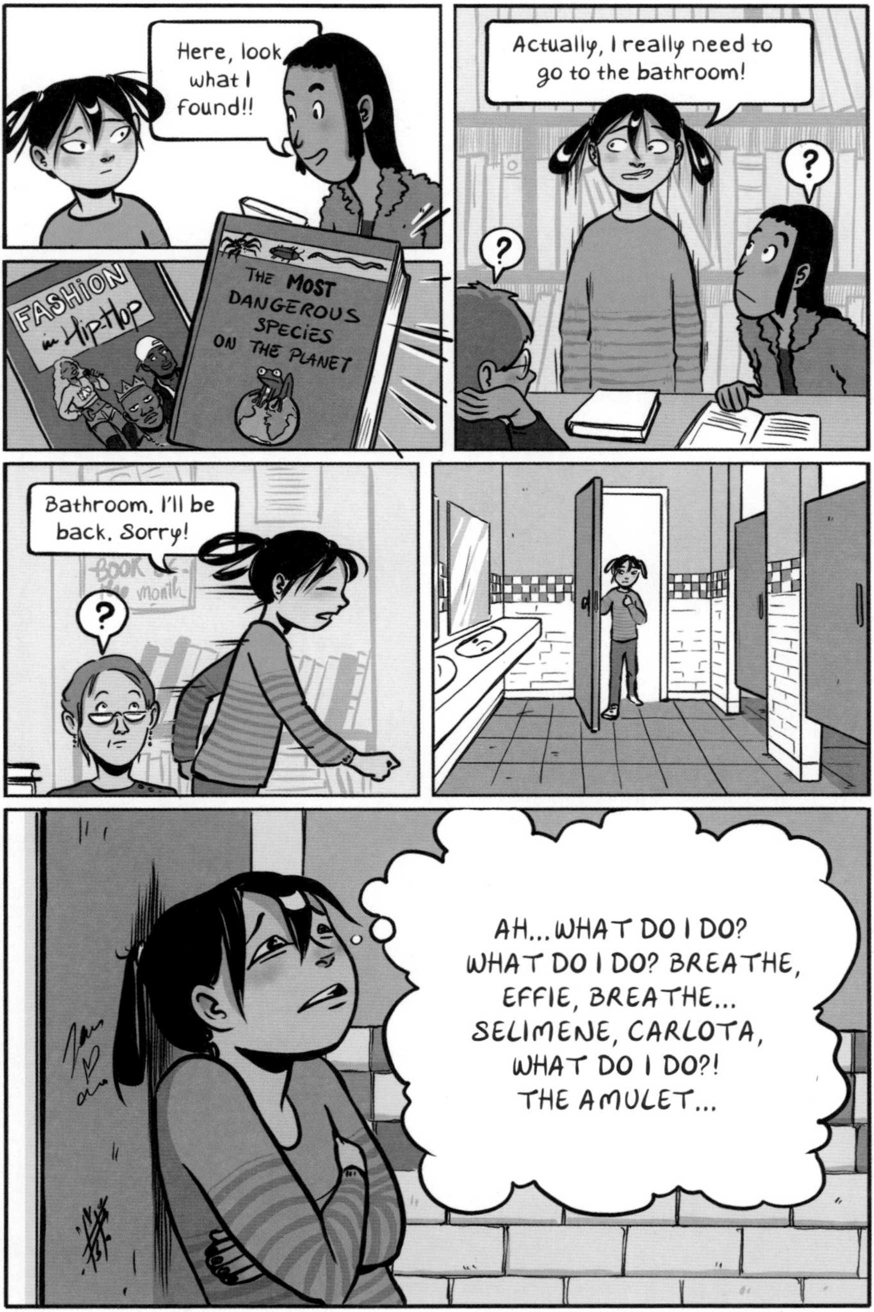

Here, look what I found!!
FASHION in Hip-Hop
THE MOST DANGEROUS SPECIES ON THE PLANET
Actually, I really need to go to the bathroom!
?
?
Bathroom. I'll be back. Sorry!
?
AH...WHAT DO I DO? WHAT DO I DO? BREATHE, EFFIE, BREATHE... SELIMENE, CARLOTA, WHAT DO I DO?! THE AMULET...

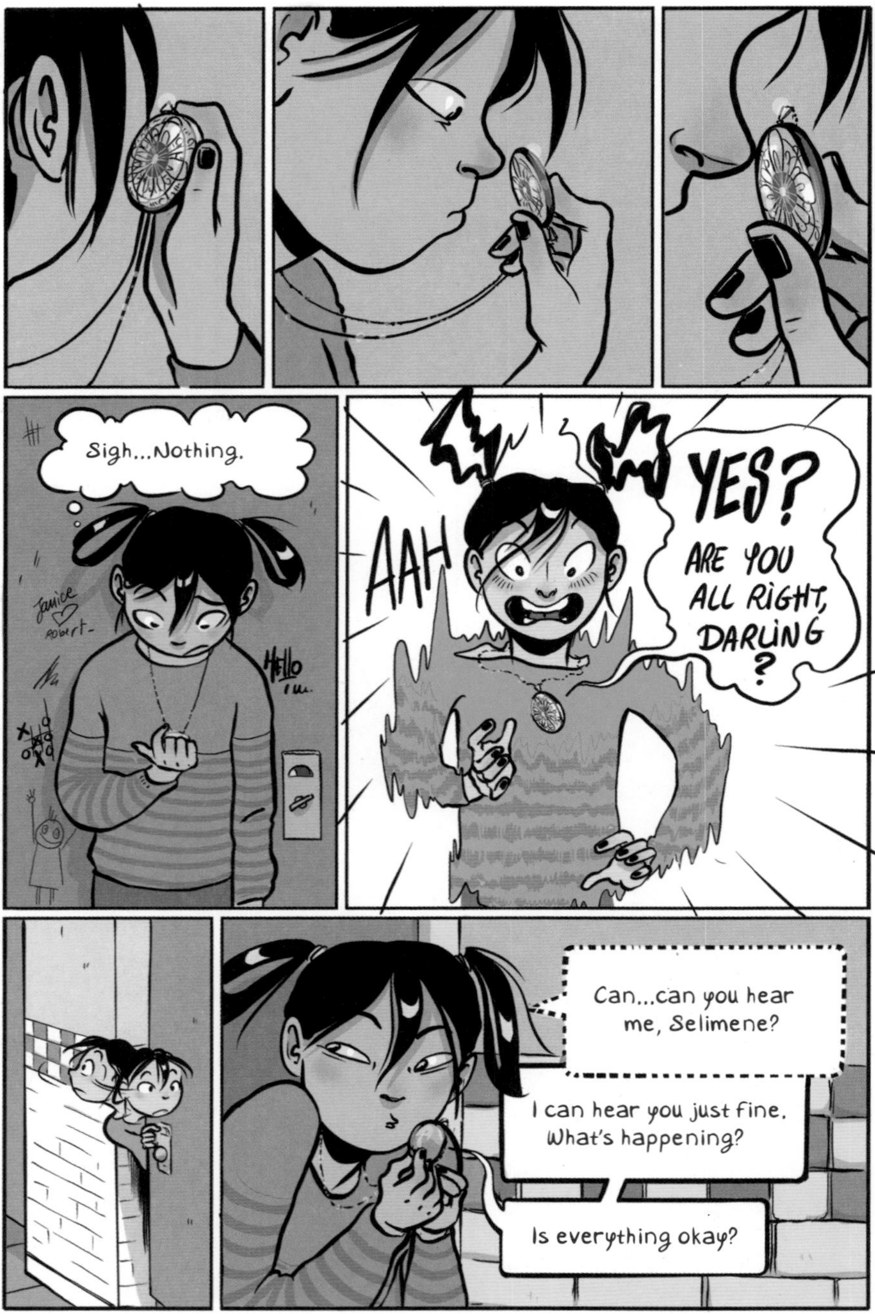
Sigh...Nothing.
AAH
YES? ARE YOU ALL RIGHT, DARLING?
Can...can you hear me, Selimene?
I can hear you just fine. What's happening?
Is everything okay?

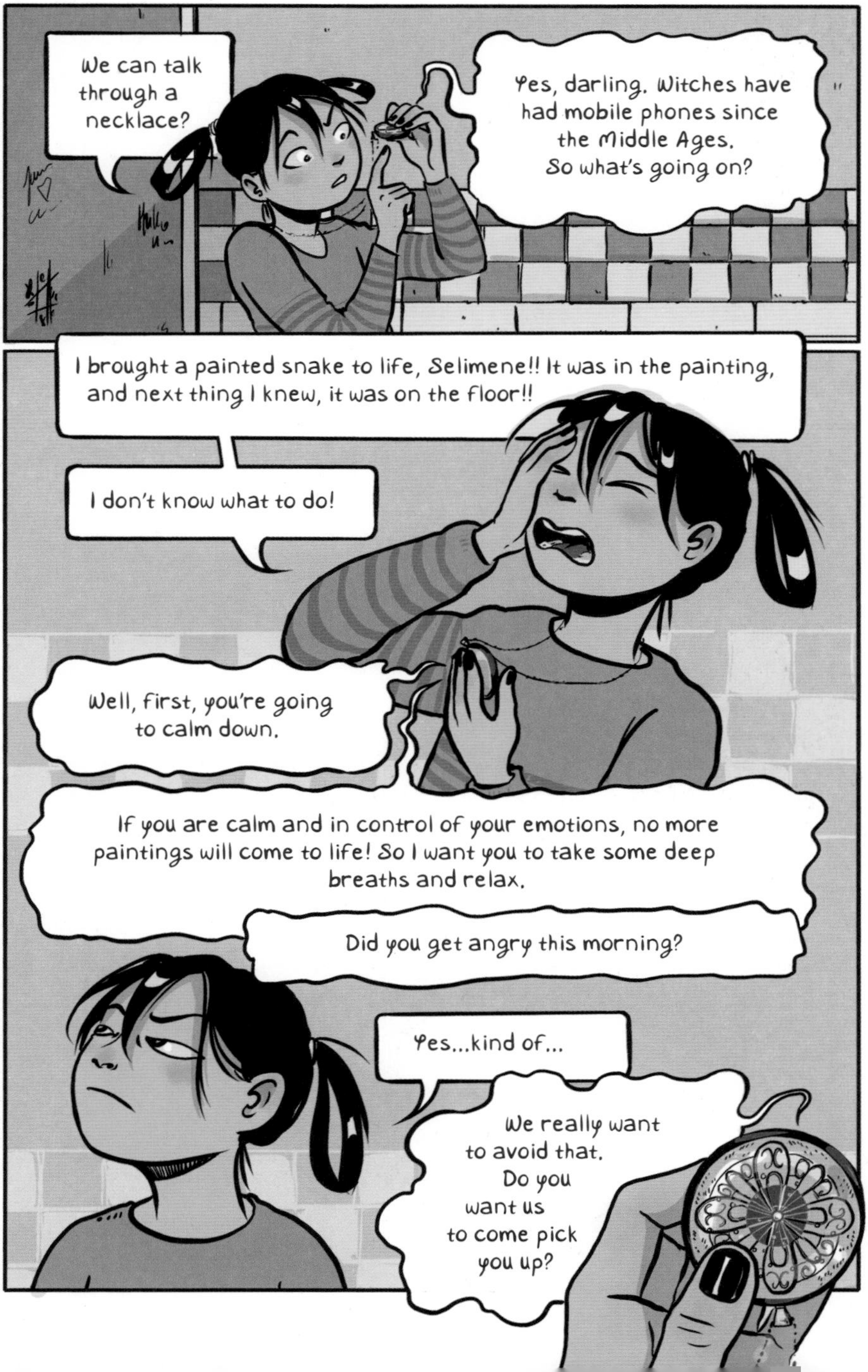
We can talk through a necklace?
Yes, darling. Witches have had mobile phones since the Middle Ages. So what's going on?
I brought a painted snake to life, Selimene!! It was in the painting, and next thing I knew, it was on the floor!!
I don't know what to do!
Well, first, you're going to calm down.
If you are calm and in control of your emotions, no more paintings will come to life! So I want you to take some deep breaths and relax.
Did you get angry this morning?
Yes...kind of...
We really want to avoid that. Do you want us to come pick you up?

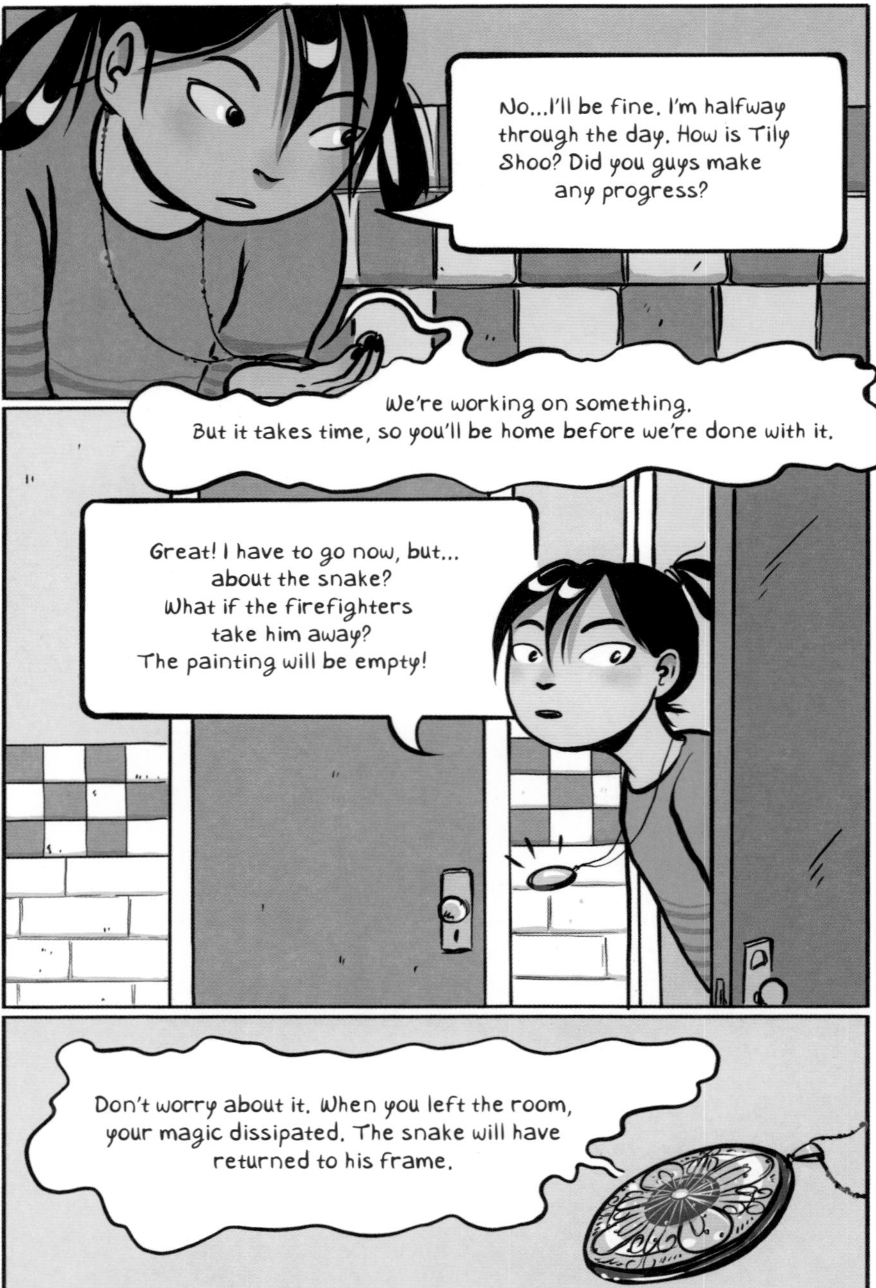
No...I'll be fine. I'm halfway through the day. How is Tily Shoo? Did you guys make any progress?
We're working on something. But it takes time, so you'll be home before we're done with it.
Great! I have to go now, but... about the snake? What if the firefighters take him away? The painting will be empty!
Don't worry about it. When you left the room, your magic dissipated. The snake will have returned to his frame.

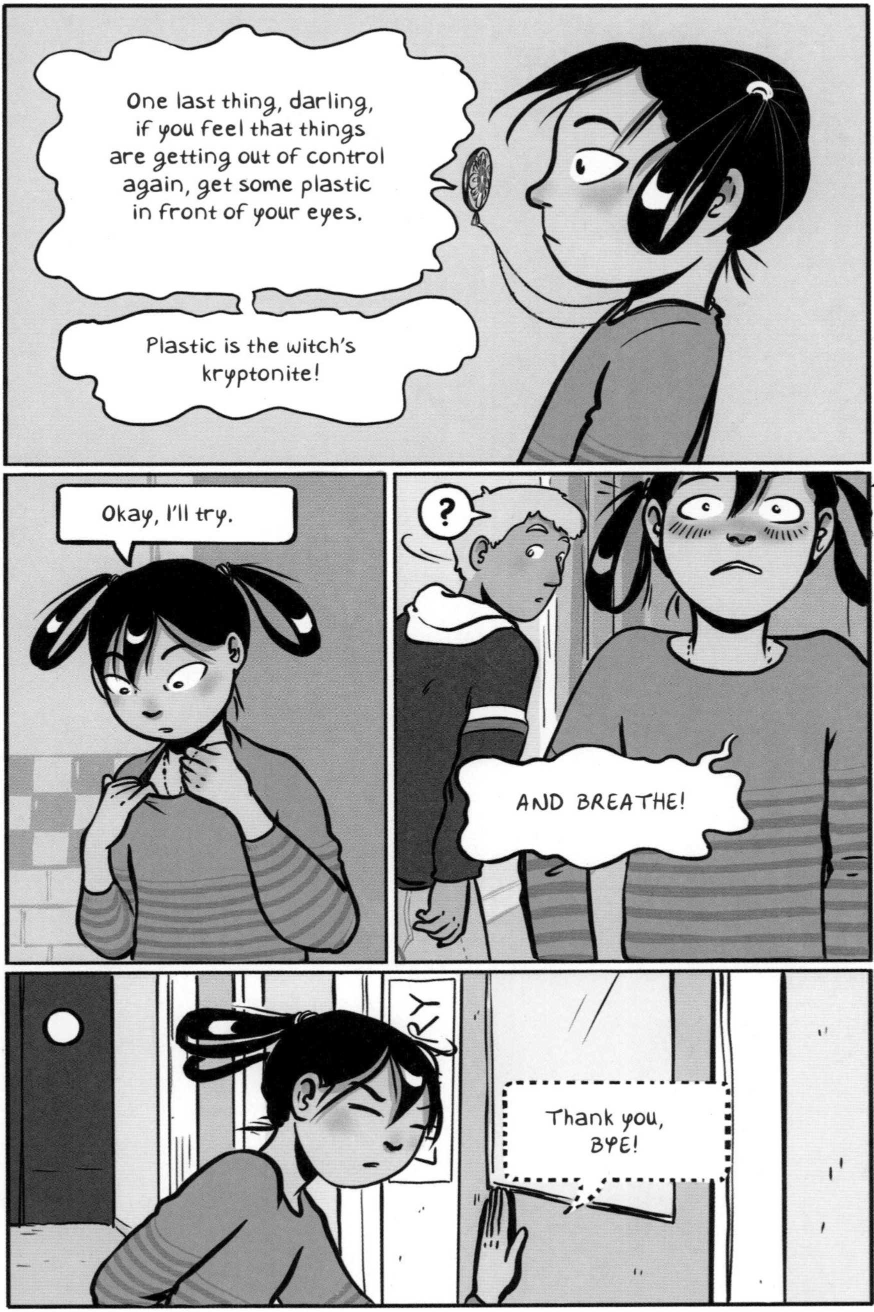
One last thing, darling, if you feel that things are getting out of control again, get some plastic in front of your eyes.
Plastic is the witch's kryptonite!
Okay, I'll try.
?
AND BREATHE!
Thank you, BYE!

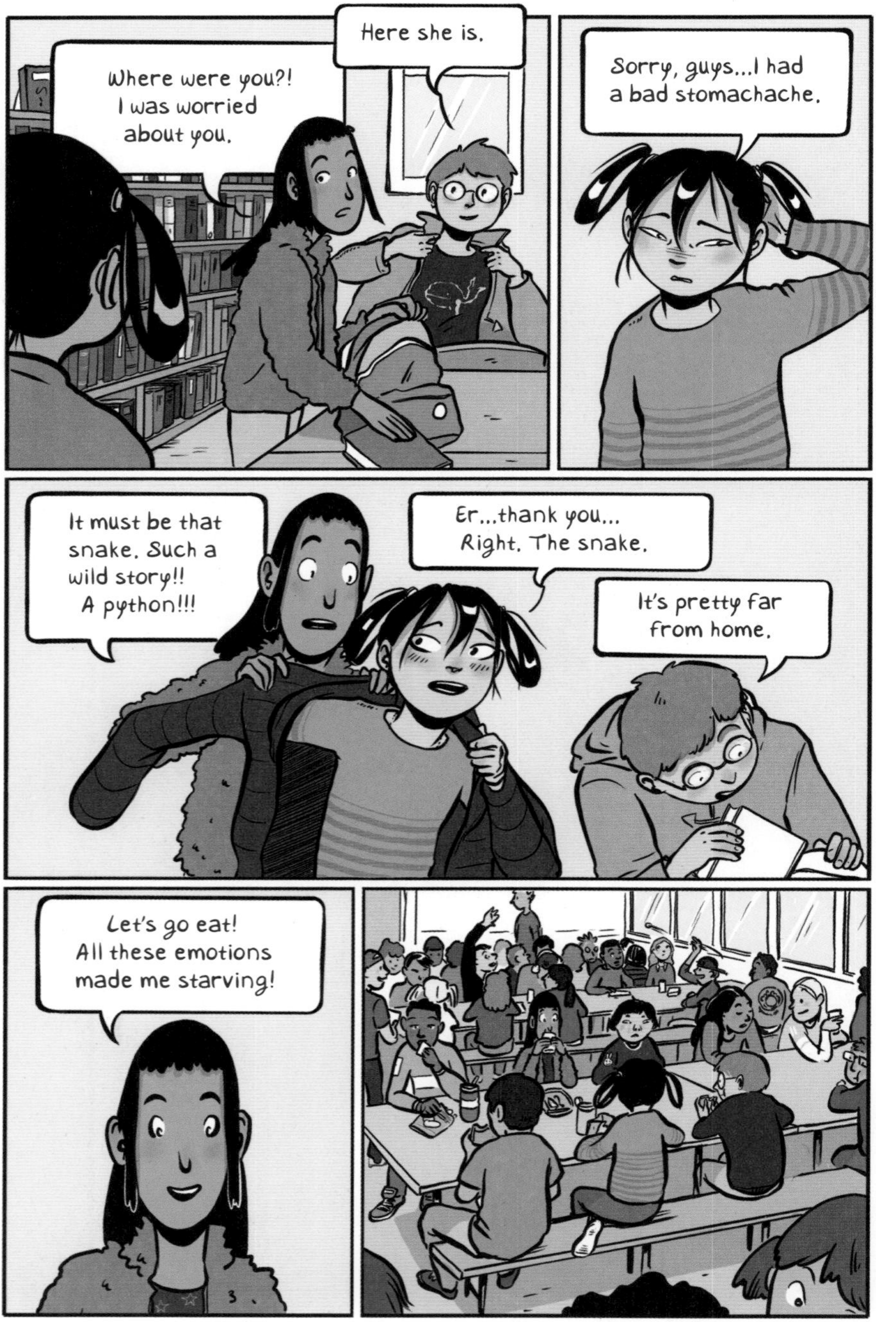
Where were you?! I was worried about you.
Here she is.
Sorry, guys...I had a bad stomachache.
It must be that snake. Such a wild story!! A python!!!
Er...thank you... Right. The snake.
It's pretty far from home.
Let's go eat! All these emotions made me starving!

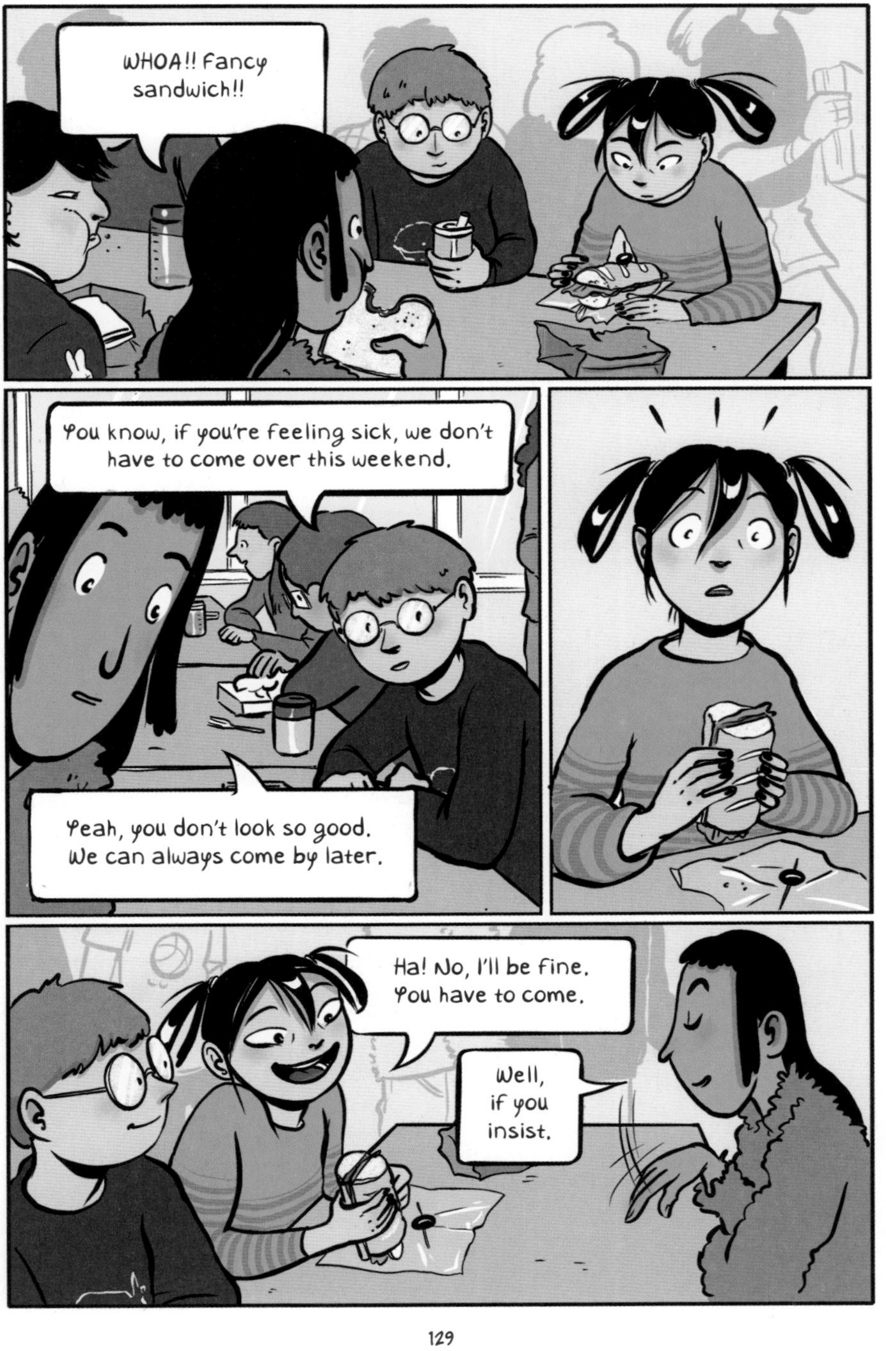
WHOA!! Fancy sandwich!!
You know, if you're feeling sick, we don't have to come over this weekend.
Yeah, you don't look so good. We can always come by later.
Ha! No, I'll be fine. You have to come.
Well, if you insist.

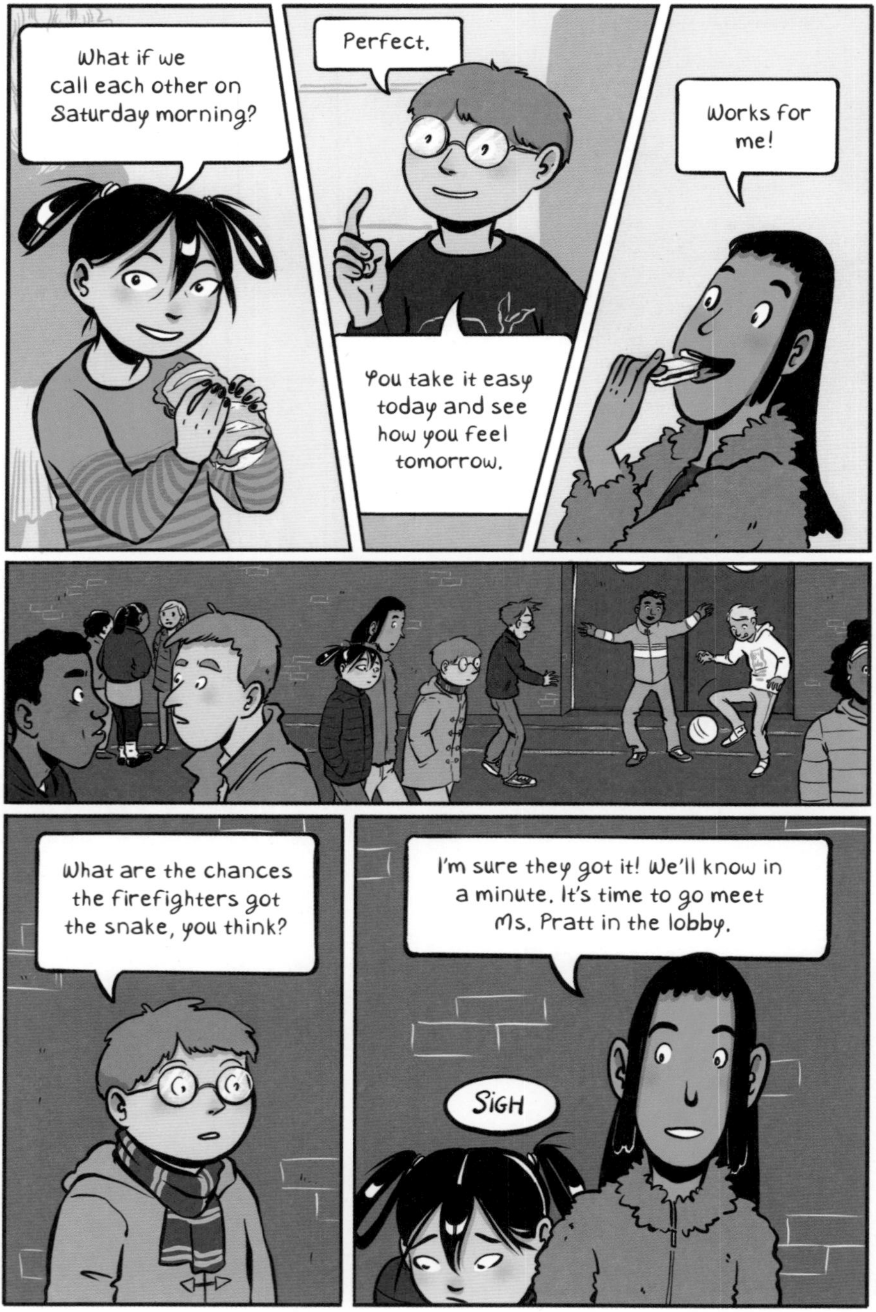
What if we call each other on Saturday morning?
Perfect.
You take it easy today and see how you feel tomorrow.
Works for me!
What are the chances the firefighters got the snake, you think?
I'm sure they got it! We'll know in a minute. It's time to go meet Ms. Pratt in the lobby.
SIGH

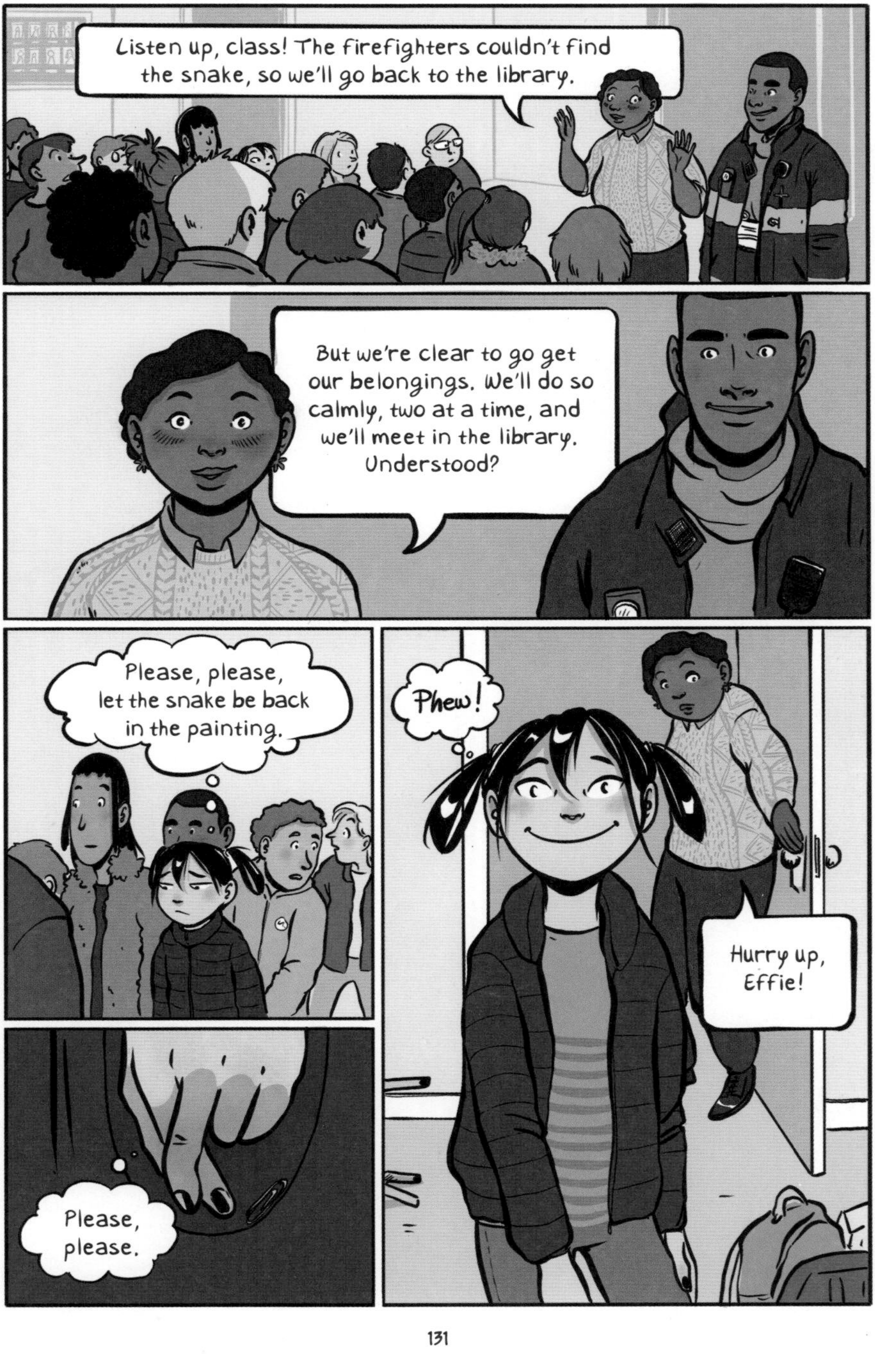
Listen up, class! The firefighters couldn't find the snake, so we'll go back to the library.
But we're clear to go get our belongings. We'll do so calmly, two at a time, and we'll meet in the library. Understood?
Please, please, let the snake be back in the painting.
Please, please.
Phew!
Hurry up, Effie!

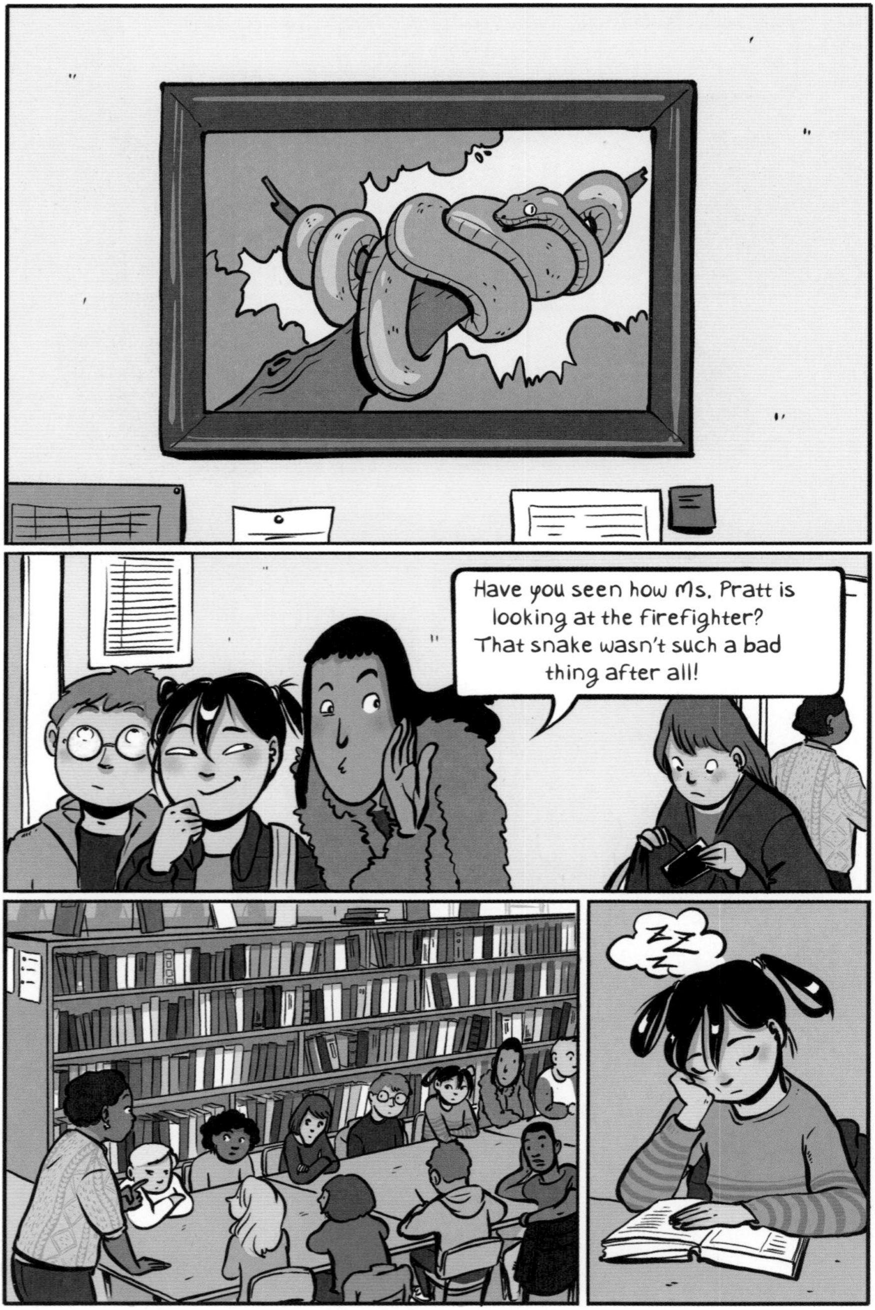
Have you seen how Ms. Pratt is looking at the firefighter? That snake wasn't such a bad thing after all!
ZZZ

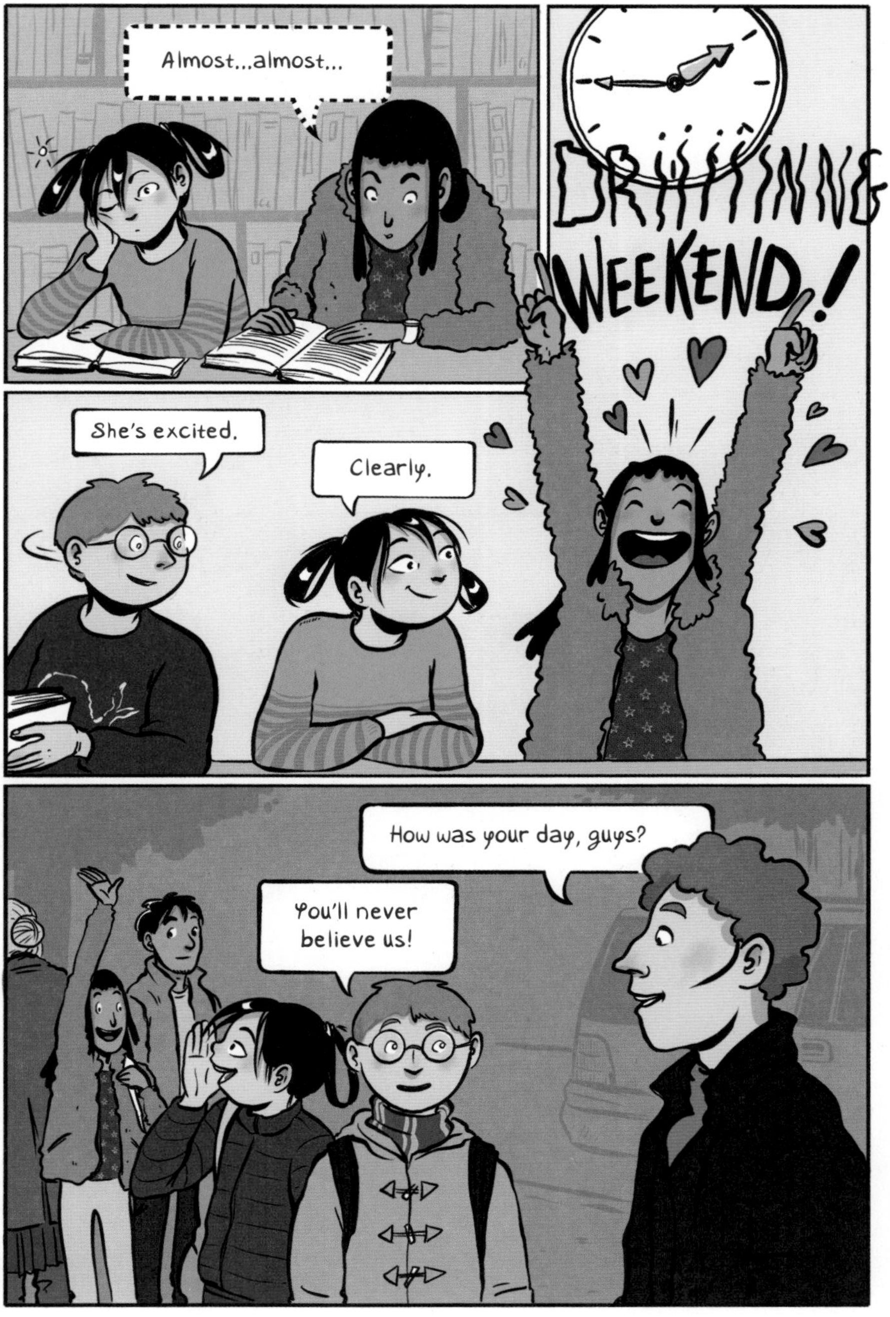
Almost...almost...
DRIIIINNG
WEEKEND!
She's excited.
Clearly.
How was your day, guys?
You'll never believe us!

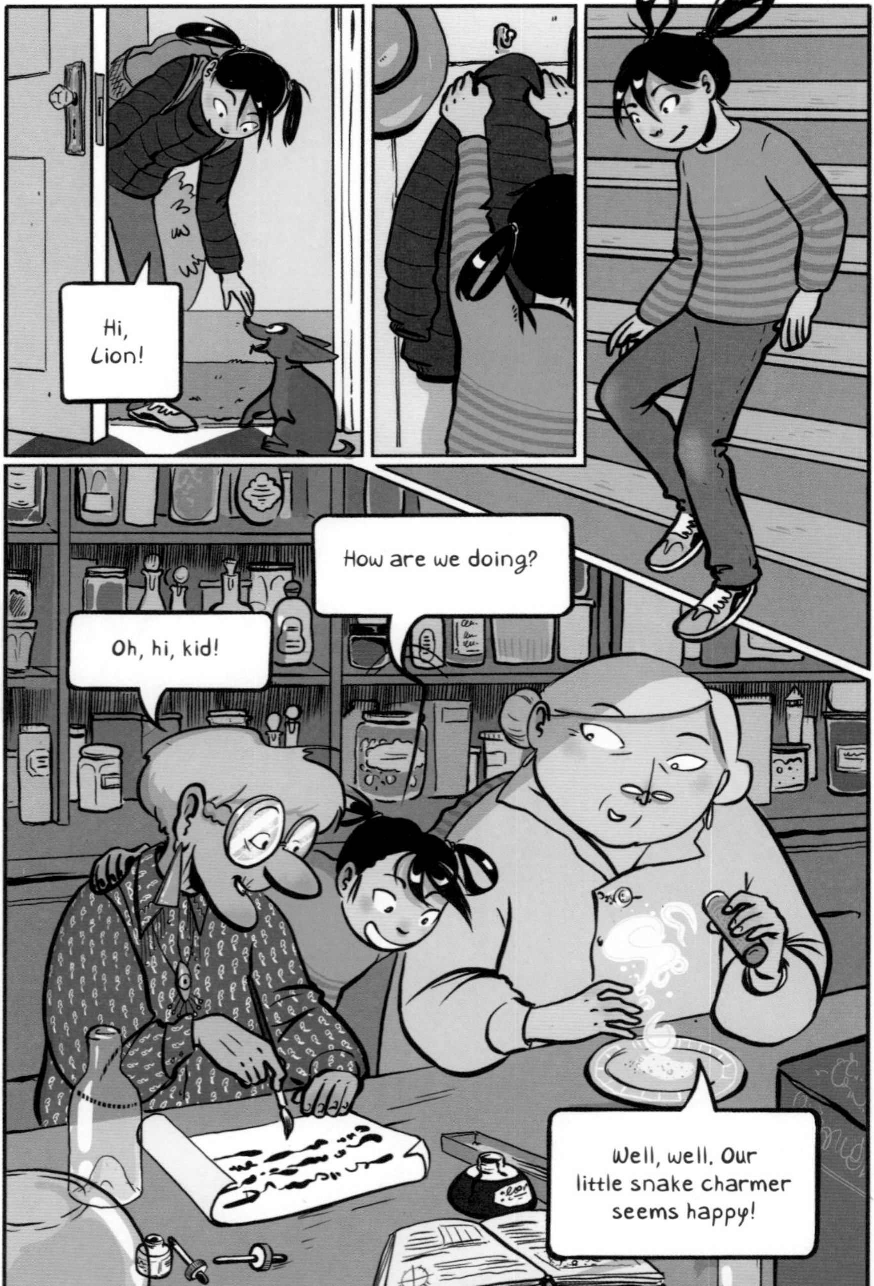
Hi, Lion!
How are we doing?
Oh, hi, kid!
Well, well. Our little snake charmer seems happy!

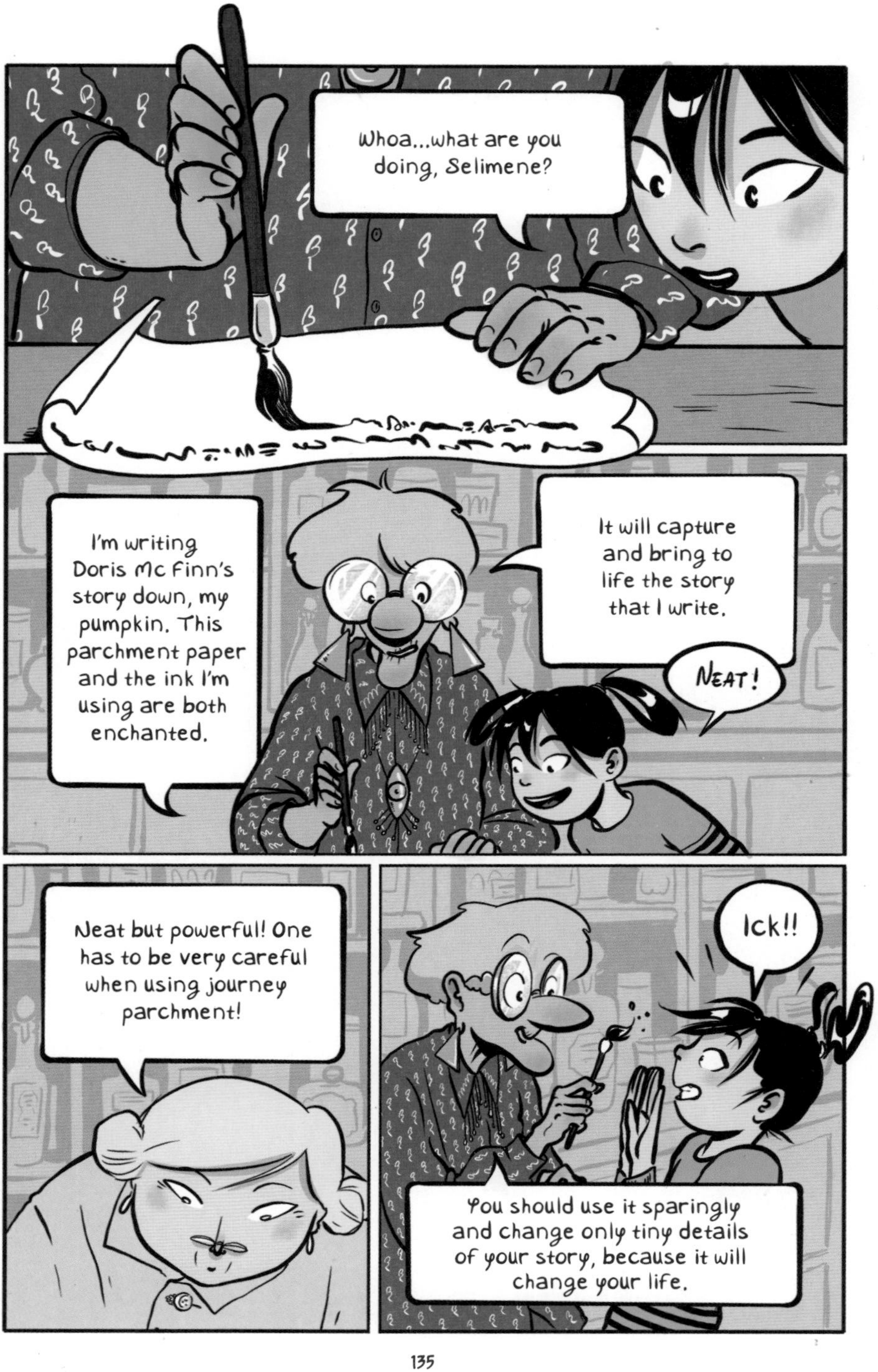
Whoa...what are you doing, Selimene?
I'm writing Doris Mc Finn's story down, my pumpkin. This parchment paper and the ink I'm using are both enchanted.
It will capture and bring to life the story that I write.
NEAT!
Neat but powerful! One has to be very careful when using journey parchment!
Ick!!
You should use it sparingly and change only tiny details of your story, because it will change your life.

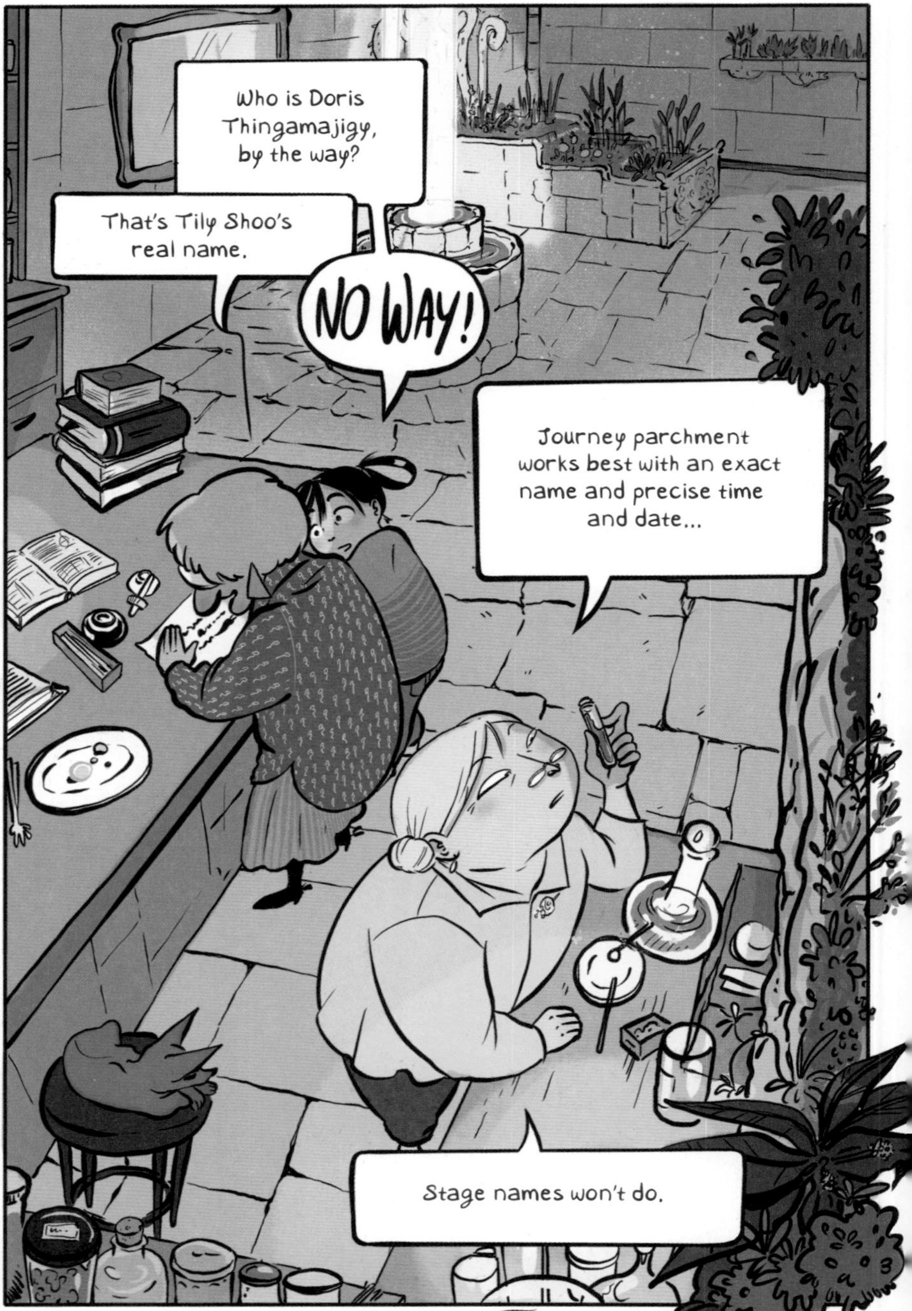
Who is Doris Thingamajigy, by the way?
That's Tily Shoo's real name.
NO WAY!
Journey parchment works best with an exact name and precise time and date...
Stage names won't do.

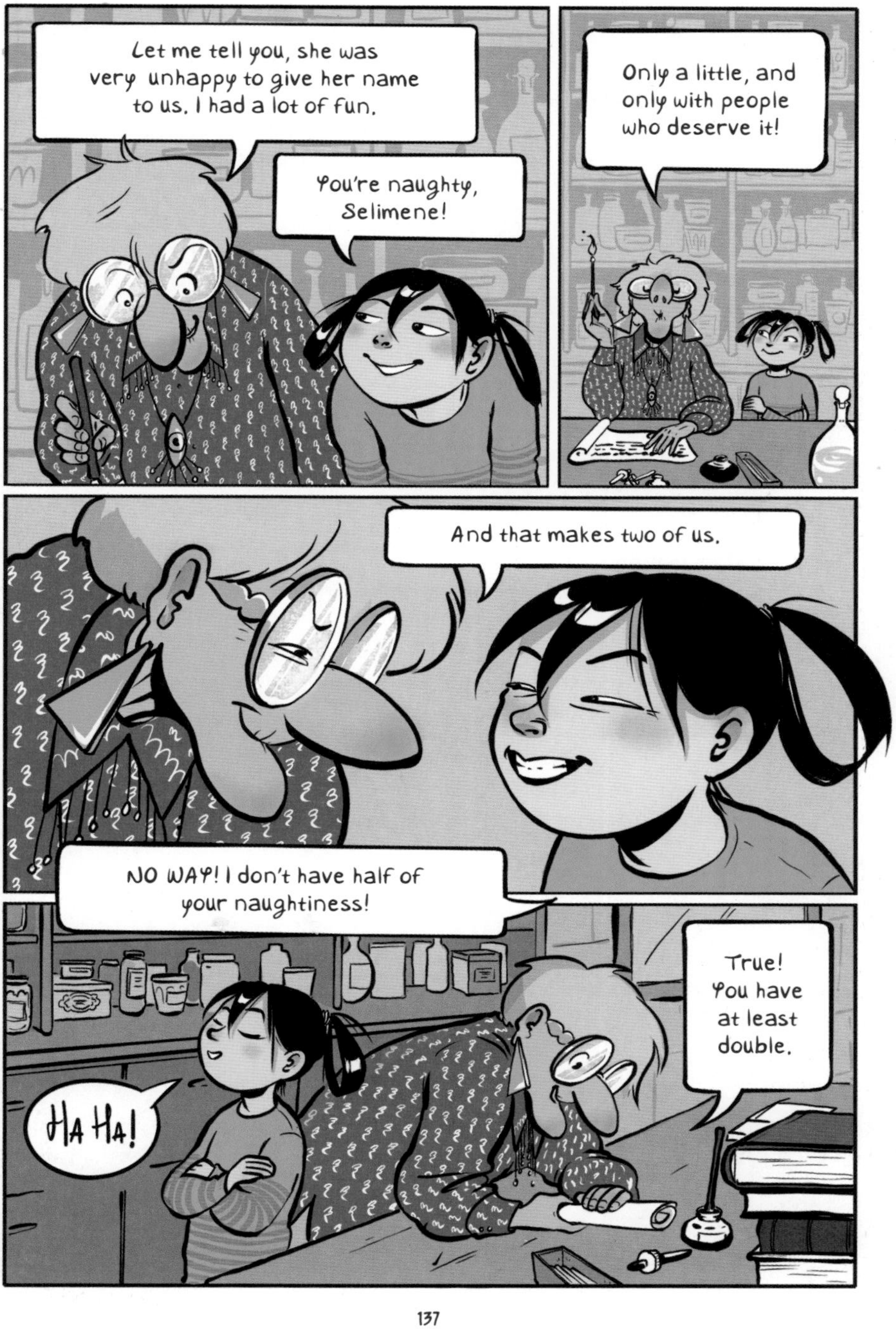
Let me tell you, she was very unhappy to give her name to us. I had a lot of fun.
You're naughty, Selimene!
Only a little, and only with people who deserve it!
And that makes two of us.
NO WAY! I don't have half of your naughtiness!
True! You have at least double.
HA HA!

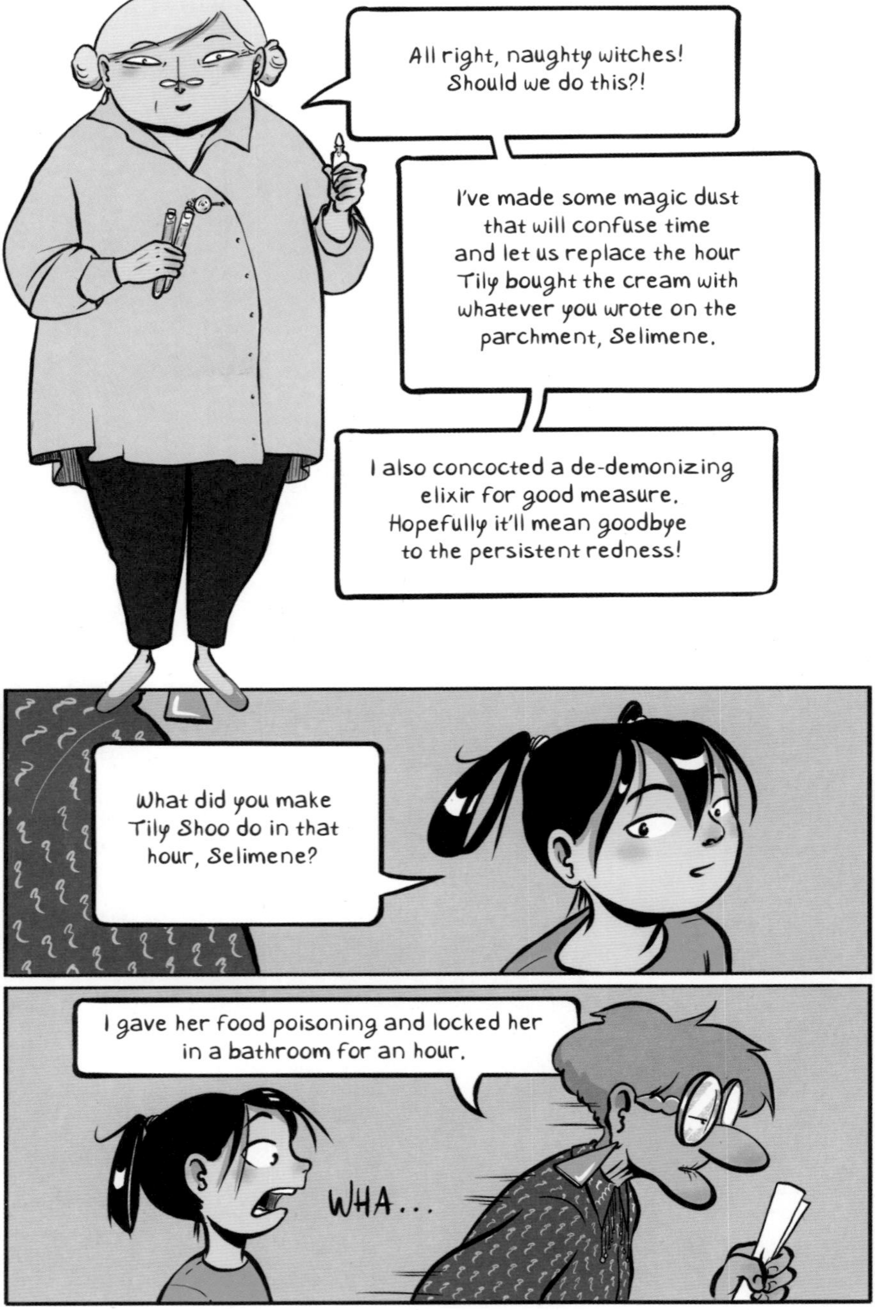
All right, naughty witches! Should we do this?!
I've made some magic dust that will confuse time and let us replace the hour Tily bought the cream with whatever you wrote on the parchment, Selimene.
I also concocted a de-demonizing elixir for good measure. Hopefully it'll mean goodbye to the persistent redness!
What did you make Tily Shoo do in that hour, Selimene?
I gave her food poisoning and locked her in a bathroom for an hour.
WHA...

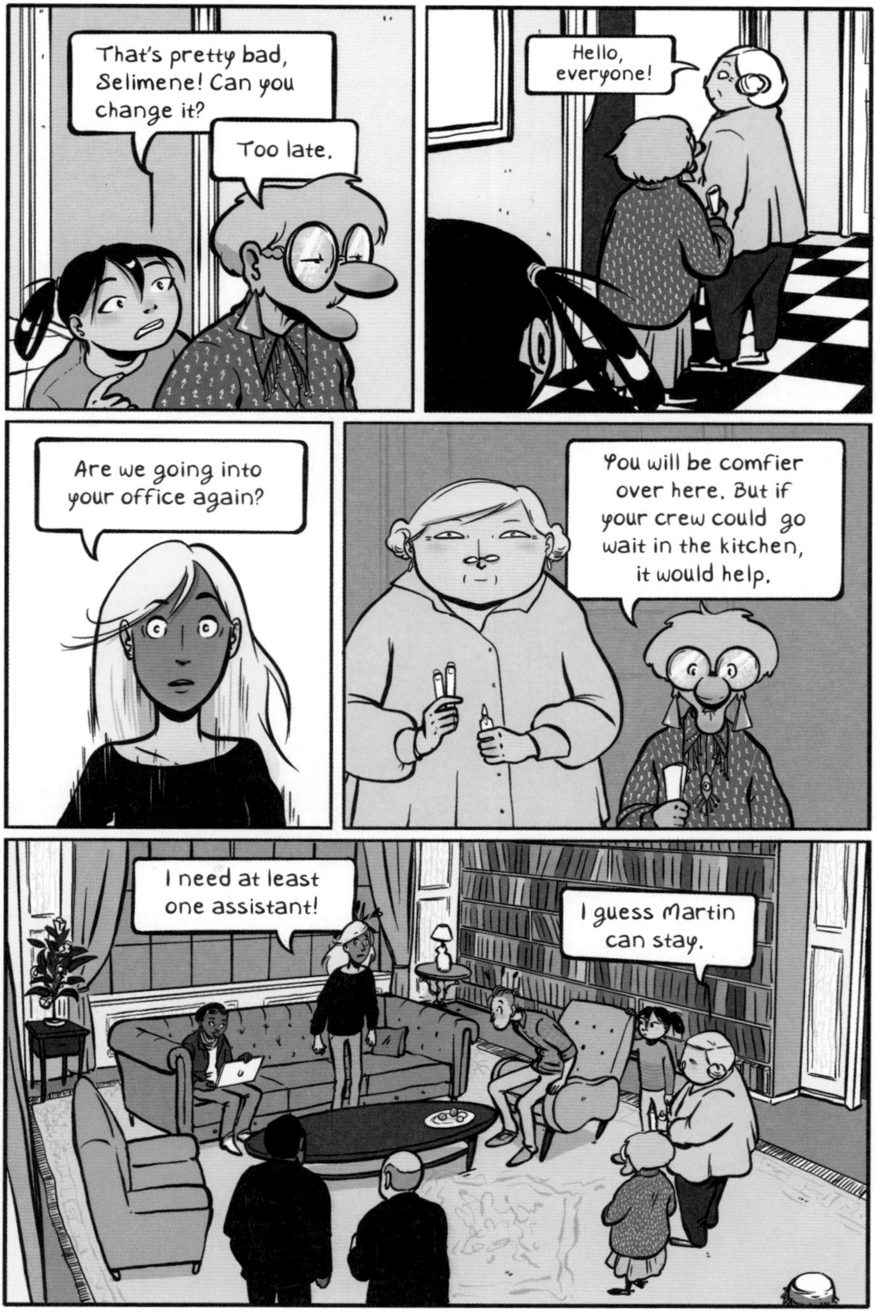
That's pretty bad, Selimene! Can you change it?
Too late.
Hello, everyone!
Are we going into your office again?
You will be comfier over here. But if your crew could go wait in the kitchen, it would help.
I need at least one assistant!
I guess Martin can stay.

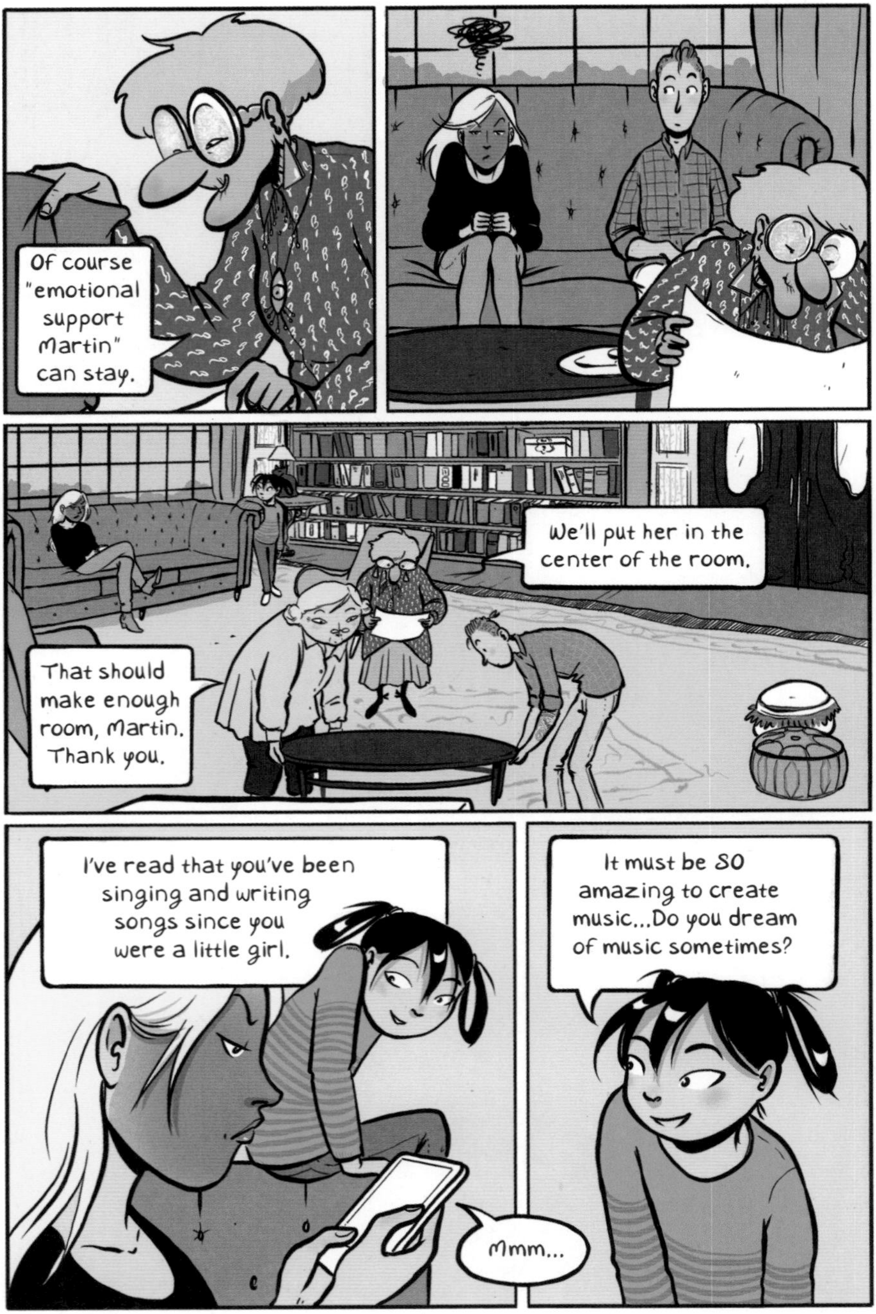
Of course "emotional support Martin" can stay.
We'll put her in the center of the room.
That should make enough room, Martin. Thank you.
I've read that you've been singing and writing songs since you were a little girl.
Mmm...
It must be SO amazing to create music...Do you dream of music sometimes?

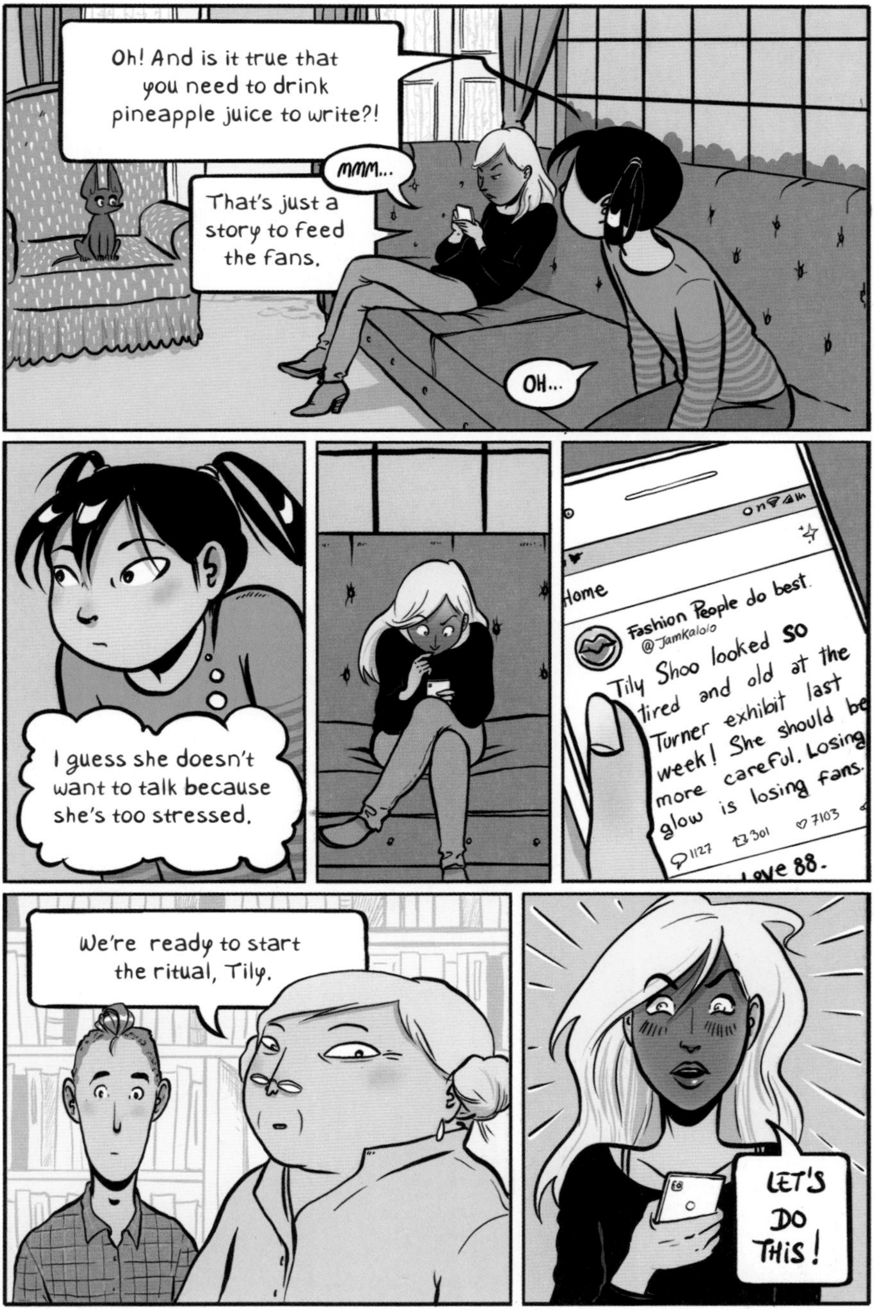
Oh! And is it true that you need to drink pineapple juice to write?!
MMM...
That's just a story to feed the fans.
OH...
I guess she doesn't want to talk because she's too stressed.
Home
Fashion People do best.
Fashion People
@JamKalolo
Tily Shoo looked SO tired and old at the Turner exhibit last week! She should be more careful. Losing glow is losing fans.
1127
301
7103
Love 88.
We're ready to start the ritual, Tily.
LET'S DO THIS!

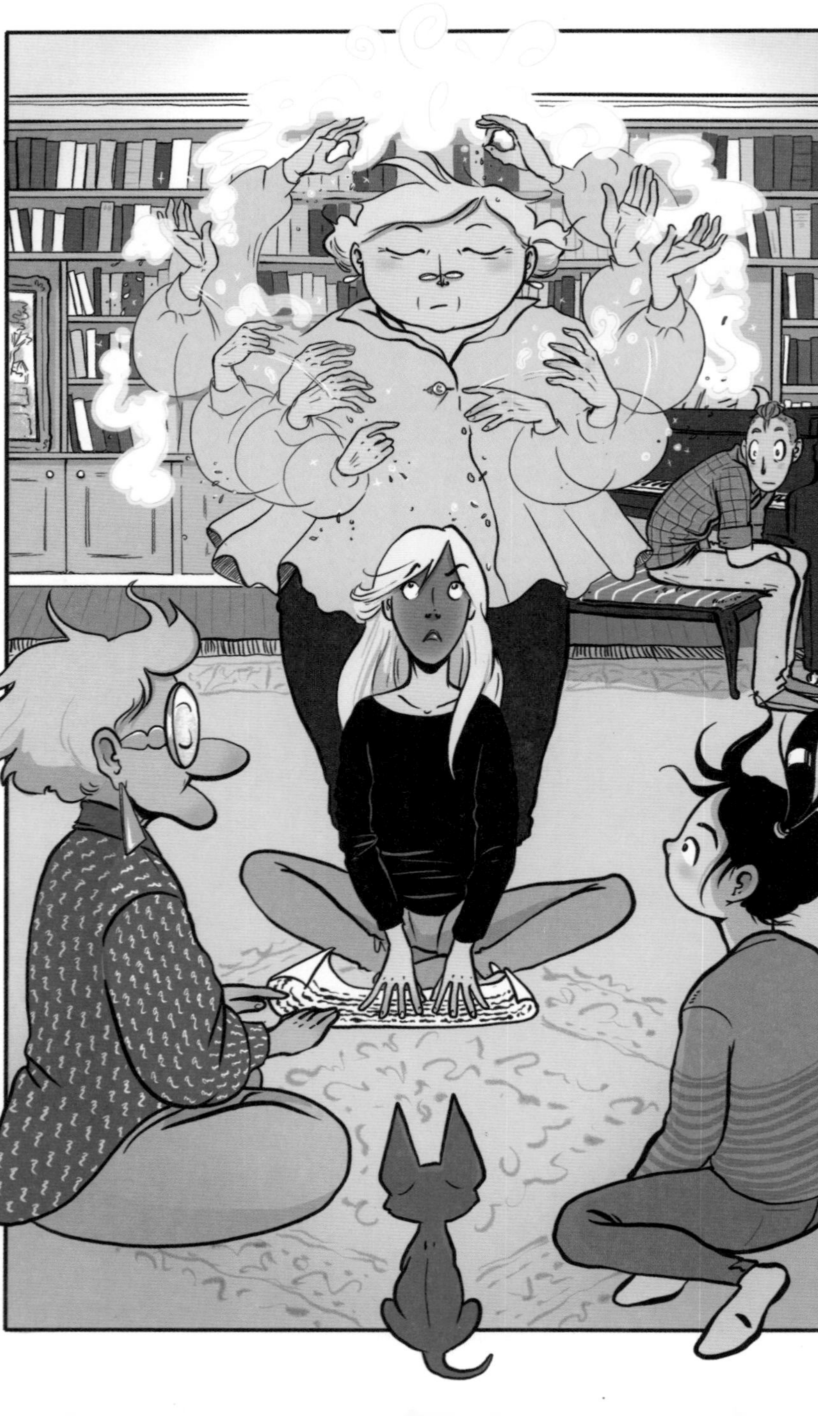

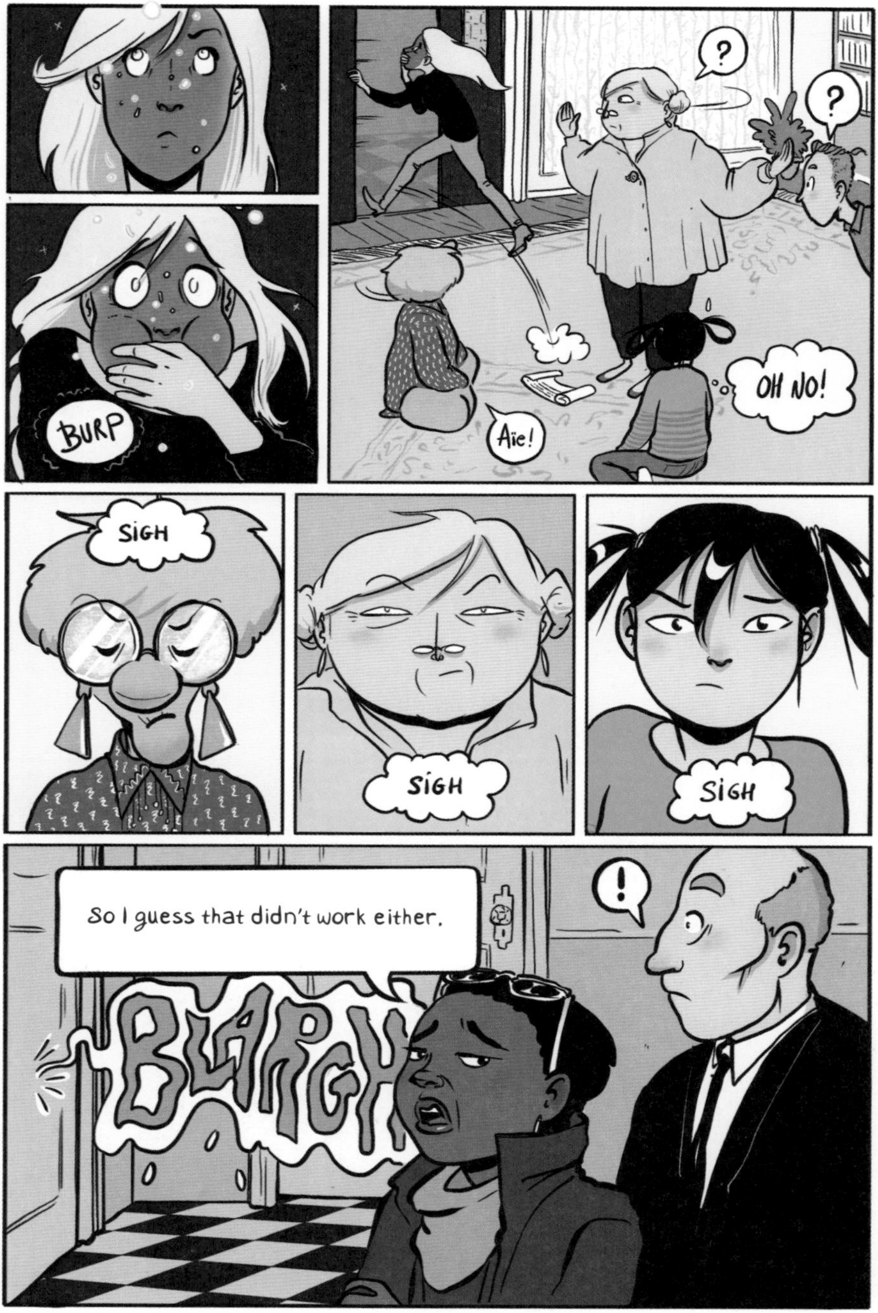
BURP
?
?
OH NO!
Aïe!
SIGH
SIGH
SIGH
!
So I guess that didn't work either.
BLARGH

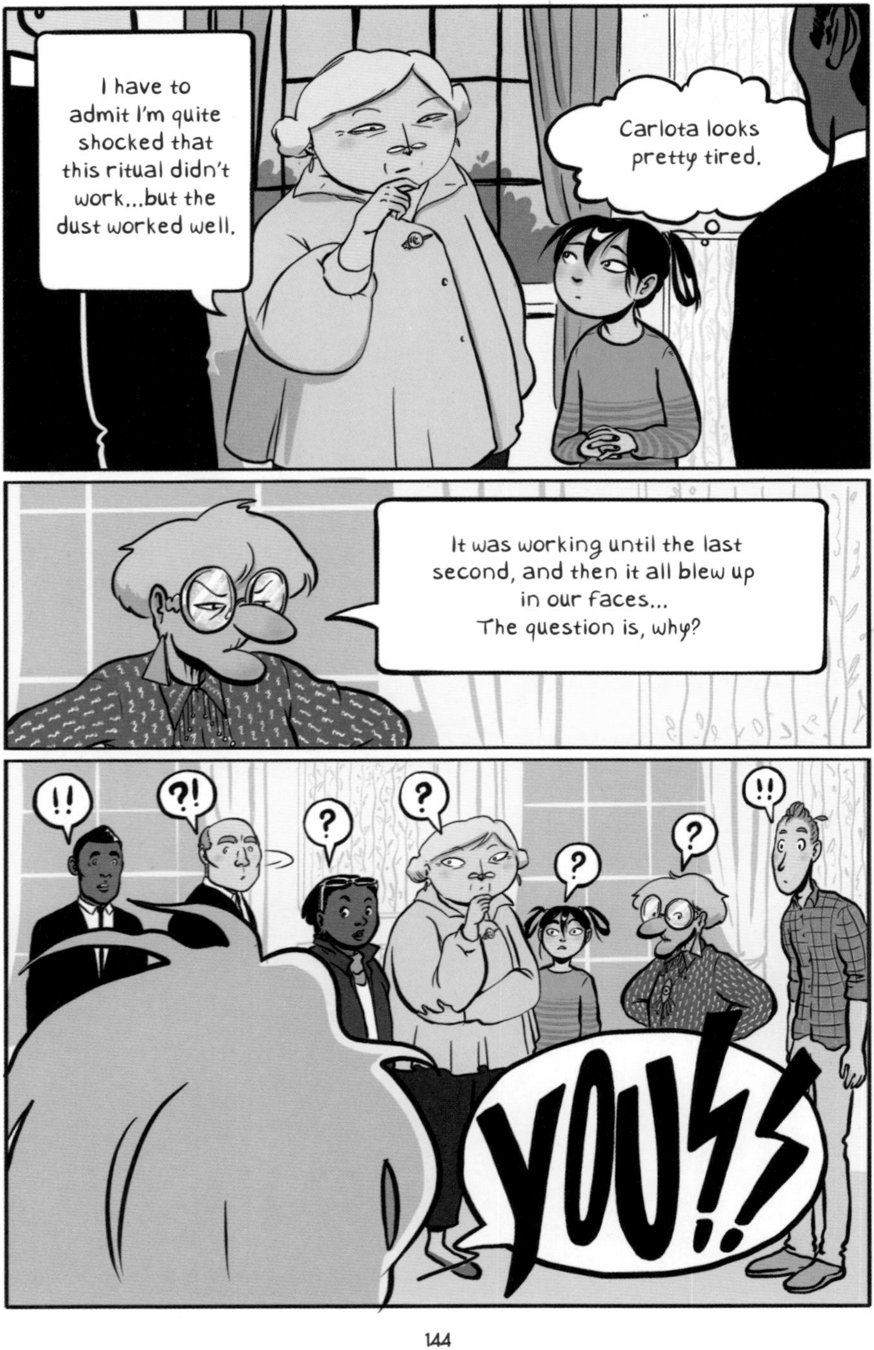
I have to admit I'm quite shocked that this ritual didn't work...but the dust worked well.
Carlota looks pretty tired.
It was working until the last second, and then it all blew up in our faces...
The question is, why?
!!
?!
?
?
?
?
!!
YOU!!

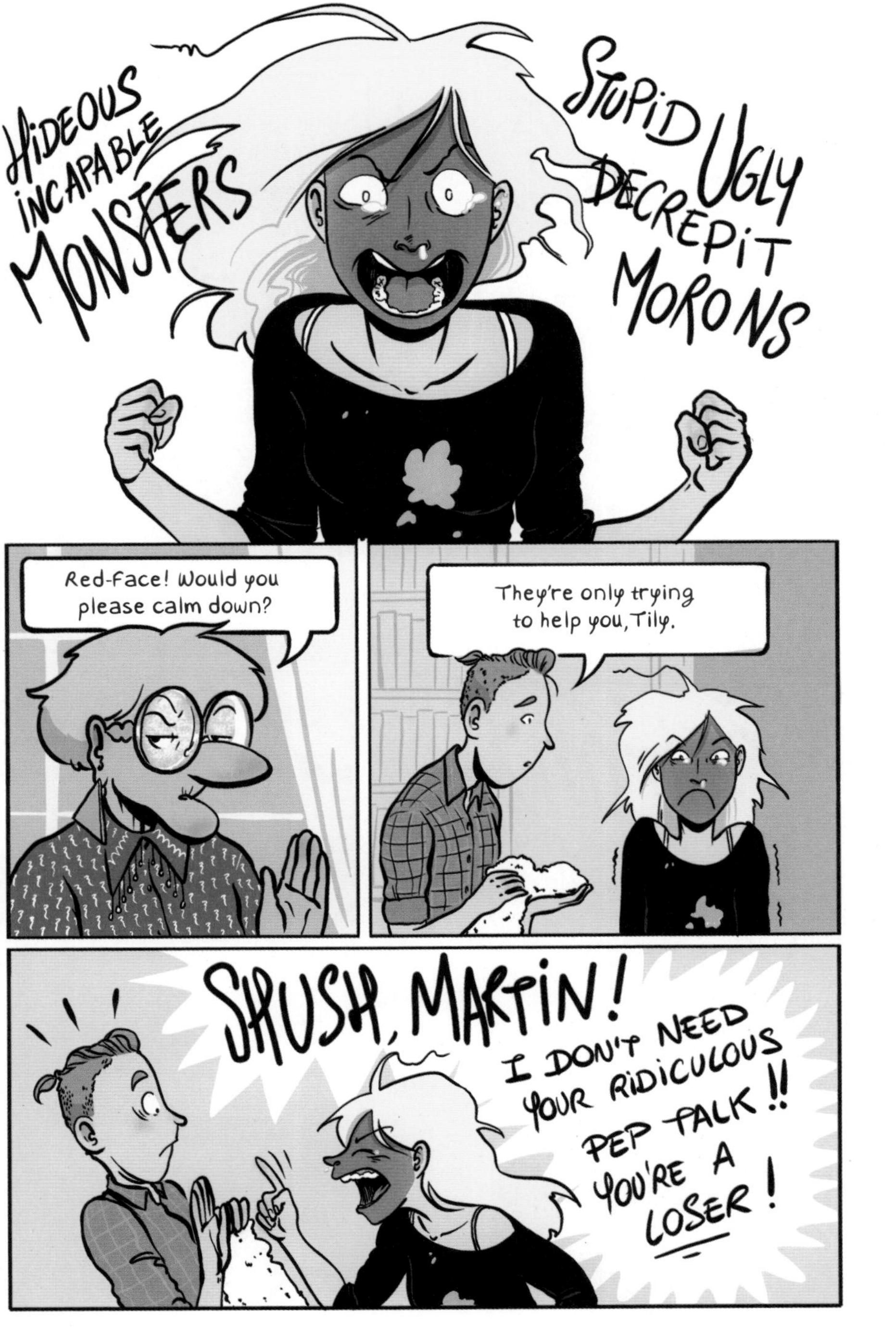

HIDEOUS INCAPABLE MONSTERS
STUPID UGLY DECREPIT MORONS
Red-Face! Would you please calm down?
They're only trying to help you, Tily.
SHUSH, MARTIN!
I DON'T NEED YOUR RIDICULOUS PEP TALK!!
YOU'RE A LOSER!

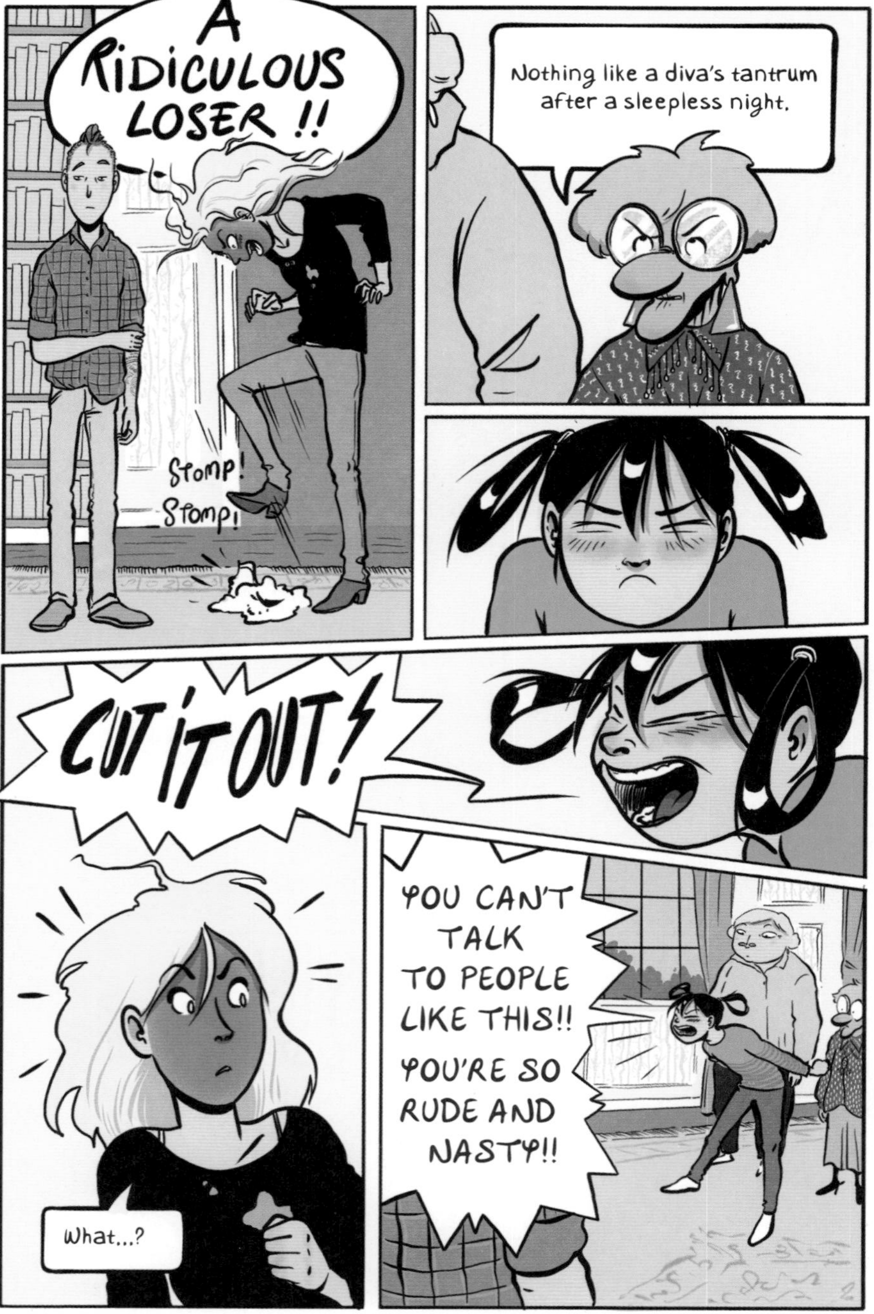
A RIDICULOUS LOSER !!
Stomp! Stomp!
Nothing like a diva's tantrum after a sleepless night.
CUT IT OUT!
What...?
YOU CAN'T TALK TO PEOPLE LIKE THIS!!
YOU'RE SO RUDE AND NASTY!!

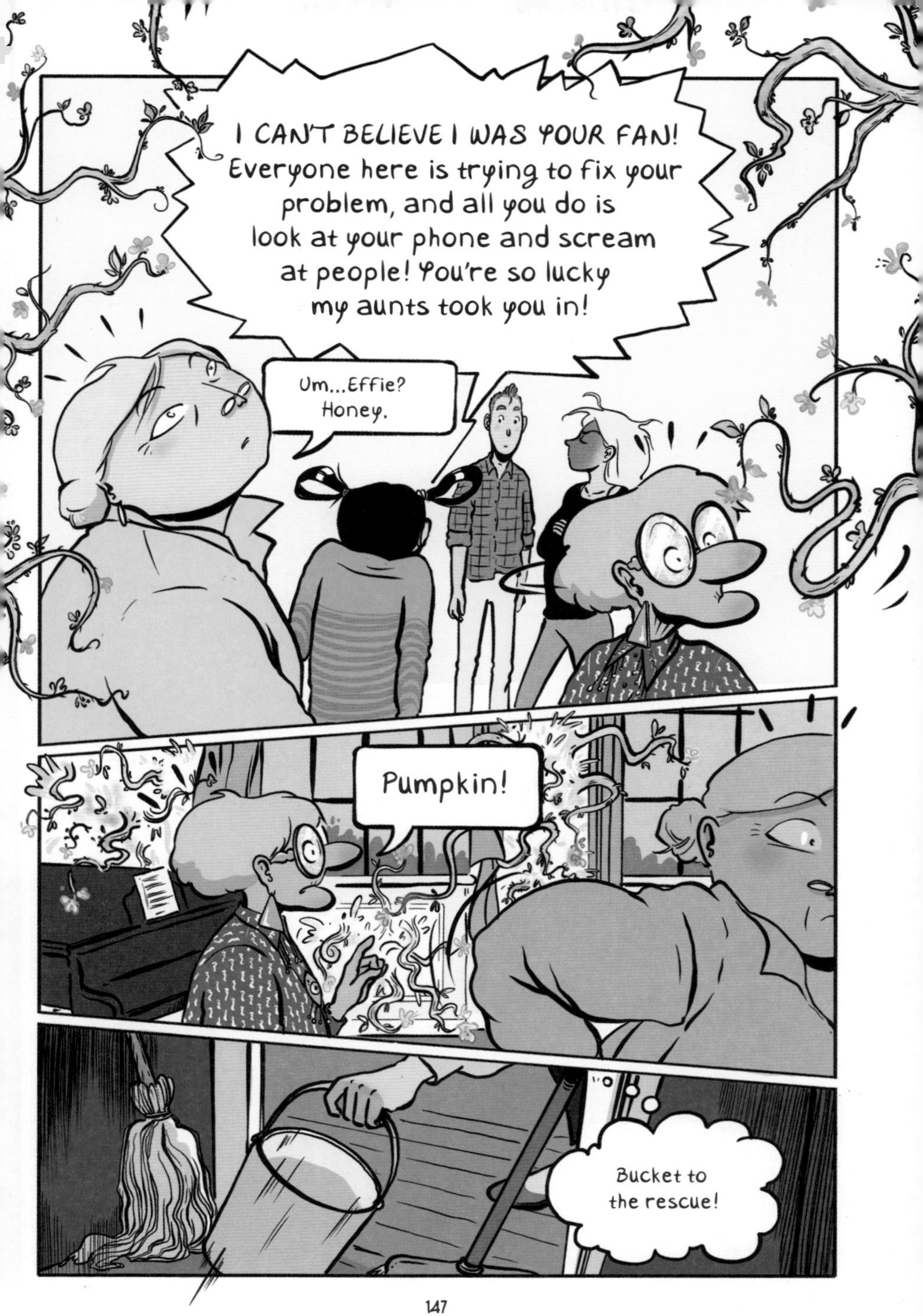
I CAN'T BELIEVE I WAS YOUR FAN! Everyone here is trying to fix your problem, and all you do is look at your phone and scream at people! You're so lucky my aunts took you in!
Um...Effie? Honey.
Pumpkin!
Bucket to the rescue!

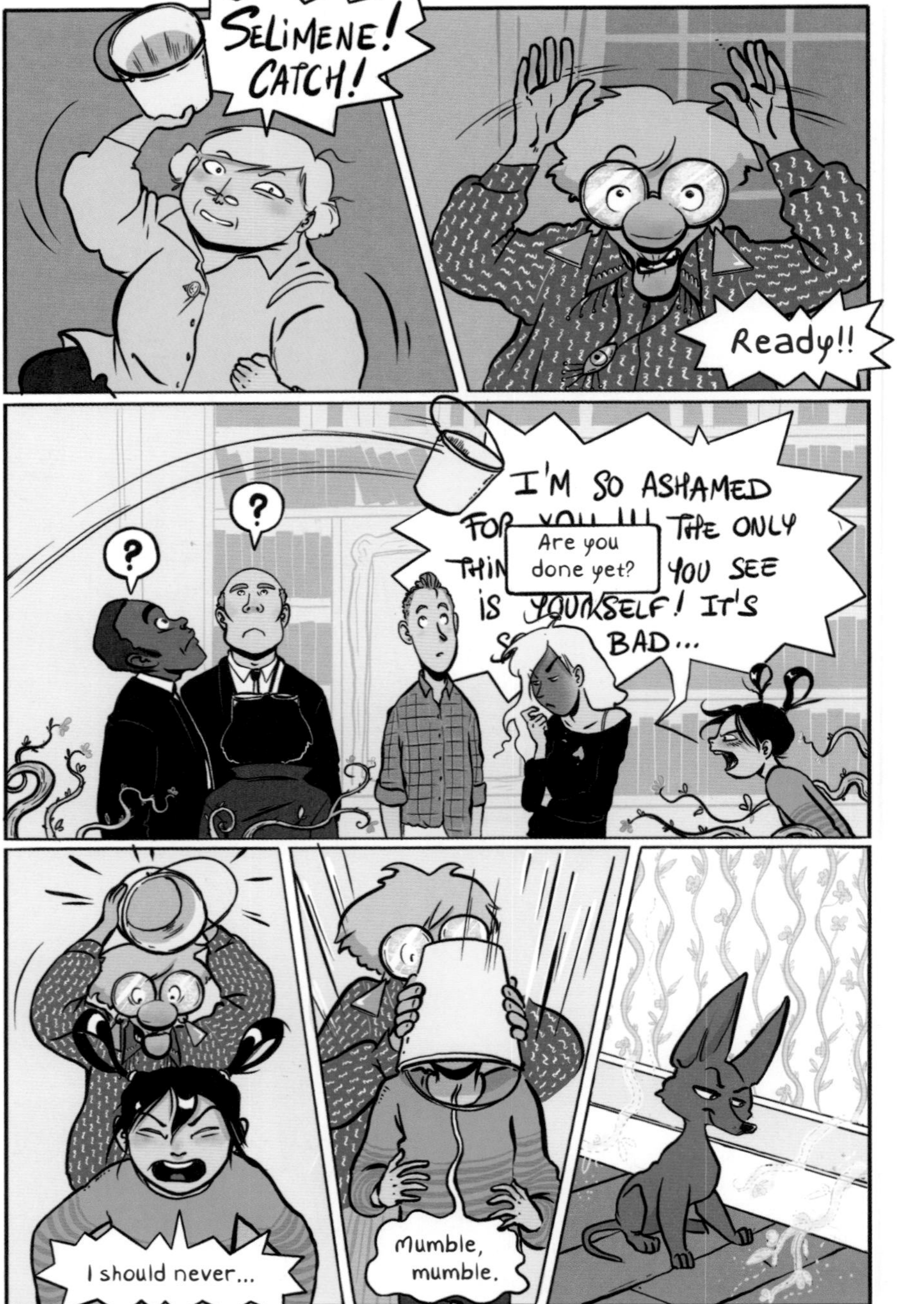
SELIMENE! CATCH!
Ready!!
?
?
I'M SO ASHAMED FOR YOU!!! THE ONLY THIN YOU SEE IS YOURSELF! IT'S BAD...
Are you done yet?
I should never...
Mumble, mumble.

Chapter 4

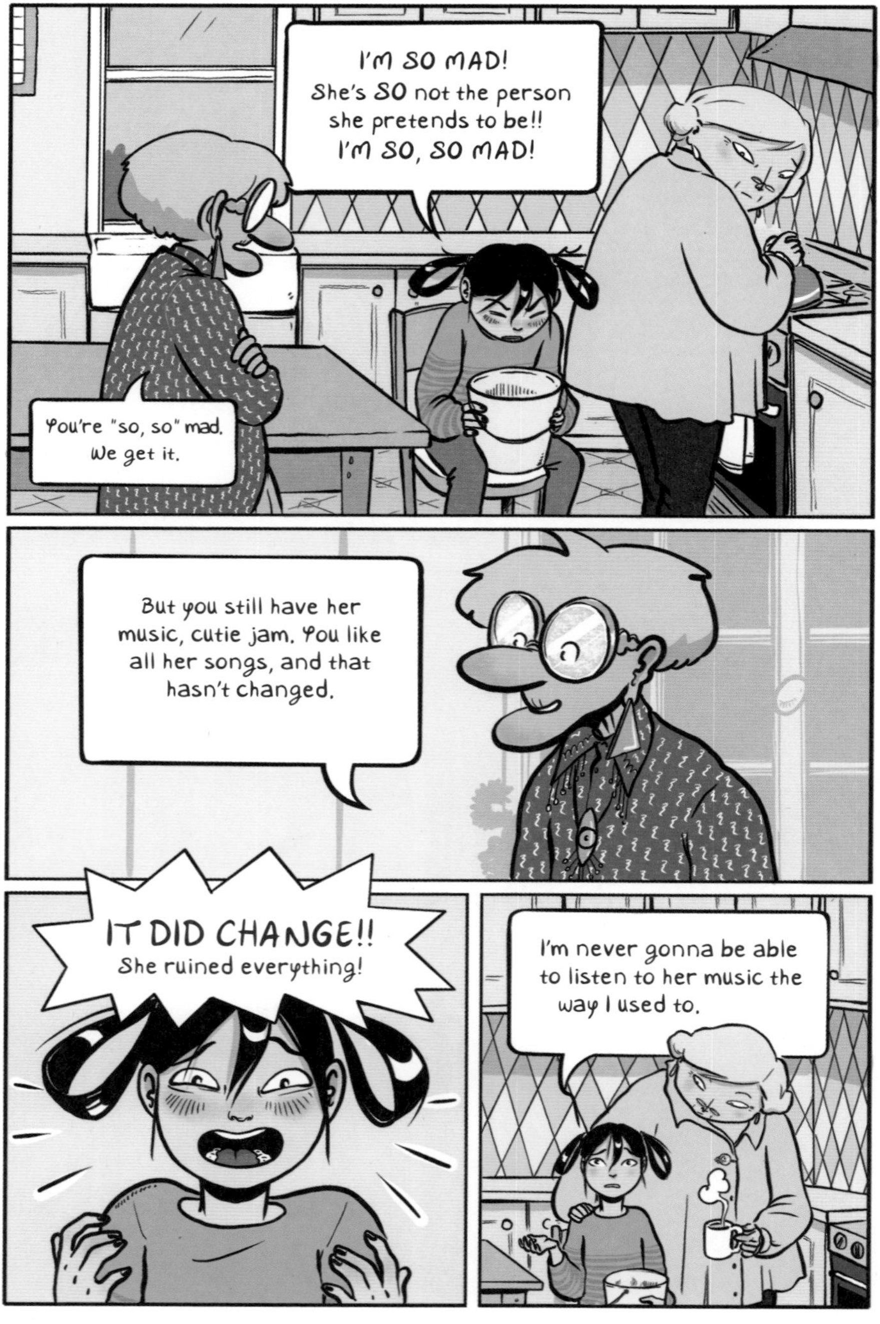
I'M SO MAD!
She's SO not the person she pretends to be!!
I'M SO, SO MAD!
You're "so, so" mad. We get it.
But you still have her music, cutie jam. You like all her songs, and that hasn't changed.
IT DID CHANGE!! She ruined everything!
I'm never gonna be able to listen to her music the way I used to.

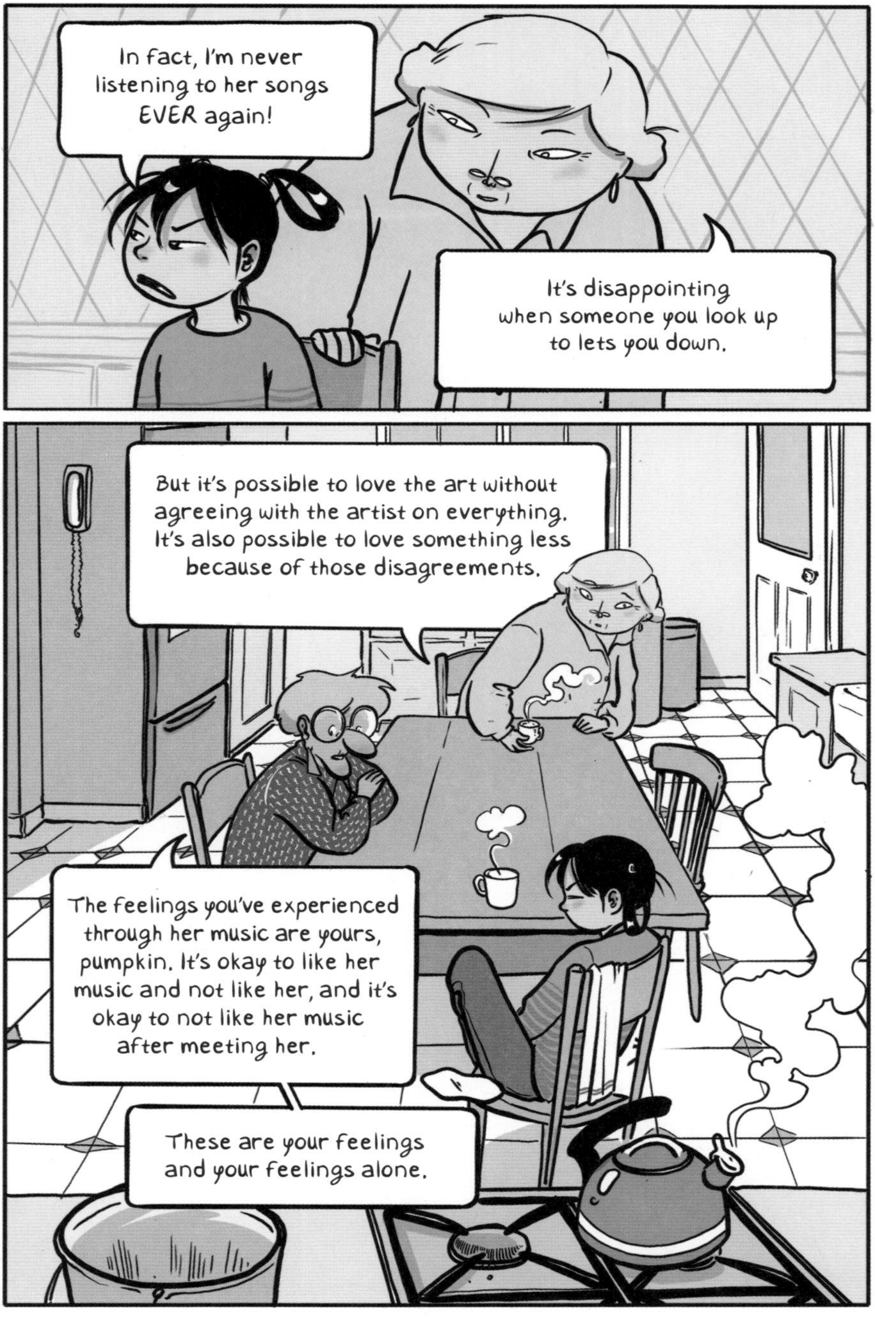
In fact, I'm never listening to her songs EVER again!
It's disappointing when someone you look up to lets you down.
But it's possible to love the art without agreeing with the artist on everything. It's also possible to love something less because of those disagreements.
The feelings you've experienced through her music are yours, pumpkin. It's okay to like her music and not like her, and it's okay to not like her music after meeting her.
These are your feelings and your feelings alone.

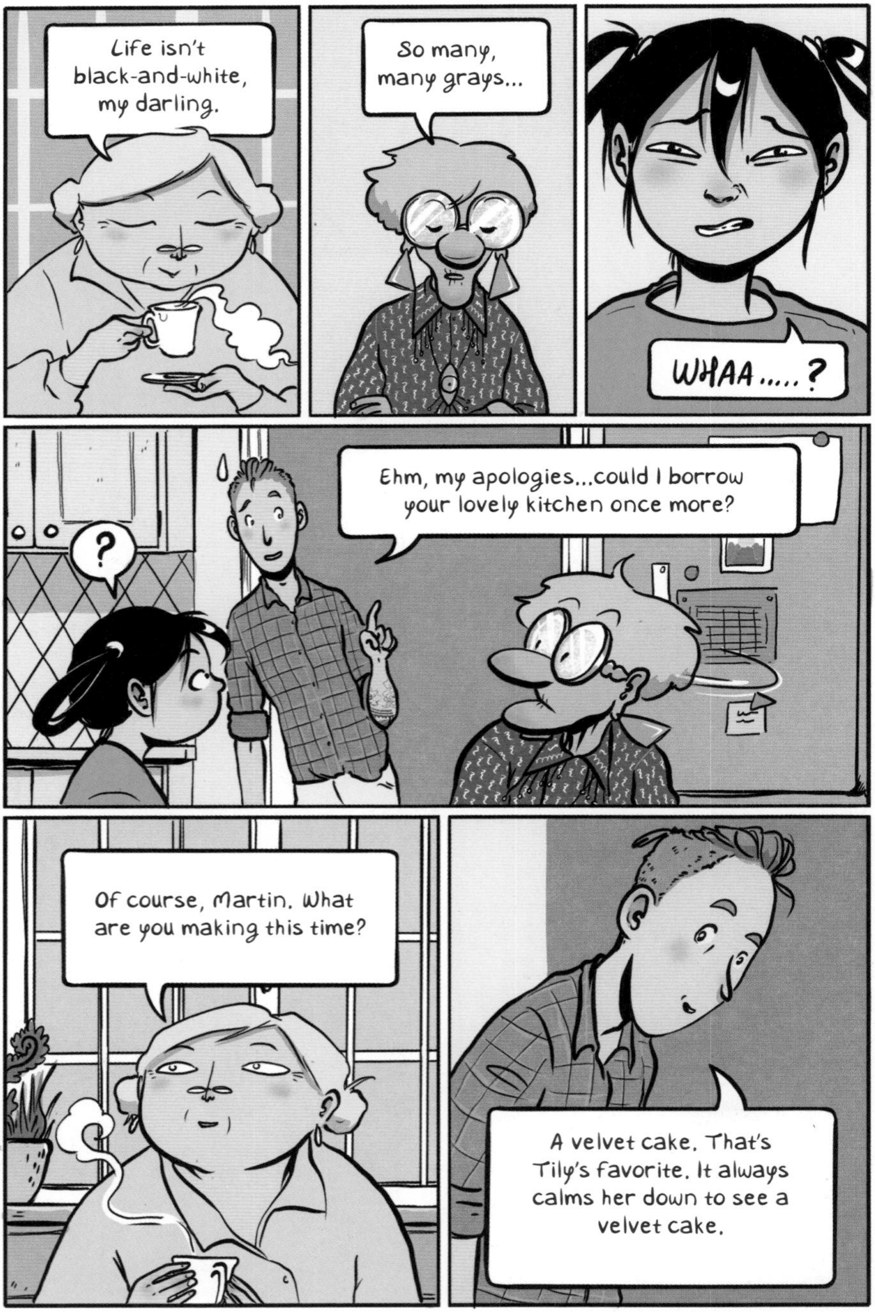
Life isn't black-and-white, my darling.
So many, many grays...
WHAA.....?
?
Ehm, my apologies...could I borrow your lovely kitchen once more?
Of course, Martin. What are you making this time?
A velvet cake. That's Tily's favorite. It always calms her down to see a velvet cake.

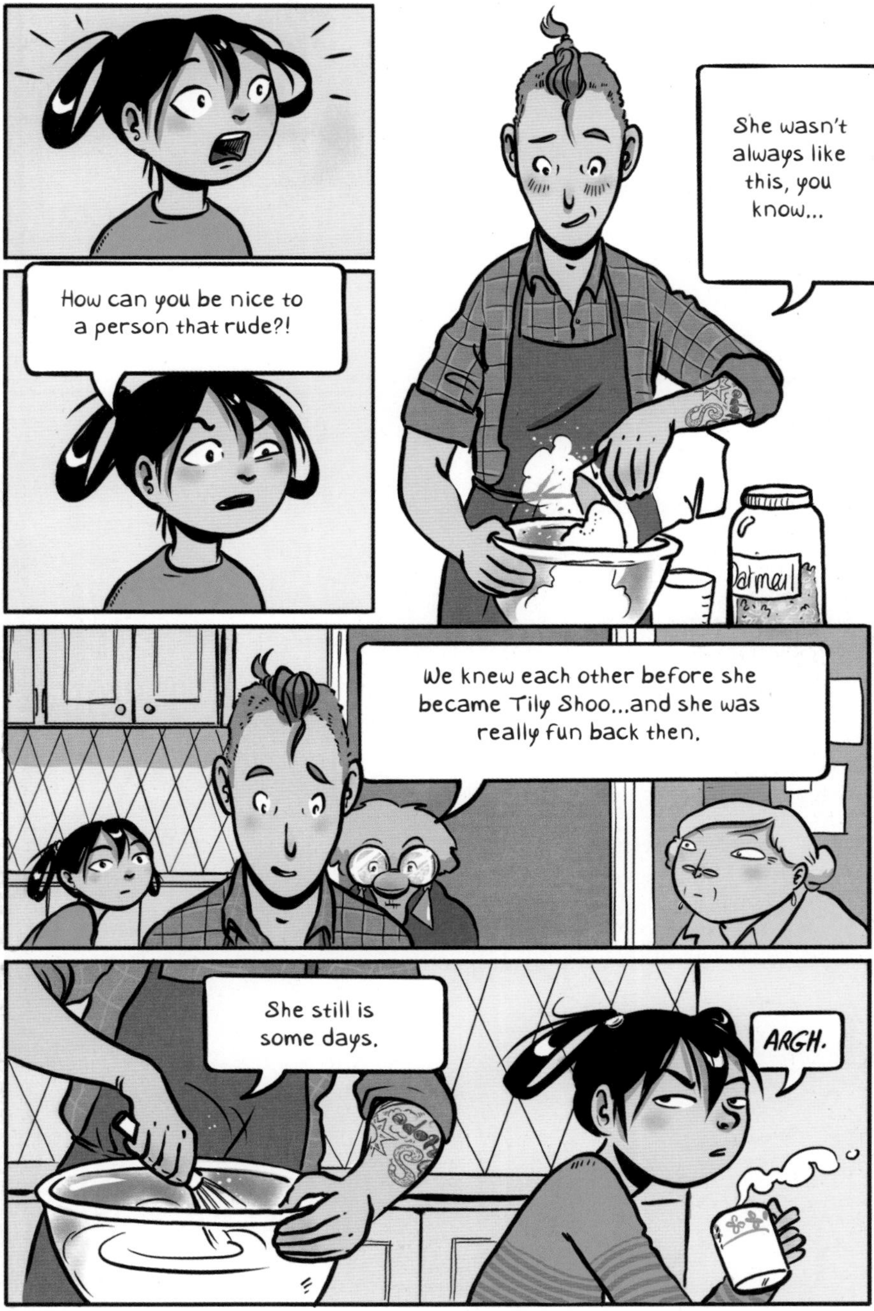
She wasn't always like this, you know...
How can you be nice to a person that rude?!
We knew each other before she became Tily Shoo...and she was really fun back then.
She still is some days.
ARGH.
Oatmeal

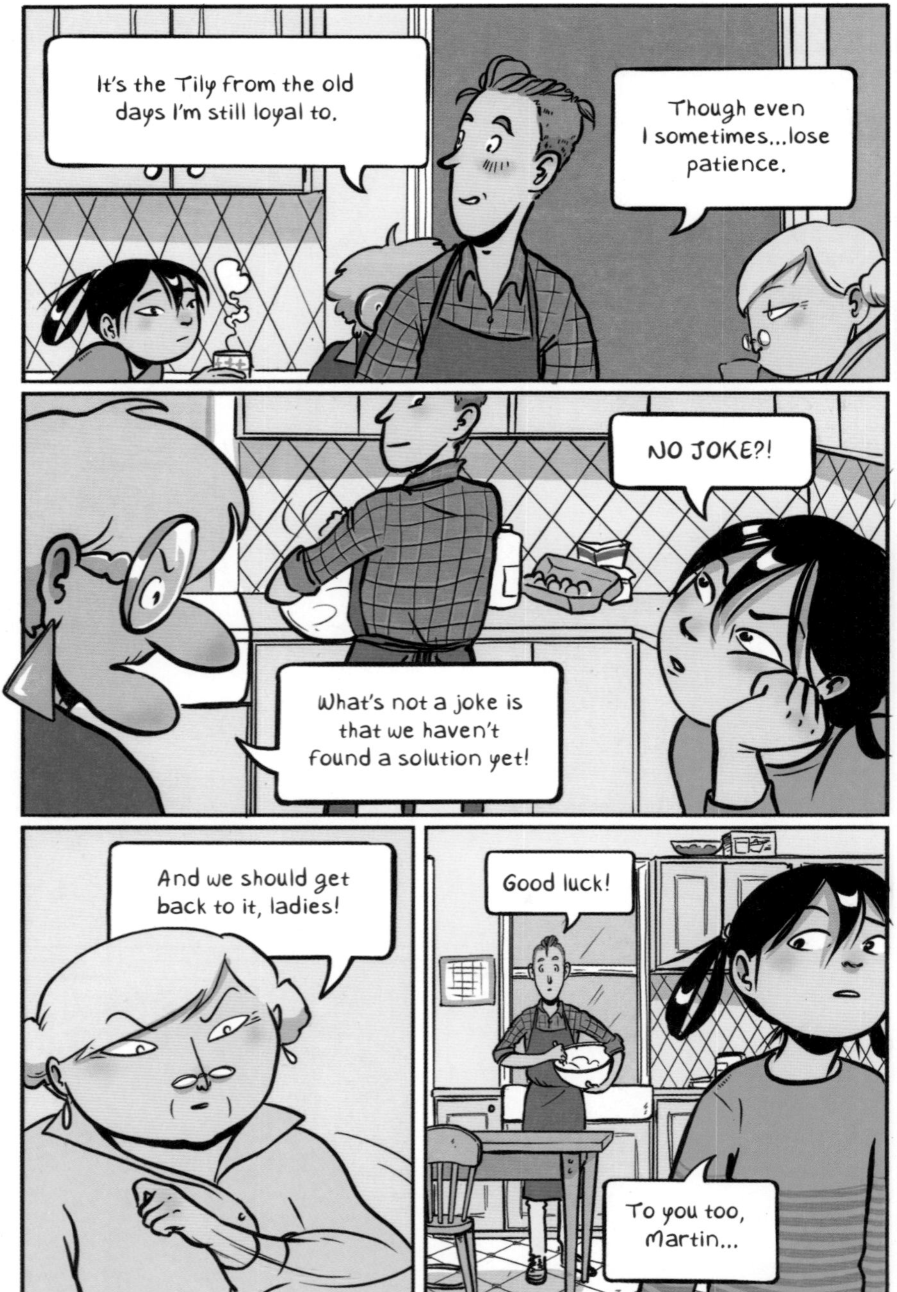
It's the Tily from the old days I'm still loyal to.
Though even I sometimes...lose patience.
NO JOKE?!
What's not a joke is that we haven't found a solution yet!
And we should get back to it, ladies!
Good luck!
To you too, Martin...

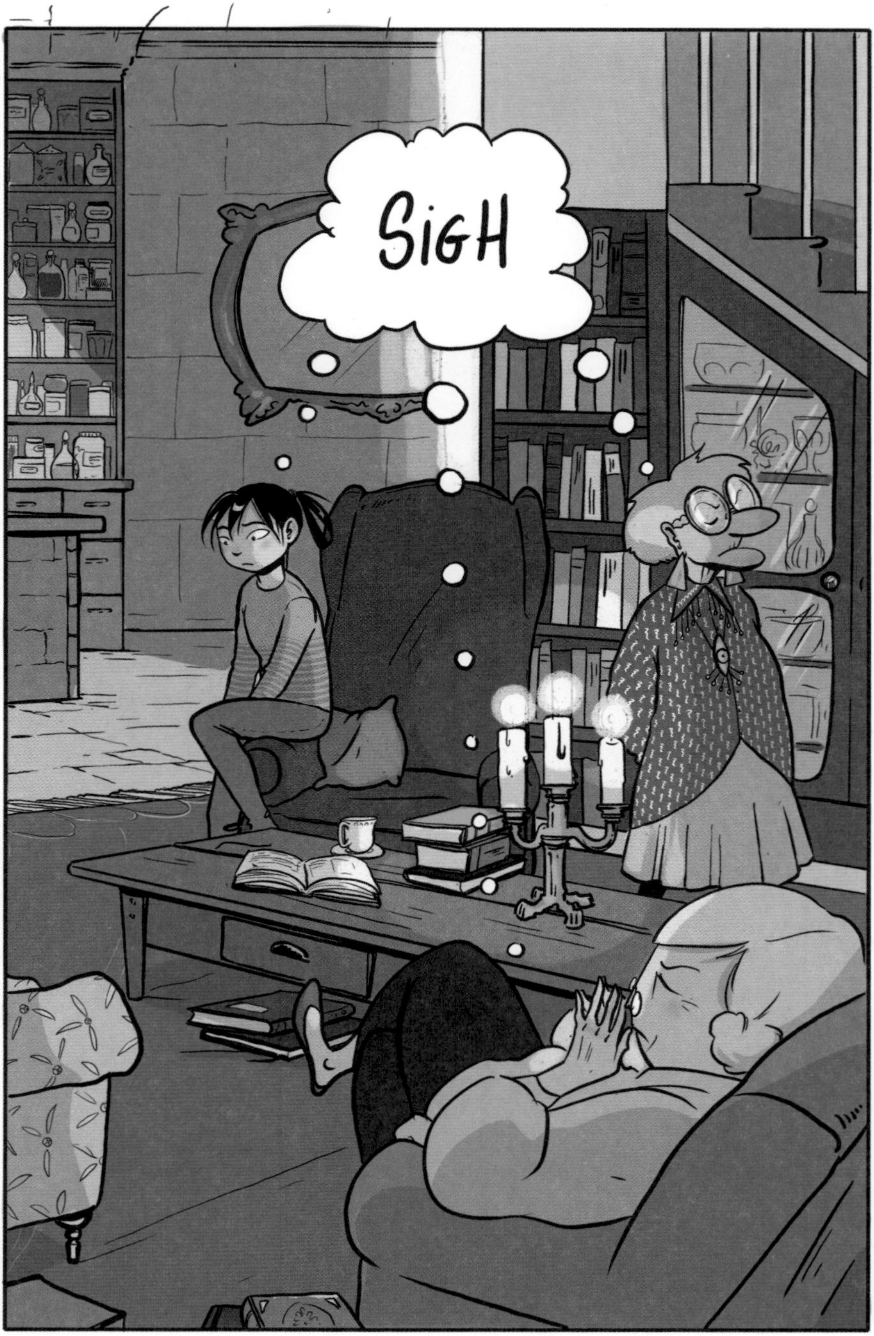
SIGH

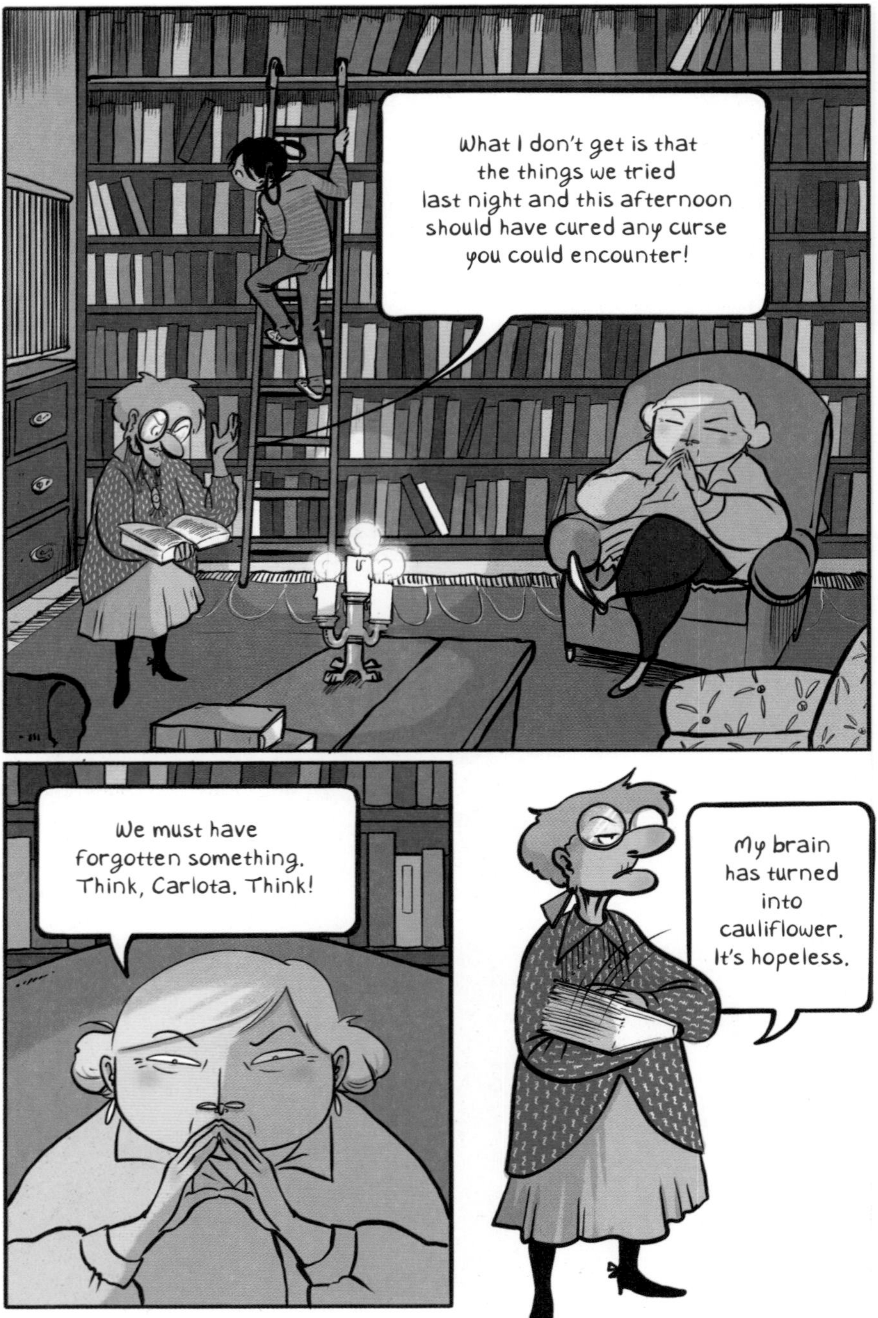
What I don't get is that the things we tried last night and this afternoon should have cured any curse you could encounter!
We must have forgotten something. Think, Carlota. Think!
My brain has turned into cauliflower. It's hopeless.

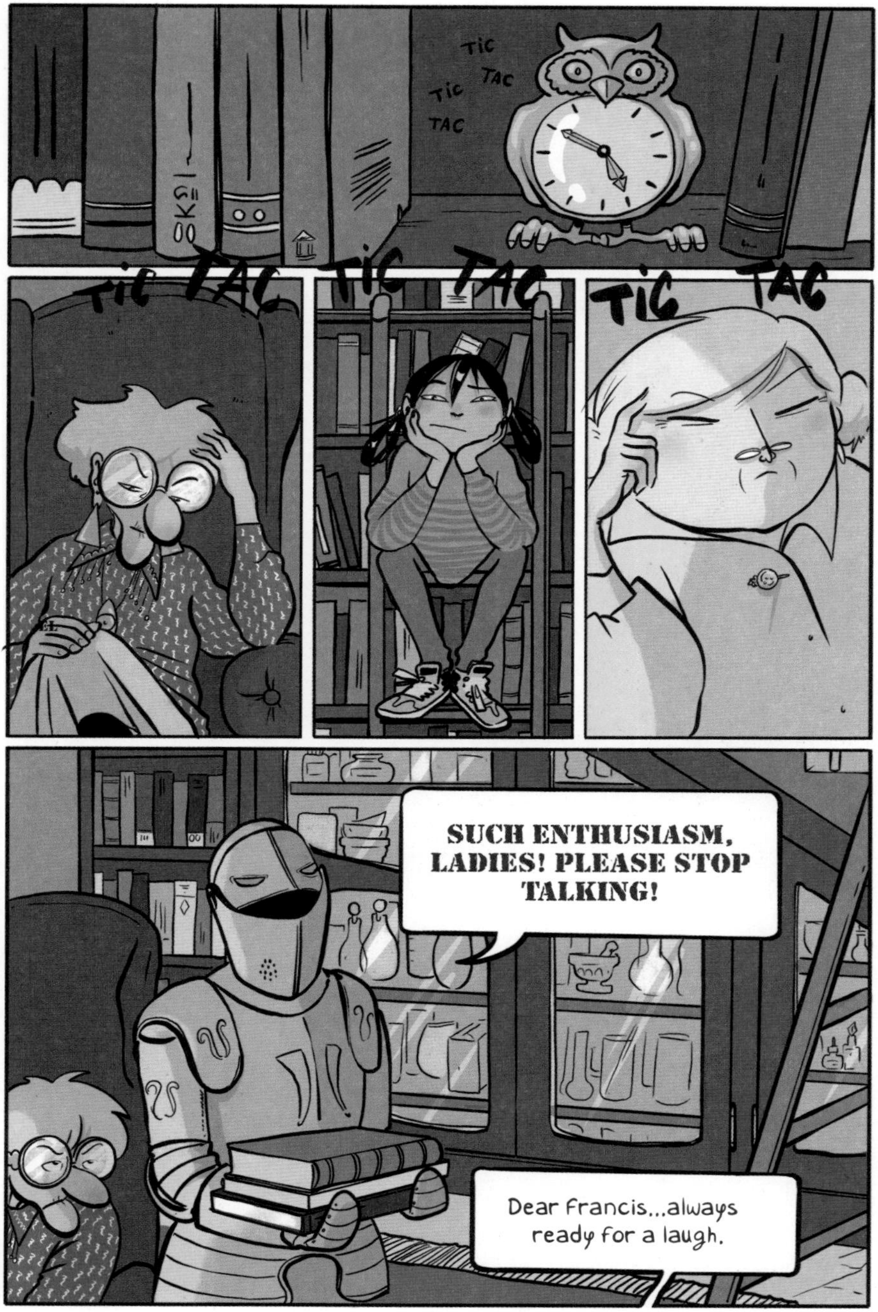
TIC
TAC
TIC
TAC
TIC TAC TIC TAC TIC TAC
SUCH ENTHUSIASM, LADIES! PLEASE STOP TALKING!
Dear Francis...always ready for a laugh.

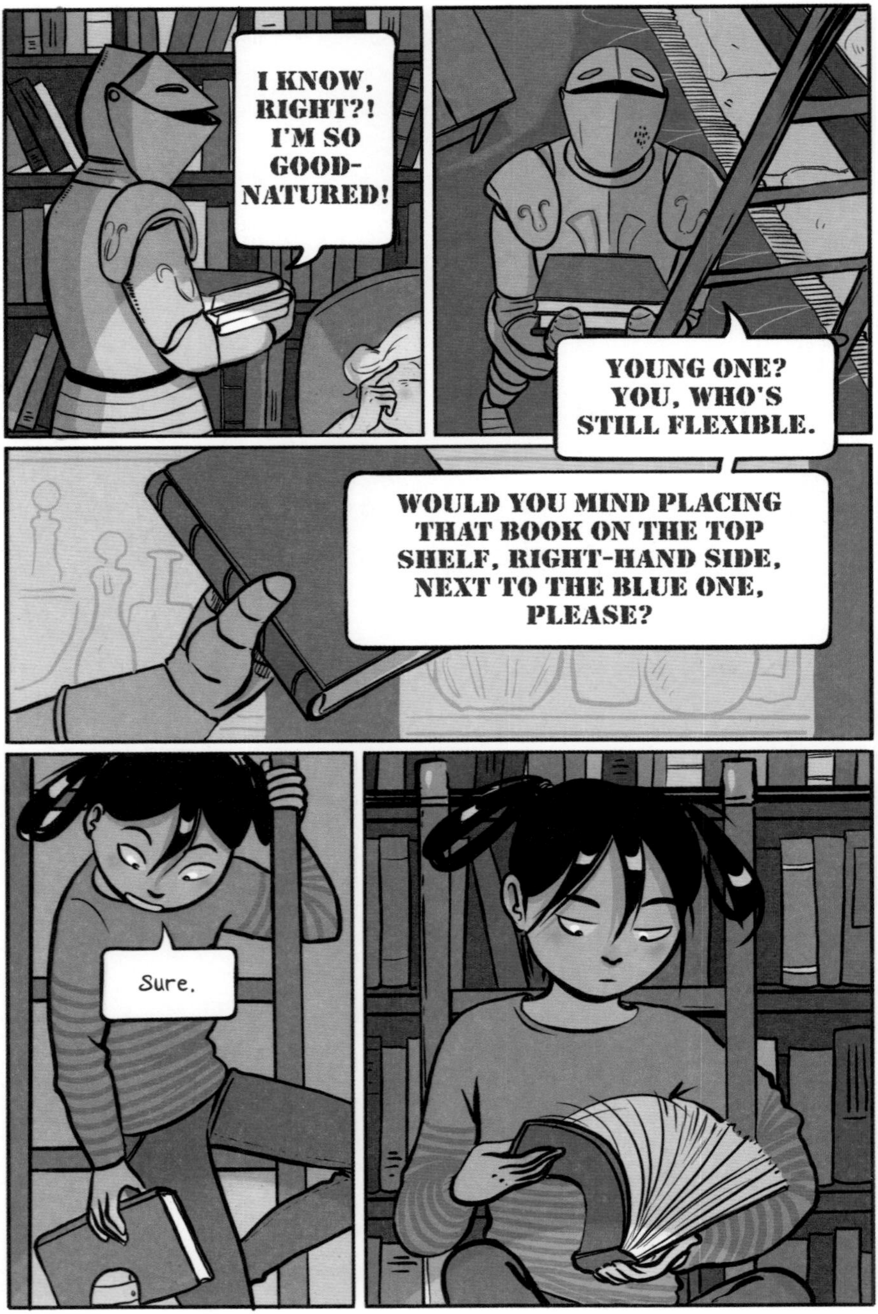
I KNOW, RIGHT?! I'M SO GOOD-NATURED!
YOUNG ONE? YOU, WHO'S STILL FLEXIBLE.
WOULD YOU MIND PLACING THAT BOOK ON THE TOP SHELF, RIGHT-HAND SIDE, NEXT TO THE BLUE ONE, PLEASE?
Sure.

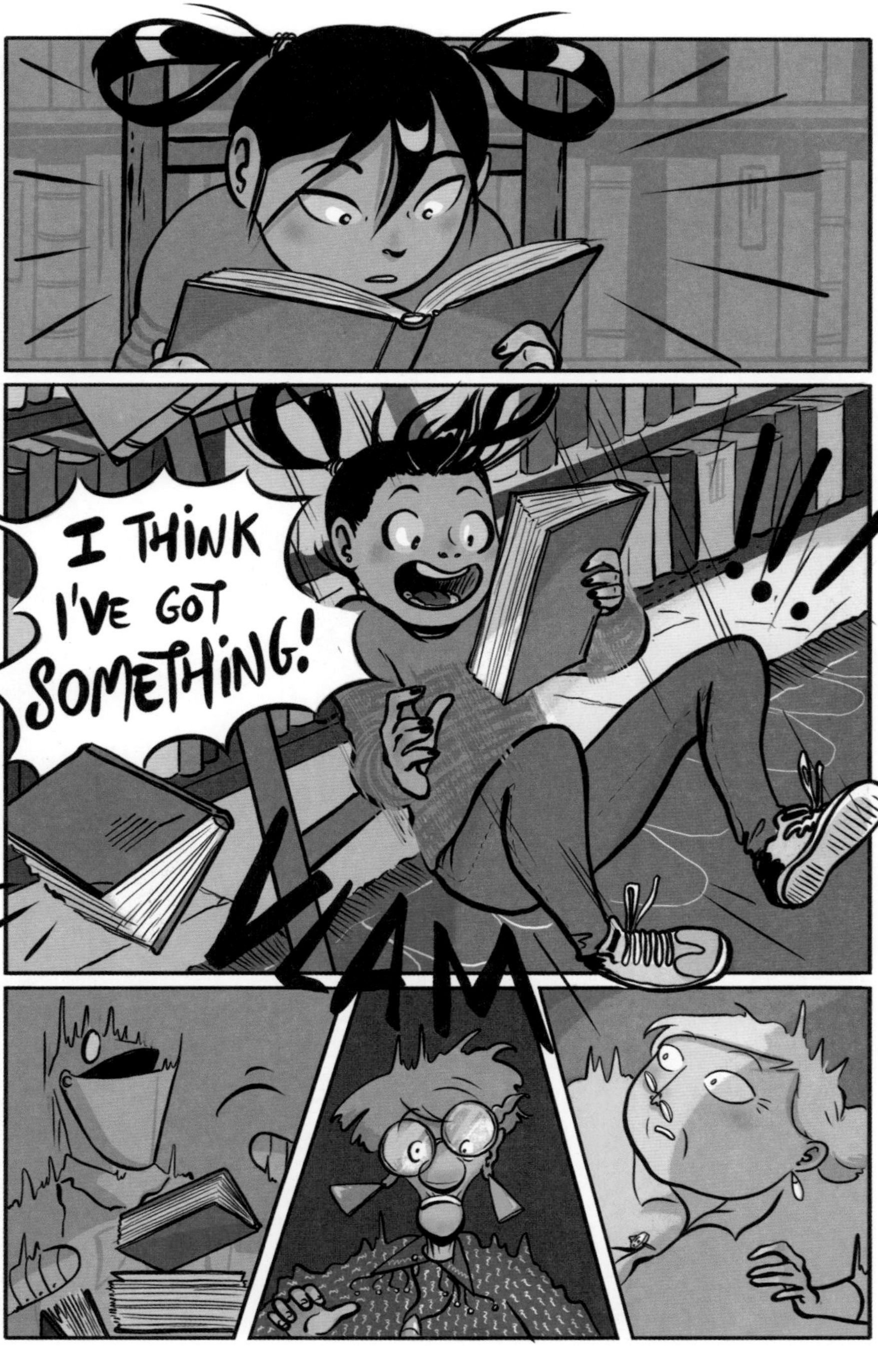
I THINK I'VE GOT SOMETHING!
!!!
WAM

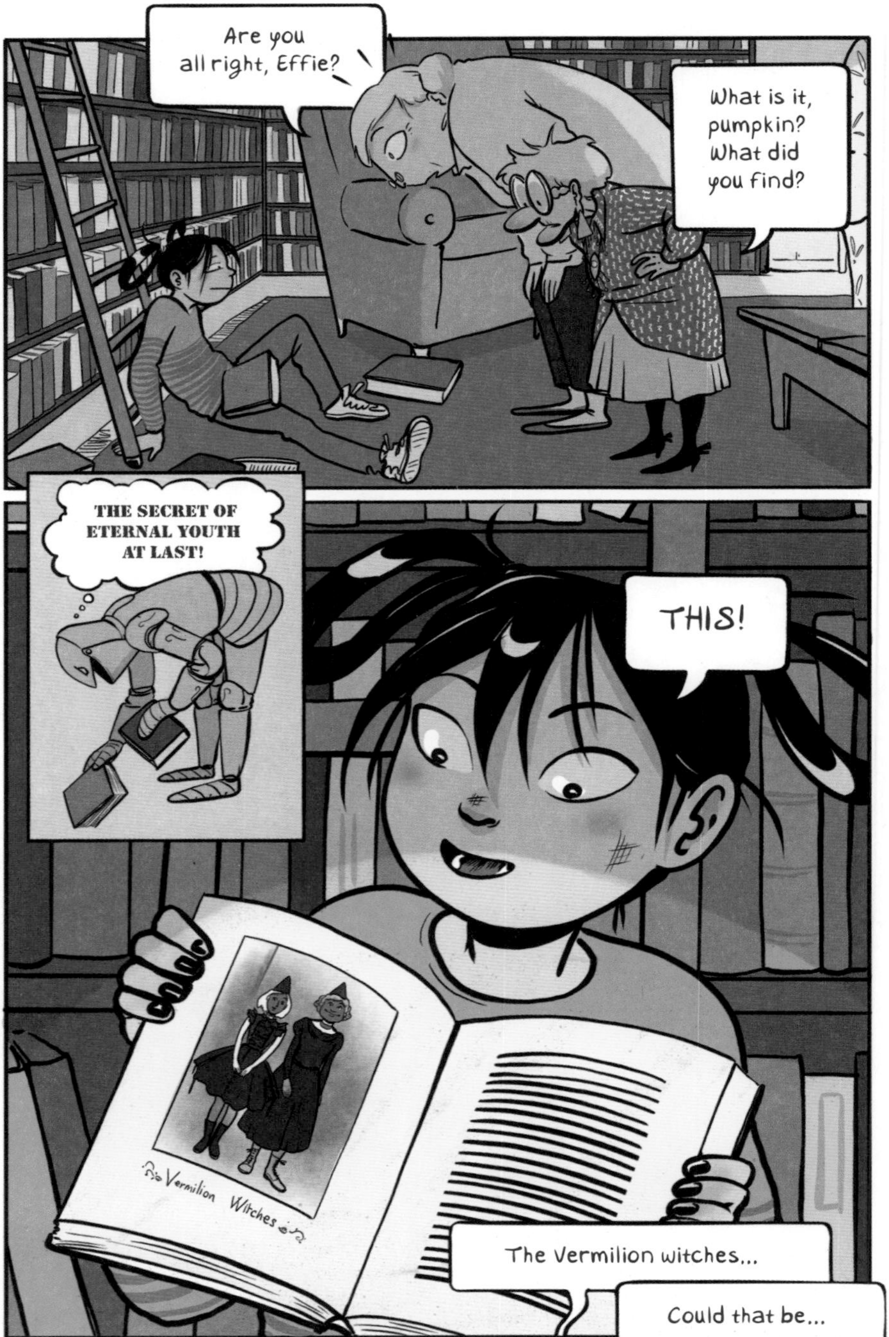
Are you all right, Effie?
What is it, pumpkin? What did you find?
THE SECRET OF ETERNAL YOUTH AT LAST!
THIS!
Vermilion Witches
The Vermilion witches...
Could that be...

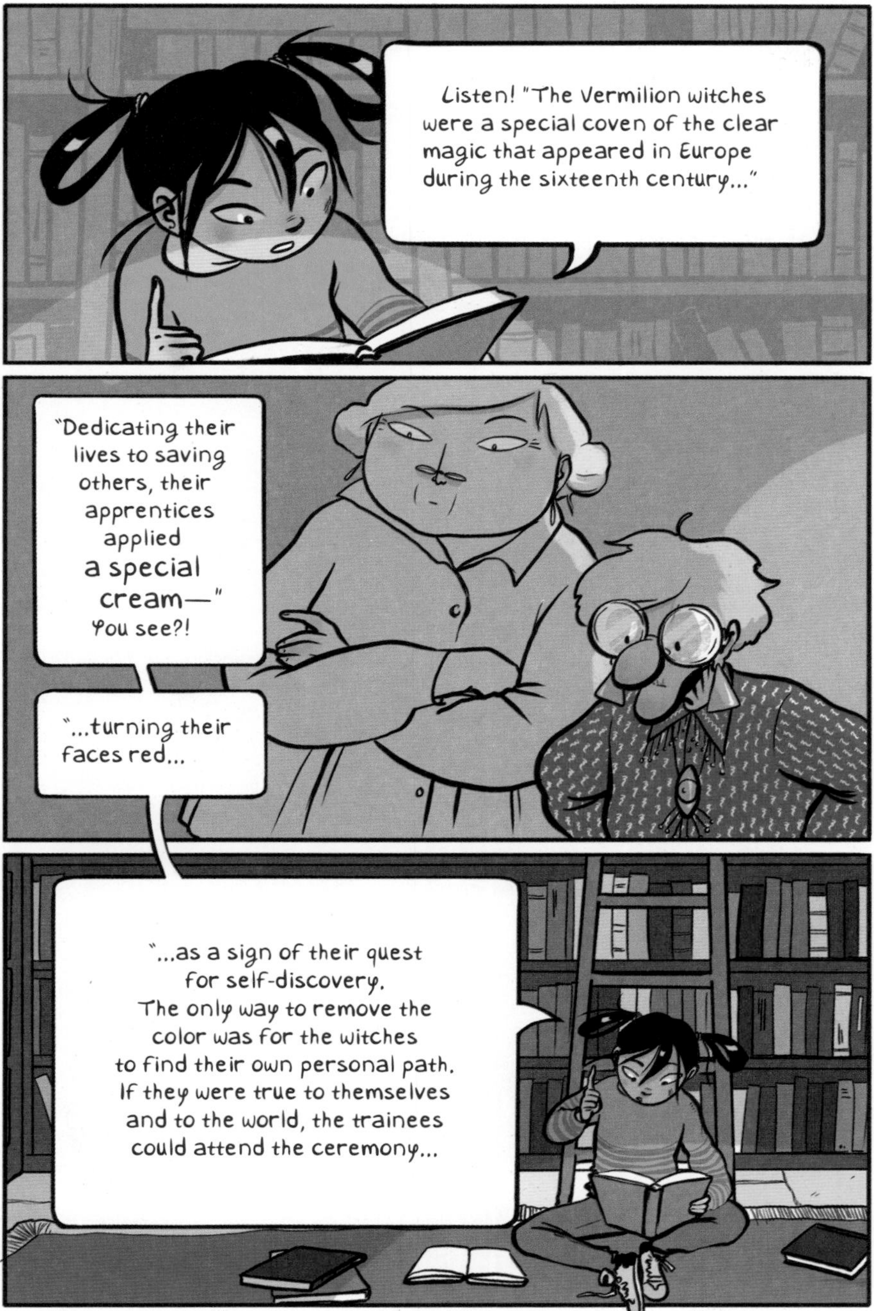
Listen! "The Vermilion witches were a special coven of the clear magic that appeared in Europe during the sixteenth century..."
"Dedicating their lives to saving others, their apprentices applied a special cream—" You see?!
"...turning their faces red...
"...as a sign of their quest for self-discovery. The only way to remove the color was for the witches to find their own personal path. If they were true to themselves and to the world, the trainees could attend the ceremony...

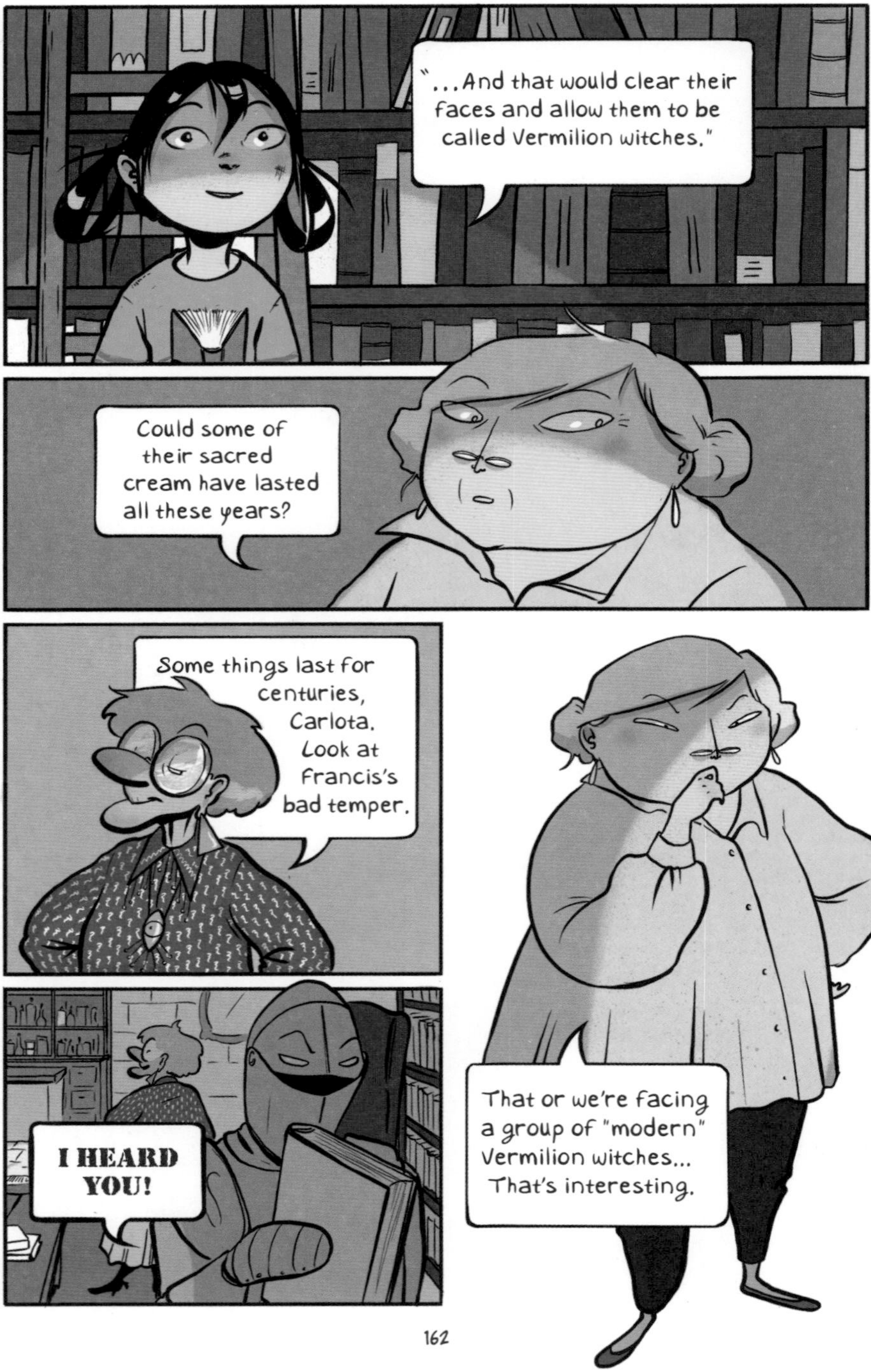
"...And that would clear their faces and allow them to be called Vermilion witches."
Could some of their sacred cream have lasted all these years?
Some things last for centuries, Carlota. Look at Francis's bad temper.
I HEARD YOU!
That or we're facing a group of "modern" Vermilion witches... That's interesting.

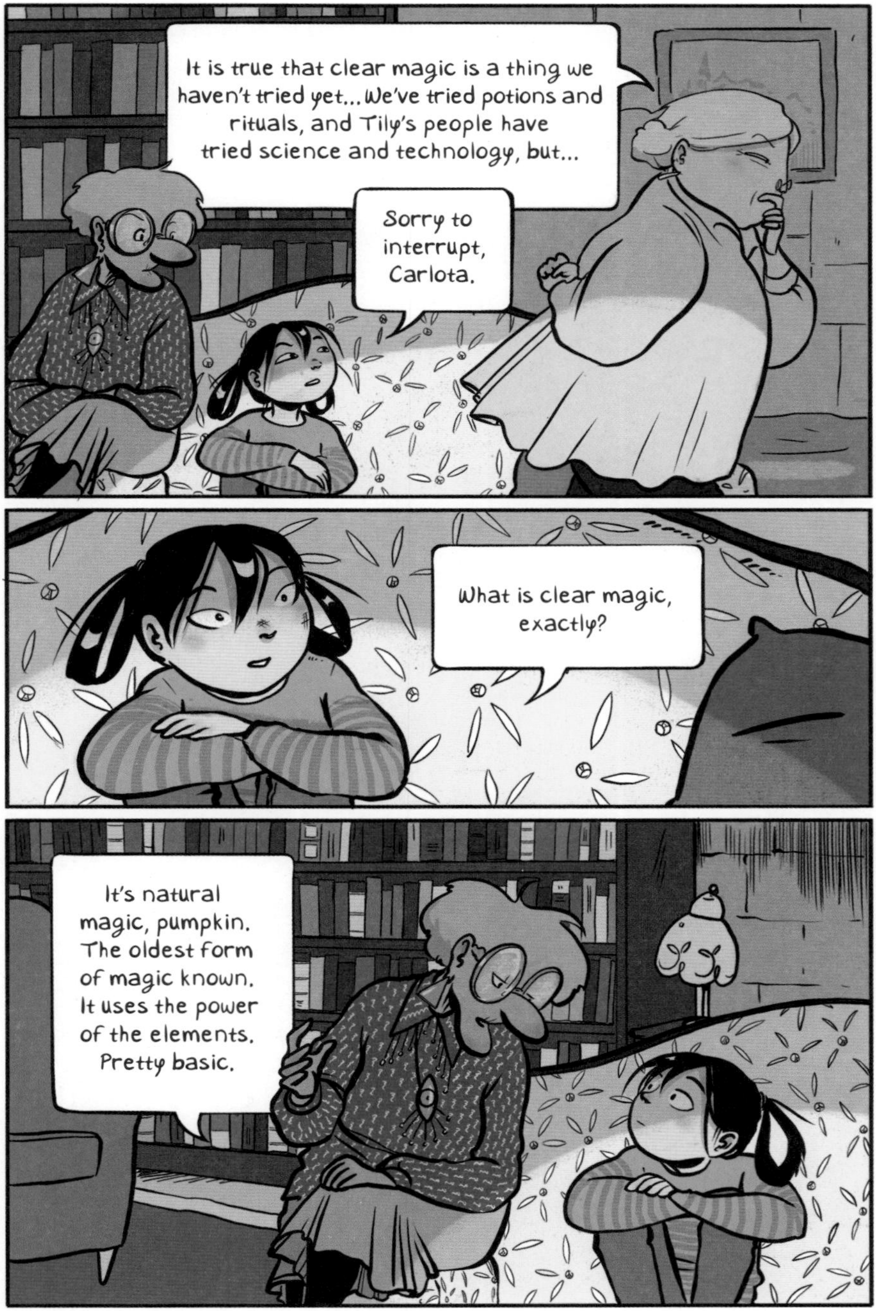
It is true that clear magic is a thing we haven't tried yet... We've tried potions and rituals, and Tily's people have tried science and technology, but...
Sorry to interrupt, Carlota.
What is clear magic, exactly?
It's natural magic, pumpkin. The oldest form of magic known. It uses the power of the elements. Pretty basic.

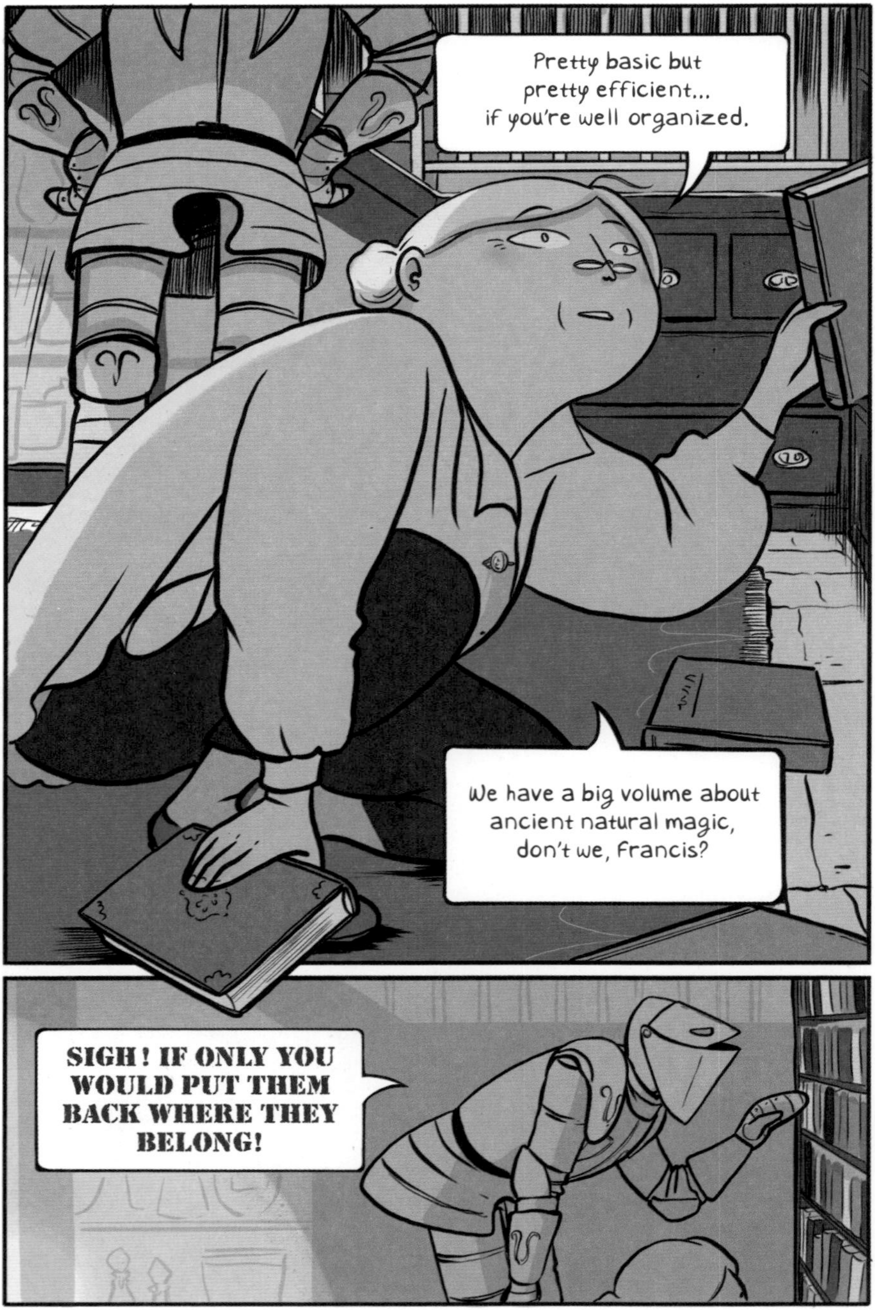
Pretty basic but pretty efficient... if you're well organized.
We have a big volume about ancient natural magic, don't we, Francis?
SIGH! IF ONLY YOU WOULD PUT THEM BACK WHERE THEY BELONG!

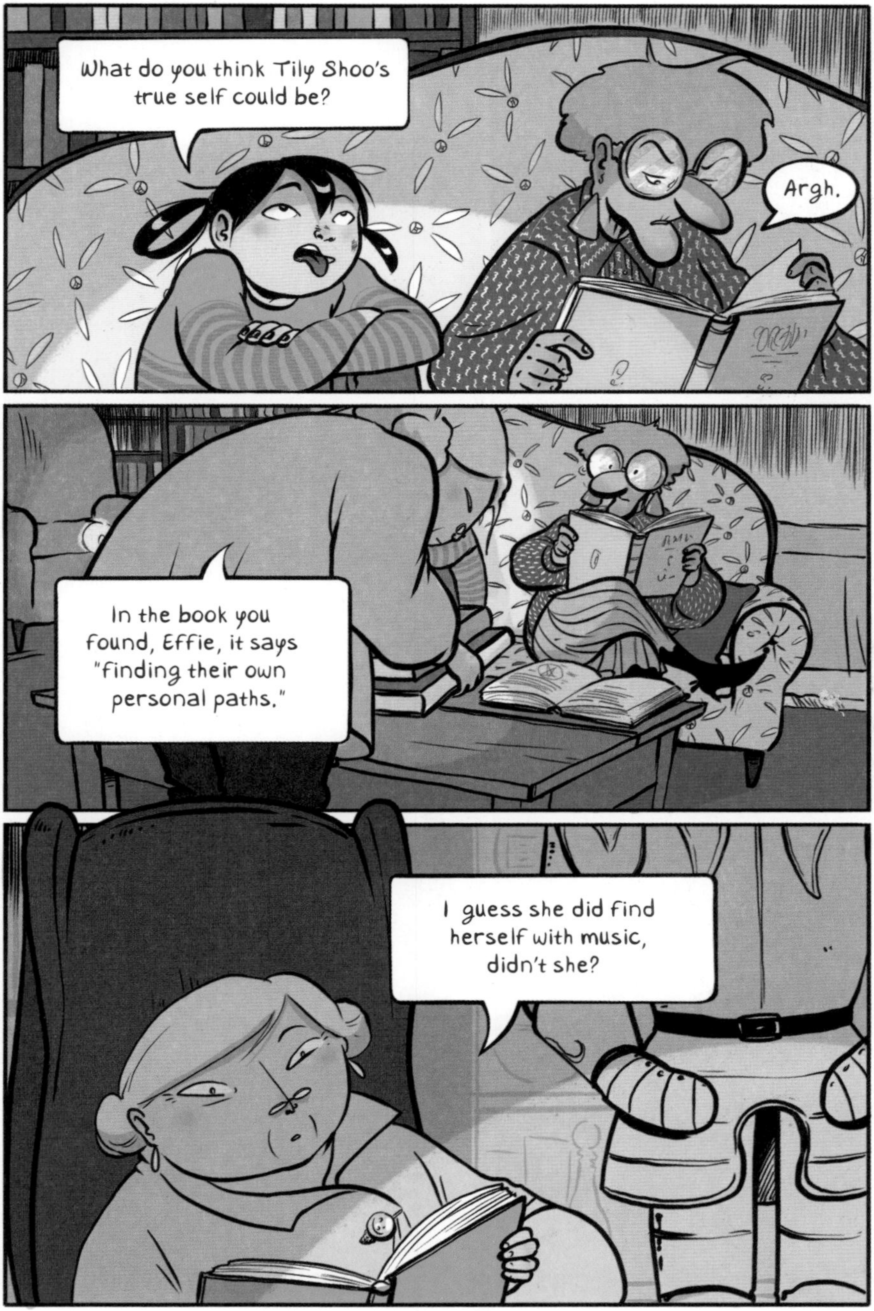
What do you think Tily Shoo's true self could be?
Argh.
In the book you found, Effie, it says "finding their own personal paths."
I guess she did find herself with music, didn't she?

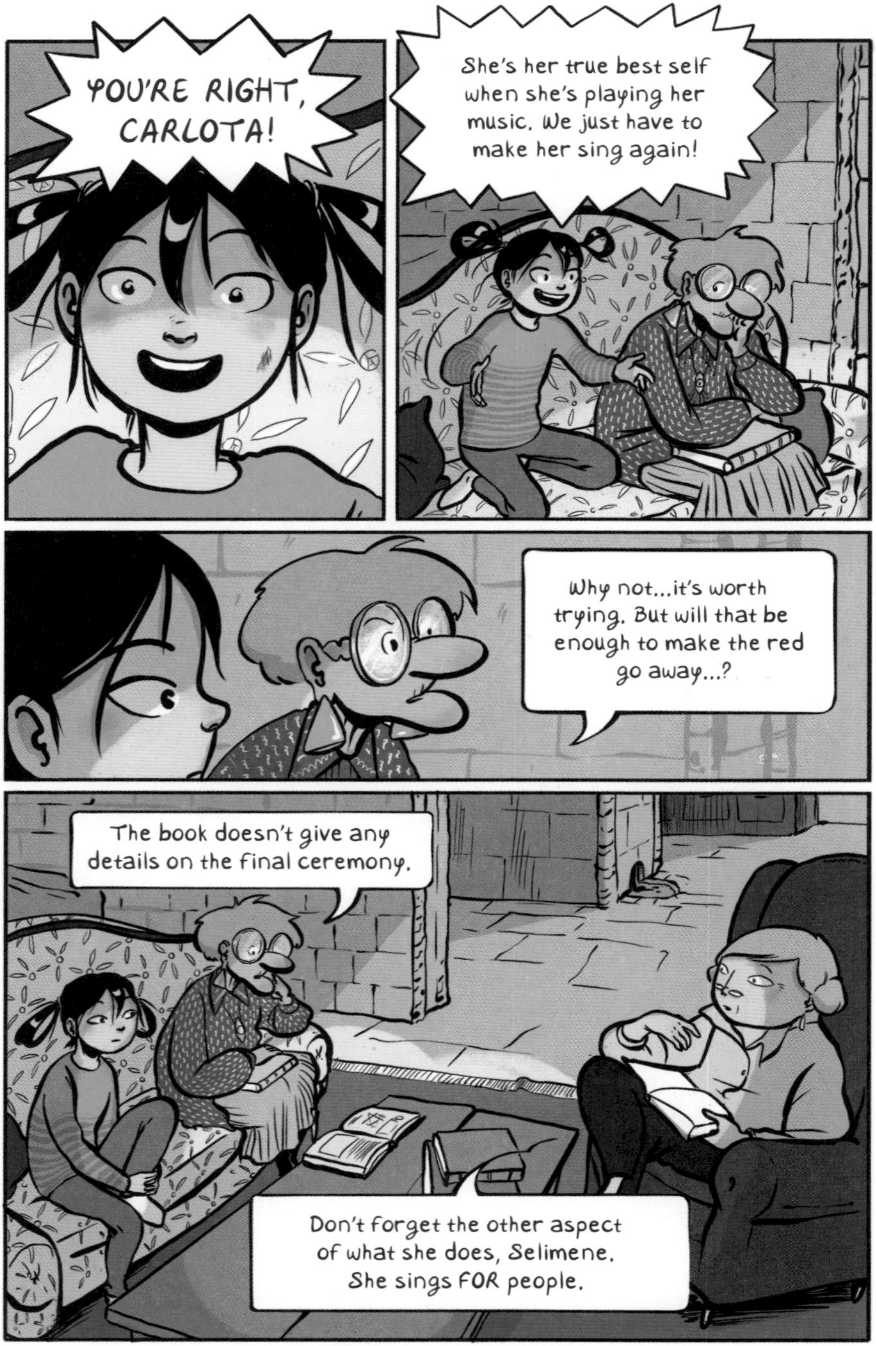
YOU'RE RIGHT, CARLOTA!
She's her true best self when she's playing her music. We just have to make her sing again!
Why not...it's worth trying. But will that be enough to make the red go away...?
The book doesn't give any details on the final ceremony.
Don't forget the other aspect of what she does, Selimene. She sings FOR people.

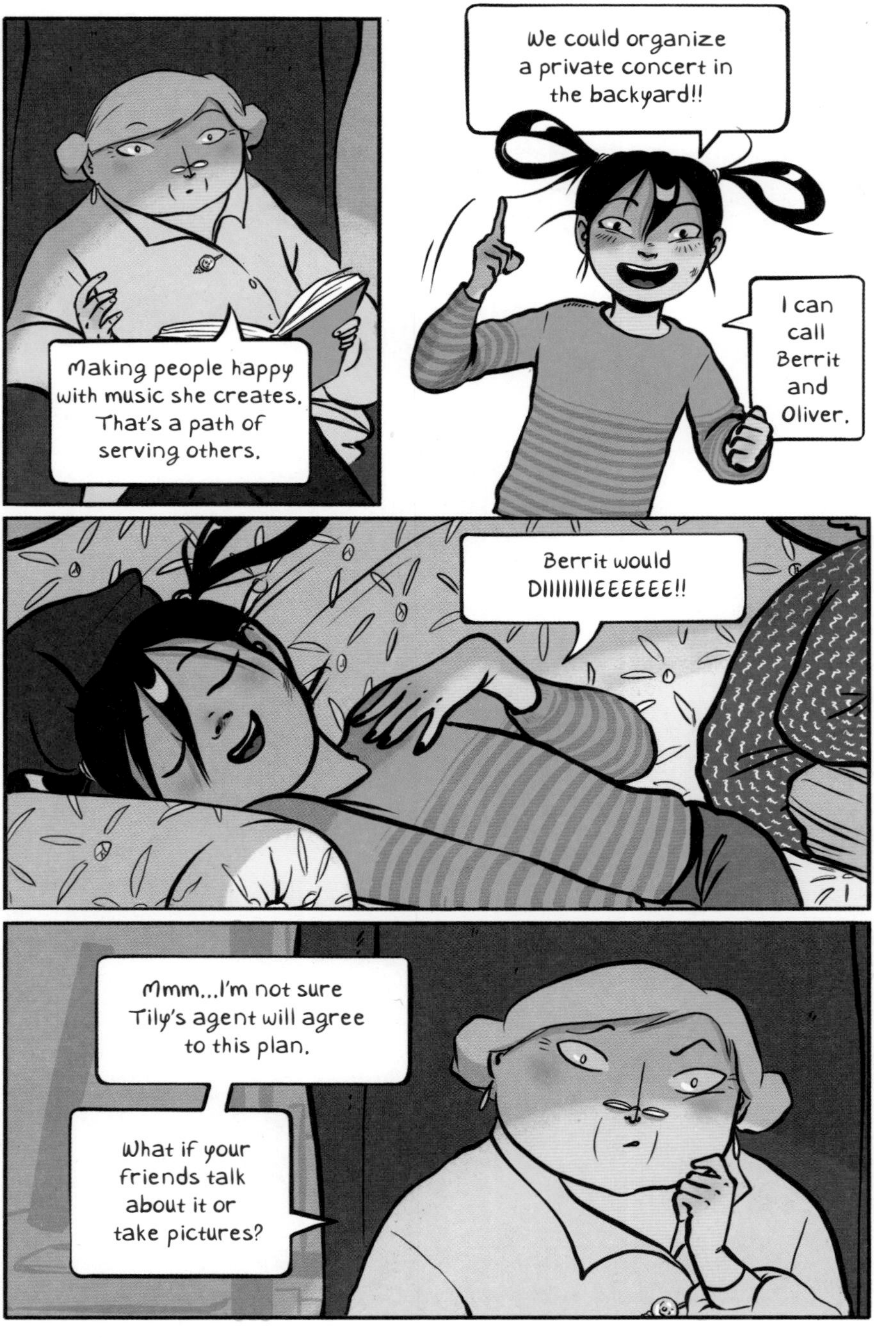
Making people happy with music she creates. That's a path of serving others.
We could organize a private concert in the backyard!!
I can call Berrit and Oliver.
Berrit would DIIIIIIIEEEEEE!!
Mmm...I'm not sure Tily's agent will agree to this plan.
What if your friends talk about it or take pictures?

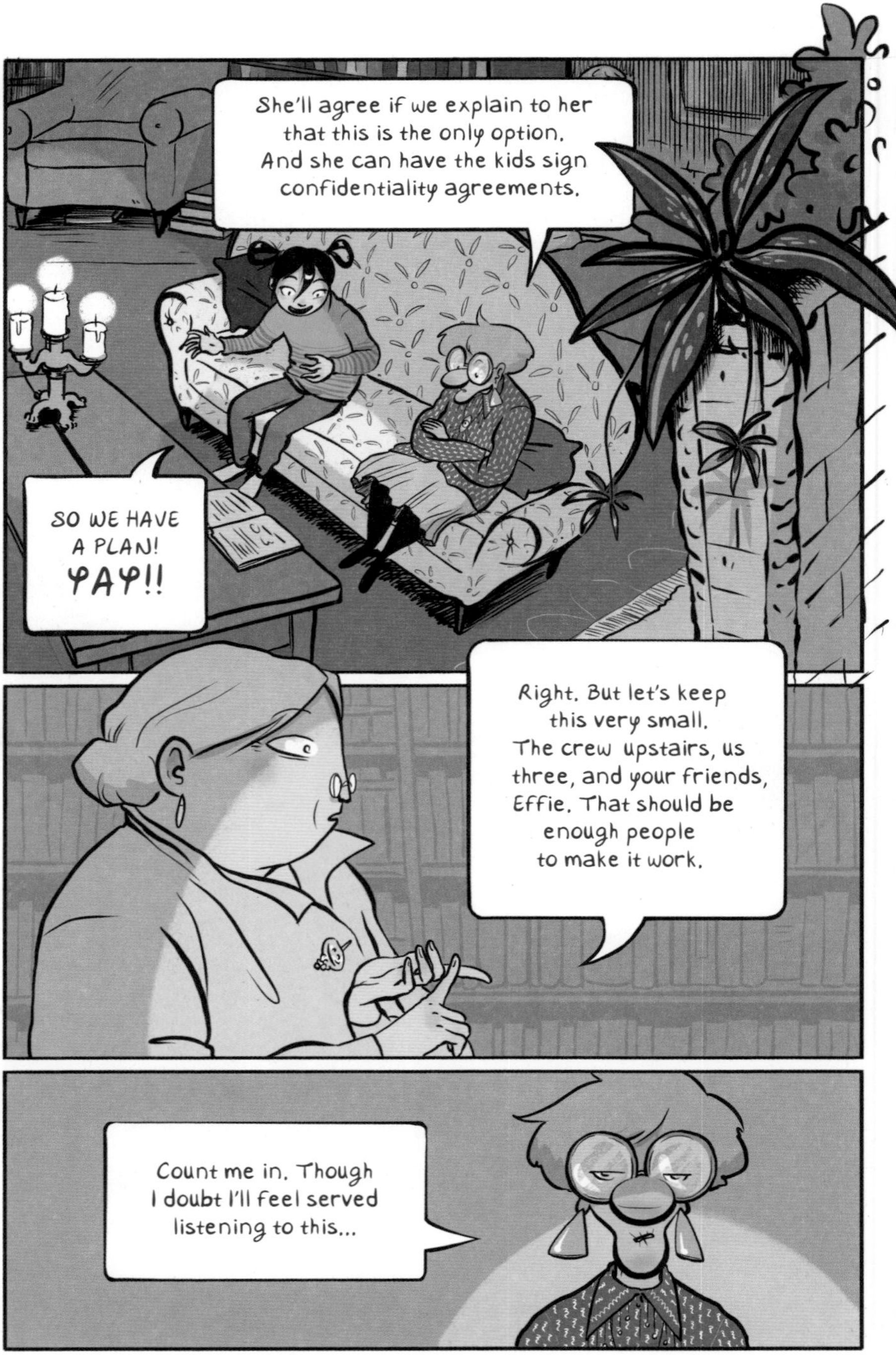

She'll agree if we explain to her that this is the only option. And she can have the kids sign confidentiality agreements.
SO WE HAVE A PLAN! YAY!!
Right. But let's keep this very small. The crew upstairs, us three, and your friends, Effie. That should be enough people to make it work.
Count me in. Though I doubt I'll feel served listening to this...

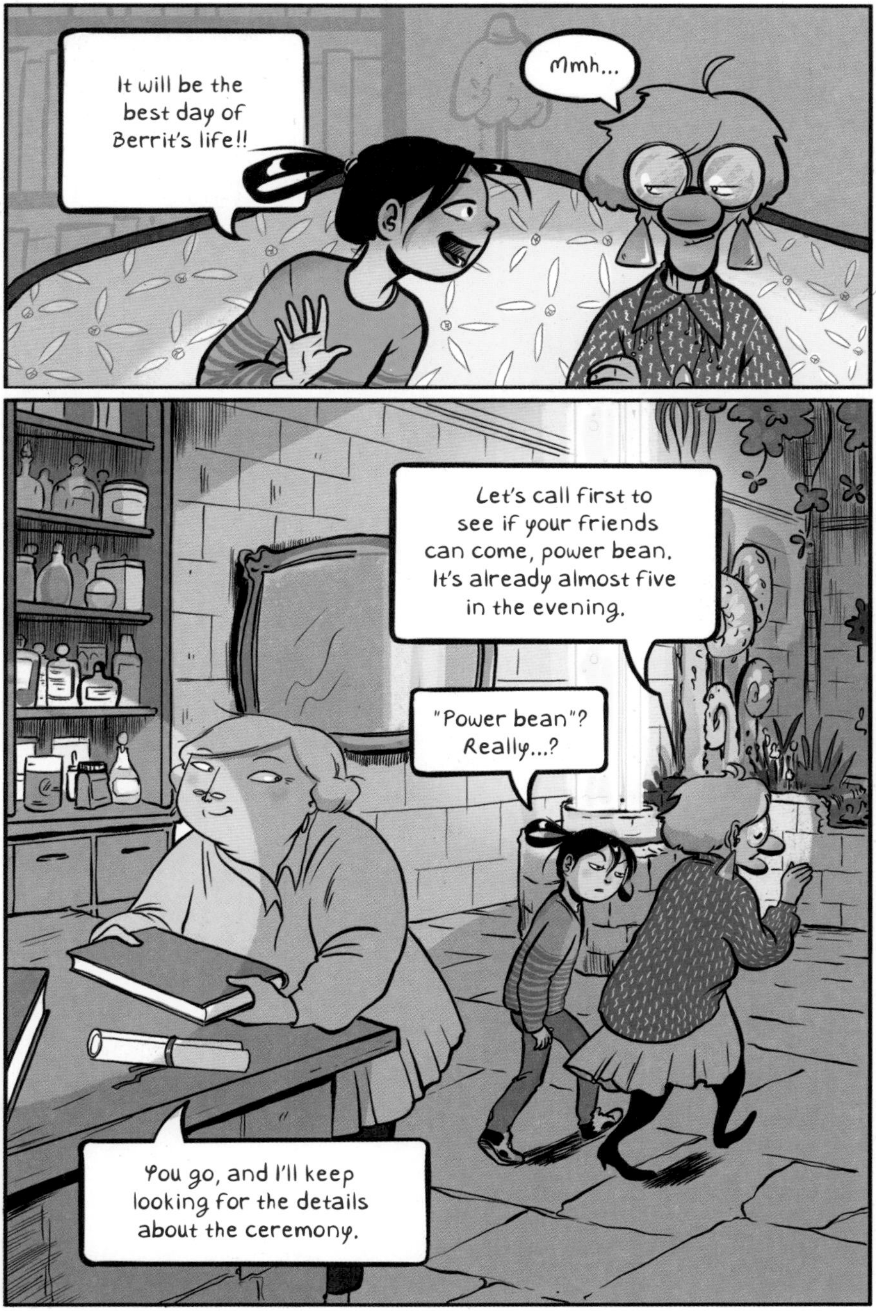
It will be the best day of Berrit's life!!
Mmh...
Let's call first to see if your friends can come, power bean. It's already almost five in the evening.
"Power bean"? Really...?
You go, and I'll keep looking for the details about the ceremony.

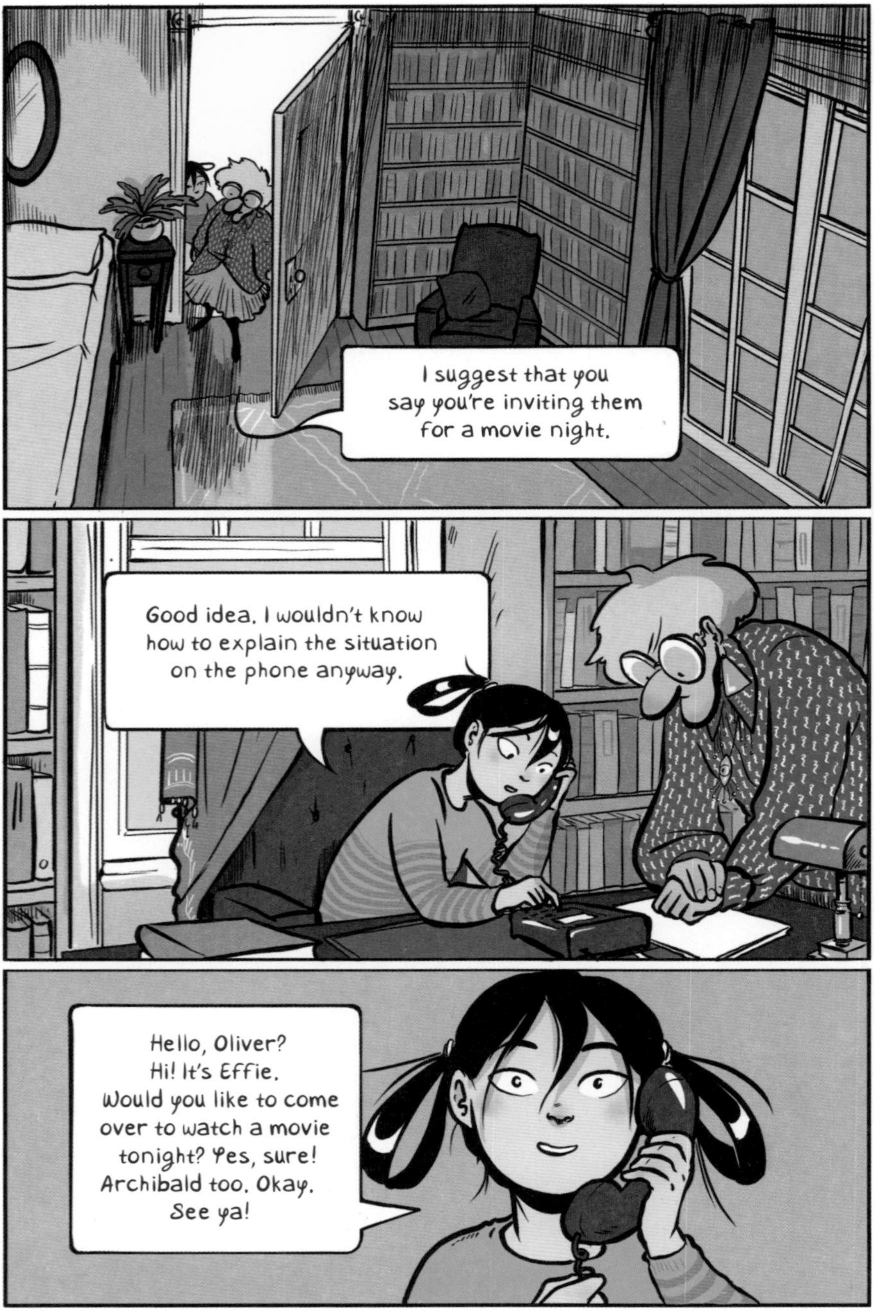
I suggest that you say you're inviting them for a movie night.
Good idea. I wouldn't know how to explain the situation on the phone anyway.
Hello, Oliver? Hi! It's Effie. Would you like to come over to watch a movie tonight? Yes, sure! Archibald too. Okay. See ya!

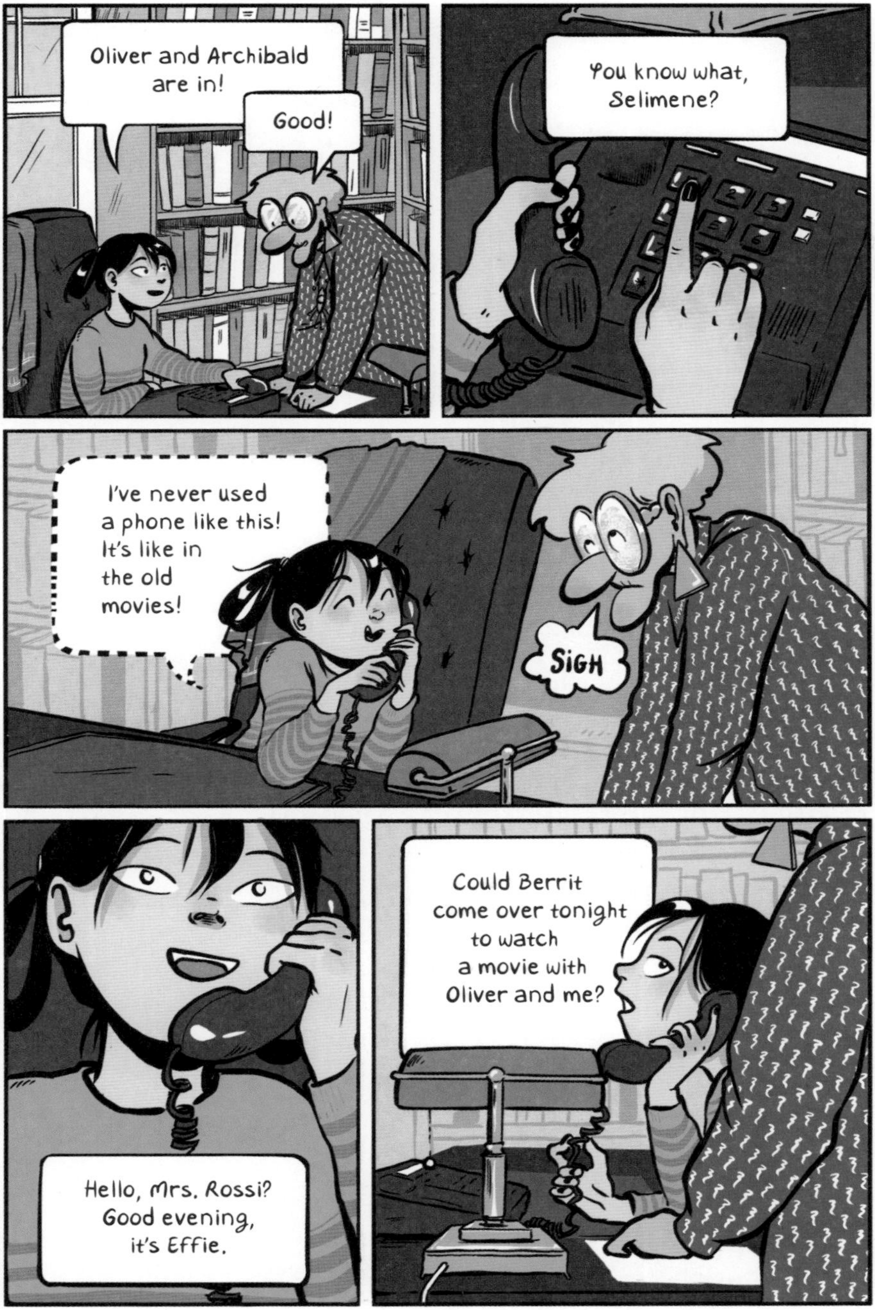
Oliver and Archibald are in!
Good!
You know what, Selimene?
I've never used a phone like this! It's like in the old movies!
SIGH
Hello, Mrs. Rossi? Good evening, it's Effie.
Could Berrit come over tonight to watch a movie with Oliver and me?

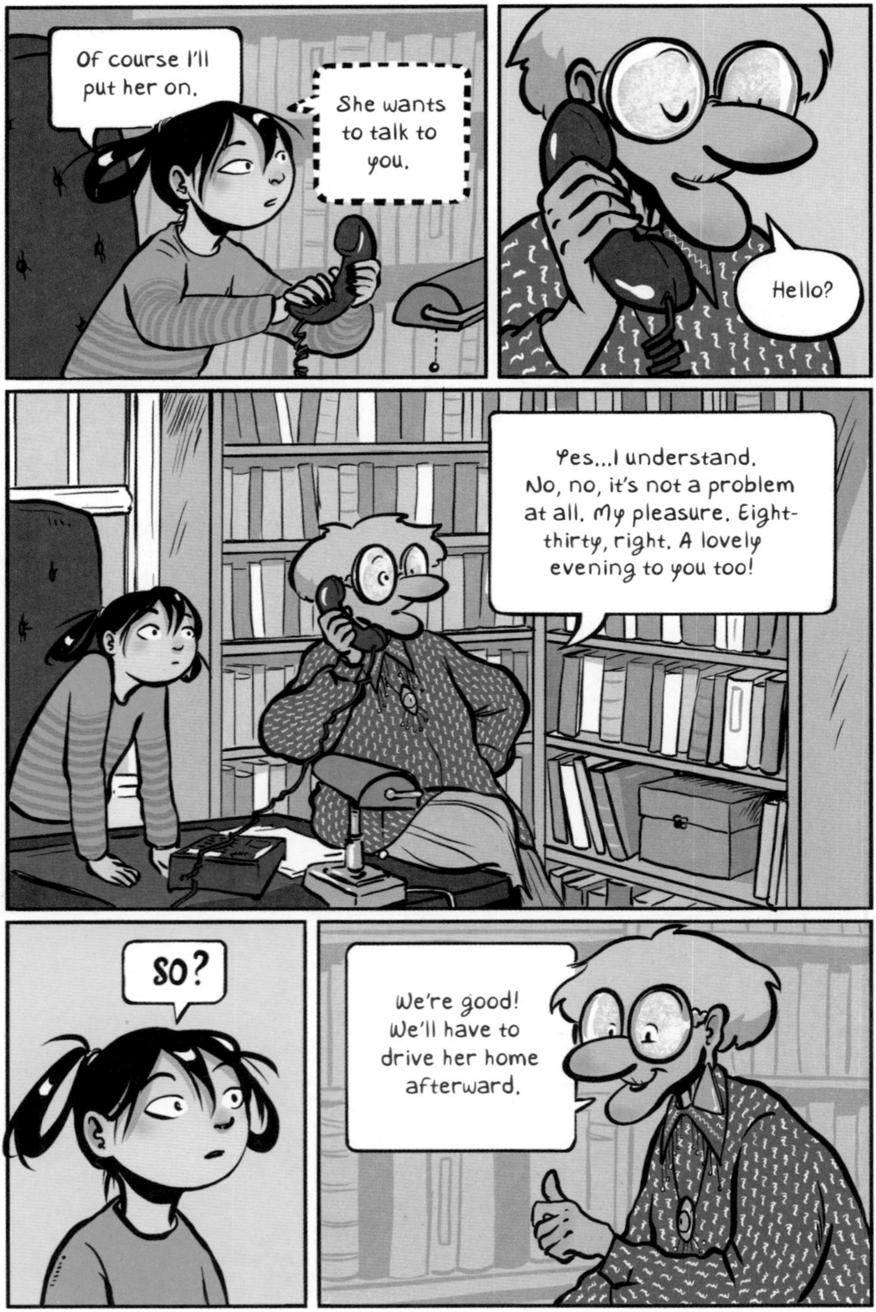
Of course I'll put her on.
She wants to talk to you.
Hello?
Yes...I understand. No, no, it's not a problem at all. My pleasure. Eight-thirty, right. A lovely evening to you too!
SO?
We're good! We'll have to drive her home afterward.

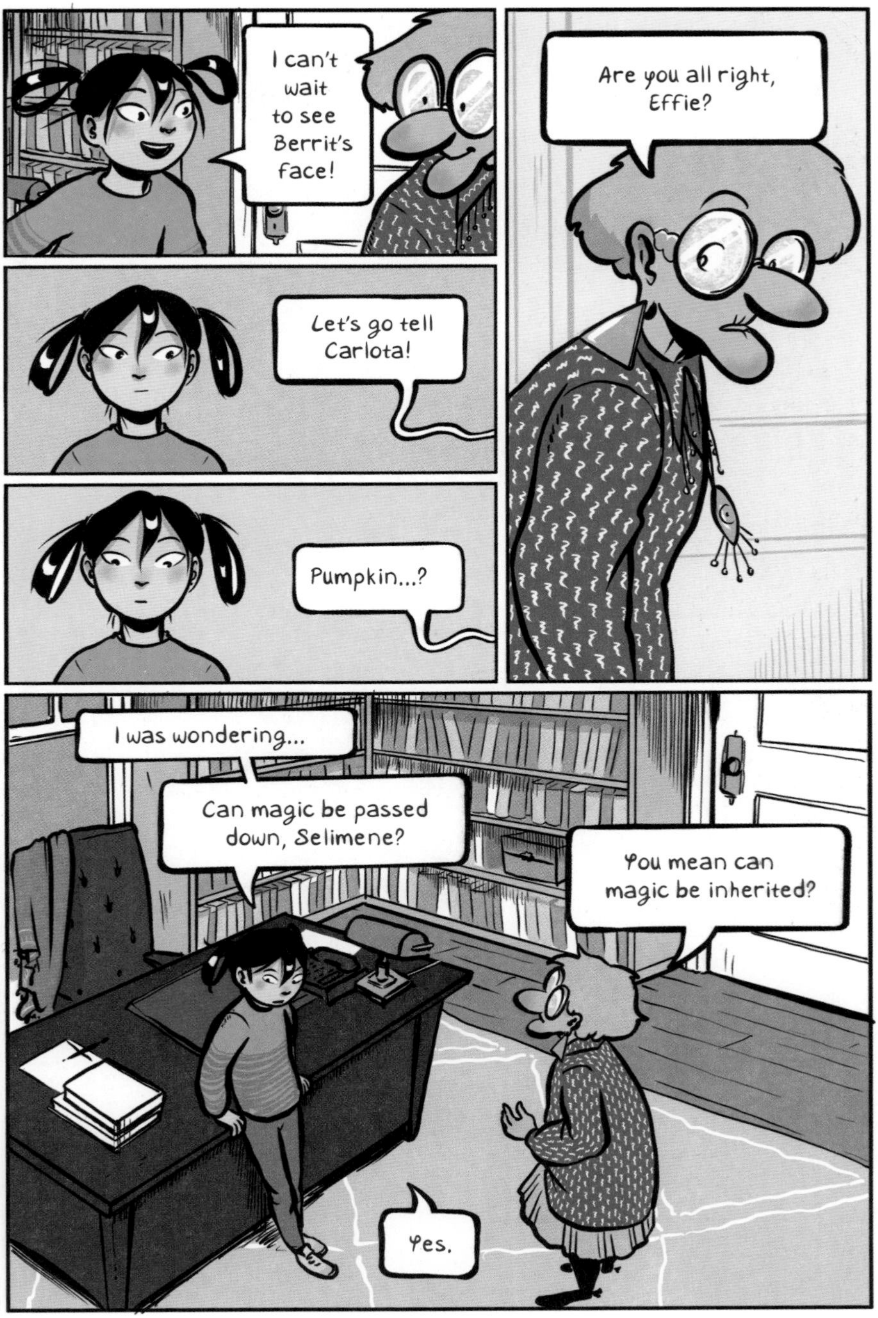
I can't wait to see Berrit's face!
Are you all right, Effie?
Let's go tell Carlota!
Pumpkin...?
I was wondering...
Can magic be passed down, Selimene?
You mean can magic be inherited?
Yes.

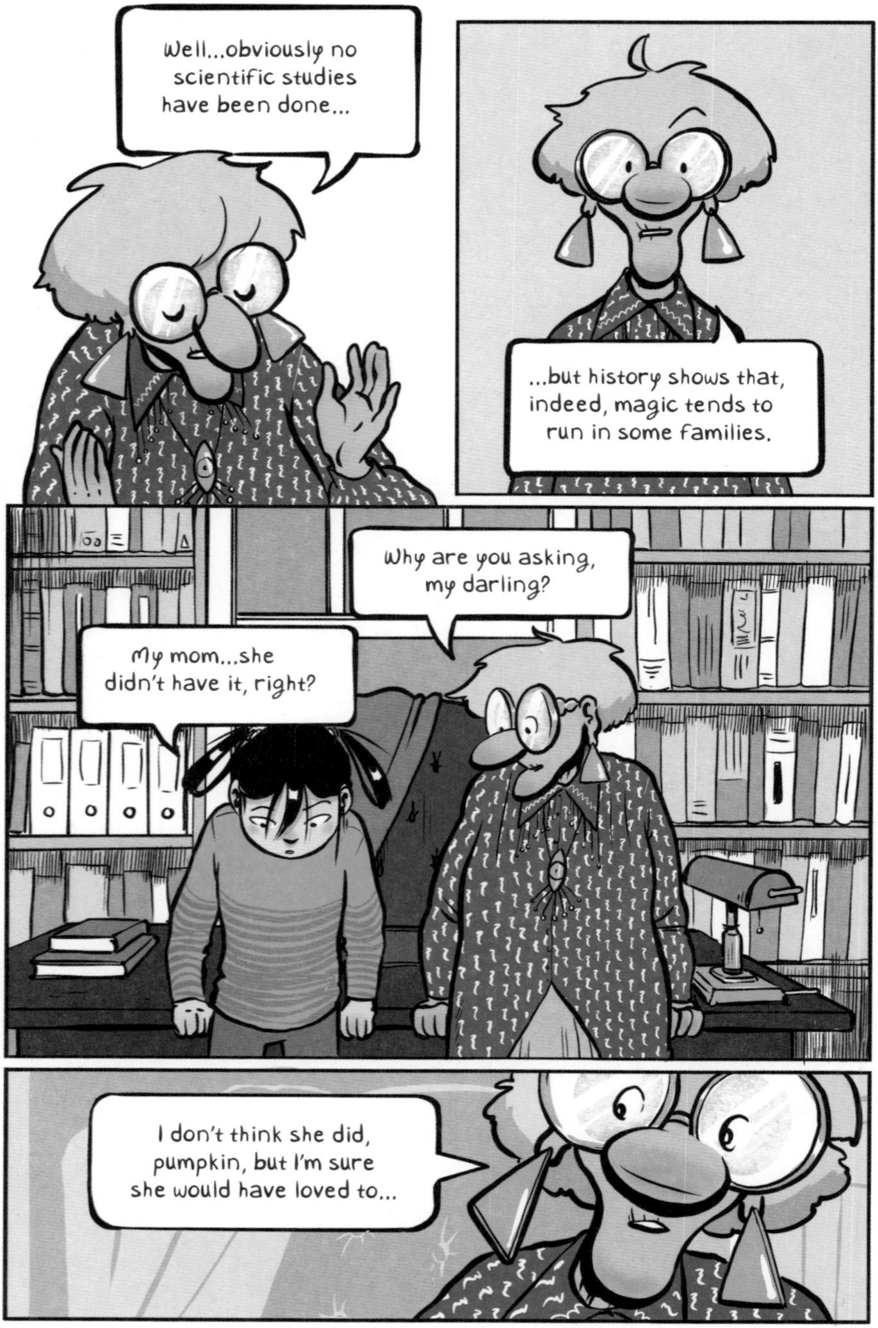
Well...obviously no scientific studies have been done...
...but history shows that, indeed, magic tends to run in some families.
Why are you asking, my darling?
My mom...she didn't have it, right?
I don't think she did, pumpkin, but I'm sure she would have loved to...

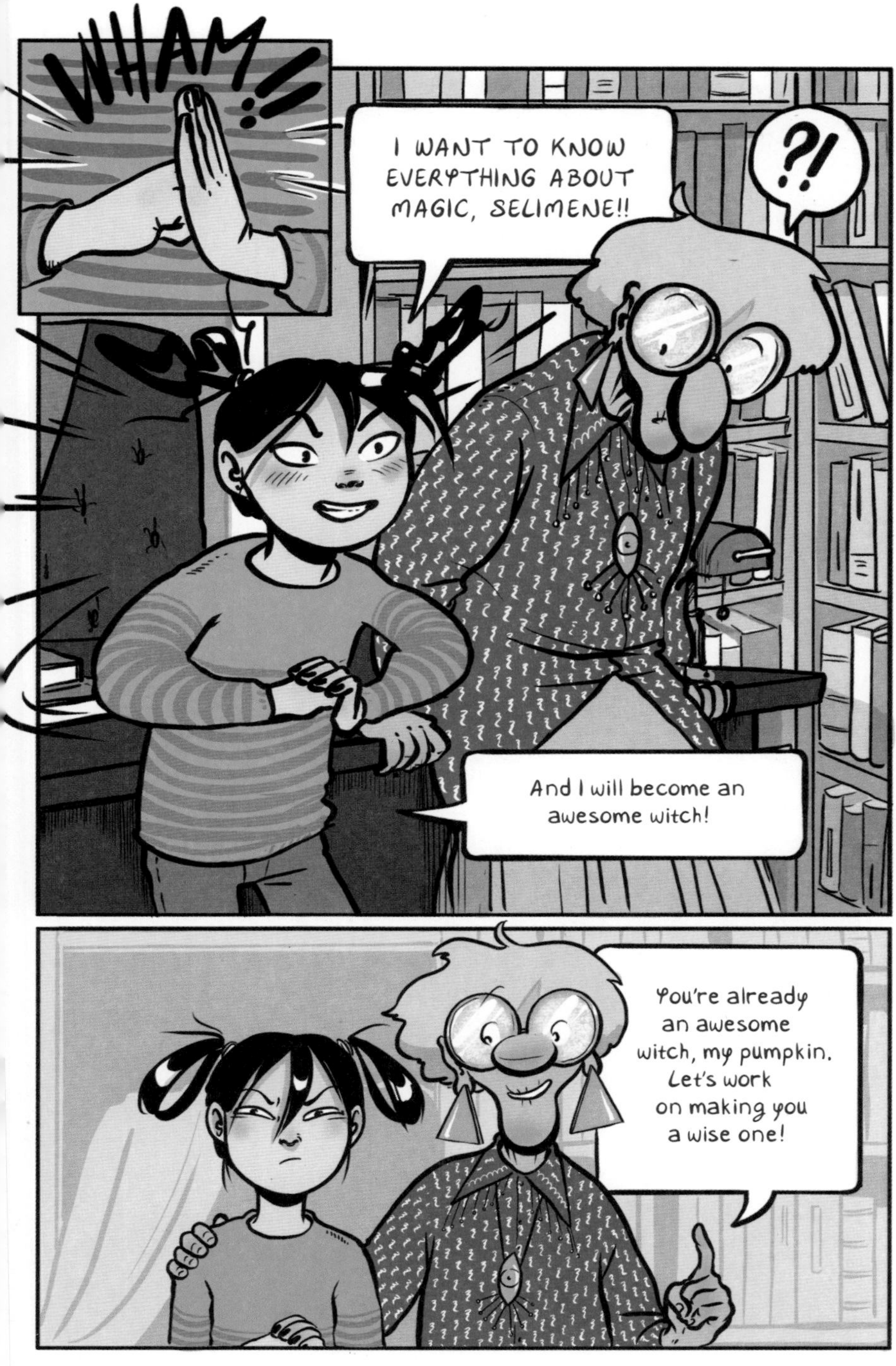
WHAM!!
I WANT TO KNOW EVERYTHING ABOUT MAGIC, SELIMENE!!
?!
And I will become an awesome witch!
You're already an awesome witch, my pumpkin. Let's work on making you a wise one!

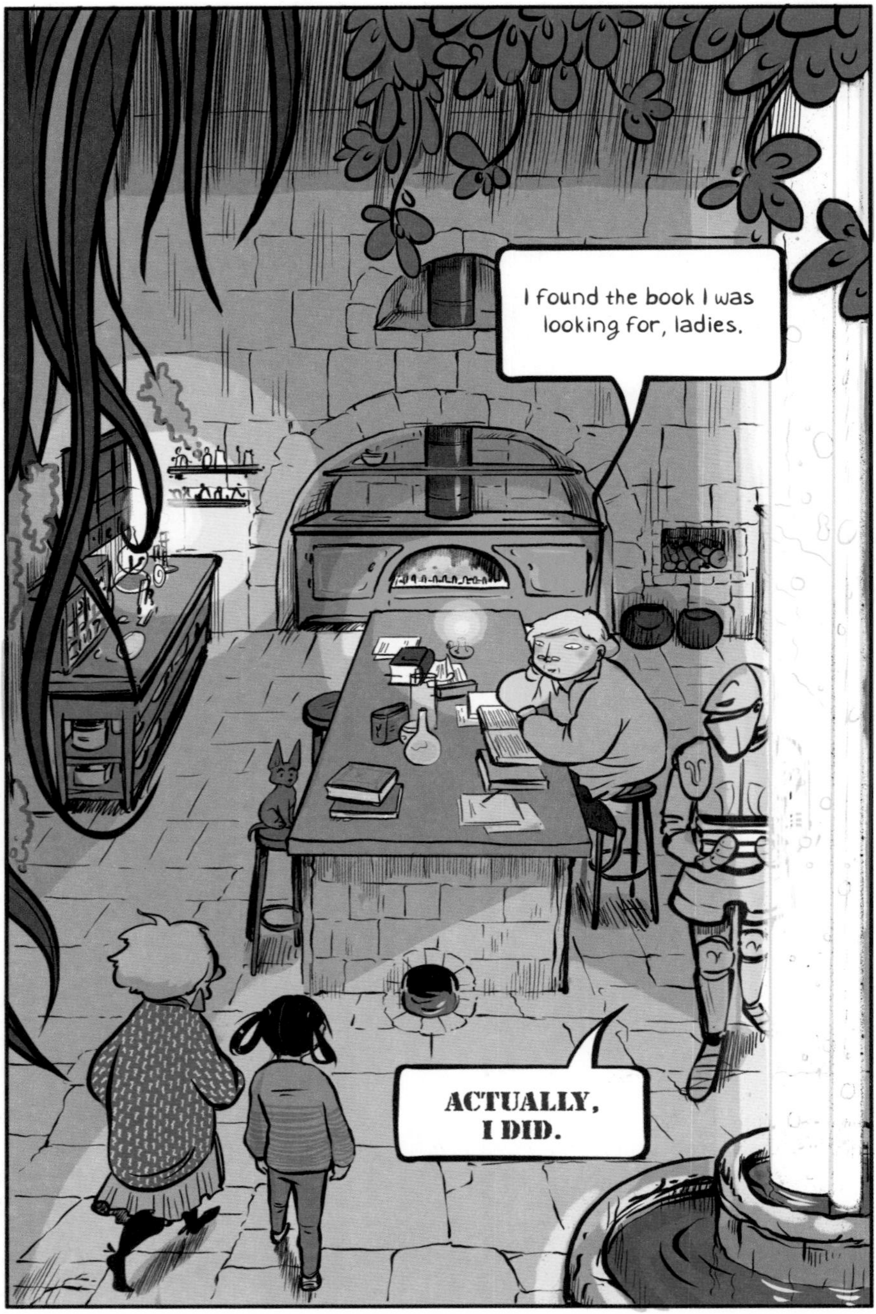
I found the book I was looking for, ladies.
ACTUALLY, I DID.

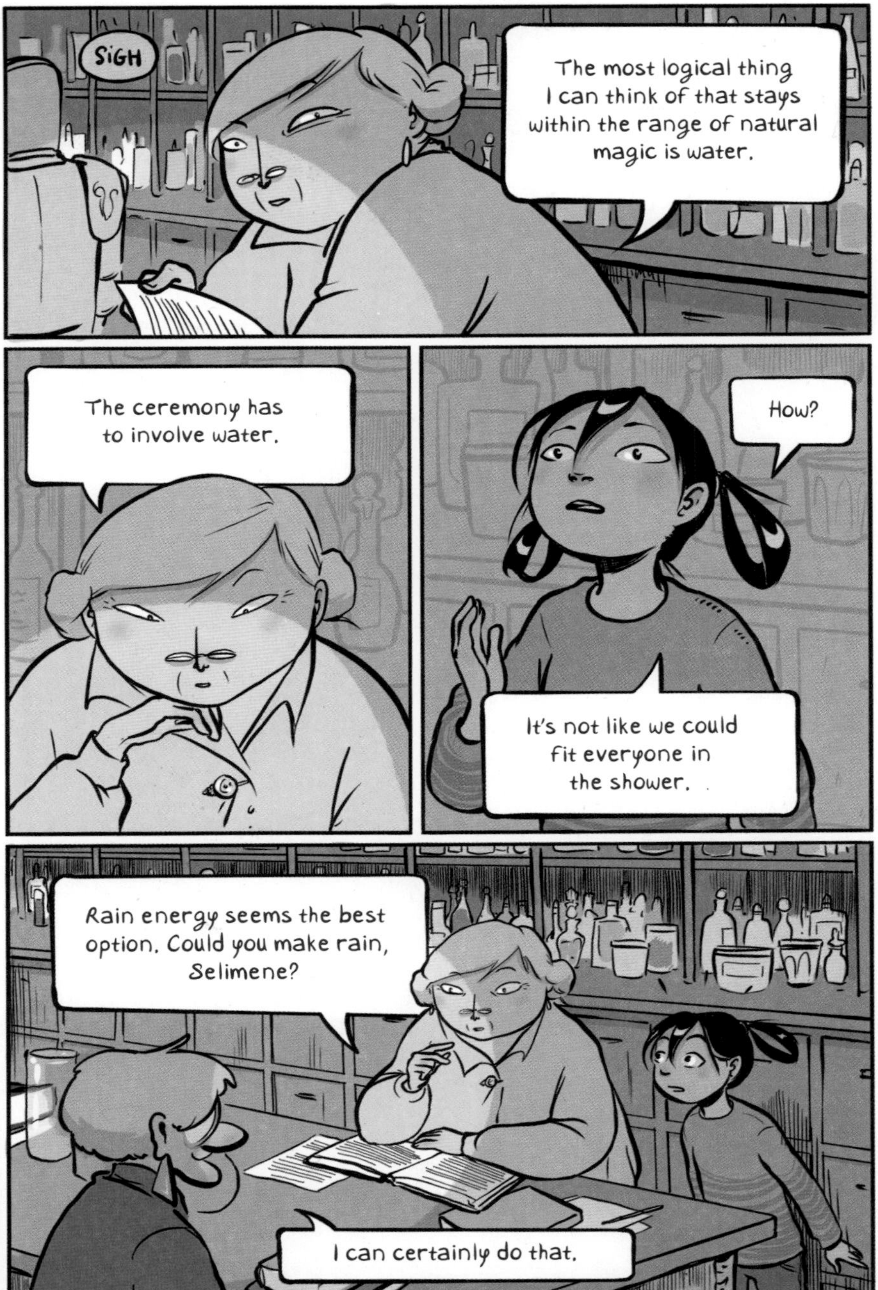

SIGH
The most logical thing I can think of that stays within the range of natural magic is water.
The ceremony has to involve water.
How?
It's not like we could fit everyone in the shower.
Rain energy seems the best option. Could you make rain, Selimene?
I can certainly do that.

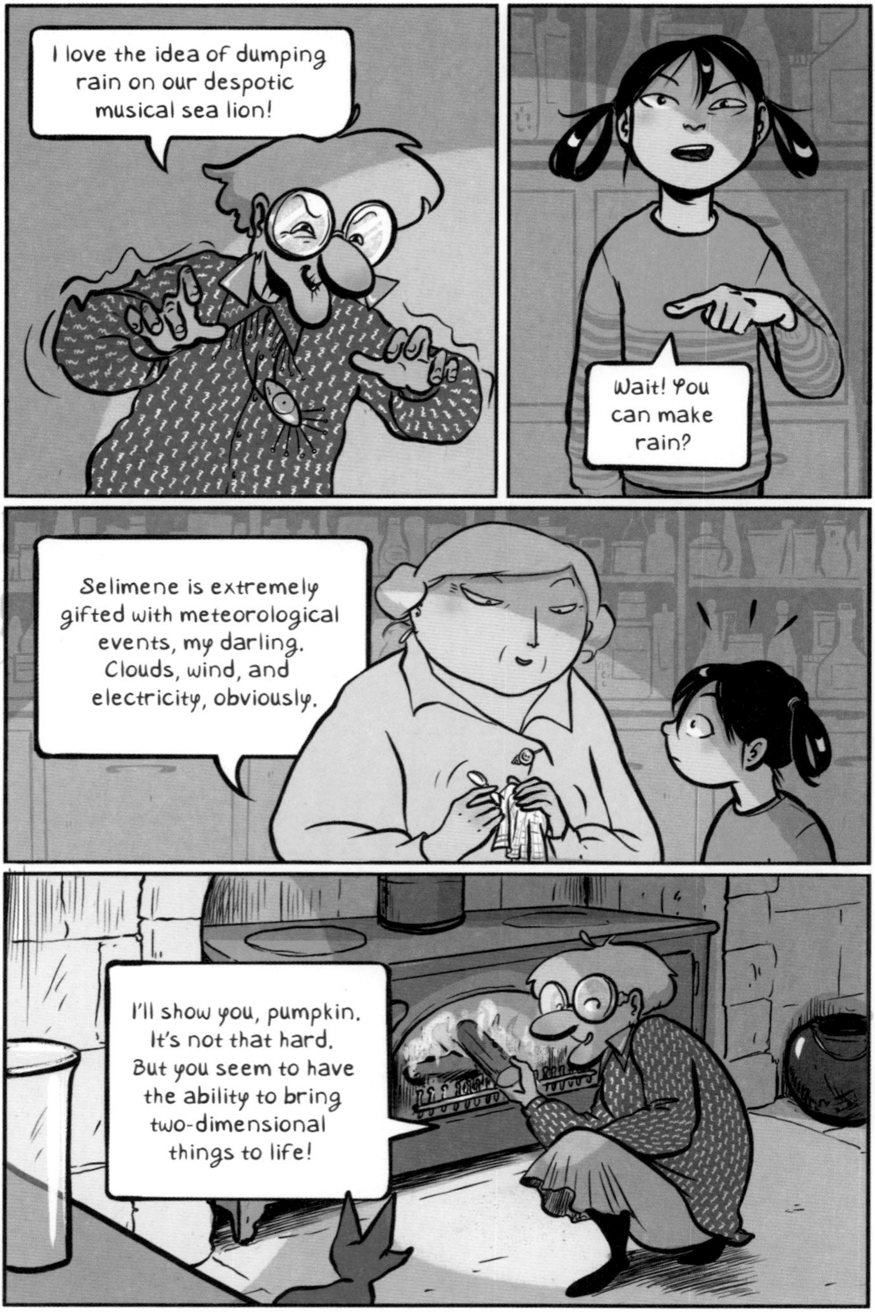
I love the idea of dumping rain on our despotic musical sea lion!
Wait! You can make rain?
Selimene is extremely gifted with meteorological events, my darling. Clouds, wind, and electricity, obviously.
I'll show you, pumpkin. It's not that hard. But you seem to have the ability to bring two-dimensional things to life!

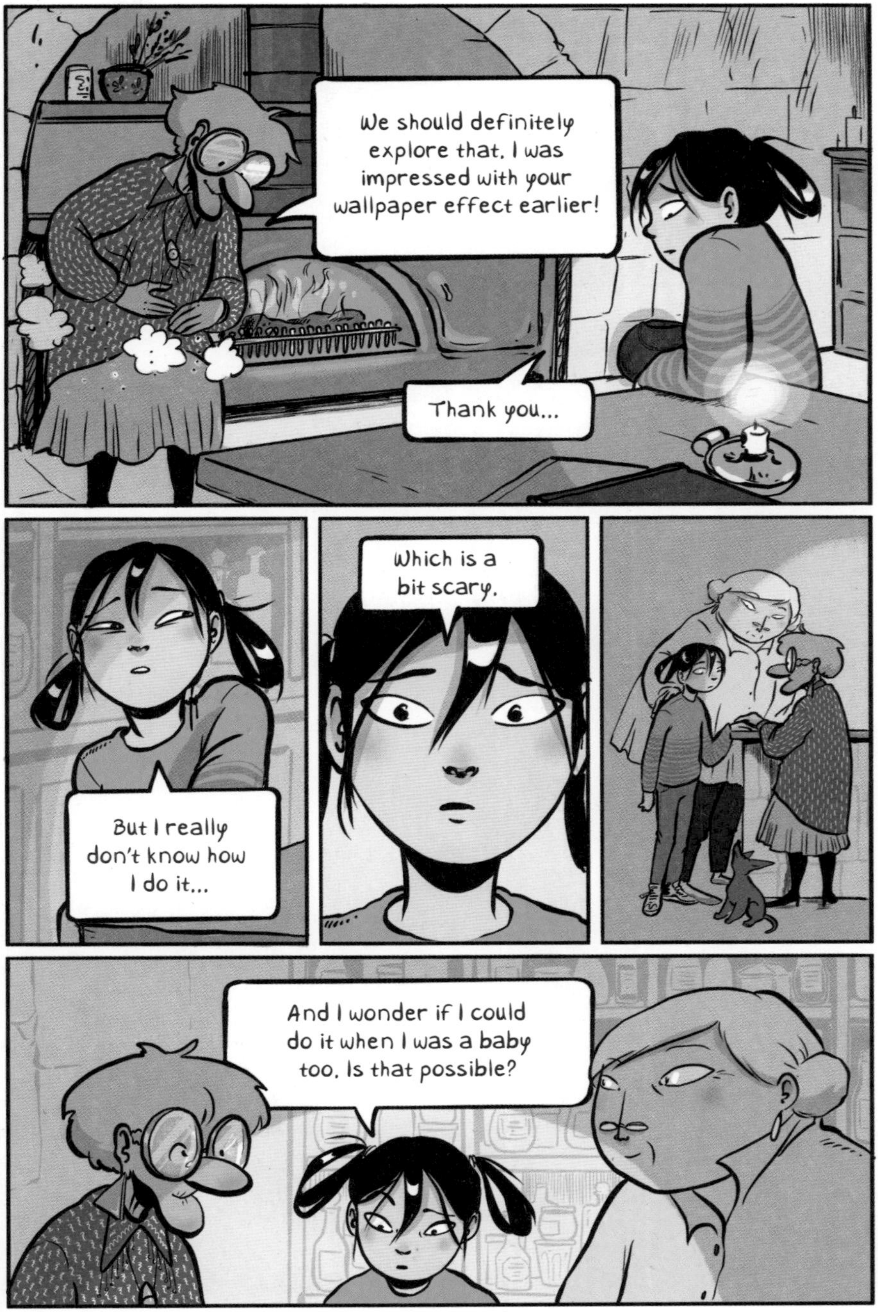

We should definitely explore that. I was impressed with your wallpaper effect earlier!
Thank you...
But I really don't know how I do it...
Which is a bit scary.
And I wonder if I could do it when I was a baby too. Is that possible?

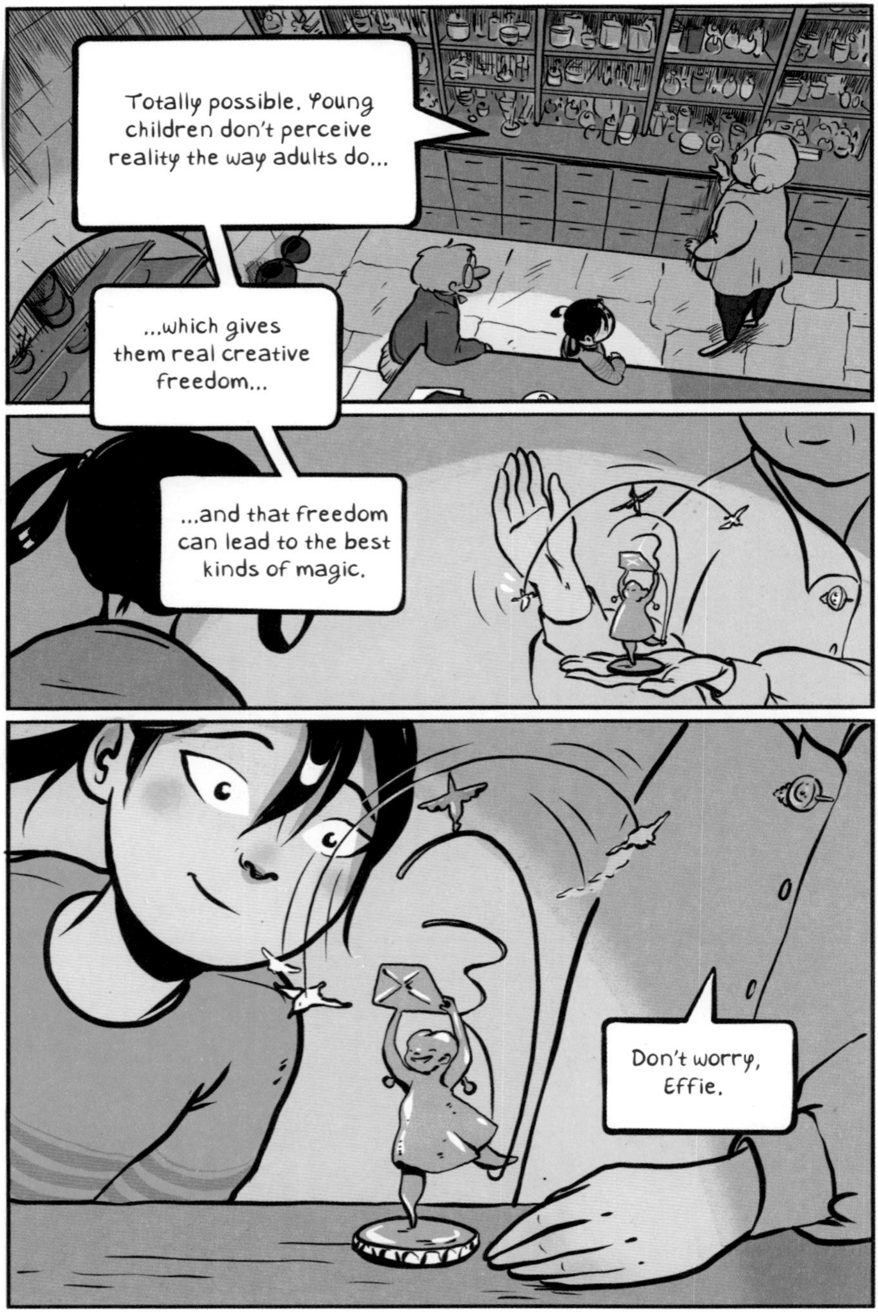
Totally possible. Young children don't perceive reality the way adults do...
...which gives them real creative freedom...
...and that freedom can lead to the best kinds of magic.
Don't worry, Effie.

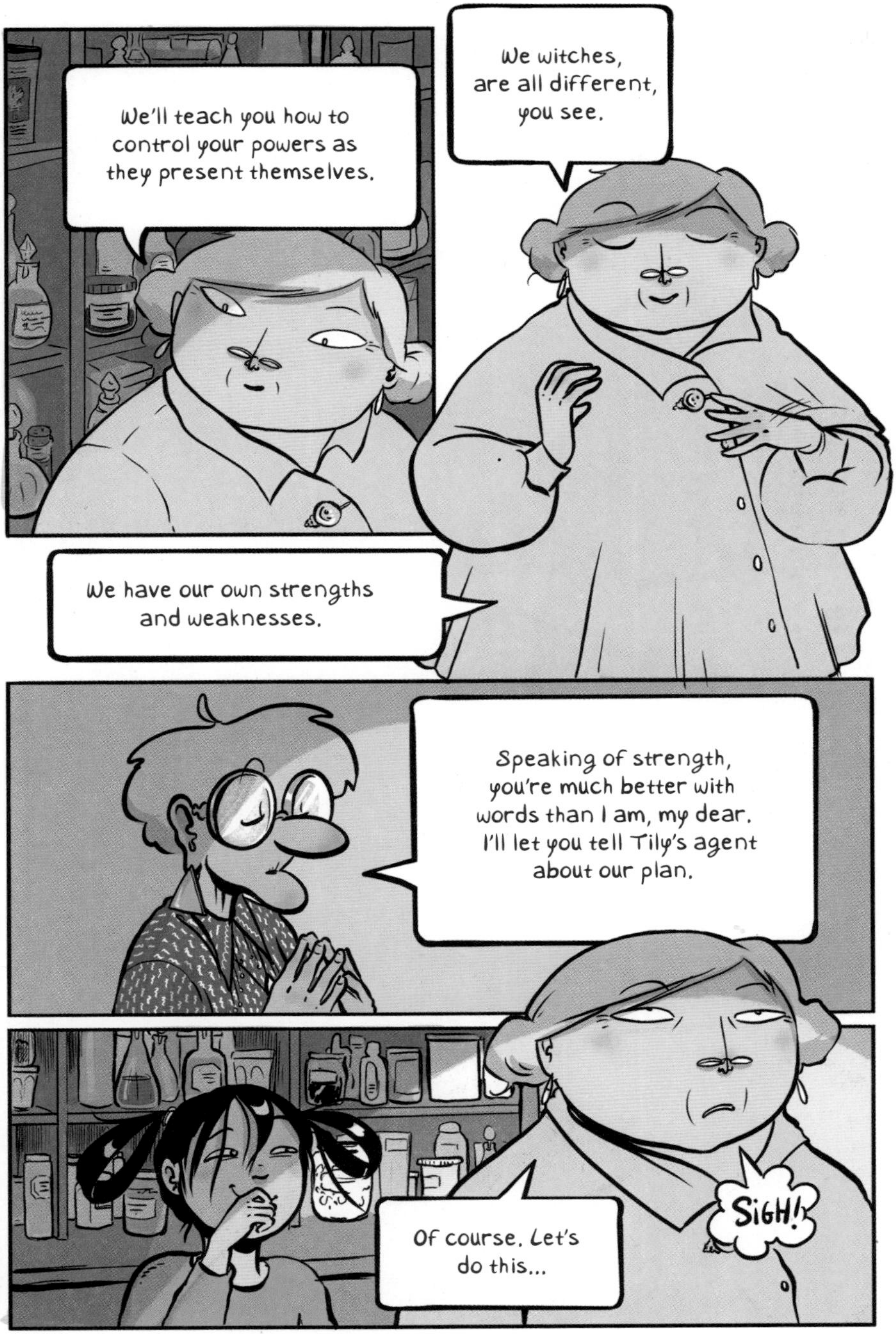
We'll teach you how to control your powers as they present themselves.
We witches, are all different, you see.
We have our own strengths and weaknesses.
Speaking of strength, you're much better with words than I am, my dear. I'll let you tell Tily's agent about our plan.
Of course. Let's do this...
SIGH!

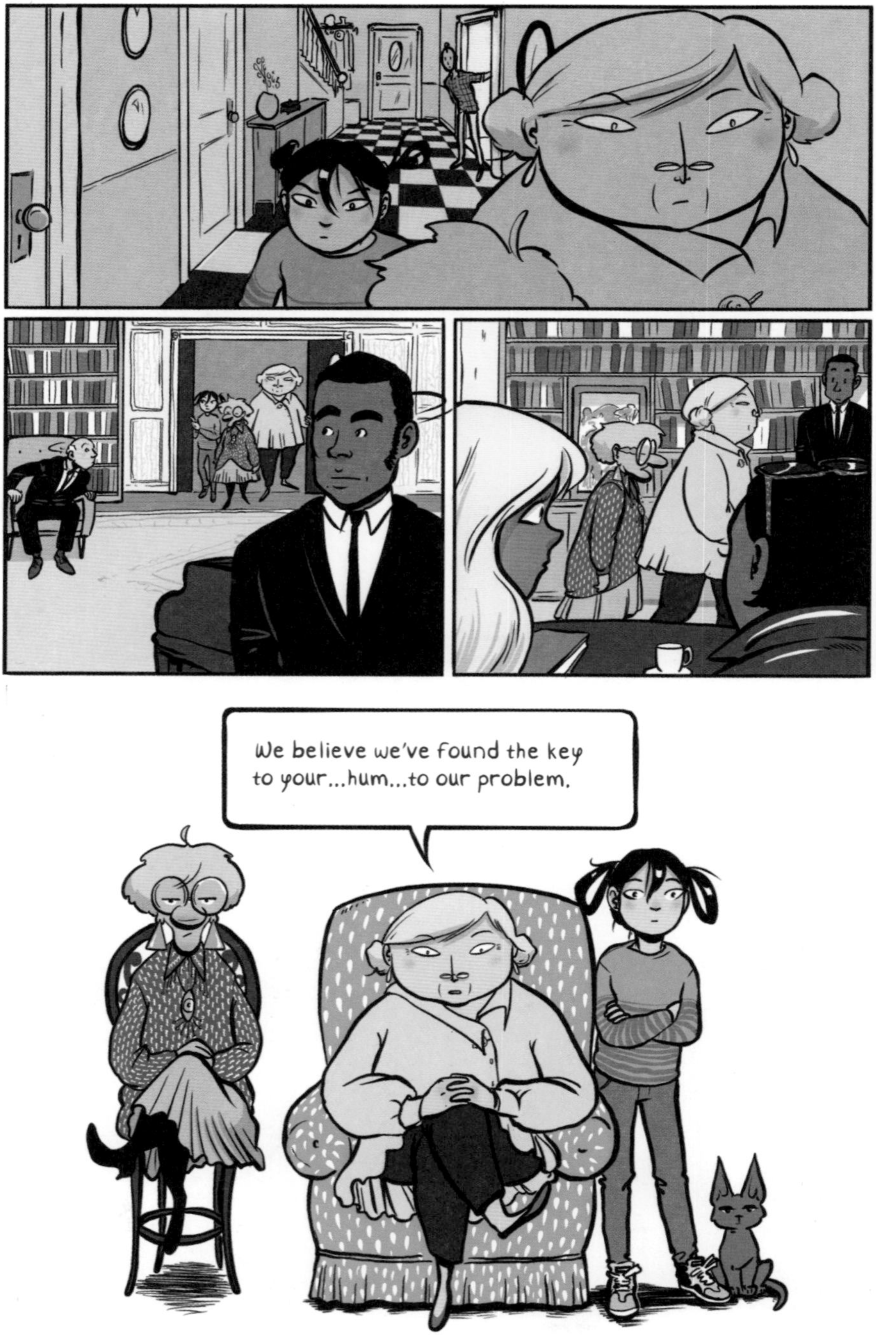
We believe we've found the key to your...hum...to our problem.

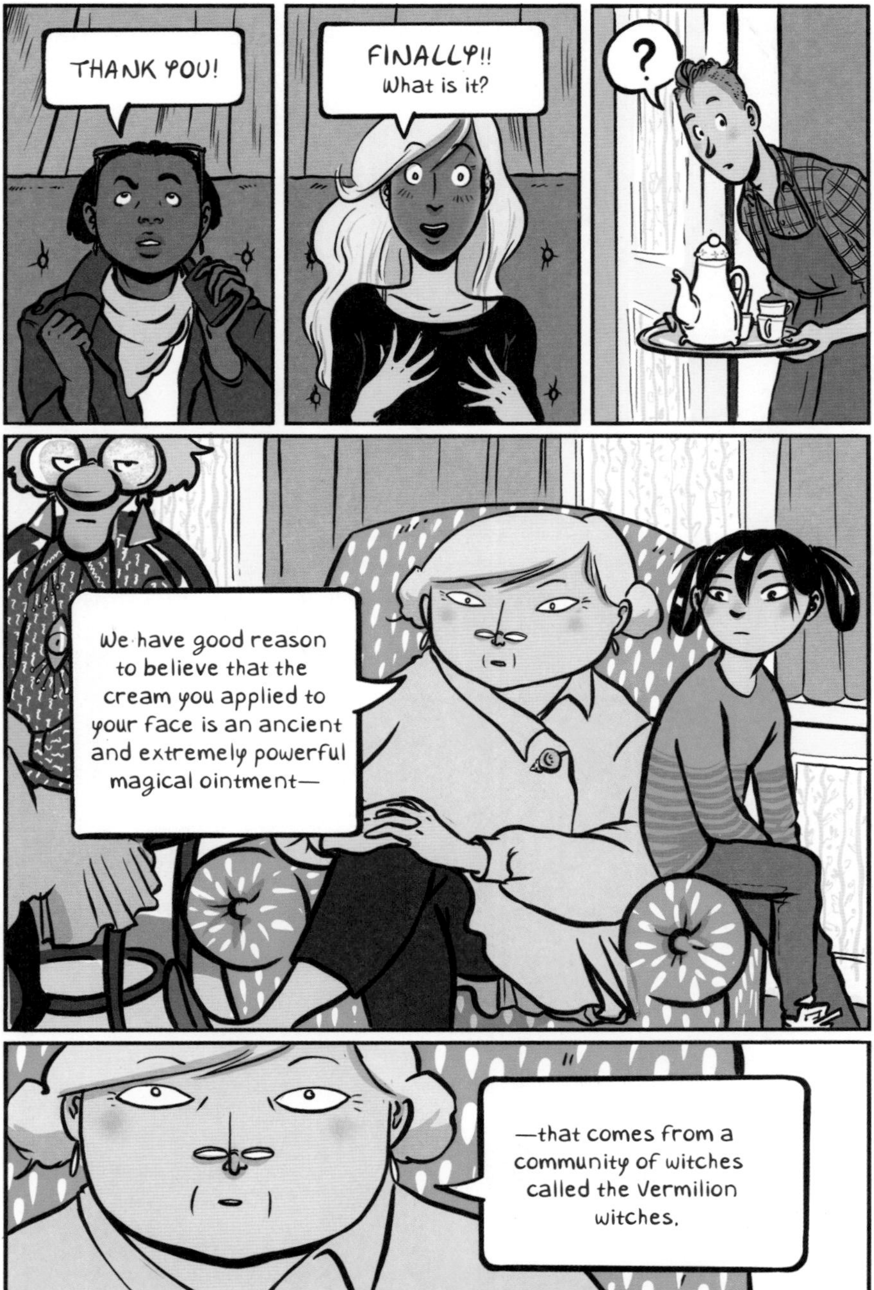
THANK YOU!
FINALLY!! What is it?
?
We have good reason to believe that the cream you applied to your face is an ancient and extremely powerful magical ointment—
—that comes from a community of witches called the Vermilion witches.

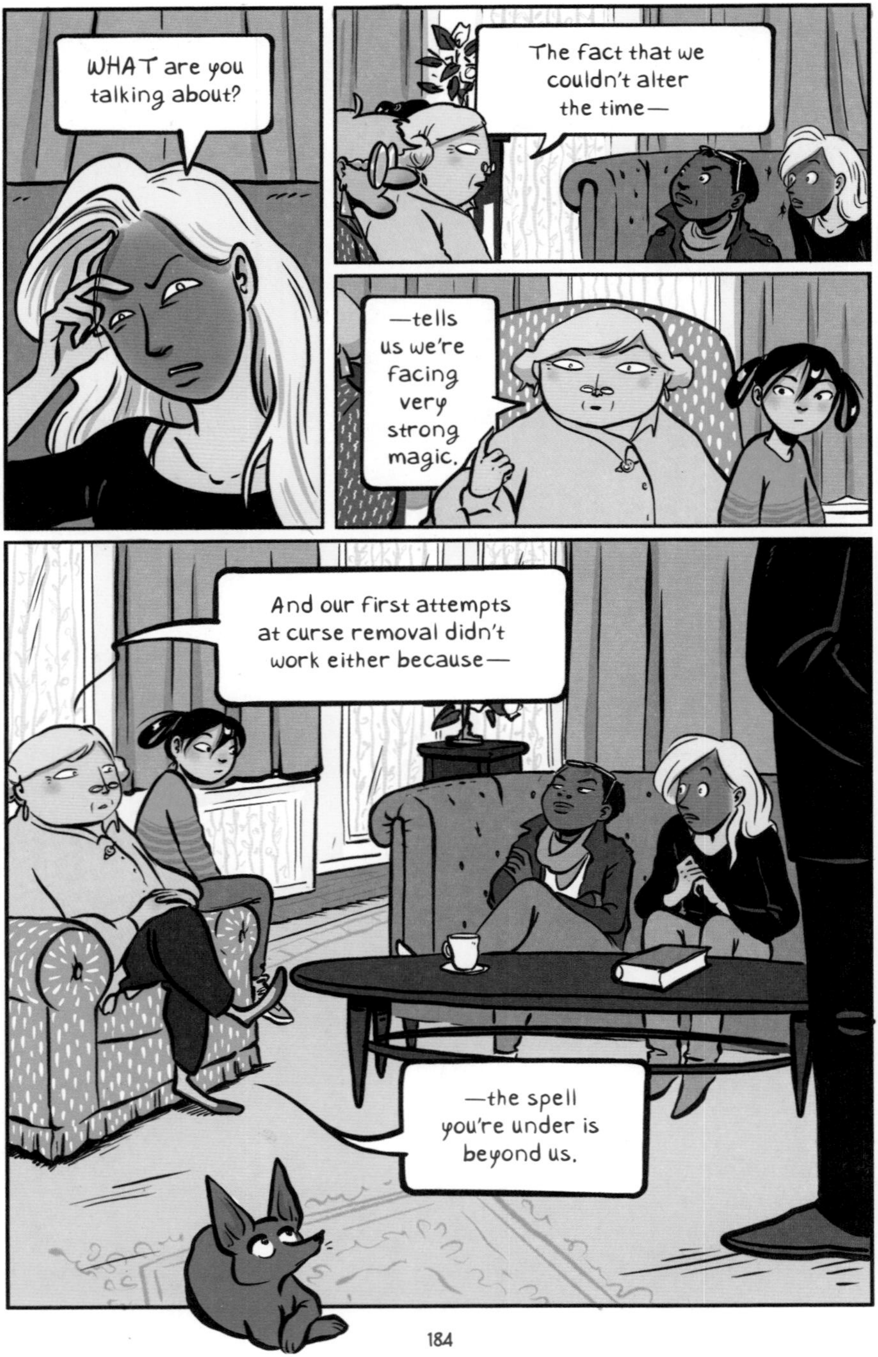
WHAT are you talking about?
The fact that we couldn't alter the time—
—tells us we're facing very strong magic.
And our first attempts at curse removal didn't work either because—
—the spell you're under is beyond us.

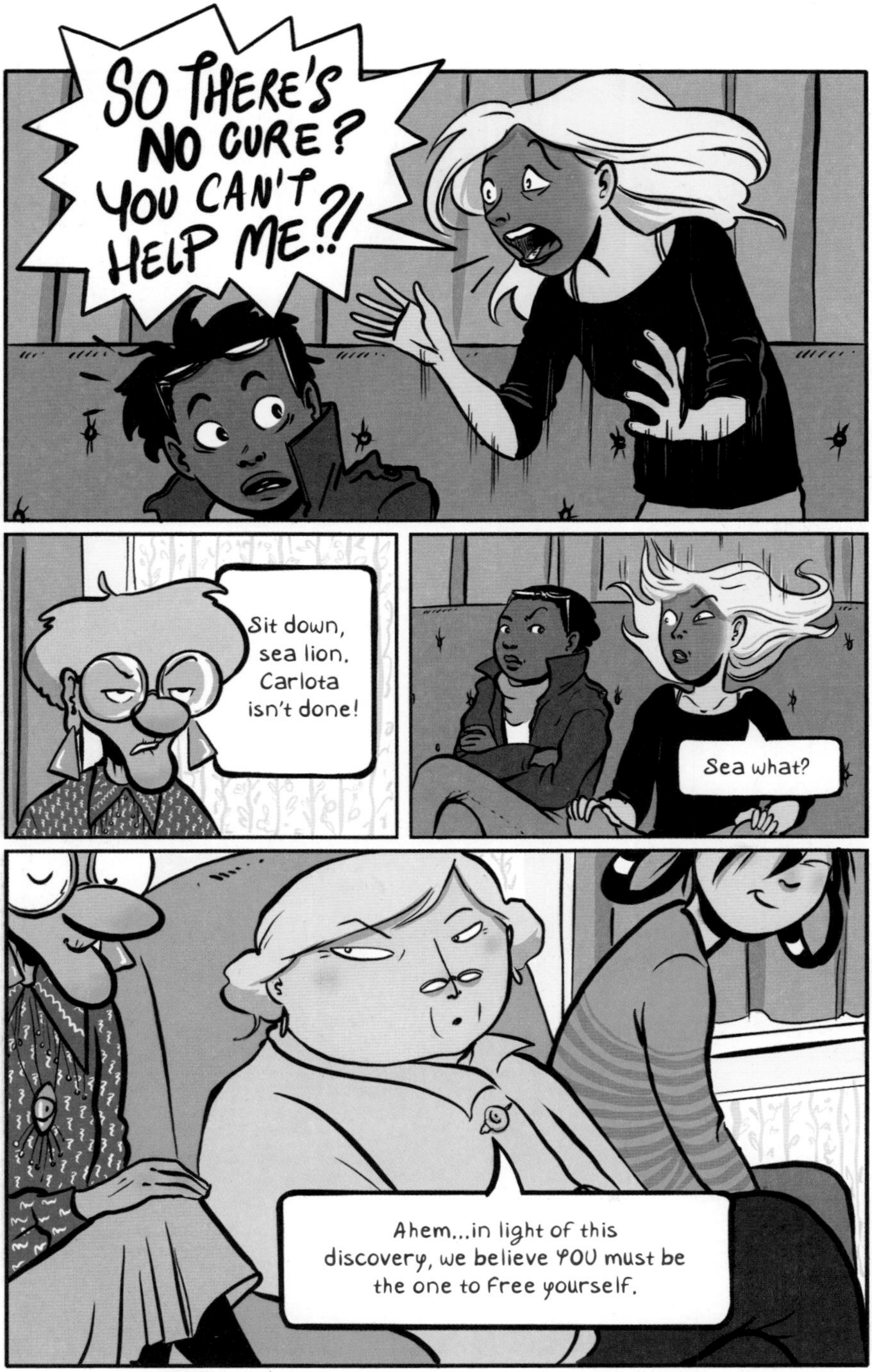
SO THERE'S NO CURE? YOU CAN'T HELP ME?!
Sit down, sea lion. Carlota isn't done!
Sea what?
Ahem...in light of this discovery, we believe YOU must be the one to free yourself.

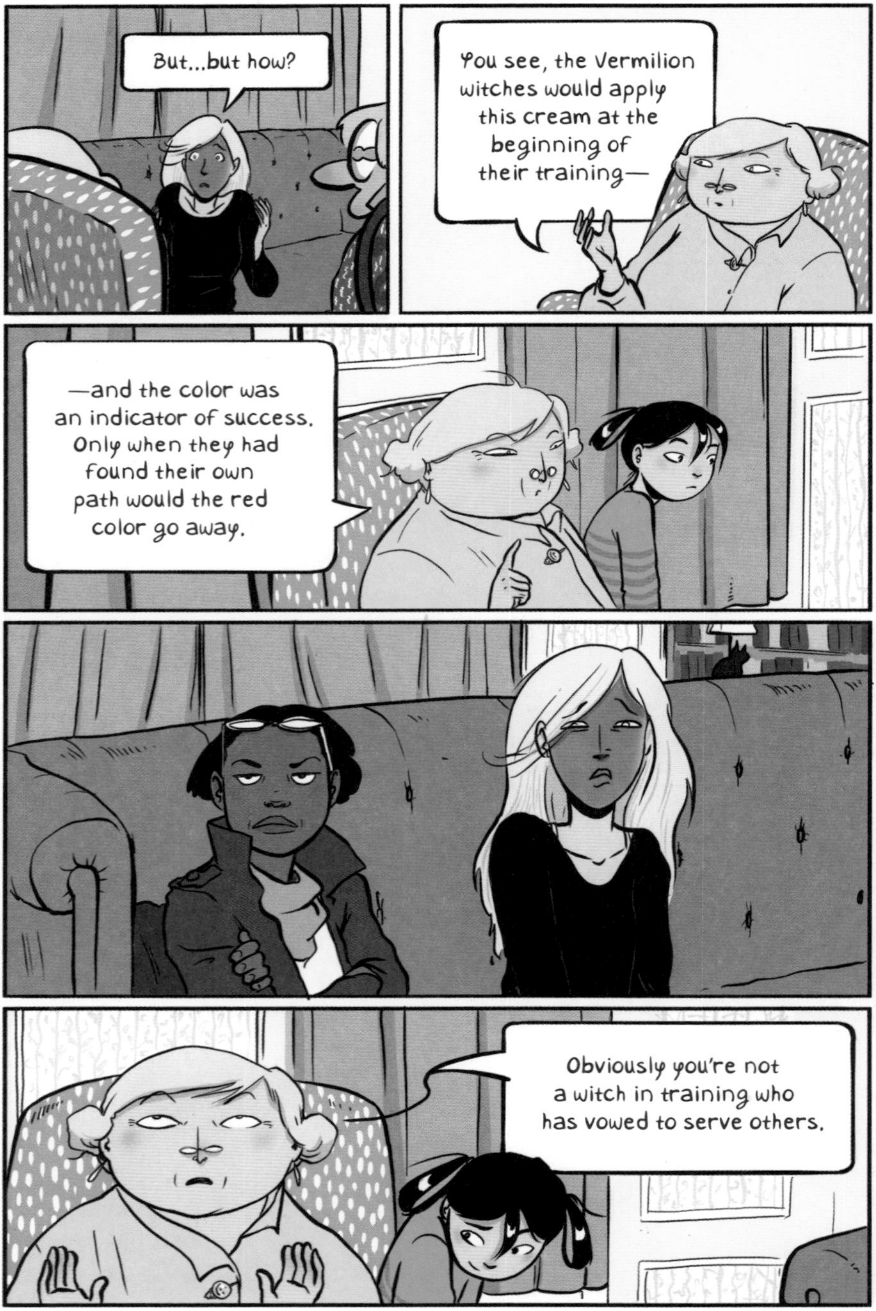
But...but how?
You see, the Vermilion witches would apply this cream at the beginning of their training—
—and the color was an indicator of success. Only when they had found their own path would the red color go away.
Obviously you're not a witch in training who has vowed to serve others.

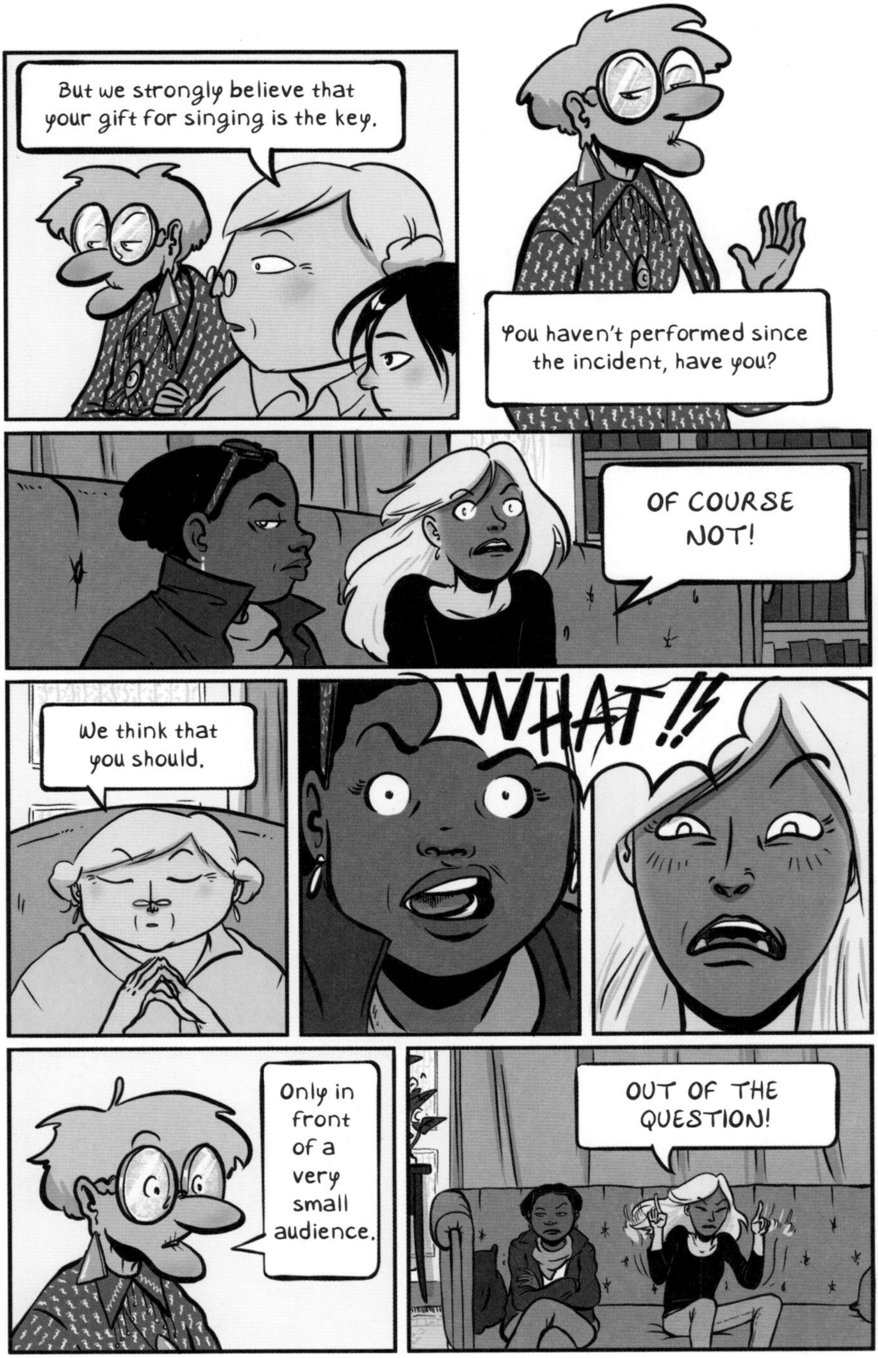
But we strongly believe that your gift for singing is the key.
You haven't performed since the incident, have you?
OF COURSE NOT!
We think that you should.
WHAT!!
Only in front of a very small audience.
OUT OF THE QUESTION!

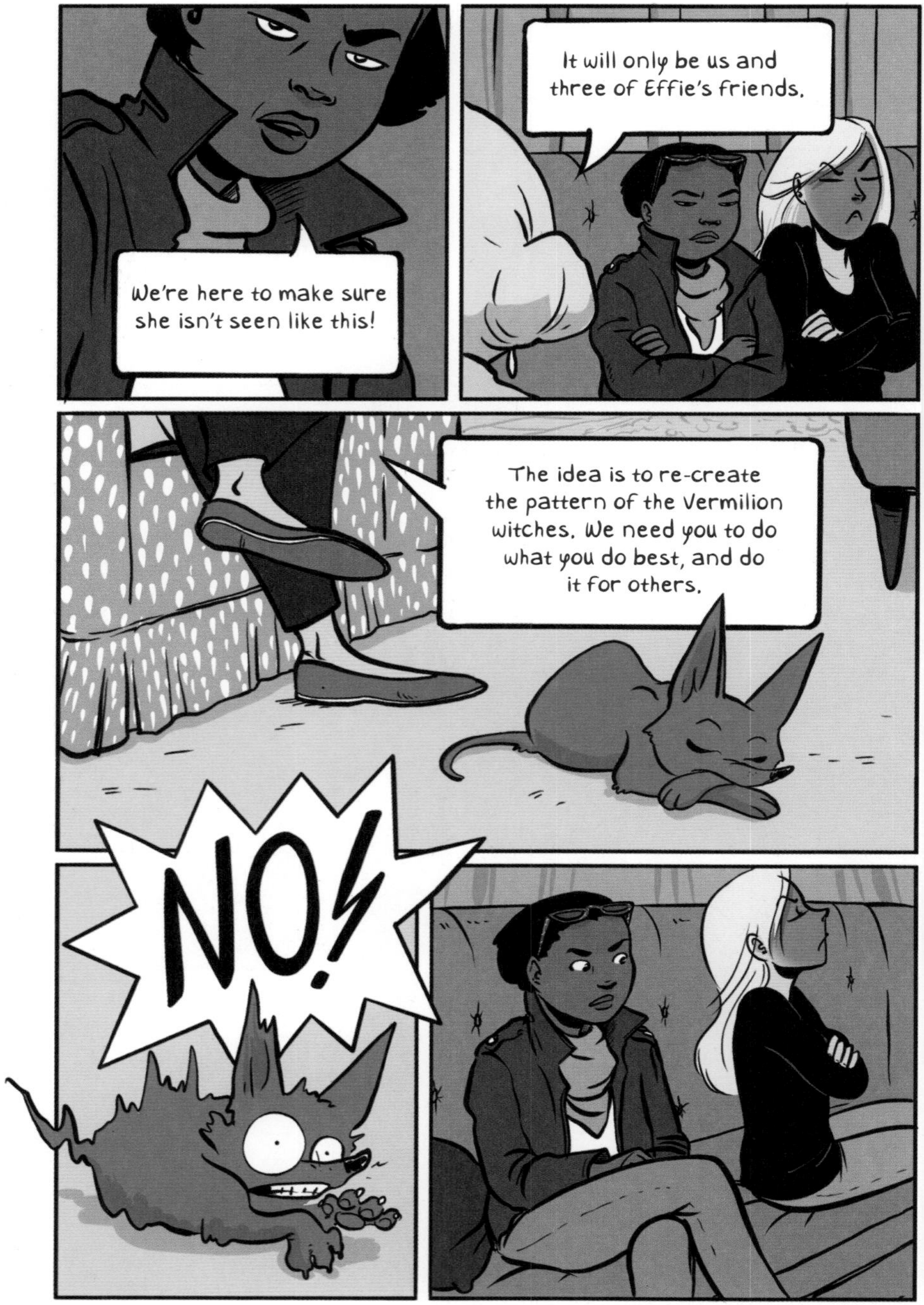
We're here to make sure she isn't seen like this!
It will only be us and three of Effie's friends.
The idea is to re-create the pattern of the Vermilion witches. We need you to do what you do best, and do it for others.
NO!

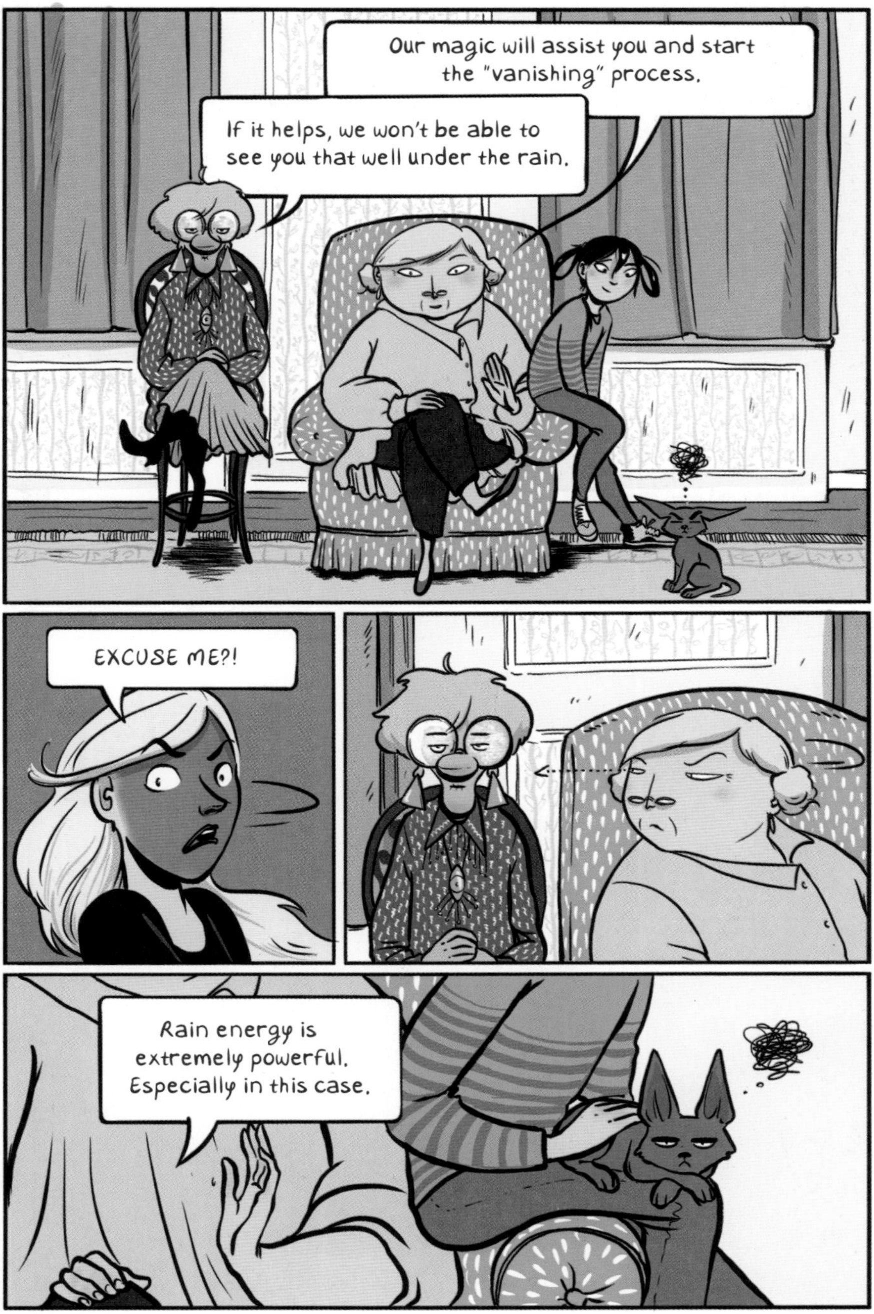
If it helps, we won't be able to see you that well under the rain.
Our magic will assist you and start the "vanishing" process.
EXCUSE ME?!
Rain energy is extremely powerful. Especially in this case.

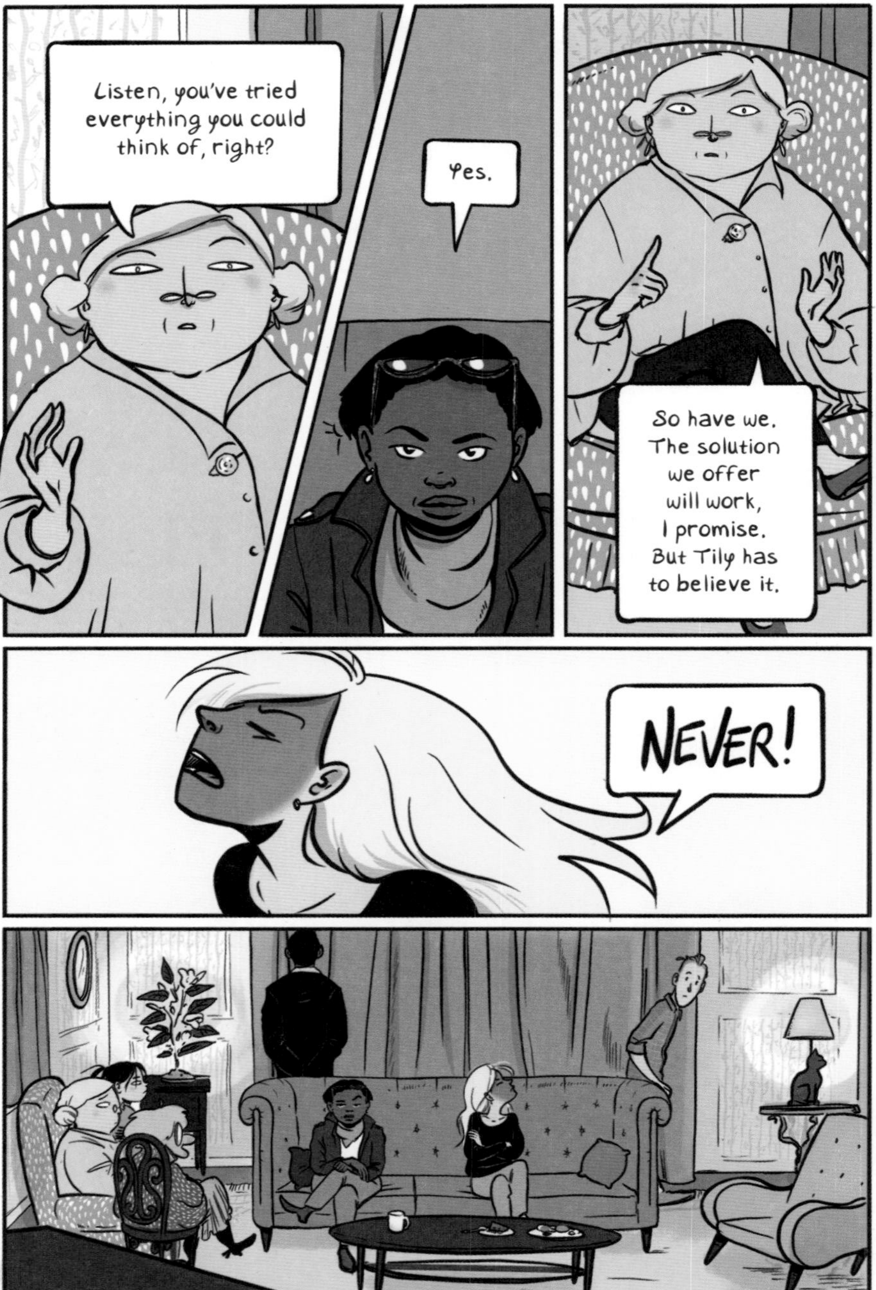
Listen, you've tried everything you could think of, right?
Yes.
So have we. The solution we offer will work, I promise. But Tily has to believe it.
NEVER!

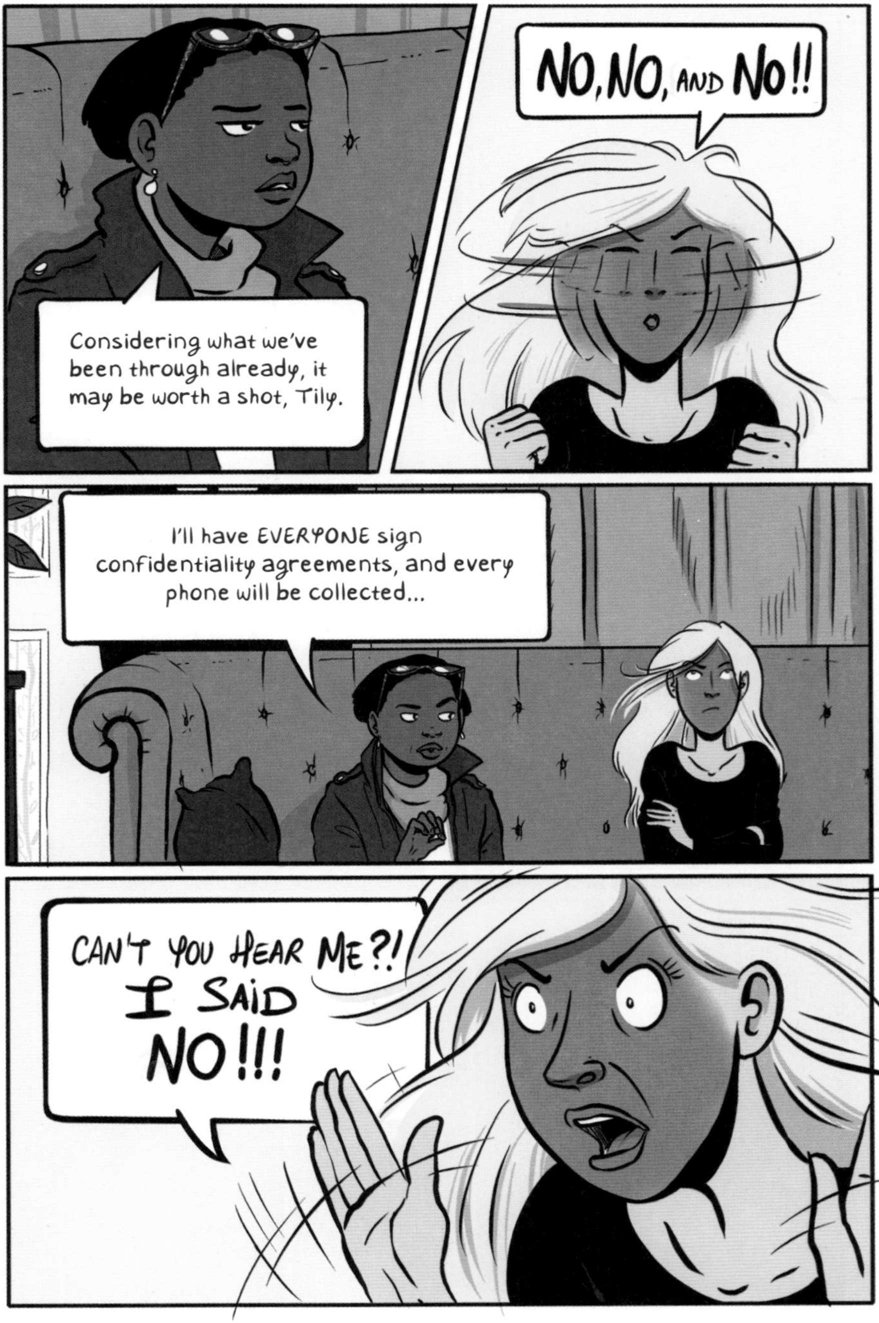
Considering what we've been through already, it may be worth a shot, Tily.
NO, NO, AND NO!!
I'll have EVERYONE sign confidentiality agreements, and every phone will be collected...
CAN'T YOU HEAR ME?! I SAID NO!!!

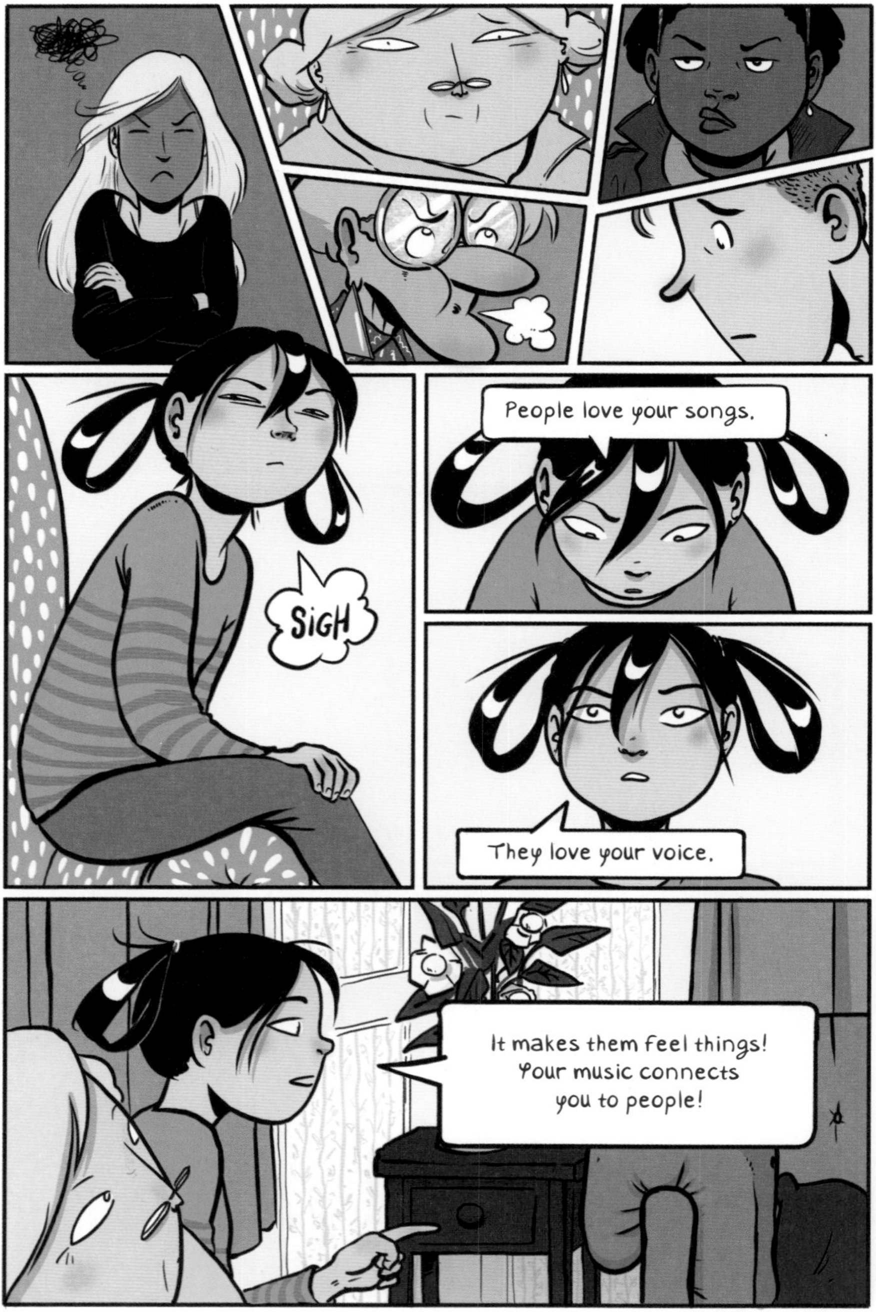
People love your songs.
SIGH
They love your voice.
It makes them feel things! Your music connects you to people!

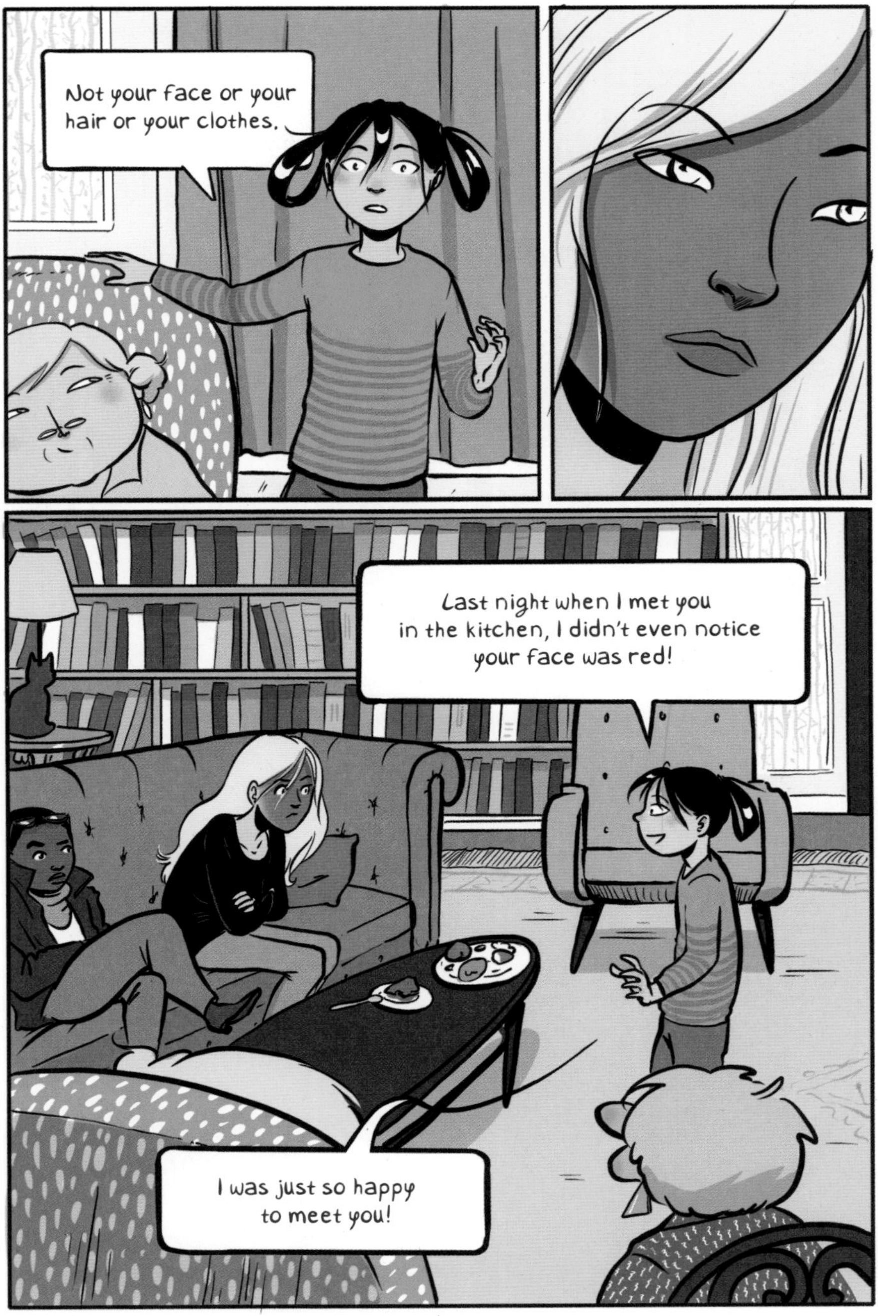
Not your face or your hair or your clothes.
Last night when I met you in the kitchen, I didn't even notice your face was red!
I was just so happy to meet you!

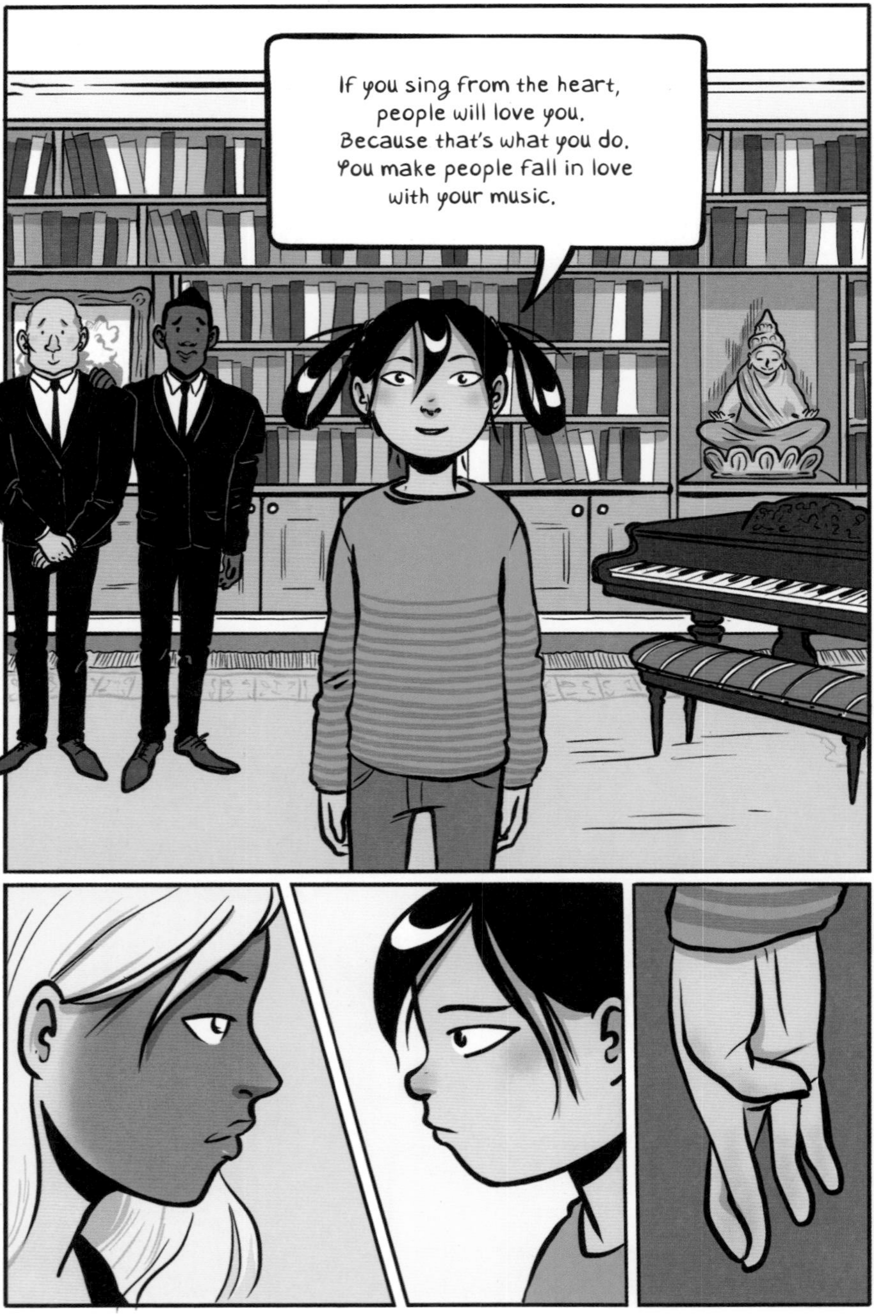
If you sing from the heart, people will love you. Because that's what you do. You make people fall in love with your music.

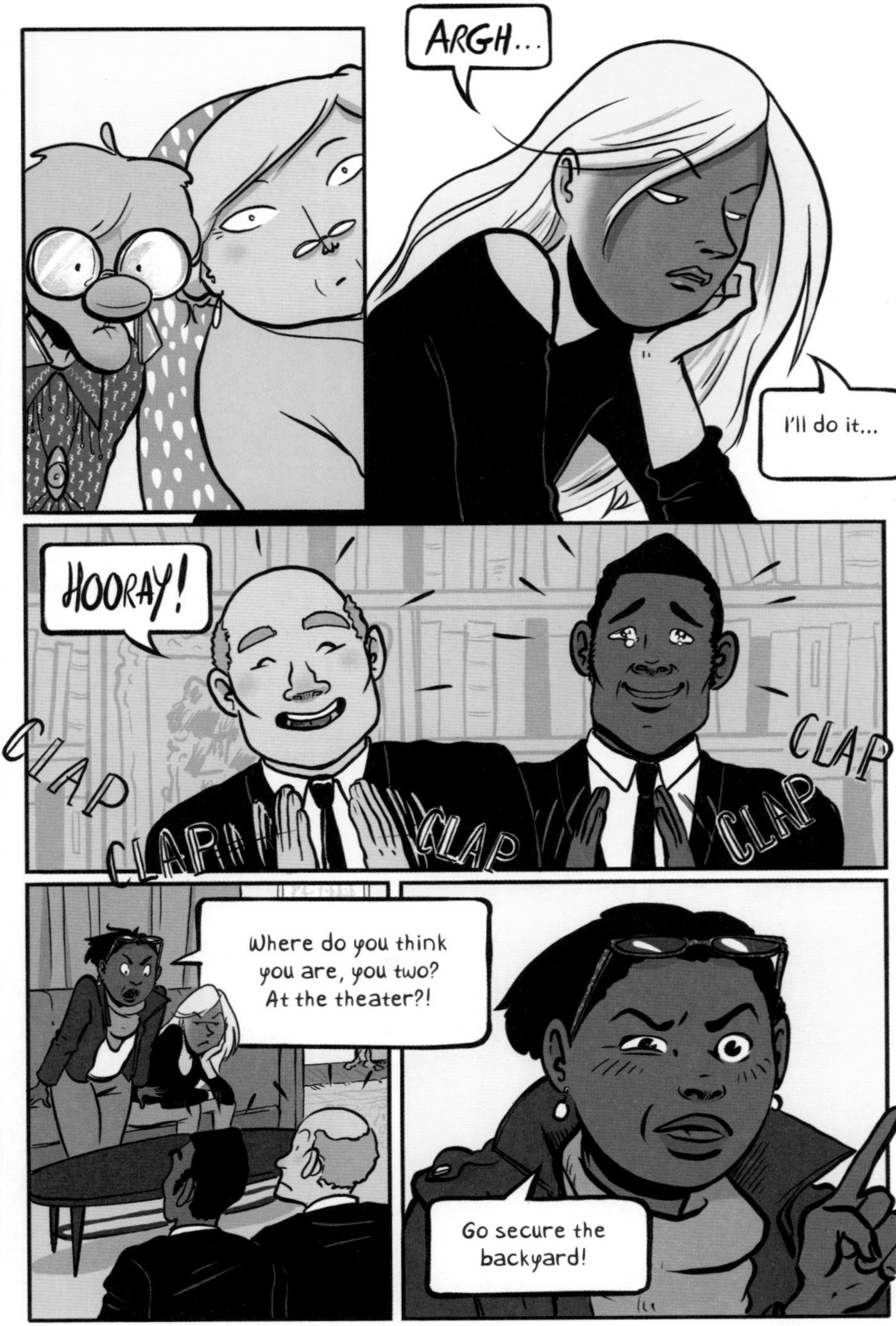
ARGH...
I'll do it...
HOORAY!
CLAP
CLAP
CLAP
CLAP
CLAP
Where do you think you are, you two? At the theater?!
Go secure the backyard!

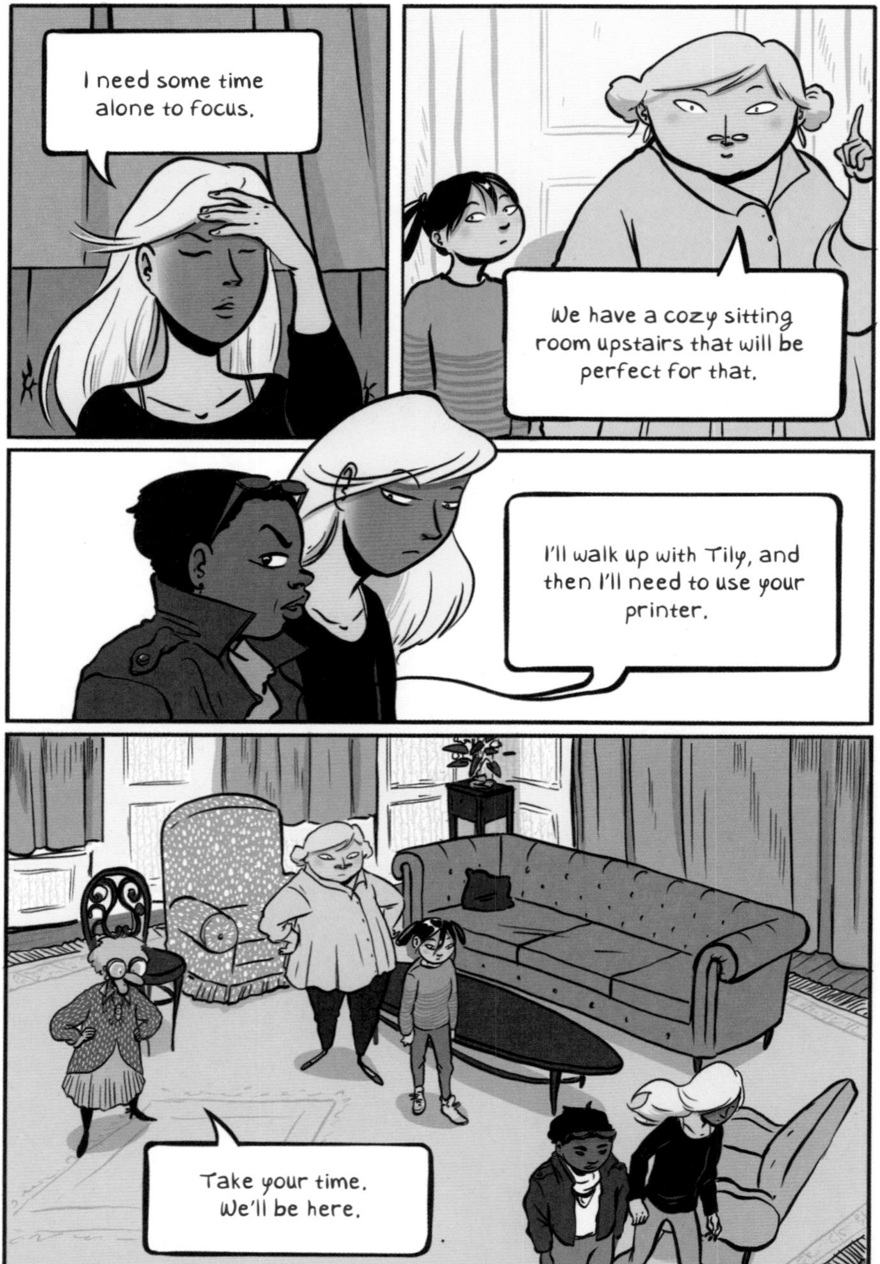
I need some time alone to focus.
We have a cozy sitting room upstairs that will be perfect for that.
I'll walk up with Tily, and then I'll need to use your printer.
Take your time. We'll be here.

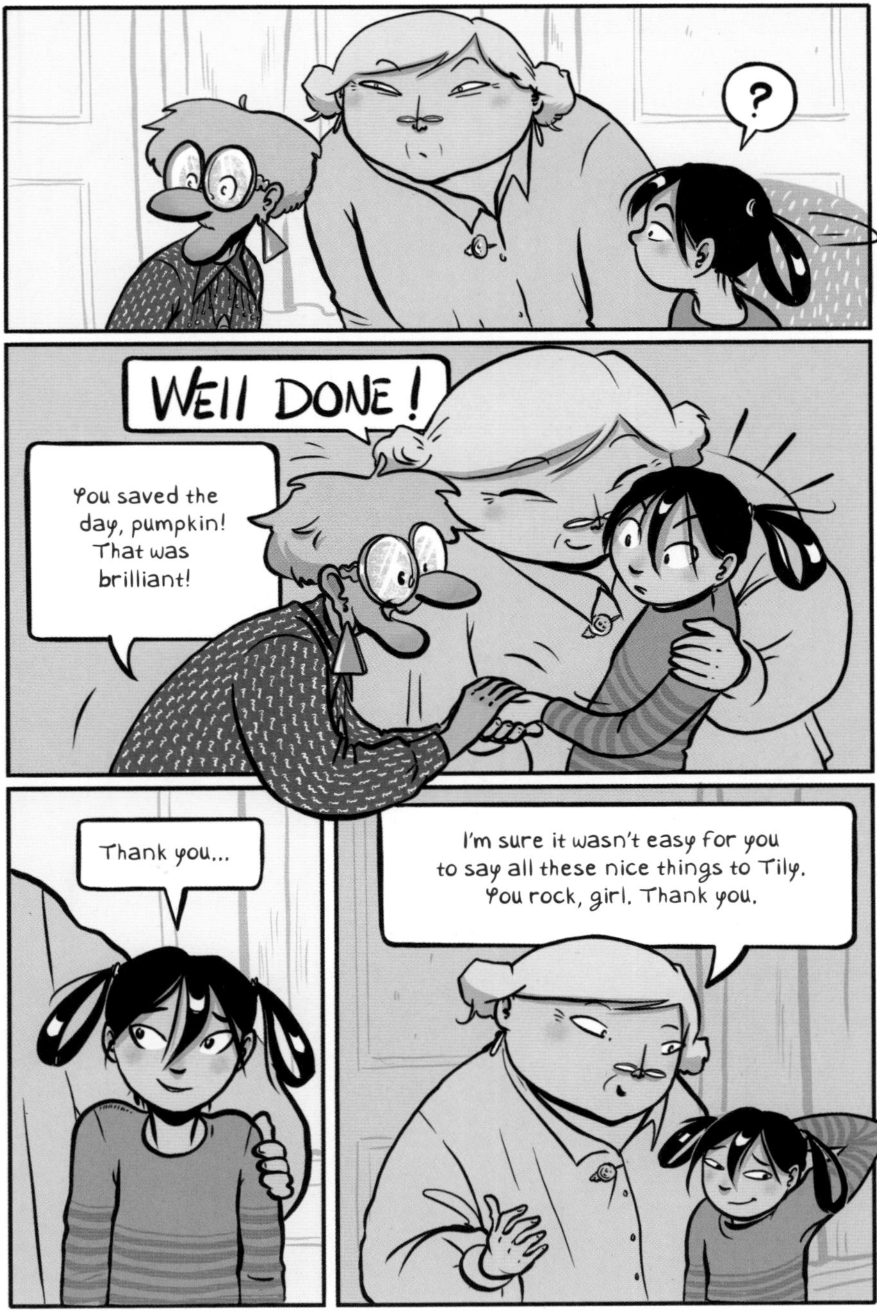
?
WEll DONE!
You saved the day, pumpkin! That was brilliant!
Thank you...
I'm sure it wasn't easy for you to say all these nice things to Tily. You rock, girl. Thank you.

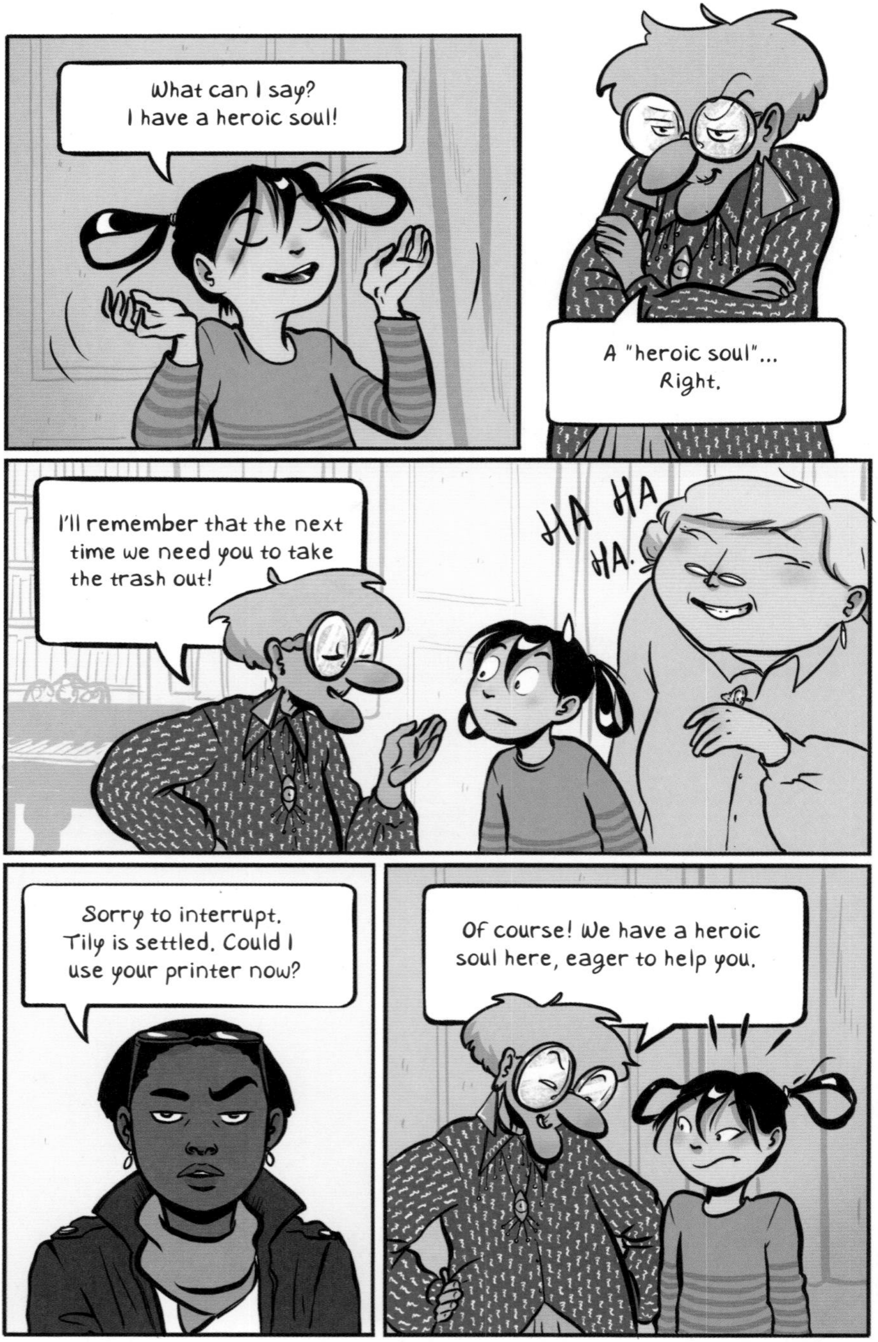
What can I say? I have a heroic soul!
A "heroic soul"... Right.
I'll remember that the next time we need you to take the trash out!
HA HA HA.
Sorry to interrupt. Tily is settled. Could I use your printer now?
Of course! We have a heroic soul here, eager to help you.

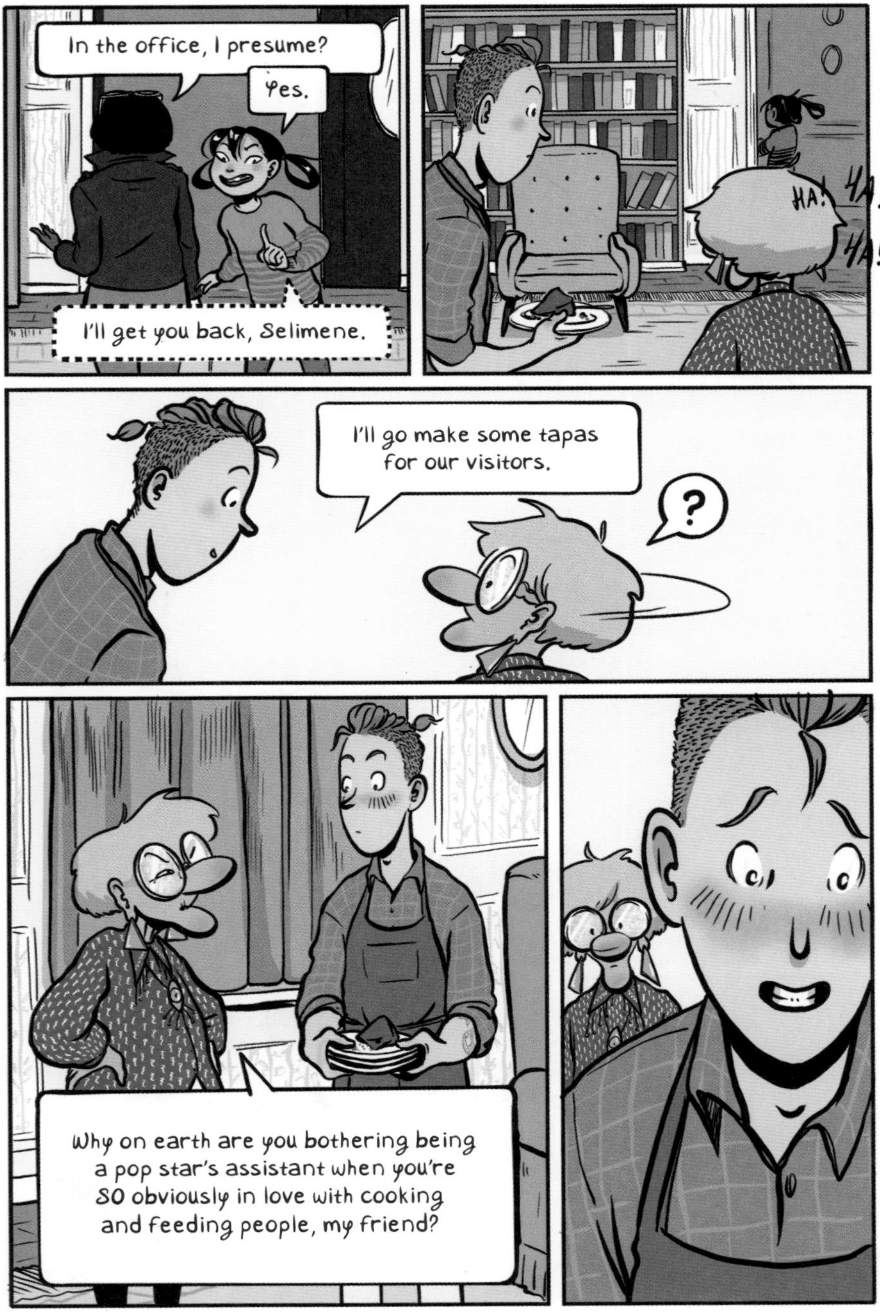
In the office, I presume?
Yes.
I'll get you back, Selimene.
HA! HA! HA!
I'll go make some tapas for our visitors.
?
Why on earth are you bothering being a pop star's assistant when you're SO obviously in love with cooking and feeding people, my friend?

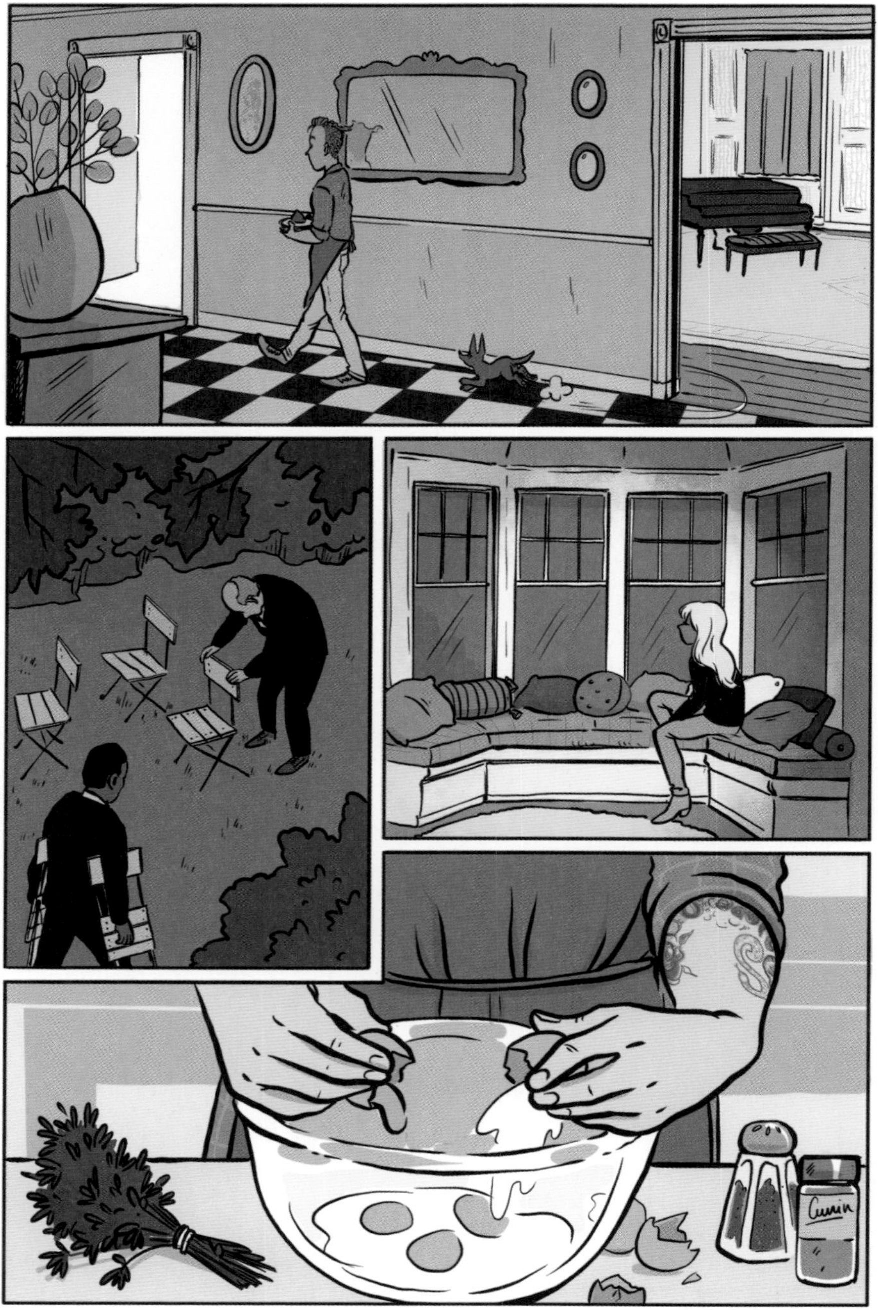
Cumin

Chapter 5

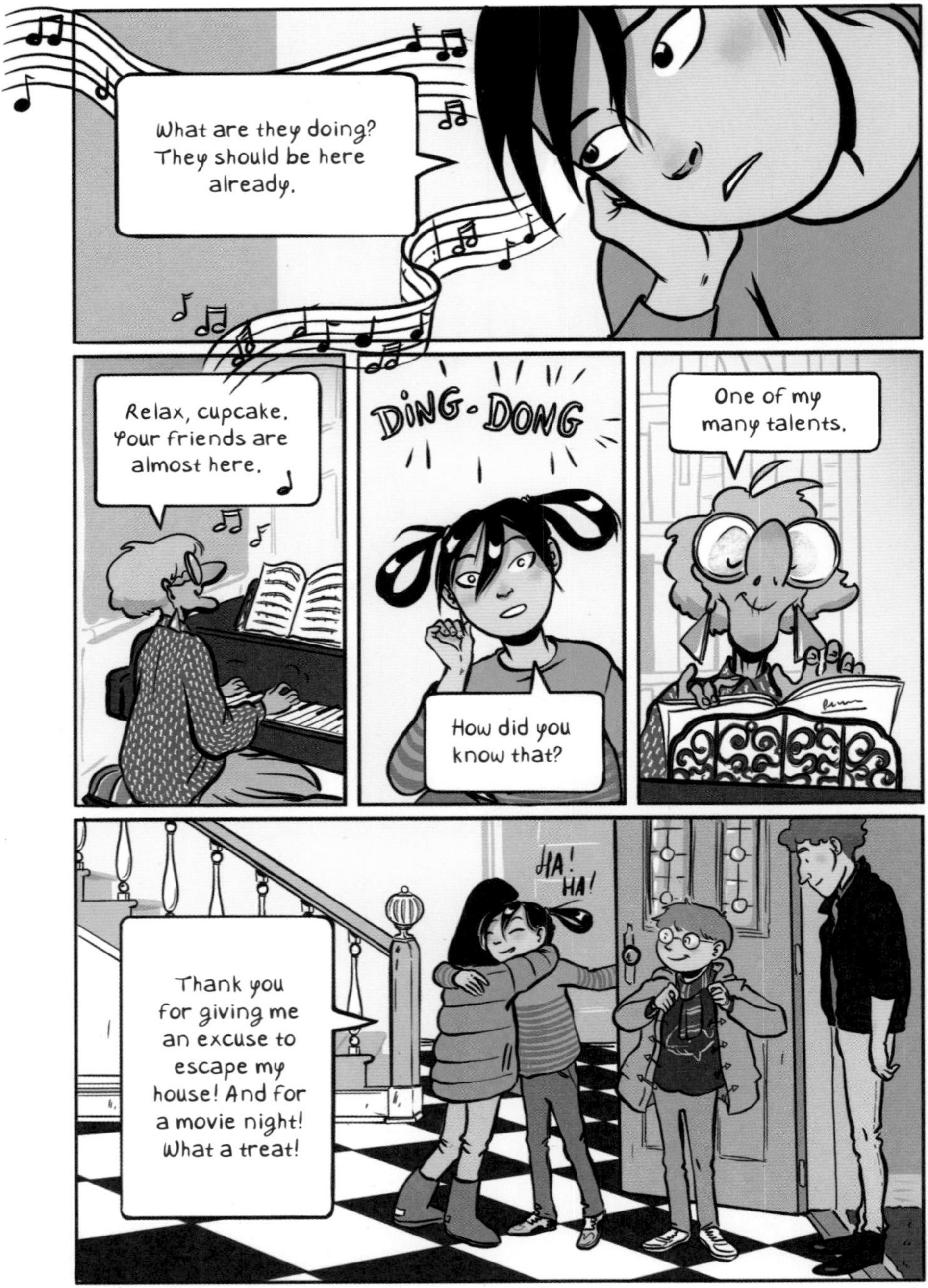
What are they doing? They should be here already.
Relax, cupcake. Your friends are almost here.
DING-DONG
How did you know that?
One of my many talents.
HA! HA!
Thank you for giving me an excuse to escape my house! And for a movie night! What a treat!

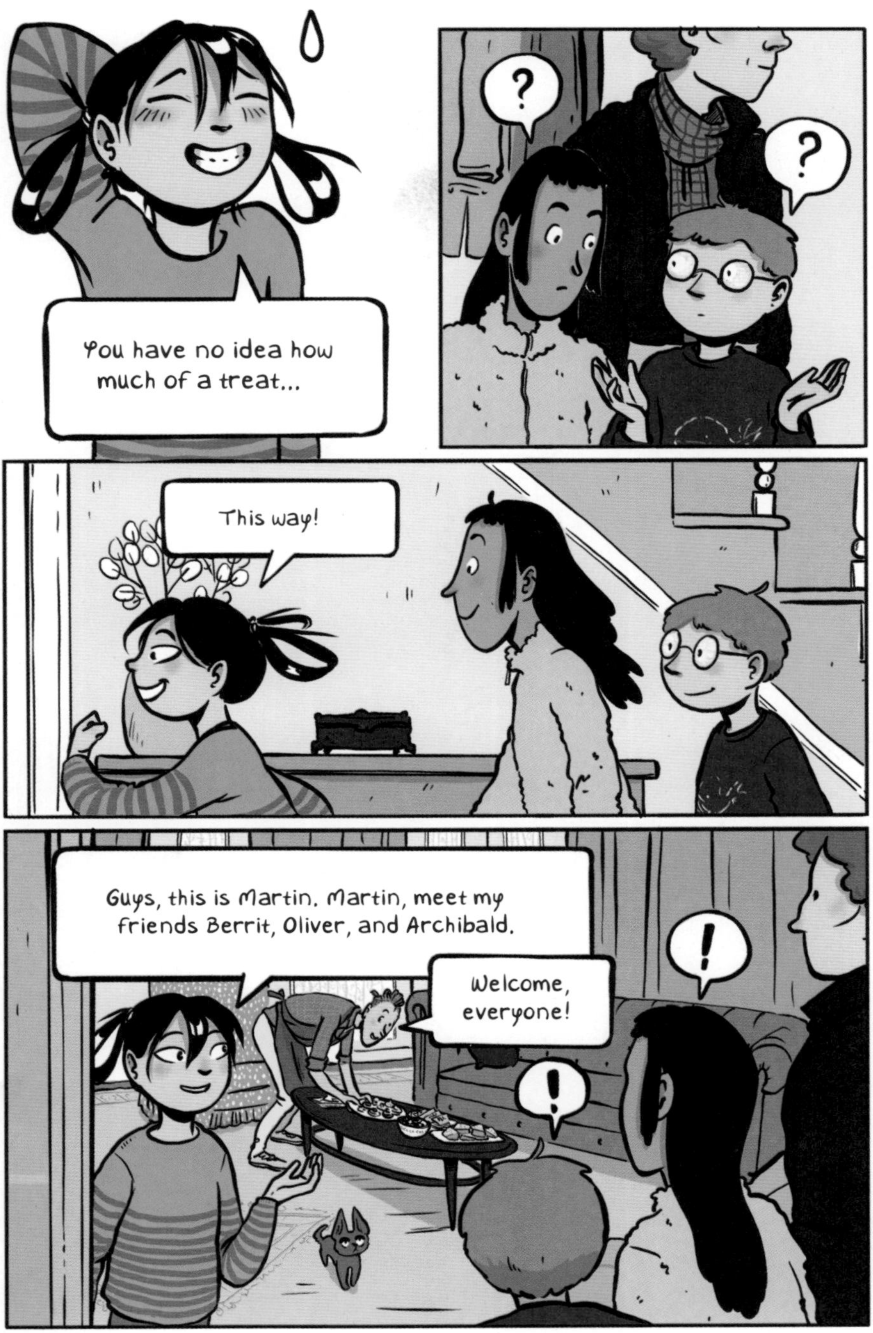
You have no idea how much of a treat...
?
?
This way!
Guys, this is Martin. Martin, meet my friends Berrit, Oliver, and Archibald.
Welcome, everyone!
!
!

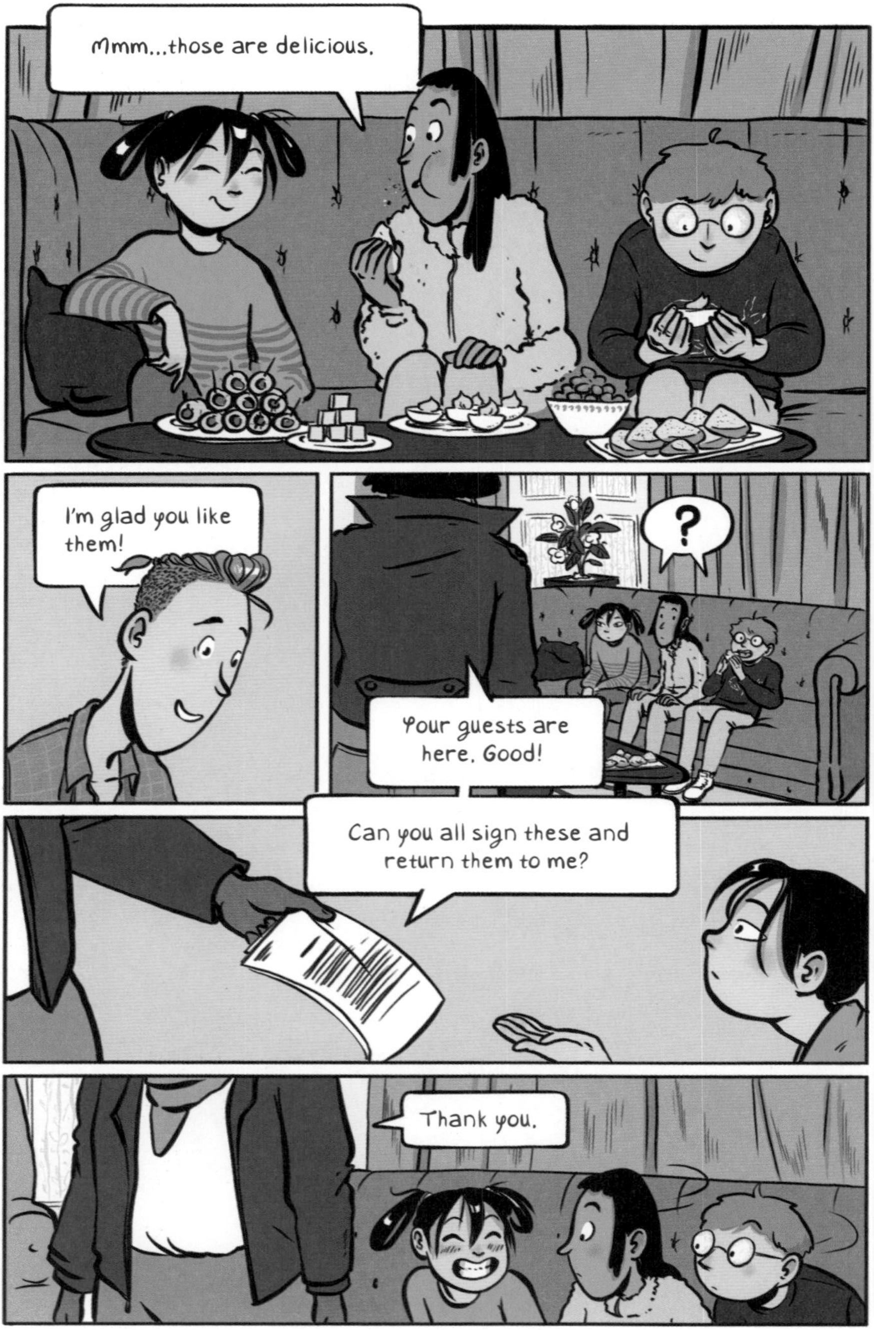
Mmm...those are delicious.
I'm glad you like them!
?
Your guests are here. Good!
Can you all sign these and return them to me?
Thank you.

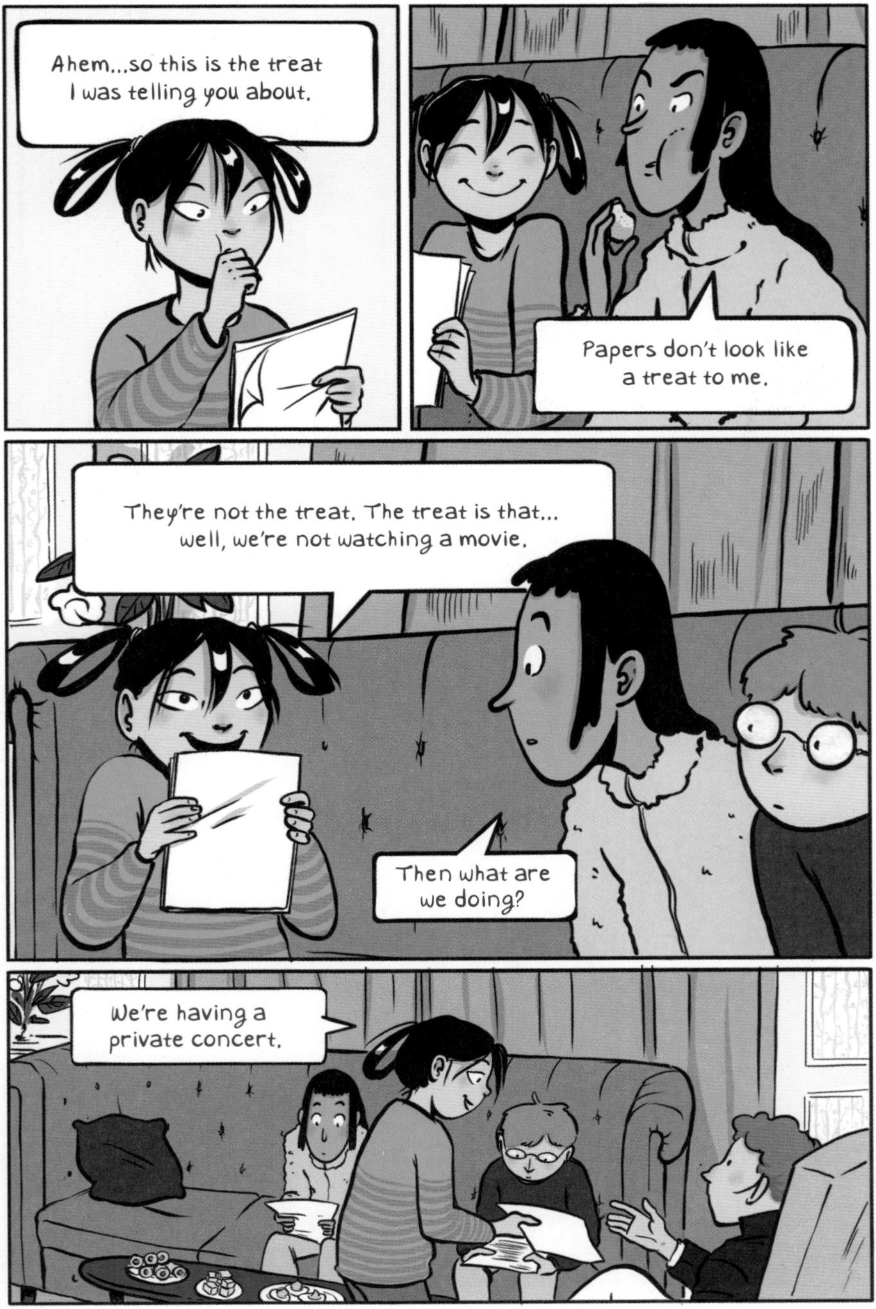
Ahem...so this is the treat I was telling you about.
Papers don't look like a treat to me.
They're not the treat. The treat is that... well, we're not watching a movie.
Then what are we doing?
We're having a private concert.

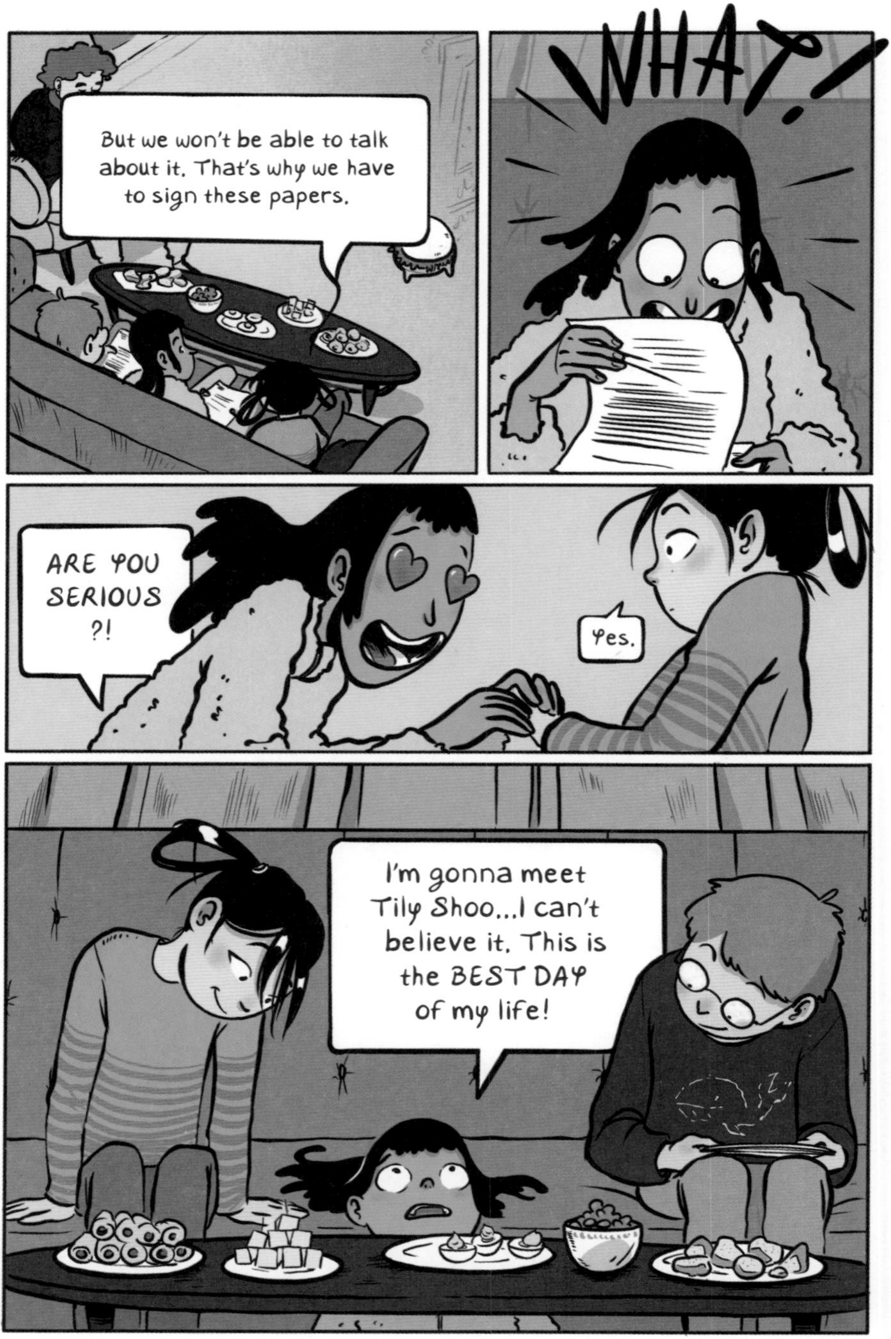
But we won't be able to talk about it. That's why we have to sign these papers.
WHAT?!
ARE YOU SERIOUS ?!
Yes.
I'm gonna meet Tily Shoo...I can't believe it. This is the BEST DAY of my life!

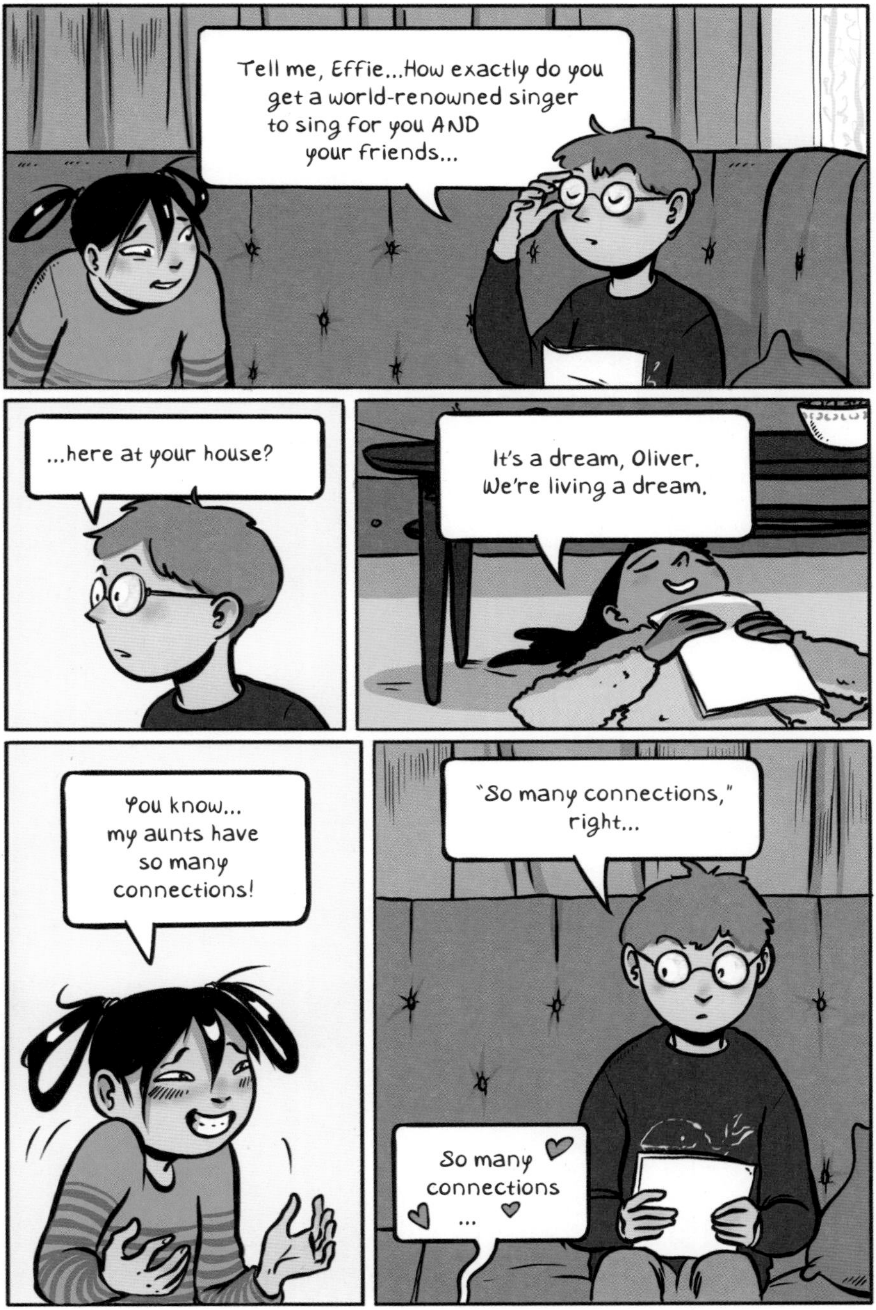
Tell me, Effie...How exactly do you get a world-renowned singer to sing for you AND your friends...
...here at your house?
It's a dream, Oliver. We're living a dream.
You know... my aunts have so many connections!
"So many connections," right...
So many connections ...

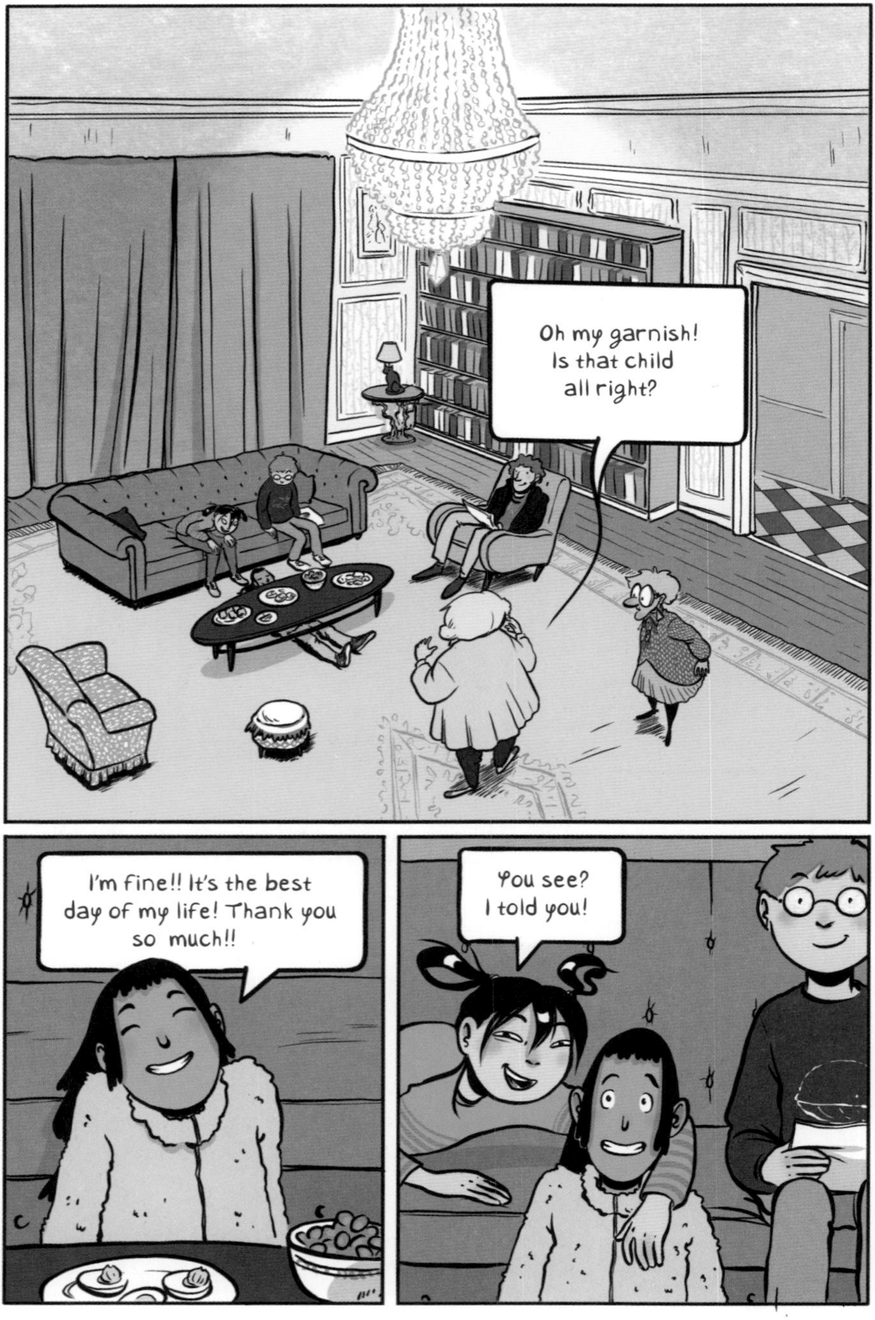
Oh my garnish! Is that child all right?
I'm fine!! It's the best day of my life! Thank you so much!!
You see? I told you!

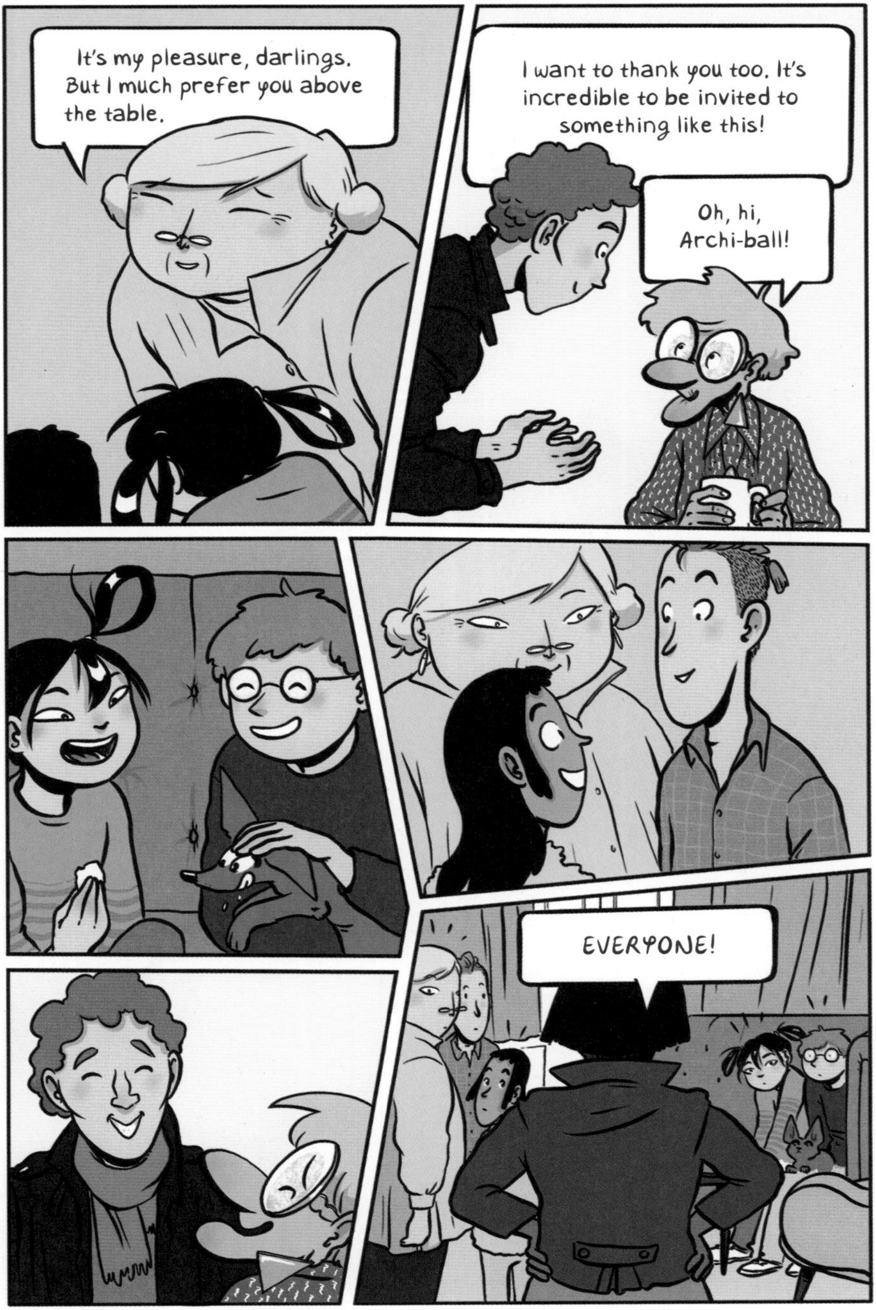
It's my pleasure, darlings. But I much prefer you above the table.
I want to thank you too. It's incredible to be invited to something like this!
Oh, hi, Archi-ball!
EVERYONE!

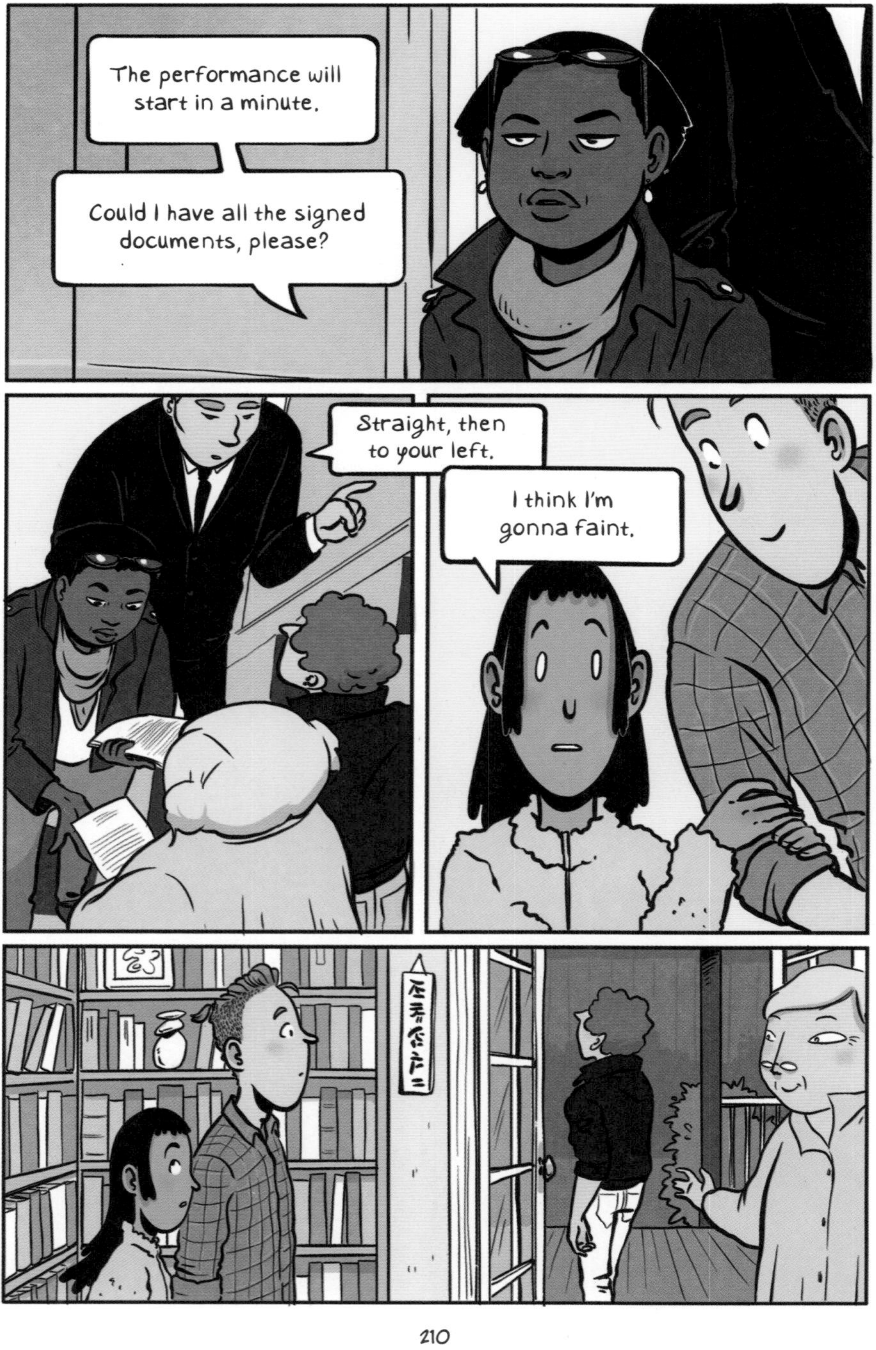
The performance will start in a minute.
Could I have all the signed documents, please?
Straight, then to your left.
I think I'm gonna faint.

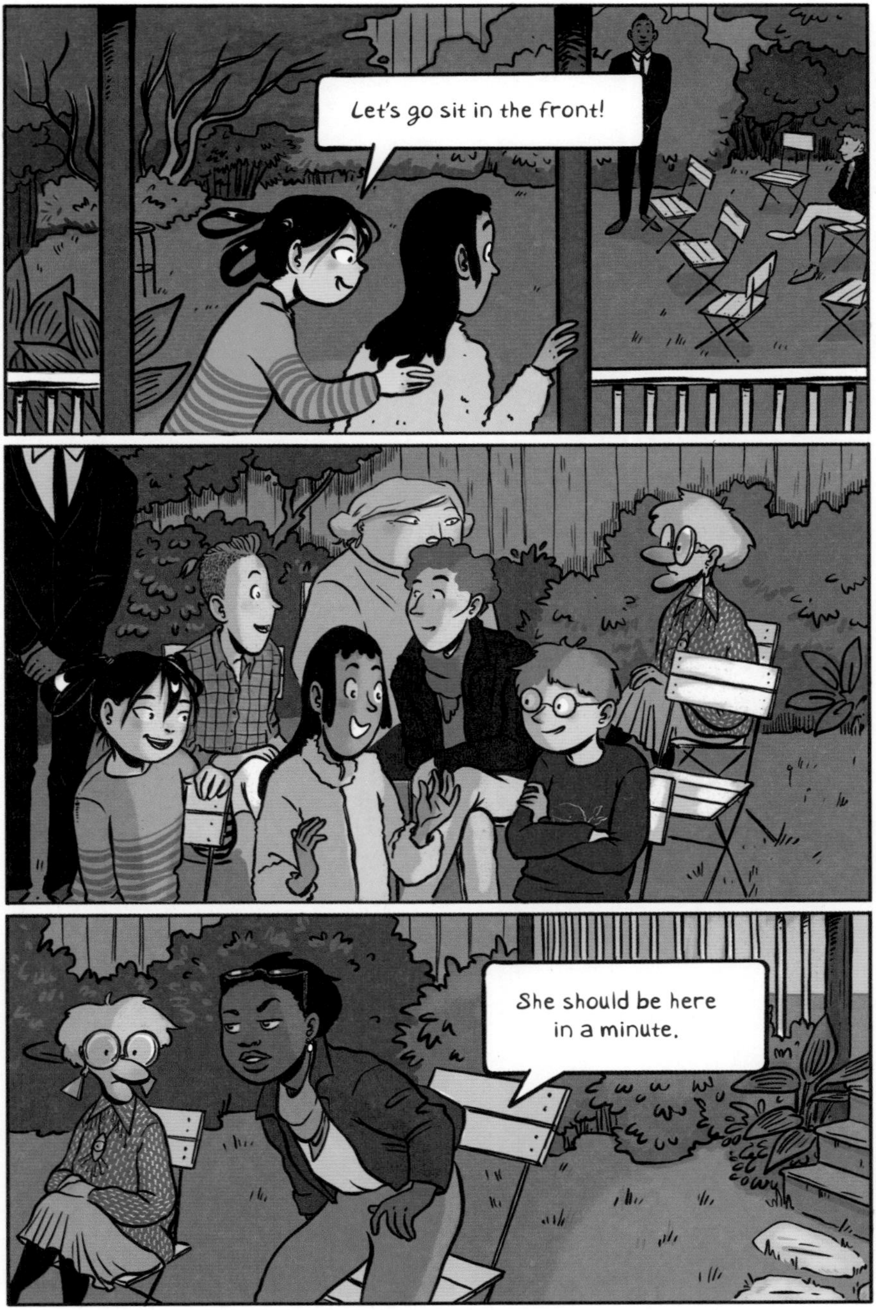
Let's go sit in the front!
She should be here in a minute.

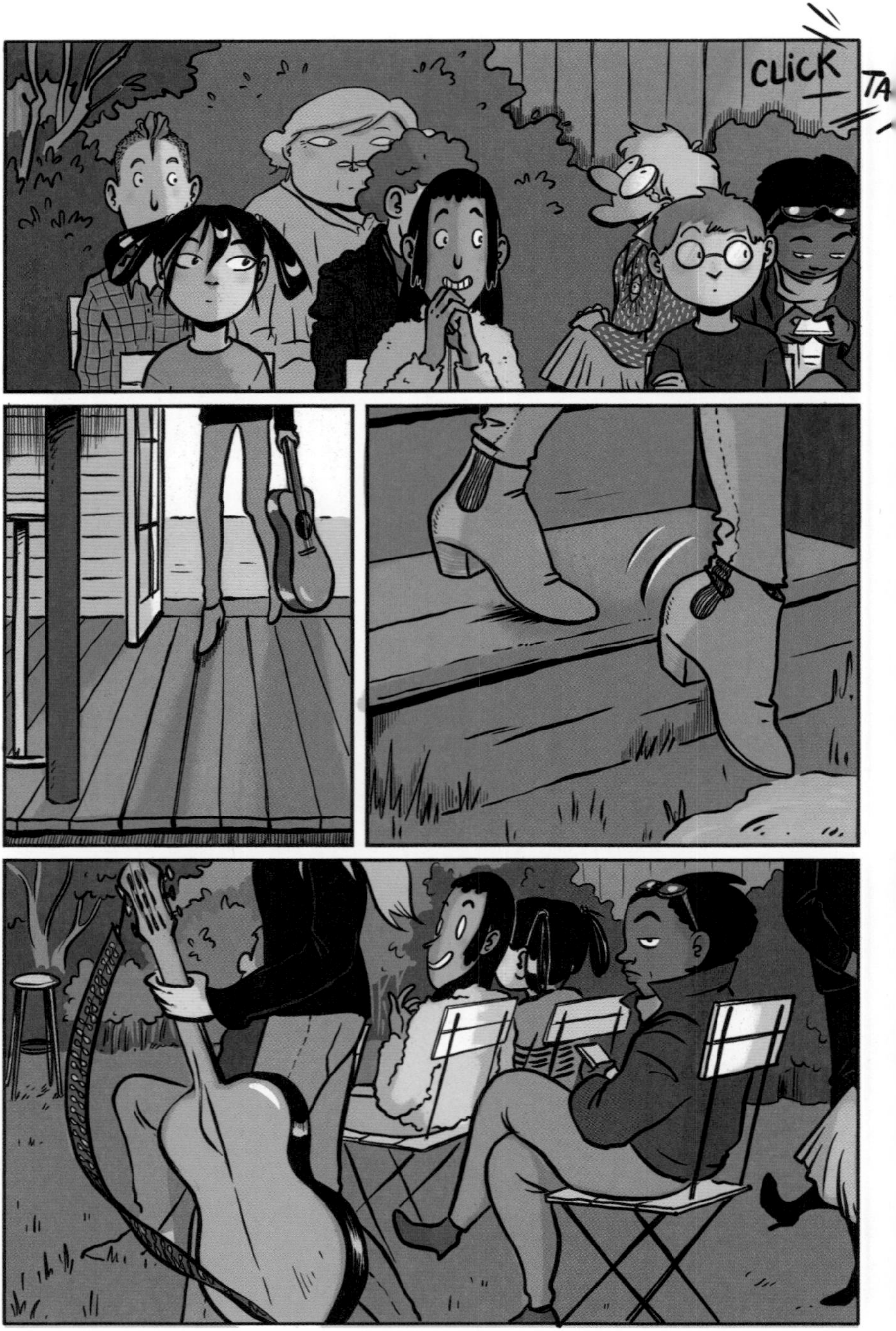
CLICK
TA

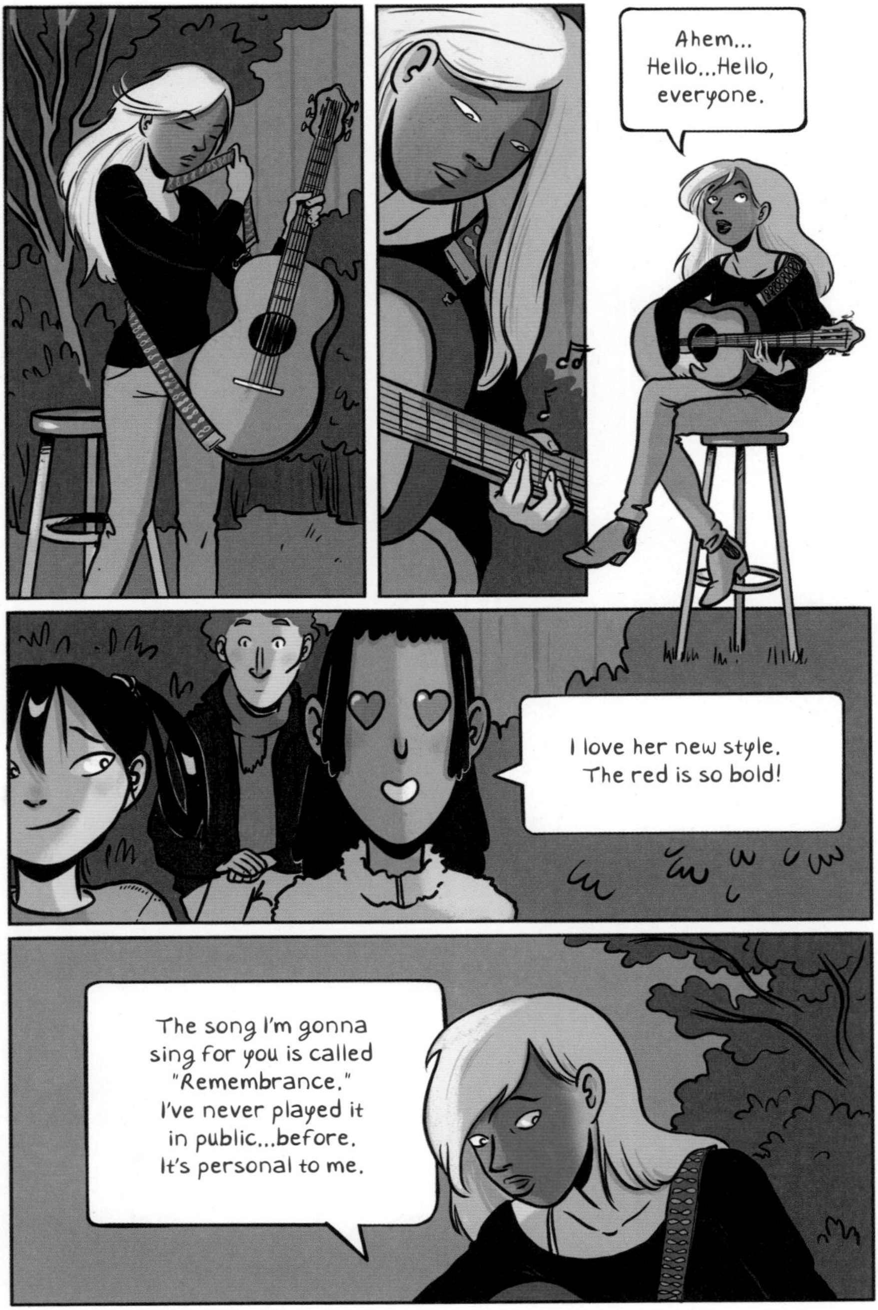
Ahem... Hello...Hello, everyone.
I love her new style. The red is so bold!
The song I'm gonna sing for you is called "Remembrance." I've never played it in public...before. It's personal to me.

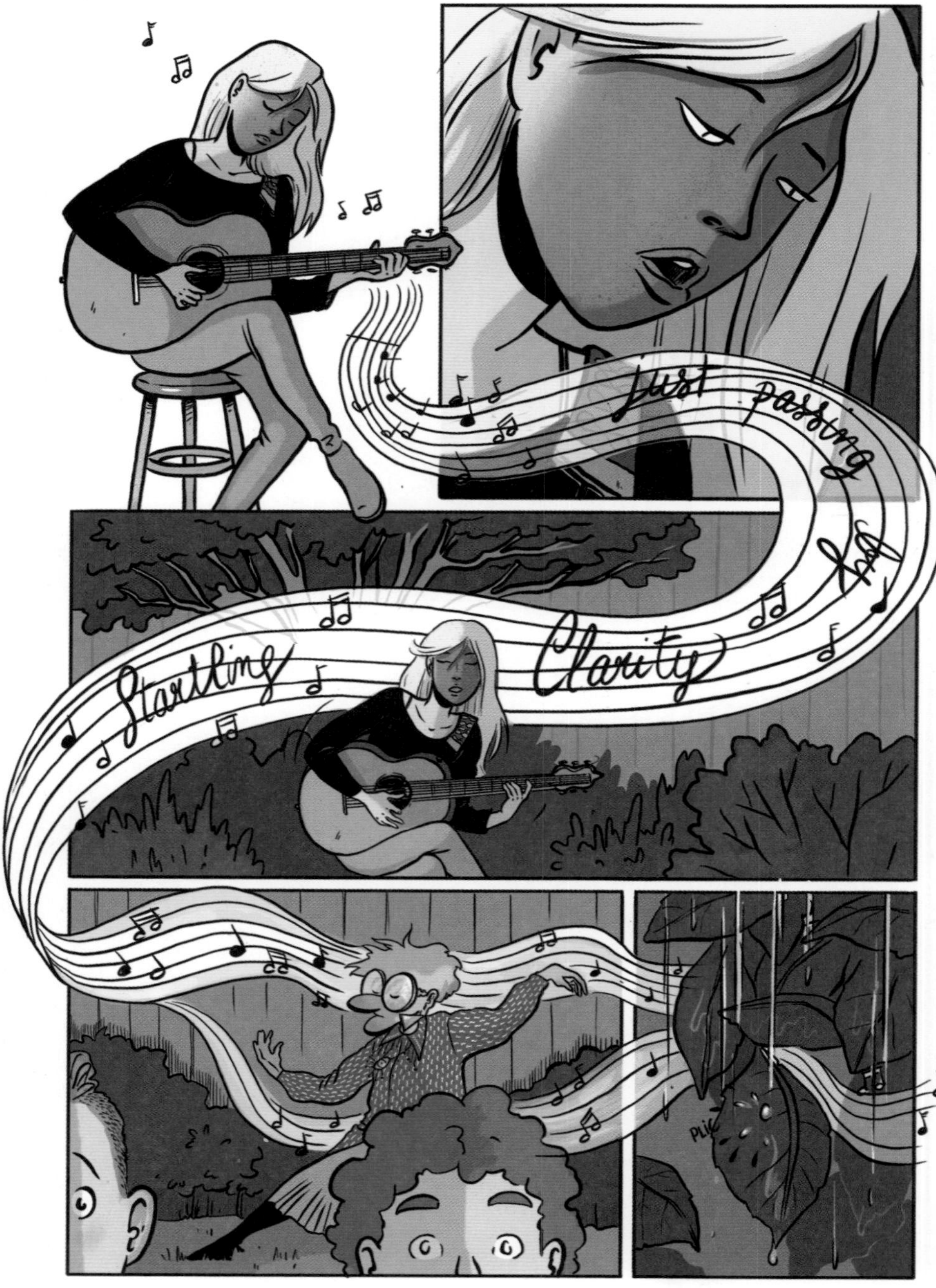
just passing
Startling
Clarity
PLIC

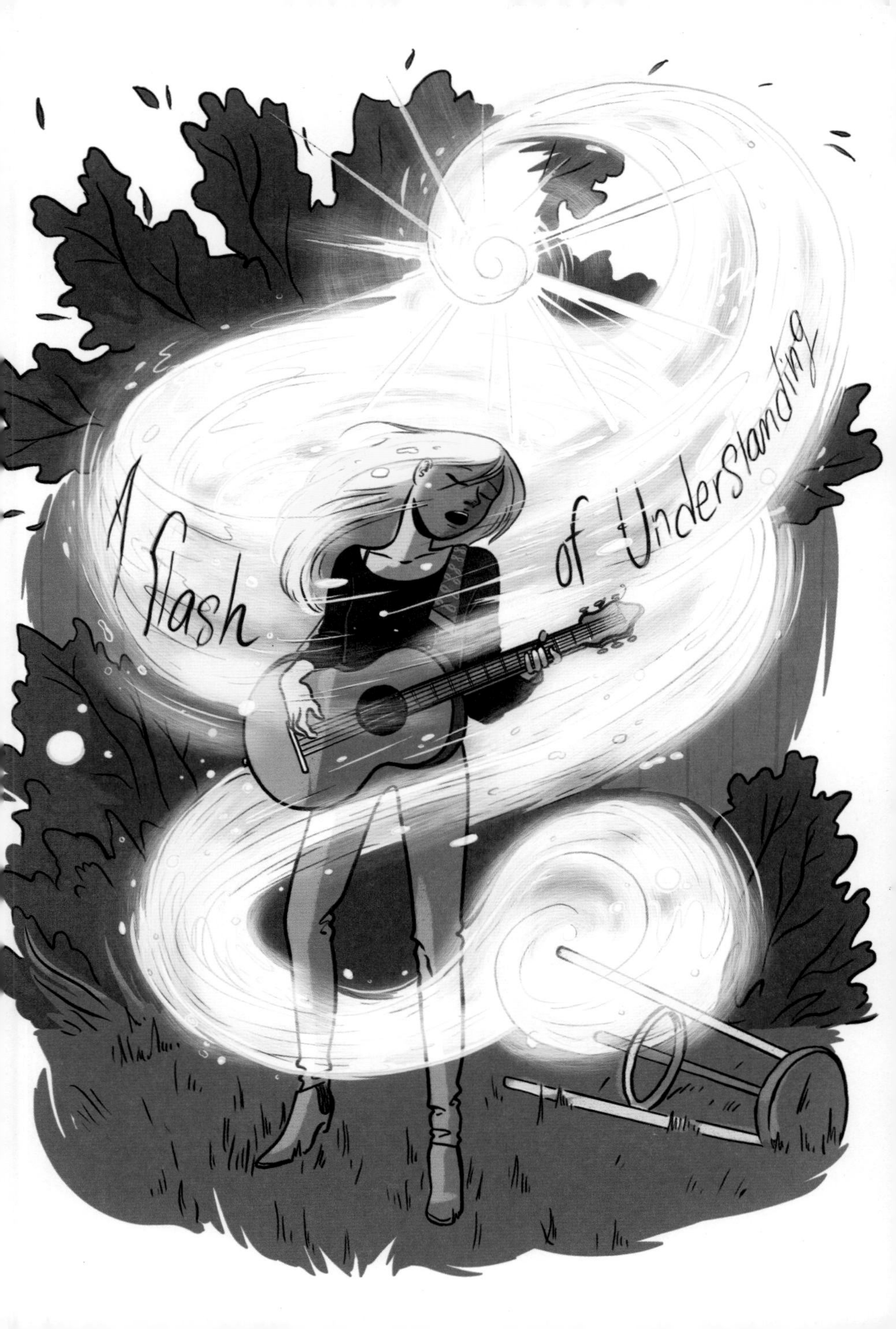
A flash of Understanding

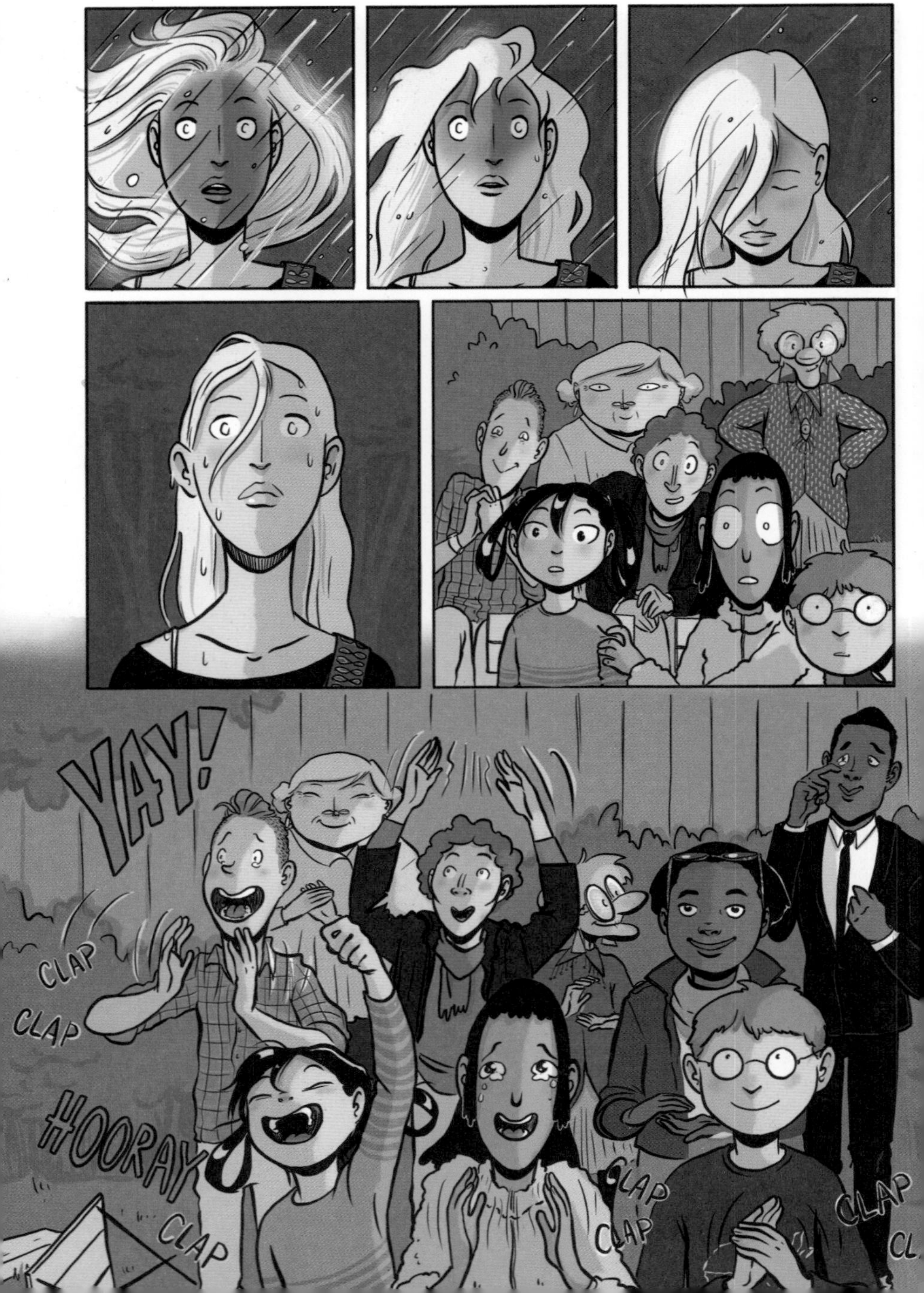

YAY!
CLAP
CLAP
HOORAY
CLAP
CLAP
CLAP
CLAP

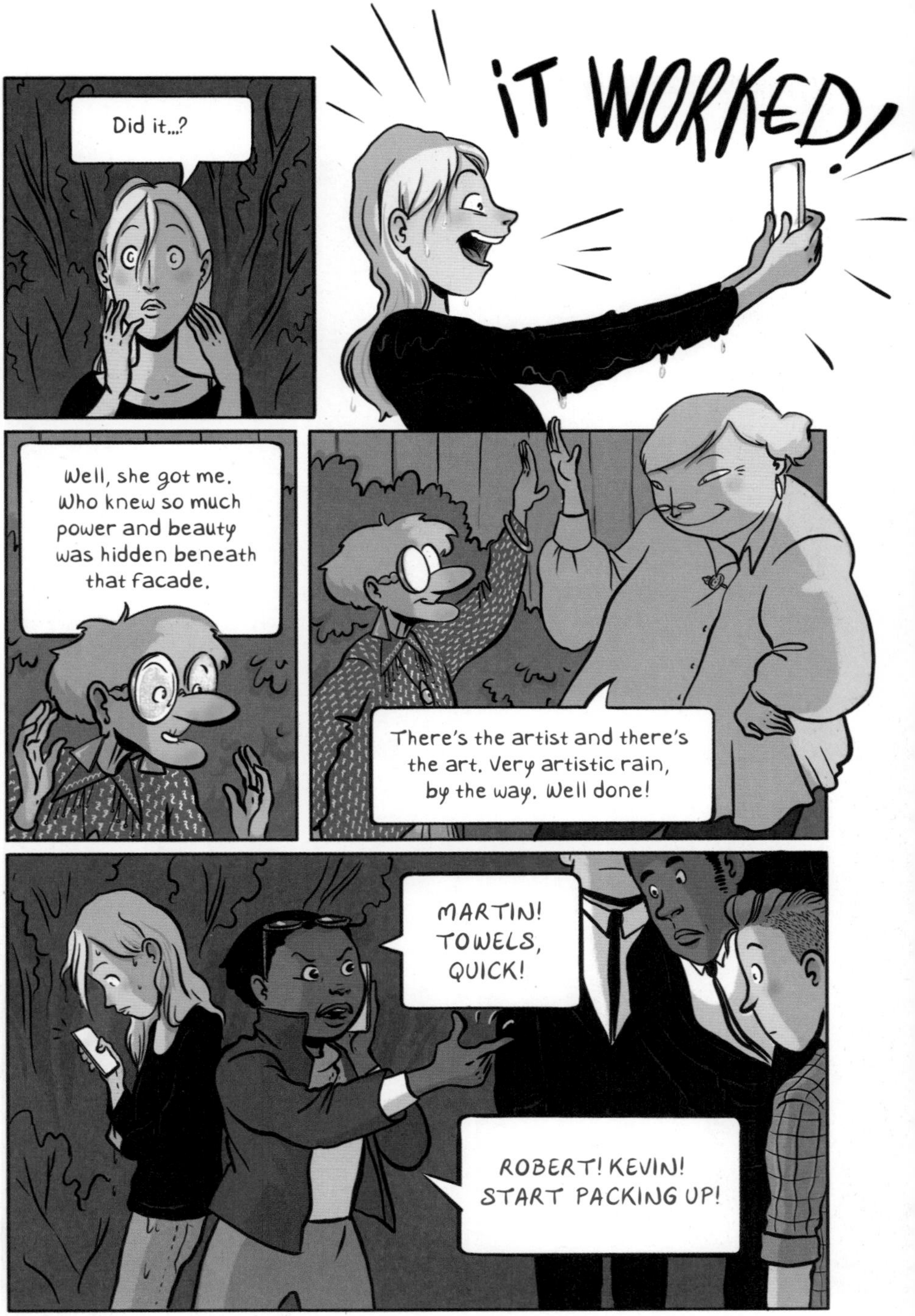
Did it...?
IT WORKED!
Well, she got me. Who knew so much power and beauty was hidden beneath that facade.
There's the artist and there's the art. Very artistic rain, by the way. Well done!
MARTIN! TOWELS, QUICK!
ROBERT! KEVIN! START PACKING UP!

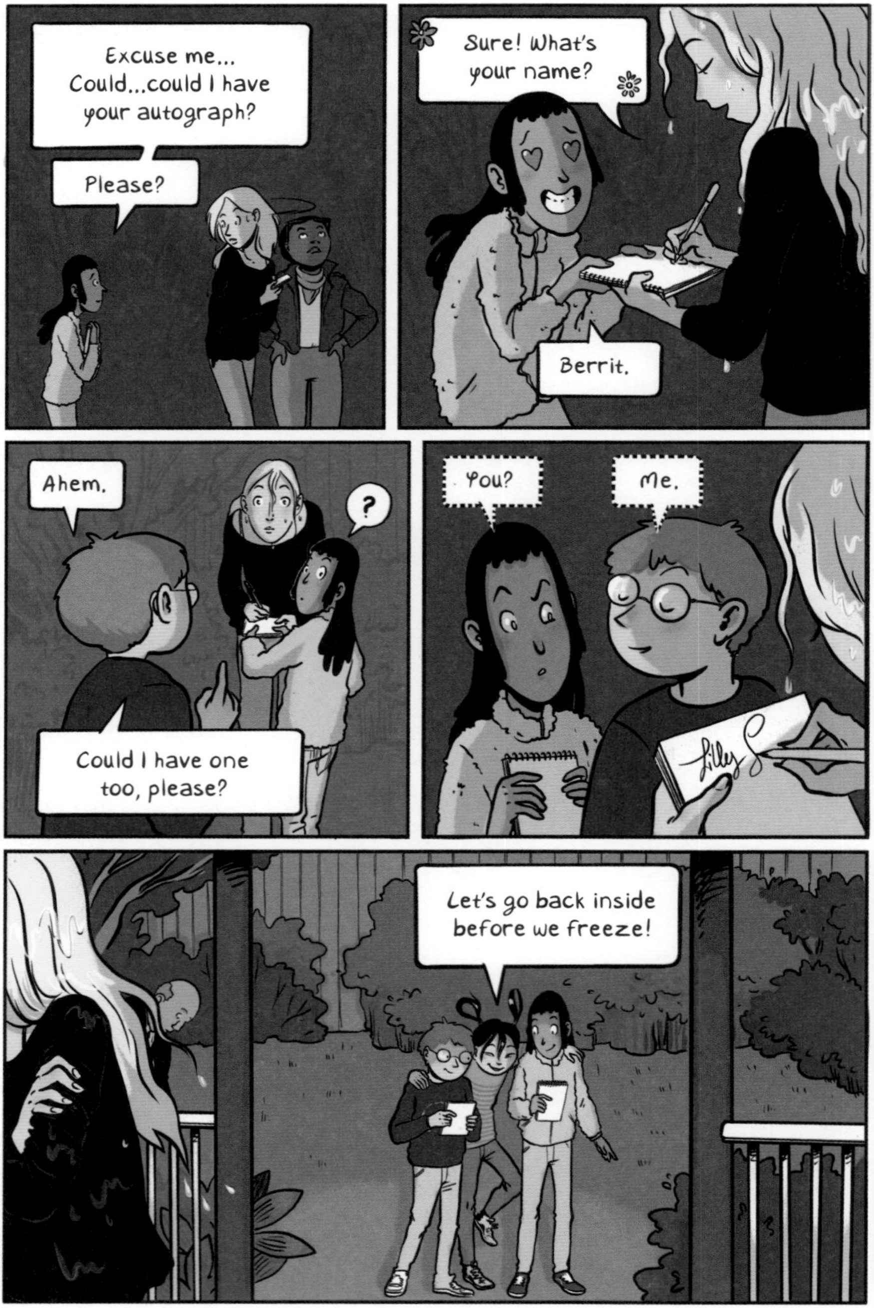
Excuse me... Could...could I have your autograph?
Please?
Sure! What's your name?
Berrit.
Ahem.
?
Could I have one too, please?
You?
Me.
Lilly S
Let's go back inside before we freeze!

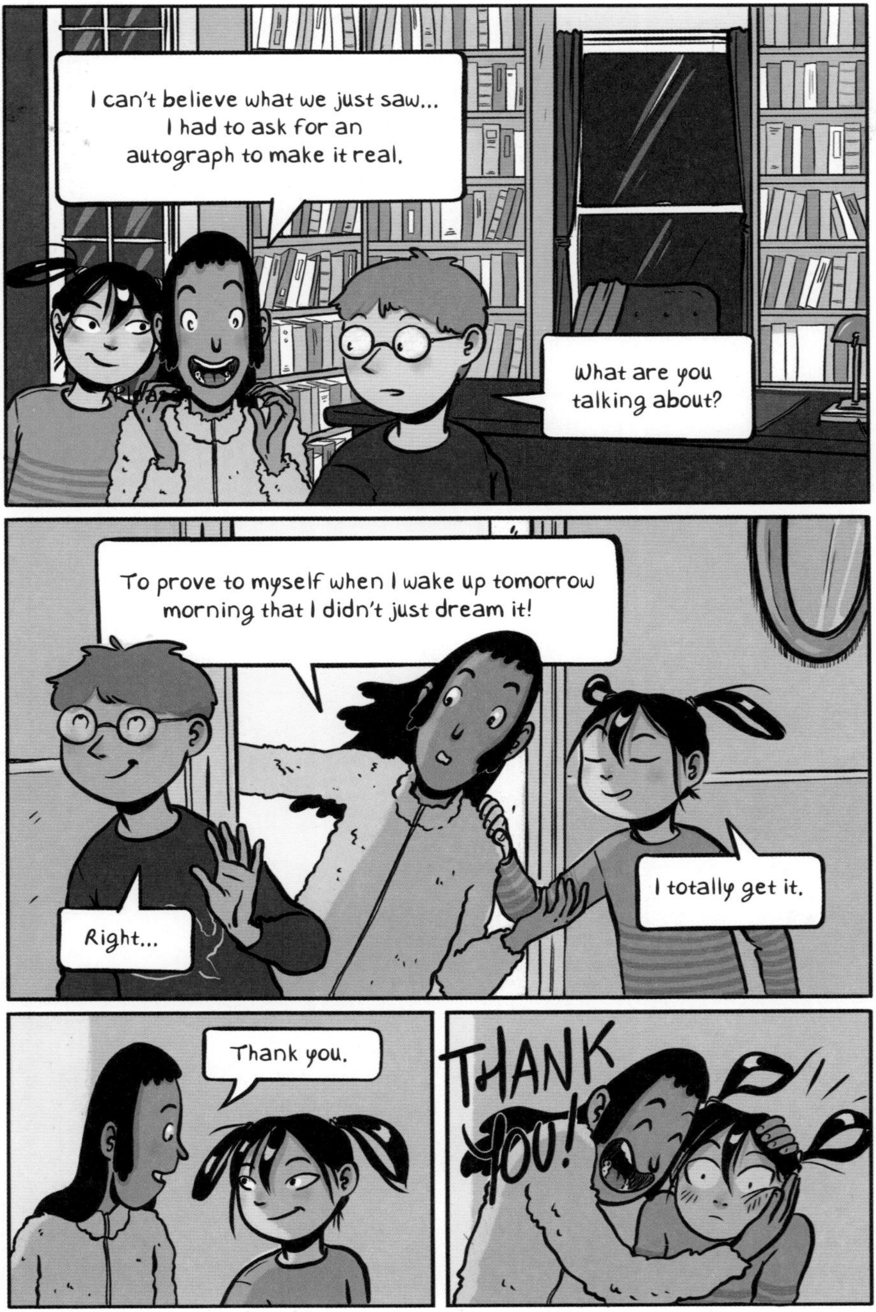
I can't believe what we just saw... I had to ask for an autograph to make it real.
What are you talking about?
To prove to myself when I wake up tomorrow morning that I didn't just dream it!
Right...
I totally get it.
Thank you.
THANK YOU!

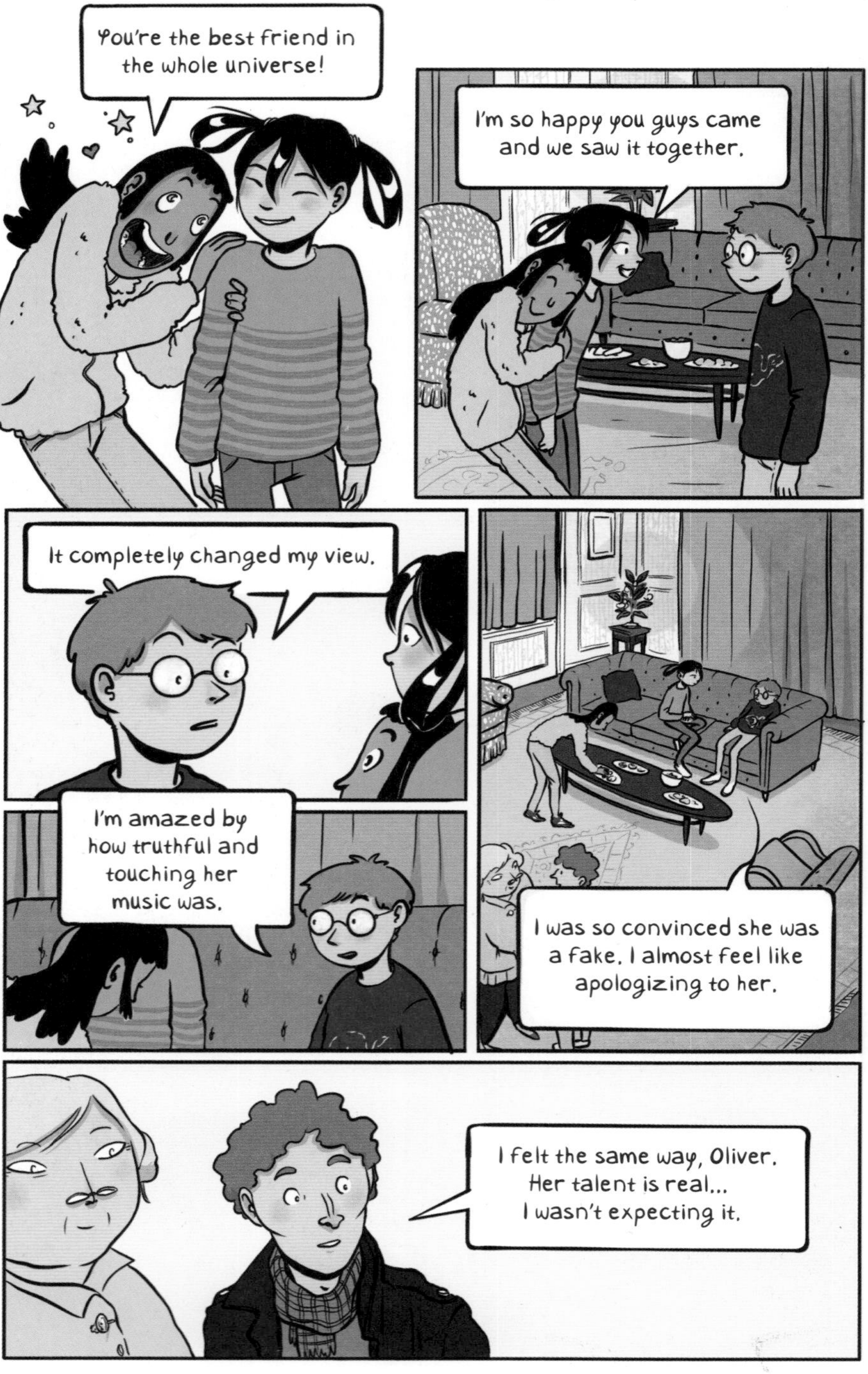
You're the best friend in the whole universe!
I'm so happy you guys came and we saw it together.
It completely changed my view.
I'm amazed by how truthful and touching her music was.
I was so convinced she was a fake. I almost feel like apologizing to her.
I felt the same way, Oliver. Her talent is real... I wasn't expecting it.

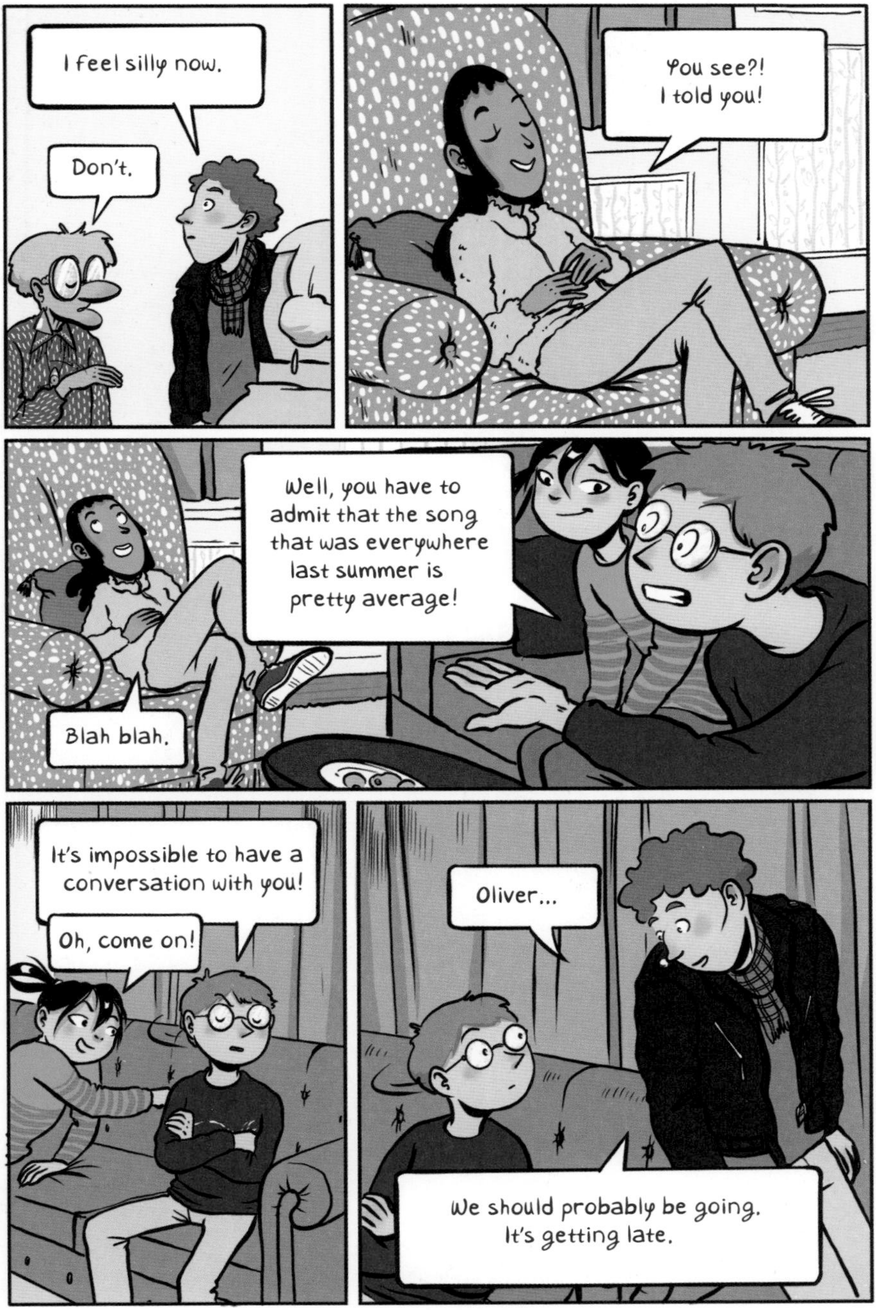
I feel silly now.
Don't.
You see?!
I told you!
Well, you have to admit that the song that was everywhere last summer is pretty average!
Blah blah.
It's impossible to have a conversation with you!
Oh, come on!
Oliver...
We should probably be going.
It's getting late.

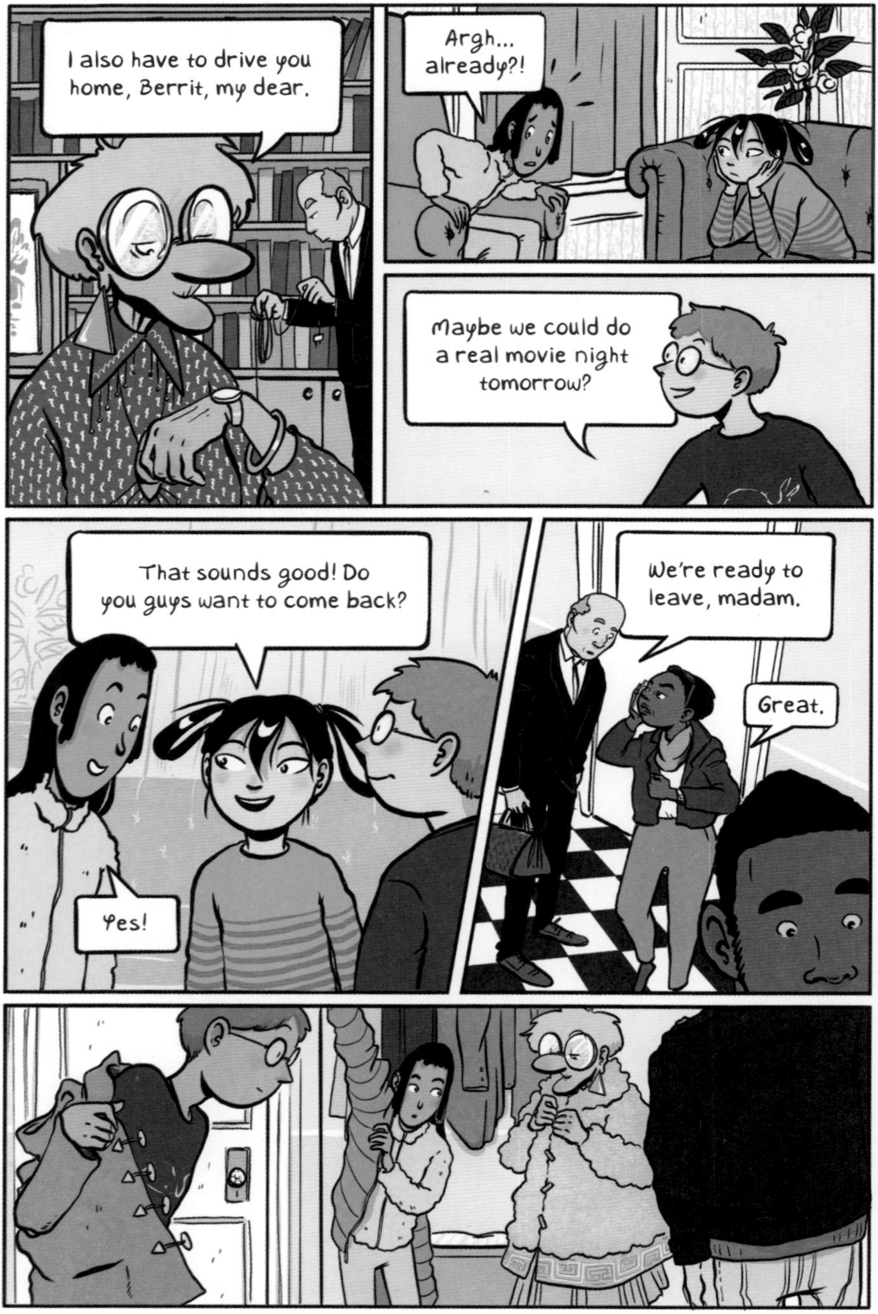
I also have to drive you home, Berrit, my dear.
Argh... already?!
Maybe we could do a real movie night tomorrow?
That sounds good! Do you guys want to come back?
Yes!
We're ready to leave, madam.
Great.

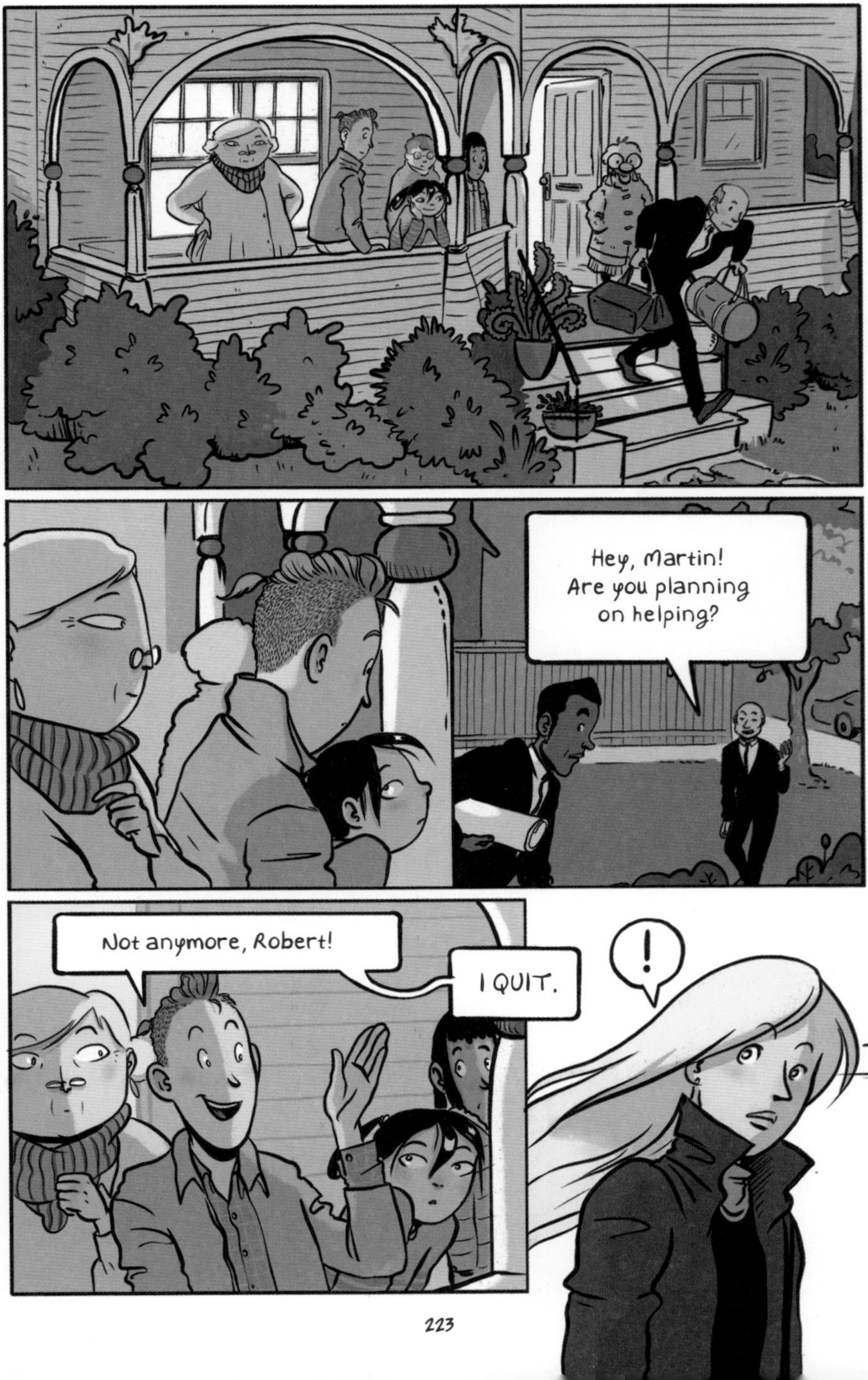
Hey, Martin! Are you planning on helping?
Not anymore, Robert!
I QUIT.
!

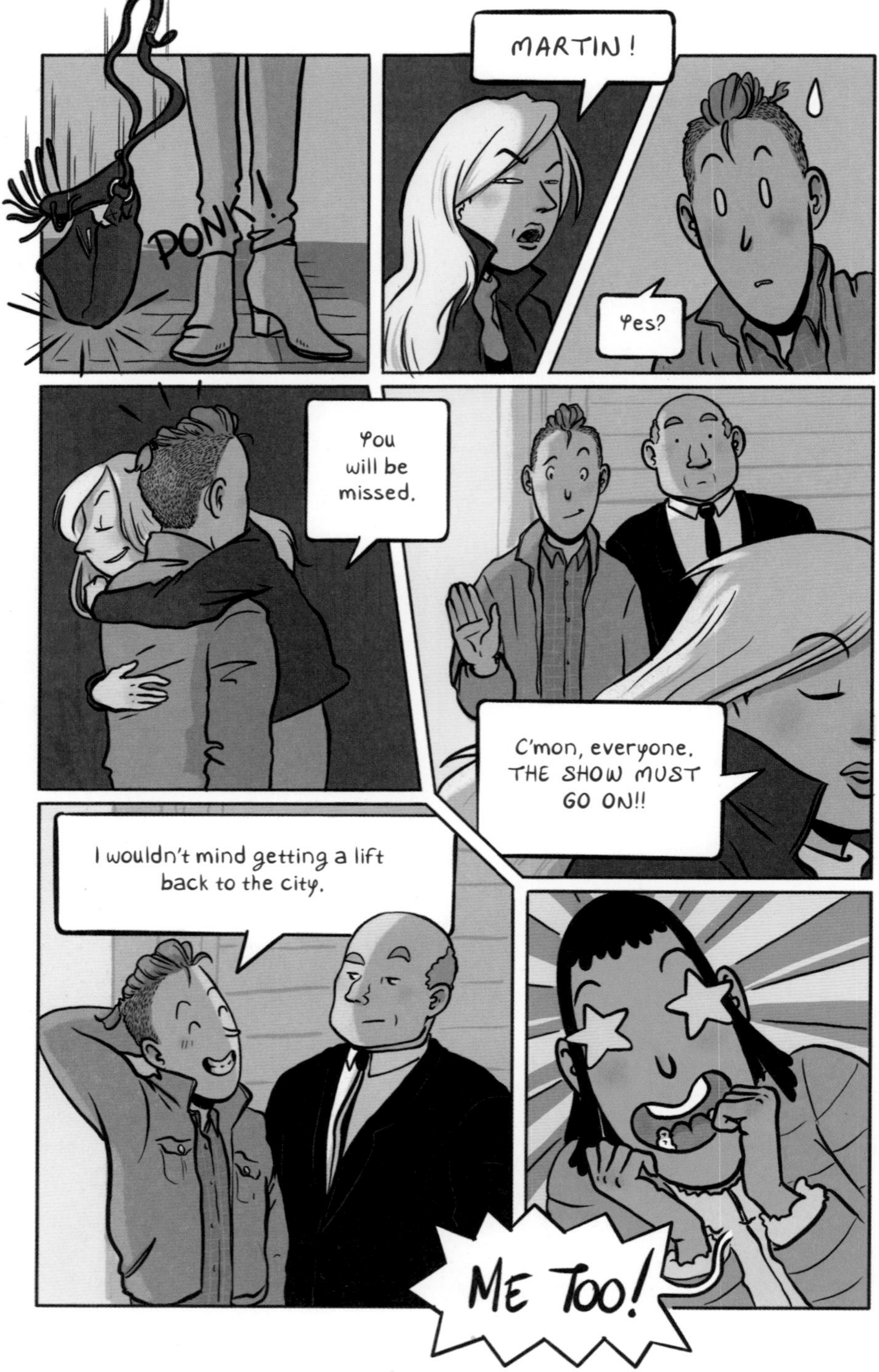
PONK!
MARTIN!
Yes?
You will be missed.
C'mon, everyone. THE SHOW MUST GO ON!!
I wouldn't mind getting a lift back to the city.
ME TOO!

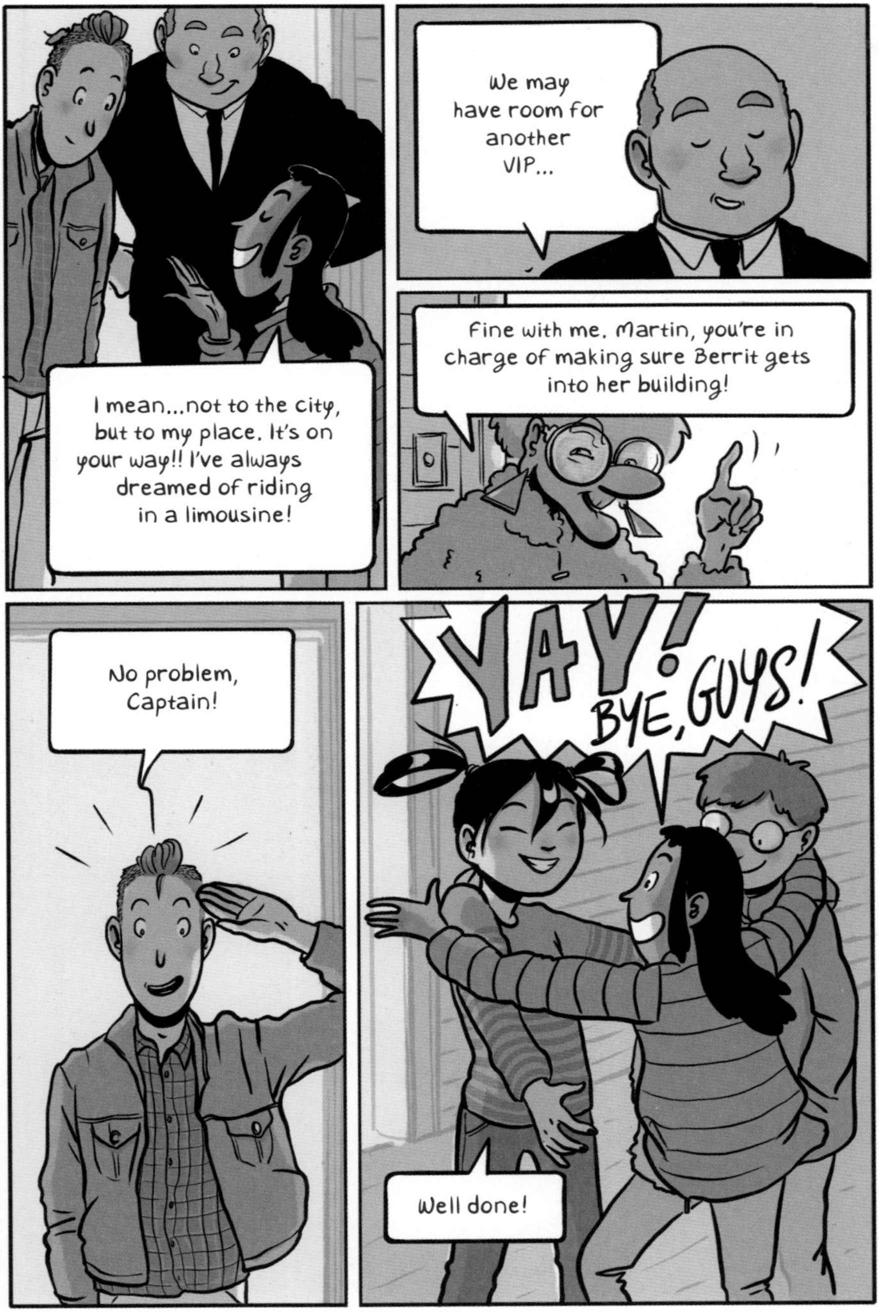
We may have room for another VIP...
I mean...not to the city, but to my place. It's on your way!! I've always dreamed of riding in a limousine!
Fine with me. Martin, you're in charge of making sure Berrit gets into her building!
No problem, Captain!
YAY!
BYE, GUYS!
Well done!

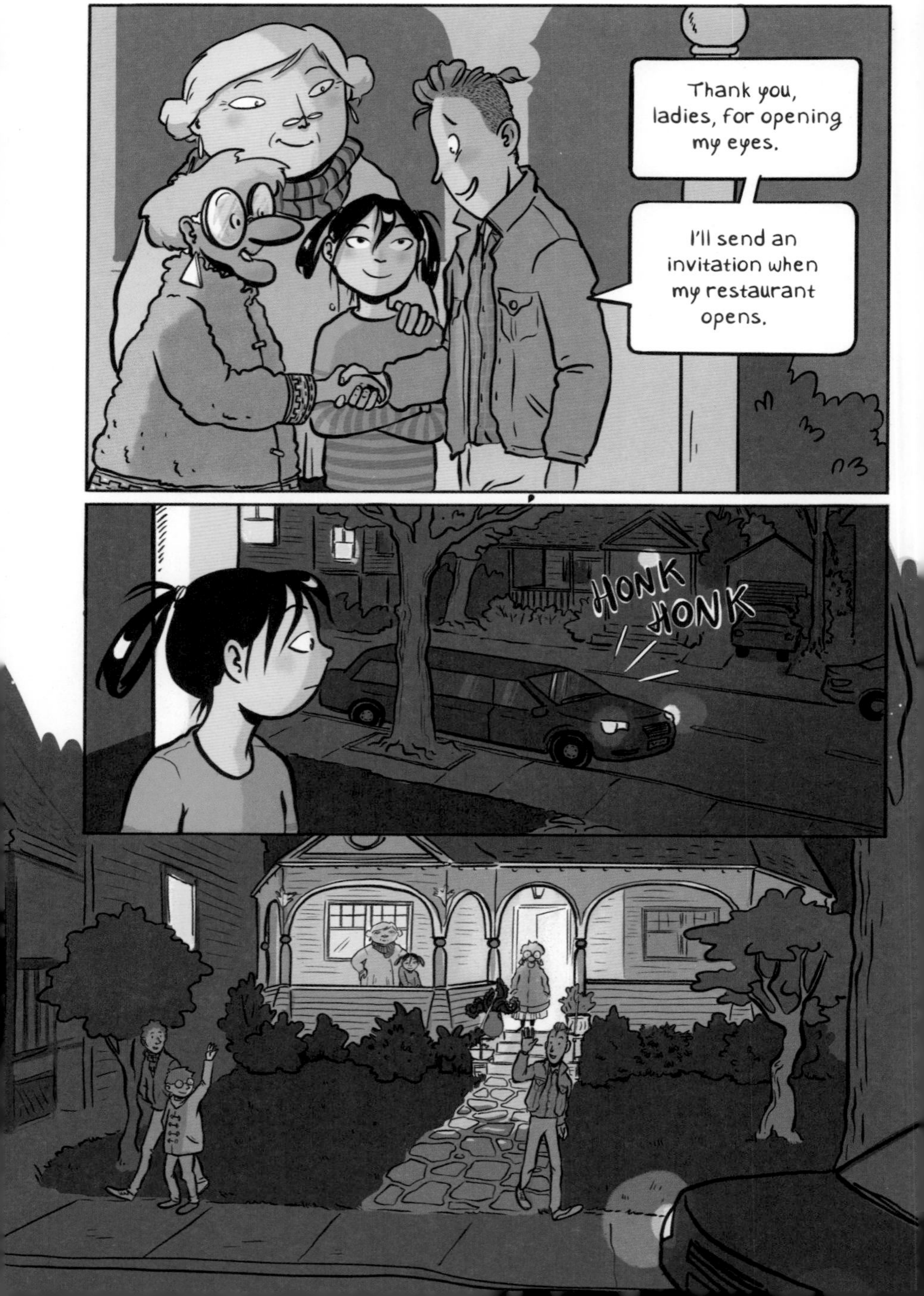
Thank you, ladies, for opening my eyes.
I'll send an invitation when my restaurant opens.
HONK HONK

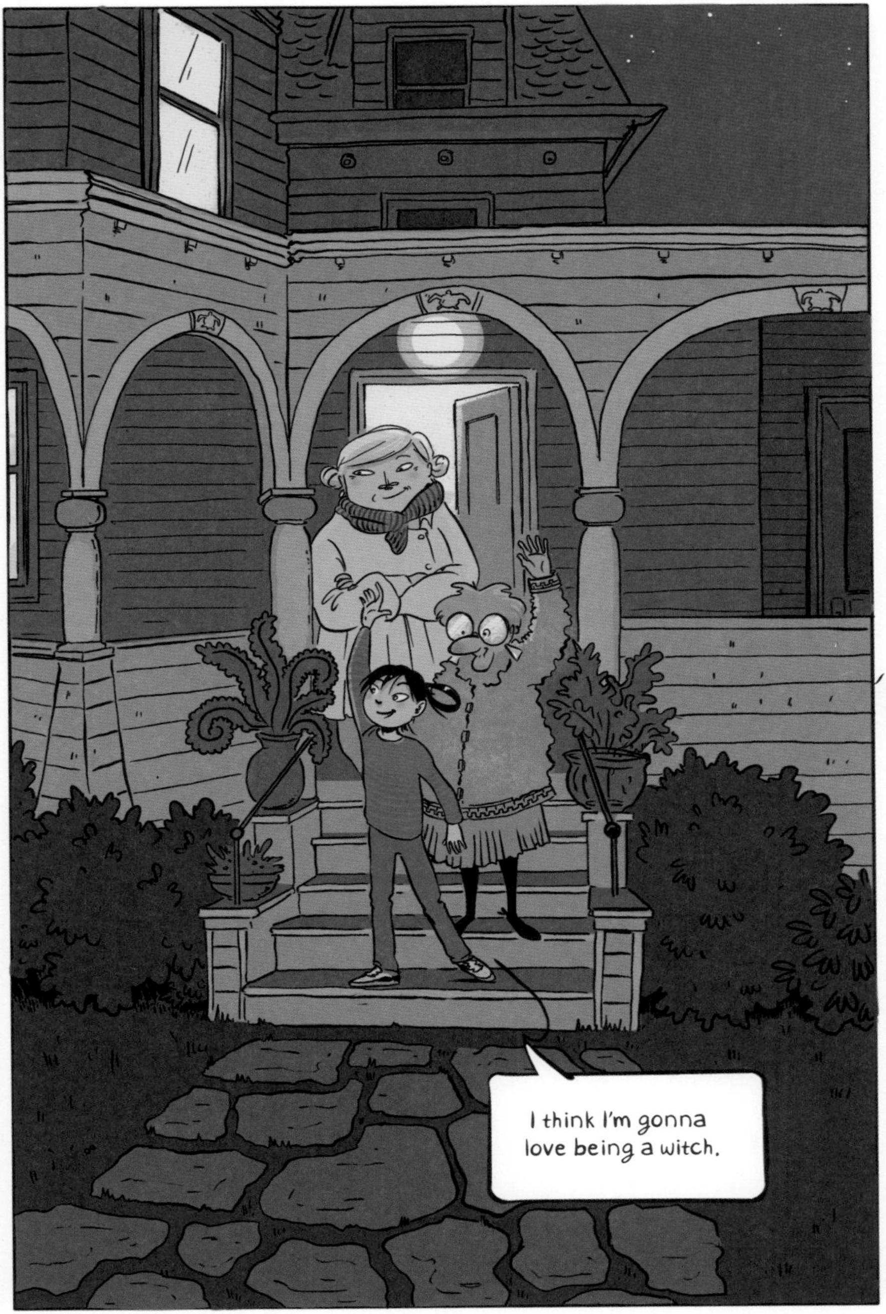
I think I'm gonna love being a witch.

Acknowledgments

Thank you to Kelly Sonnack, my extraordinary, amazing agent, for her support, guidance, and wisdom. This book wouldn't exist if our paths hadn't crossed. Thank you for believing in me—I am so grateful to you for being my agent.

Thanks to the Random House team, especially to Gina Gagliano for being such an amazing human being and believing in me and the Witches of Brooklyn from the beginning.

Thank you to Whitney Leopard for her incredible work editing this book. Thank you for your patience and kindness with all my questions and typos.

I am also very grateful to Patrick Crotty for his help shaping this book and bringing it to life. And for recommending so many cool graphic novels to me.

Thank you to my husband, Patrick Flynn, for loving and supporting me and being by my side through all the ups and downs of the birth of this book. (Another birth!)

Thanks to my incredible children, Ella, Josephine, and Arthur, for being the best and for being so enthusiastic about everything I draw.

Thank you to my amazing, loving parents for being my first cheerleaders and for introducing me to the work of André Franquin (a Belgian comic artist who made me fall in love, once and for all, with comics).

And finally, thanks to Crouton for her unwavering love and support.

Sophie Escabasse is a French illustrator and comic artist living in Brooklyn, New York, with her husband and three children. She has illustrated books for middle-grade readers, including Kenzie Kickstarts a Team (The Derby Daredevils #1) by Kit Rosewater and the Spotlight Club Mysteries series by Florence Parry Heide and Roxanne Heide Pierce.

Sophie studied graphic design at the École nationale supérieure des Arts Décoratifs in Paris and at Central Saint Martins College of Art and Design. She worked in advertising in Paris and New York for a couple of years before fully embracing illustration as a career.

Hailing from a family of graphic novel lovers, Sophie has been enjoying comics since she learned to read. Today she's happily juggling being a mom of three and a comic artist of a new trilogy. It's a lot of sweat but a lot of fun!

Witches of Brooklyn is her graphic novel debut.

THERE GOES THE NEIGHBORHOOD!

EFFIE (AND HER MAGICAL AUNTS!) RETURNS IN A BRAND-NEW SEQUEL

RH GRAPHIC

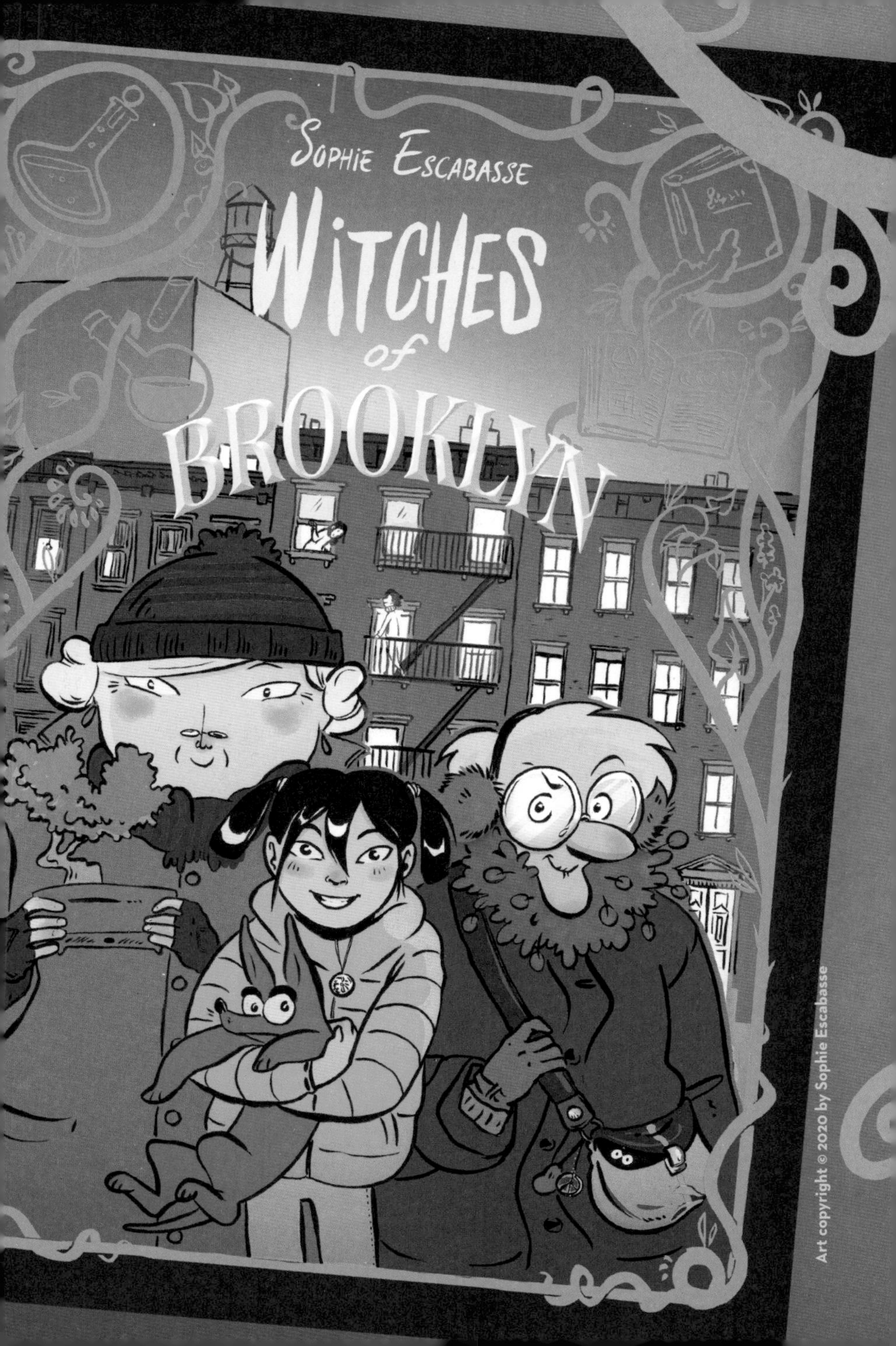
Sophie Escabasse
Witches of Brooklyn

MAGIC, FANTASY, AND WONDER—
ALL IN A GRAPHIC NOVEL

Aster and the Accidental Magic
by Thom Pico and Karensac

After a trickster spirit gives Aster three wishes, her new home suddenly gets interesting!

Kerry and the Knight of the Forest
by Andi Watson

There's a deep, dark forest on Kerry's way home. Will he find his way through or be trapped there forever?

Séance Tea Party
by Reimena Yee

Lora doesn't want to grow up—can her new ghost-friend, Alexa, change her mind?

Doodleville
by Chad Sell

Drew's art is getting out of control . . . and escaping off the page!

Witches of Brooklyn
by Sophie Escabasse

Life in Brooklyn takes a strange turn when Effie discovers MAGIC runs in the family. . . .

5 Worlds
by Mark Siegel, Alexis Siegel, Xanthe Bouma, Matt Rockefeller, and Boya Sun

The Five Worlds are in danger. Can three unlikely heroes come together to save everyone?

VISIT US AT RHKIDSGRAPHIC.COM